Praise for Er

'The perfect read for
Canats

'Funny, heart-wrenching and simply brilliant.'
Beth Reekles, bestselling author of _The Kissing Booth_

'Heart-warming and emotional.'
My Weekly

'Romantic, hopeful and uplifting.'
Emily Stone

'A beautifully written, emotionally rich story about
hope, love and new beginnings.'
Lynsey James

'A charming page-turner of a romance.'
Laura Jane Williams

'Perfect for a sunny afternoon.'
Daily Mail

'A light-hearted read to get lost in.'
The UpComing

Emily Houghton was a digital specialist, but is now a full-time creative writer. Originally from Essex, she now lives in London. Emily is a trained yoga and spin teacher, is completely obsessed with dogs and has dreamt of being an author ever since she could hold a pen.

Also by Emily Houghton

BEFORE I SAW YOU
LAST TIME WE MET

TAKE A CHANCE ON ME

Emily Houghton

PENGUIN BOOKS

TRANSWORLD PUBLISHERS
Penguin Random House, One Embassy Gardens,
8 Viaduct Gardens, London SW11 7BW
www.penguin.co.uk

Penguin
Random House
UK

Transworld is part of the Penguin Random House group of companies
whose addresses can be found at global.penguinrandomhouse.com

First published in Great Britain in 2024 by Penguin Books
an imprint of Transworld Publishers

Extract on p. 1 from *Lonely on the Mountain* by Louis L'Amour
(Random House, 1999)
Extract on p. 105 from *Your Light is the Key* by Mimi Novic
(Aspiring Hope Publishing, 2018)
Extract on p. 215 from *The Story of My Life* by Helen Keller
(Simon & Schuster, 2005)
Extract on p. 327 from *An Intimate Collision* by Craig D. Lounsbrough
(Ambassador-Emerald, 2013)

A CIP catalogue record for this book
is available from the British Library.

ISBN
9781804992647

Typeset in 10.75/14.4pt Sabon by Jouve (UK), Milton Keynes.
Printed and bound in Great Britain by Clays Ltd, Elcograf S.p.A.

The authorized representative in the EEA is Penguin Random House Ireland,
Morrison Chambers, 32 Nassau Street, Dublin D02 YH68.

Penguin Random House is committed to a sustainable future
for our business, our readers and our planet. This book is made
from Forest Stewardship Council® certified paper.

MIX
Paper | Supporting
responsible forestry
FSC® C018179

This book is a love letter to a country that stole my heart and changed my life. India, you are majestic and magical and I will love you for ever.

To my sister. I never want to imagine a world without you. Thanks for being my person. Friends by choice always . . . x

I

*There will come a time when you believe everything
is finished; that will be the beginning*
Louis L'Amour

Jacob

Jacob didn't need to check his diary to see today's date. There were some things that simply couldn't be forgotten, no matter how hard one tried. And God, had he been trying. For the past five years, he had been doing his best to convince himself that it was just another day. As remarkably unremarkable as the ones that lay either side of it. A day he could pretend had little to no importance in his life. Except this year, it did. This year it fell on one of the most important days of his week: a Monday.

Jacob downed the dregs of his tea and moved the empty cup to the side, making sure there was enough space for him to work. Like every other Monday morning, he had gone to his favourite spot in town, ordered a tea and a delicious breakfast, and prepared to plan his next adventure. The tools for the job were already laid out in front of him: his tattered notebook and trusted pair of dice.

'Are we all done here, sir?'

No sooner had Jacob's hand released itself from the saucer than a kind-faced waiter appeared next to him.

'Can I get you anything else?'

Jacob looked out over the terrace; he had deliberately seated himself at the front of the restaurant so as to get the best view possible. The crystal ocean lapped lazily at the expanse of golden sand. The sun, edging its way higher and higher through the bundles of cotton clouds, gently warmed his face. How lucky he was to be here.

In more ways than one.

The thought lashed him like a red-hot band across his brain, and he physically recoiled in response.

'Sir? Anything else for you?'

'Yes!' Jacob clapped his hands together, forcing himself back to reality. 'I think I will get something.' He promised himself that the sentiment of the day wouldn't get the better of him. 'You only turn thirty once, after all!'

Although it didn't seem humanly possible, the waiter's smile grew larger on his face. 'It's your birthday, sir? Oh my, why didn't you say earlier!' He threw his hands in the air with unfettered joy. 'Whatever you want is on the house! And may I recommend the banana bread – it's our best-seller.'

Jacob couldn't help but be infected by the man's enthusiasm. 'Well then, in that case I'll take two slices and another tea, please.'

'Coming right up!' The man gave a small bow and disappeared.

Jacob settled back into his chair and let the salty breeze dance across his skin. How had this day come around so soon? It seemed impossible that he'd already spent three decades on this planet. That thirty years ago he'd come into the world kicking, screaming, red-faced and wrinkled – into a life that now felt so far away it could belong to just about anybody. Could he even count those years as his? And more importantly, did he want to?

A tug behind his navel made Jacob aware that he'd spent too long reflecting. There was no more time to waste. Sri Lanka had been beautiful, but he was ready to move on. To explore somewhere new, become another nameless face in a brand-new crowd. This would be his fifth birthday by himself; each one spent in a different place, a different country. Surrounded by different people, most of whom didn't even know he existed. Total anonymity, just the way he had planned.

Jacob reached for the dice, clenching them tightly in his fist and allowing the worn edges to dig into his flesh. It was time to roll.

'Haaaaappy biiiiirthday to you . . .'

A tray of tea and cake was suddenly thrust in front of him, along with the jubilant waiter and his very out-of-tune singing.

'. . . happy birthday to you!' he finished proudly. 'Enjoy!'

Jacob took the tray and placed it to the side, noting the chocolate icing that decorated his plate with another happy birthday message. The sentiment was so touching that, for the briefest of seconds, Jacob felt lost for words.

'Thank you,' he managed after some time. 'It means a lot.'

'My pleasure.' The waiter nodded. 'Now I will leave you to enjoy your birthday treats and to play your game in peace.'

'My game?'

'The dice.' The man pointed to the pair clasped in Jacob's hand. 'They are for a game, no?'

'Oh – yes.' Jacob's thoughts were thankfully directed back to the present. 'Well . . . I guess you could call it a game.' Jacob unfurled his fingers and laid his palm flat. 'It's the game of my life.'

Confusion etched itself deeper on to the young man's face. 'I don't understand.'

Jacob sat up taller, pulling the diary towards him and flicking to the back pages. 'I'm a traveller, a nomad if you will. I use these dice to tell me where I should go next. If it's an odd number, I have to stay where I am. If it's an even number, I get to leave. Then I roll again, and whatever number I throw corresponds to a place on my list.' He pushed the scrawled page towards the waiter. 'See . . .?'

The waiter's confusion morphed rapidly into disbelief.

'You're joking with me?' he gasped, running his finger down the list of destinations.

Jacob burst out laughing; other people's reactions to his method never failed to amuse him. 'I'm not joking, I promise.'

'Wow,' the waiter breathed, his eyes wider than the plates in front of them. 'You must be very brave. Very brave indeed, sir.'

'Most people go for "crazy", so that makes a nice change.'

'Crazy people can still be brave!' He chuckled. 'Now I shall leave you to it. Enjoy your treats and good luck with your game. I wish you only the best.'

And with that, Jacob was left alone. He closed his palm around the dice and took a deep inhale. Excitement began to bubble beneath the surface of his sun-darkened skin, adrenaline sparking like fireworks.

Two shakes and a roll. Show me, Universe, where I should go . . .

As he released the dice on to the table, his heart skipped a beat. He resisted the urge to celebrate out loud as he stared down at his results.

A two and a four.

Permission to go.

Jacob reached for the dice again, feeling the sense of anticipation building once more. He knew he was leaving, but now the question was, where to?

Nerves churned in the pit of his stomach as he released the dice once more.

Two fives.

Something about that felt familiar. Number ten. What on earth was number ten?

Jacob grabbed the diary and scanned down the list of destinations. As his eyes found the answer, he couldn't help but note his pang of disappointment. The number ten was so familiar because he had already been to the country it represented. Not once, but twice before.

He tapped his finger to the page. 'Hello, India, my old friend.'

And a friend, it truly was. In fact, it was one of his favourite countries in the world. The chaos, the colour, the full sensory experience that greeted you around every corner. It was the perfect place to lose yourself, and it certainly wasn't for the faint-hearted. Maybe the waiter was right. Maybe he was braver than he thought.

Jacob took a large mouthful of sweet tea and steadied himself. There was another task to complete before the job was finished. One more throw. One more answer to find. For every country came with its own specific list of places to visit. He had the diary open at his list for India. He was ready.

Two shakes and a roll. Show me, Universe, where I should go . . .

The dice clattered across the table.

A three and a four.

Lucky number seven.

Delhi.

A third visit to India and a third for Delhi, too. A place made for only the bravest.

Jacob leant back in his chair and let the sights and sounds of Delhi burst free from his catalogue of memories. Already he felt his heartbeat quicken and the adrenaline surge through his veins. It was a far cry from his tranquil Sri Lankan beach, but he knew deep down there must be a reason for it.

If he was to commit fully to the life he'd chosen, he had to believe that.

'Oh, Universe,' he sighed, digging his fork into one of the thick slabs of banana bread, 'what on earth have you got planned for me next, I wonder . . .' And as he bit down on the soft, sweet cake, he couldn't ignore the prickle of electricity that spread through him.

It's something big.

It's got to be something big . . .

Olivia

Olivia checked the time. How was it half past six already?

'I have to leave. I really have to leave,' she told herself, throwing her barely eaten bowl of granola into the sink and downing the dregs of her espresso, before hurriedly shoving another capsule into the machine.

'Right.' She stood up tall and shot back the searing hot coffee. 'I *think* we are good to go.' She grabbed her laptop bag and slung it over her shoulder, the weight of it nearly causing her to stumble. Phil had been promising her a new computer for the past year, but so far he'd managed to spend all their technology budget on a gigantic flat-screen TV for the office, and Olivia had remained lumbered with this brick. She hoisted her handbag up and was about to open the front door when her phone began to ring.

'Please don't be Phil with more changes . . . *please* don't be Phil with more changes,' she prayed under her breath.

From the moment the board presentation had been announced, her boss Phil had been in overdrive. The entire team had been working on it for months now. In fact, they had gone over it so many times that whenever Olivia closed her eyes, all she could see were graphs and data points. Surely there was nothing more that needed to be done?

She pulled the phone free, her stomach dropping at the name flashing up on her screen.

Don't answer it. You can call him back later.

Olivia hesitated, her finger hovering over the reject button.

But he never calls this early.

In fact, he never calls at all . . .

Panic gripped her and she answered the phone immediately.

'Kyle, what's wrong?' she barked.

'Wow, that wasn't the friendly greeting I was expecting this fine Monday morning.'

'What do you expect? It's like . . .' Olivia glanced down at her watch. 'Quarter to seven. Why are you even awake?'

As if on cue, her brother let out an exaggerated yawn. 'I pulled a double shift at work. The kitchen was seriously understaffed, so I said I'd help out. You know me, always a giver.'

'And always slightly delusional.' Olivia rolled her eyes. 'Is everything OK? Are you all right? Is Mum OK?'

'Yes, yes, we're all fine. Calm down. How many coffees have you had? You sound wired.'

Olivia felt the caffeine pulsing through her.

'I'm not in the mood for messing around, Kyle. I have a big day at work, and I need my energy.'

She checked the time again, a nervous habit which only served to make her more anxious.

'I know you do, that's why I was calling.'

'Huh?'

'I wanted to wish you luck. You've got that big presentation thing today, don't you?'

'Yes . . .' A spark of suspicion flared up inside her. It was a stretch for Kyle to wish her a happy birthday, let alone remember one of her work meetings.

'So, I wanted to call and wish you luck. You seemed spun out about it the last time I saw you, so I knew it was probably a big deal.'

'The last time I saw you, I was "spun out" about quite a few things,' she fired back, a little too harshly.

'Weren't we all.'

A pang of guilt. A surge of grief.

'I'm sorry – that wasn't fair of me.'

'It's fine. We can blame it on the espresso hitting.' He gave a sad half-laugh. 'On that note, though, have you spoken to Mum and Dad?'

Olivia's guilt grew in intensity.

'No . . . I've been meaning to, but I . . . I've just been too busy with work.' She winced at her poor excuse. 'Have you?'

'Yeah, they seem OK. Well, as OK as they can be, I suppose.'

'I promise I'll ring them as soon as this presentation's over.' Olivia bent down and hauled her bags up from the floor. 'But right now, I have to g—'

'Have you done it yet?' Kyle interrupted.

'Done what?'

'Come on, don't play dumb. It doesn't suit you.'

Olivia closed her eyes and felt her heart sink towards her feet. 'Really? You're going to do this now?'

'Surely not even *you* can have this much self-restraint?'

Olivia's eyes fell instinctively on the sealed envelope that was sitting on top of the microwave.

'I think you'll find I can.'

'Just . . .' Kyle hesitated. 'Just don't leave it too long, OK?

I know out of the two of us, I'm rarely the one that's right. But trust me on this. You're going to want to open that letter sooner rather than later.'

An uncomfortable thought dawned on her.

Does he know?

When Olivia had first brought the letter home, it had stayed hidden in her jacket pocket. Then it got moved to the windowsill in her bedroom. But staring at your dead sister's handwriting first thing every morning turned out to be a rather triggering wake-up call. After much shifting and re-arranging around her flat, it had finally found its resting place on top of the microwave. Not completely hidden from sight, but not screaming out for attention every five minutes either.

'Anyway, Big Sis, I'd better leave you to it. I stink. I need a shower and a McDonald's breakfast muffin, pronto.'

Olivia felt a slight ease return to her tight chest. No. There was no way Leah would trust Kyle to help her out with this. She loved her brother, she really did, but if you wanted a job done, the truth was you never went to Kyle.

But then who had been the one to place the letters on the mantelpiece the morning of the funeral? Who had been the one her little sister had trusted with her parting words? It wasn't just Olivia who had been shocked by their presence; everyone had seemed completely taken aback by the final gift from Leah. A series of perfectly sealed envelopes, one for each member of the family.

'Charming as ever.' She smirked, balancing the phone pre-cariously on her shoulder whilst she attempted to open the front door.

'Damn straight. You may have got the successful gene, but I won out on charisma.'

'Again, delusional.' Olivia hooked her bags over her

shoulders. 'Right, I'm not messing around now, Kyle. I *really* have to go.'

'*Fine*. Good luck and let me know how it goes.'

'OK, bye.'

She hung up the phone, and just before she closed the door, she stole one last glance at the unopened letter.

Soon, Leah.

I promise, I'll read you soon.

*

By the time Olivia sat down at her desk, she was already an hour behind schedule. Of course, today would be the day that London's entire transport system decided to turn to complete and utter shit; and then when she finally got to the office, the queue for the coffee shop was practically out the door.

'Running a little late for you, Jackson. What happened?' her colleague Rob sneered at her from across the floor. 'Decided to get some beauty sleep before the big meeting?'

Don't rise to it. You don't have the time.

Olivia offered a pathetic half-laugh and threw her bags down.

'Ooh, too serious to even have a little joke, are we? Someone's nervous about the presentation! Don't worry, you'll be fine,' he added rather bitterly. 'You always are.'

Rob had been at the company for fifteen years and hadn't taken kindly to Olivia's rapid rise through the ranks. He was older than she was and at least three levels below. Olivia had tried to empathize with him – until she had discovered, when tasked with doing his review last year, that he was paid nearly double her salary.

'Classic corporate bullshit,' her friend Kate had shouted when Olivia had revealed her findings. 'I don't know why you stay working for such complete and utter tosspots.'

'Because it's—'

'Part of your plan – I know, I *know*,' Kate had cried.

Olivia and Kate had been best friends since secondary school, and yet it would be hard to find two more opposite people. For all of Kate's carefree, restless creativity, Olivia was focused, prepared and detailed. Olivia's career path had been mapped out since she was sixteen years old, whereas Kate seemed to treat her jobs as carelessly as her boyfriends, never able to keep one for more than two years before getting bored and moving on. Currently she was trying her hand at landscape gardening, but it didn't seem to be going that well.

'Shit!' Olivia cursed, bringing herself back to the present moment and grabbing a pack of Post-it notes. *Text Kate back ASAP*, she scrawled, underlining the words three times and sticking the note to the top of her computer screen. In her defence, she had been busy; but then again, she spent her entire life being busy.

'Hope you're ready, Jackson' – Rob's snarky voice cut through her thoughts – 'because here comes the big man!'

Olivia snapped her head up to see her boss emerge, stomach first, from the corridor.

'*Liv!*' Phil's voice boomed, echoing around the office. 'There you are! I was surprised you weren't here at dawn preparing! I thought, it's not like our Liv to be later than me.' He chuckled, his belly wobbling threateningly at her. 'Are we all ready to go?'

Olivia swallowed down the knot of emotions that had gathered in her throat. She wasn't sure what was worse: her boss's insistence on calling her Liv, or the nerves that were running their icy fingers against the inside of her stomach.

'I'm as ready as I'll ever be.' She grinned falsely.

'Good. Because you know how important this is, don't you?' Phil bumbled, tucking his white and surprisingly unstained shirt into his trousers. For a man deemed competent enough to manage a team of twenty people and a multi-million-pound budget, Phil seemed totally useless at keeping his clothes clean. Every day, as sure as the sun would rise in the sky, a stain would appear on Phil's shirt. 'If we get their approval, we sign the biggest client in the past three years.'

'Uh-huh.' Olivia nodded, feeling a small wave of nausea crash over her.

'And that means big bonuses – for you, and more importantly, for me.' A grotesque Cheshire cat grin appeared on his face. Olivia's queasiness intensified tenfold. 'Got your laptop?'

'Yes.' She held the cumbersome silver computer aloft.

'Fantastic.' Phil's piggy eyes flickered up to the large clock on the wall. 'Shall we head up? It's always good to be a little early, isn't it.'

'Sure. Let's go,' she agreed, standing up and adjusting her rather snug-fitting suit. There were many things Olivia enjoyed about her job, but wearing a suit was not one of them. The first thing she would do when she ran her own business was banish formal dress entirely.

'Fantastic.' Phil began to walk briskly ahead. 'Oh, and Lisa,' he barked at his assistant. 'Don't put any meetings in over lunch today. I'm going to have to brief the team after this and I don't want any clashes. You know what happened the last time you rescheduled my day – you got it totally wrong and the whole thing ended up a complete disaster.'

The second thing Olivia would do, as her own boss, was never speak to anyone the way Phil did. Unless it was to Phil himself, of course.

'And make sure I have a coffee waiting for me when I come out. I'm going to need something before the next meeting. Yesterday I was late because I had to get my own from downstairs.'

Olivia tried to offer Lisa a consolatory smile as they passed, but the assistant's eyes were firmly fixed on the screen in front of her, a mild look of panic dawning on her face.

'Good luck, guys!' Rob called brightly, giving them an awkwardly exaggerated thumbs up as they approached the exit to the lifts.

'Thanks,' Olivia replied, trying to ignore the beating of her heart that seemed to be growing louder and more violent with every step they took.

'After you.' Phil stopped abruptly, holding open the door and ushering Olivia through. Three lifts stood to attention on each side. Flustered-looking people were hurrying this way and that, jabbing the call buttons as though their lives depended on it.

'Thirty-second floor for us today, Liv. All the way to the top.'

Her insides squirmed, but she smiled sweetly and hit the button.

Press on. Push forward.
You have a job to do.

*

The room was hot and stuffy, despite its size. A table of thirteen rather stern, bored-looking people sat waiting for them. Eyes wide and unblinking. Suits, every shade of grey, rustling impatiently.

'Just one moment, we seem to be having a little technical trouble. Nothing to worry about, though, nothing at all!'

Phil babbled, sweat beading across his reddening forehead. '*What the hell is wrong with this thing?*' he hissed out of the corner of his mouth.

The brick of a laptop, which had been working fine only moments ago, was now making a disturbingly loud whirring noise, and the whole screen had turned black.

'I don't know.' Olivia bent down to check the connections once again. 'It should be working.'

'Well, it's *not* working, is it?' Phil spat, speckles of white saliva showering Olivia's face.

'Is there a problem?' a droll voice asked from the table.

Phil stood up sharply. 'No, no, all fine. Like I said, just a little technical issue. We'll have it fixed in a jiffy.'

Jiffy? Since when has Phil ever said 'jiffy'?

He crouched down and put his now scarlet face uncomfortably close to hers. 'Do something soon or it will be the end of us.' The smell of nerves and stale coffee made Phil's breath even more putrid than usual.

'Shall we try turning the whole thing off and on again?' she asked, offering the only solution she could think of under the pressure of the executive board's intense collective stare.

'Fine. *Fine.*' Phil waved her away frantically. 'You do that, and I'll start the introduction. That man there looks like he's already asleep.'

Olivia peered up to see an elderly gentleman towards the back, whose eyes were very much closed.

'It's because it's about a hundred degrees in here,' she whispered, resenting even more the grey fitted suit that was now sticking to her body. As great as the views were from the top of the building, the floor-to-ceiling windows made the whole room cook like a conservatory.

'Just turn the bloody computer off, will you,' Phil ordered, standing up to his full height and plastering a maniacal smile on his face. 'Ladies and gentlemen, let's make a start, shall we? I know how precious your time is and I don't want to keep you any longer. The slides' – he shot Olivia a warning look – 'will be ready shortly.'

Olivia did as she was told and switched the old, whirring laptop off and on. After a painfully long two minutes, the presentation finally burst into life on to the screen behind them. Phil's shoulders visibly relaxed, and Olivia shuffled forward to take her spot next to him.

'We've prepared the following presentation to highlight just how much we believe you could save over the next five years with a few minor tweaks to your business,' Phil continued, his bustling bravado in full swing.

Olivia had known that her job would be hard. She was prepared for the long hours and weekends working. The one thing she wasn't prepared for, however, even after seven years in the game, was just how difficult making decisions about people's lives was. For Olivia, being a business consultant was all about how to get the most from employees. How to motivate, inspire and re-energize a business so that satisfaction soared along with productivity. Unfortunately, for nearly every other person she'd met in her company, it meant streamlining and firing. Making redundancies and ending contracts. Advising on who should stay and who should go. It wasn't always an easy job, but until she'd gained enough experience to set up solo, she would keep her head down and continue to play by their rules. 'Their' essentially being Phil and his now very sweaty shirt.

'Olivia here is going to take us through the figures.' Phil gestured towards her, his broad grin still fixed in position.

Olivia took a step forward. The eyes of everyone at the table were on her.

She opened her mouth to speak but found herself unable to form the words. Her body ran cold and then instantly hot again. She tried to clear her throat, but in doing so only made it constrict harder.

Sweat was now pouring from her, and she was finding it difficult to breathe.

'Olivia?' Phil grimaced, his small watery eyes narrowing at her. 'Could you take us through the figures, please.'

Breathe.

Take a breath and speak. It's just like you practised.

But try as she might, no sound would come from Olivia's mouth. Her heart was beating loudly – so loudly, in fact, that she could hear it pulsing in her ears. The thudding was drowning out every other sound in the room.

'I . . . I . . .' she stuttered, fear slithering from the pit of her stomach up to her chest. It was as though someone had run razor blades down the inside of her windpipe, and her fingers were starting to feel oddly numb.

'I need water,' she rasped.

Her mouth was so dry, her body so hot.

'Excuse me, young lady?' A concerned voice rose from the now very blurry faces sitting in front of her. 'Are you OK?'

'Yes, you do look rather pale,' another chimed in.

Olivia's heart now felt too big for her chest. It was growing in size, and if only she could just find a way to catch her breath . . .

'Olivia, do you need to sit down?' Phil's face loomed large in front of her.

Suddenly a loud ringing began to sound in her ears.

'Liv, can you hear me?' he began to shout.

Don't call me Liv.

You aren't allowed to call me Liv.

But before she could open her mouth to answer, the room began to spin, and then everything went suddenly and sickeningly black.

Olivia

'You really don't have to come inside with me, Kate.' Olivia stopped outside her front door. 'Honestly, I'm fine.'

She had insisted she was fine the second she came to, lying prostrate on the floor of the executive boardroom. Over and over, she parroted the phrase, desperate for everyone to get back to the meeting in hand and let her do her job. But no, apparently she had to be escorted downstairs and carted off in an ambulance in front of the entire office. The mortification was too much to bear.

'Uh-huh,' her friend pouted. 'You can keep on saying it, Olivia, and I am going to keep on ignoring you. Besides, as your designated emergency contact, I have to fulfil my duties and make sure you're OK. Now, open the door.'

If Olivia weren't feeling so exhausted, she would have mustered one of her killer stares and sent it Kate's way. Maybe Kyle would have been a smarter choice as her emergency contact; it was unlikely he'd even answer his phone, let alone dash halfway across London to sit in an A&E waiting room with her for two hours. But her family had always

21

had other emergencies – *real* emergencies – to deal with. The thought made her heart drop dangerously low in her chest.

'But surely you need to be back at work? You can't take the whole afternoon off for me.'

'Keep those excuses coming. I've got all the time in the world to hear them' – Kate leant against the wall, tapping her foot for dramatic effect – 'but I'd much rather listen to them over a nice cup of tea and some Hobnobs, wouldn't you?'

Olivia bit down on the inside of her cheek. She knew there was no way out – Kate was the most stubborn human being she'd ever met – but still . . . the thought of letting her inside made Olivia feel sick.

'Come *on*.' Kate fixed her with a fierce don't-fuck-with-me look. 'I don't want to have to rugby tackle you for the keys. You're in a fragile enough state as it is.'

'*Fine!*' Olivia stuffed her key in the lock. 'But I'm warning you, it's kind of a mess in here.'

'Whatever. We both know that your version of mess is my best attempt at being clean.'

Olivia held her breath as she felt the lock click. Her head was pounding as the blood rushed through her body. This was a mistake.

She pushed on the door and let it drift open.

A gigantic mistake.

'Holy shit, what the *hell* happened!' Kate's permanently enthusiastic face dropped as she stepped across the threshold.

Mugs of half-drunk tea and coffee were lined up like toy soldiers on every available surface. Dirty dishes were piled high in the sink, the remnants of meals glued in rings around the edges, as stubborn and persistent as the anxiety that now lived permanently in Olivia's chest. Items of clothing were flung carelessly on the floor alongside empty packets of cereal bars and biscuits, the crumbs leaving speckled imprints in the carpet.

'Olivia, what *is* going on?'

'Nothing . . . I just . . .'

She stared around, as if only seeing it properly for the first time.

'Work got so busy and . . . I guess . . .' The emotion was building inside her, pressing against her skin, aching to burst free. 'I suppose I've let things get a bit on top of me, that's all.'

'A *bit* on top of you? Jesus, it looks like someone's been here and trashed the place.'

'OK, well if it's that bad you can leave, can't you?' Olivia lashed out, throwing her keys down on the table. 'I don't need your judgement on top of everyone else's today, OK?'

Olivia felt shame crawl across her skin. The memories of the day felt like a million sharp insects scuttling over her body. The look on Phil's face as he helped her into the ambulance. The doctor's concern when she burst into tears before he'd even asked what had happened. The note he wrote her, recommending she take three months off for her health. The realization that her world had officially come crashing down.

'Hey.' Kate slung her arm around Olivia's shoulder and guided her towards the sofa. 'There is no judgement here, I can promise you that. Only love and concern, and a little surprise.' She squeezed her closer. 'And it doesn't matter about anyone else; everyone else sucks.'

'Except it does matter. It's my job, Kate. It's my *life*.' Her voice broke and the tears stung her eyes.

'And you will be back there before you know it.' Kate sat down and pulled Olivia with her. 'I know it feels like a big deal right now, and you're angry and upset and feeling all the things . . . but I think, in the long term, it's for the best.'

'For the *best*?' Olivia cried. 'What's for the best is that I get back to work and start making amends for what happened, not sit here wallowing in my feelings and taking time off.'

'Olivia, you passed out because you're overworked, stressed and totally burnt out. Your little sister passed away less than two months ago, and you didn't even stop to take a breath. You've been nonstop your entire life, taking care of everybody except yourself, and quite frankly you look like shit and need a break.'

'Wow, and now I feel much better, thank you.'

'What can I say? Good friends are always there for each other, but . . .'

Kate smirked, waiting for Olivia to finish the sentence. Their silly childhood saying that had become their mantra in life.

'Come on . . . you can't leave me hanging.'

Reluctantly, and through gritted teeth, Olivia obliged. 'Only the best ones tell the truth.'

'Exactly!' Kate stood up abruptly. 'Now, here's what's going to happen. You, my friend, are going to go and have a nice long shower, because God knows you need to do something about this situation.' She gestured up and down the length of her. 'And then you're going to get into bed and sleep, whilst I sort the rest of this place out and get us some decent food. OK?'

Olivia went to protest – the thought of someone else tidying up her mess was unbearable – but Kate had already begun to frogmarch her towards the bathroom.

'And no arguing with me, Miss Jackson. For one day only, I'm in charge, all right?'

Through the depths of her exhaustion, and the thick

blanket of despair that had wrapped itself around her heart, Olivia felt a surge of affection for her friend.

'OK, but just for today, all right?'

*

Five hours later, Olivia emerged from her bedroom. The enormity of her pain still sat heavy on her shoulders, but the fog had cleared a little from her mind, and her body felt at least somewhat refreshed after the shower and sleep.

'Aha, perfect timing! I was about to come and wake you up.' Kate spun around, her mass of red hair piled on top of her head. 'I made dinner.'

The intoxicating smell of tomato, garlic and onion greeted Olivia like an old friend, and she could see big bowls piled high with pasta and cheese.

'This place . . .' She stared around at her now immaculate living room. 'It looks amazing.'

'No.' Kate strode towards her, bowls in hand. 'It looks like your flat normally does when you're not in the middle of an emotional breakdown. Now, sit and eat this, please.'

'OK, who made you my mum all of a sudden?'

'What can I say? Sometimes, even *you* need to be looked after.'

Olivia didn't argue, but only because her stomach was physically aching with hunger. She took the food and nestled down into the crumb-free, perfectly plumped sofa.

'Thank you for this.' She gestured around the room. 'All of this.'

'You're welcome. Do you feel a bit better?'

'Yeah, I can't believe how deeply I slept.'

'Your body must have needed it. Another reason why this break will be good for you.'

'About that . . .' Olivia shook her head. 'I've decided I'm going to contest it. Speak to Phil, explain how much better I feel even after one day of rest, and that maybe I could come back in a week or two.'

'You can try, my friend' – Kate wiped a fleck of tomato sauce from her chin – 'but a doctor's note is hard to go against, especially given how on edge big companies are these days about health and well-being. Trust me, I've worked in HR. Many times.'

Olivia felt her last tiny shred of hope crumple into nothing. 'But how the hell am I going to fill three months of time without work?'

'Maybe you could join an evening class. There are loads of things online now. Or you could sign up to do one of those ultramarathon things. I would offer to do it with you, but we both know that won't happen. I don't think I could manage a thirty-minute walk in my current state.'

Olivia felt her body tighten.

'How about a trip?' Kate went on. 'Ooh, maybe we could do a weekend away? Go to Paris? I've never been, which blows my mind because it's so close. I could look at flights tonight, or even the Eurostar – that's probably better for us, isn't it?'

'Stop!' Olivia shouted, dropping her fork into her bowl and spattering tomato sauce all over her lap. 'I'm sorry, I just . . . I can't process it all right now.'

If Kate was offended by Olivia's reaction she hid it well, shoving another forkful of food into her mouth and nodding in agreement. 'Of course, I'm sorry.'

The pair sat and ate the rest of their food in silence. Olivia knew the peace and quiet would be short-lived and, as suspected, the second the final mouthful was eaten, Kate piped up again.

'Do you think you should tell your mum and dad what's happened? I'm happy to call them if you're too tired.'

'No.' Her voice was firm and flat. 'They have enough going on as it is.'

'Doesn't mean they won't want to hear about your stuff too.'

'Really?' Olivia could taste the resentment building on her tongue, a sour sting against the rich tomato and basil. 'Since when have they cared about anything other than Leah from the minute she was born?'

'Hey, you know that's not true.'

And she did know, but the depths of her self-pity seemed to be clouding her judgement and sending all rational thought straight out of the window.

'Although, speaking of Leah . . .' The caution in Kate's voice made Olivia's ears instantly prick up. 'Earlier, when I was tidying up, I found this.' Kate reached into her pocket and pulled out the unopened envelope, placing it between them. 'The writing on the front looks a lot like . . . well, I thought it was from . . .'

'It is.'

Kate's mouth fell wide open.

'Really? This is from Leah?'

'Uh-huh.'

'But then why haven't you opened it yet?'

Olivia didn't even have the energy for a response, offering a measly shrug as a best attempt.

'How long have you had it?'

'Since the morning of her funeral. She left one for each of us. I came downstairs and there they were. Four of them, all lined up on the mantelpiece.'

'Jesus Christ, and you haven't even sneaked a peek at it yet?'

'I had other things going on. I wanted to get the presentation done and be in the right frame of mind before I did.'

'My love.' Kate placed her hand gently over Olivia's. 'I don't think you're ever going to be in the right frame of mind to open this letter. Do you know what was in any of the others?'

'Nope, and I don't want to ask. It's none of my business.'

'And nobody has asked what's in yours?'

'Well, obviously Kyle keeps going on at me to open it – says I shouldn't leave it so long, as if there's some kind of expiry date on it.'

Her mind was taken back to the conversation that morning with her brother. His urgency had rattled her more than she let on.

'And you know that usually I don't agree with anything your brother says, but in this case, I think I do.'

'Why? Why is everyone so obsessed with what's in that letter? It won't bring her back. It won't change anything. It's just words. Empty fucking words.'

'But they are *her* words, Olivia. They're Leah's words for *you*.'

A weariness crept up into Olivia's heart. Was she going to keep fighting this? Could she really carry on convincing herself that she wasn't intrigued by Leah's letter?

'And what if they're bad?' The childlike voice escaped from her lips.

'Bad? Why on earth would they be bad?'

'I don't know. Maybe I wasn't there enough. Maybe I didn't do enough.' Her words began to spiral, along with her thoughts. 'Maybe she was angry at me. Maybe she felt like I didn't care enough.'

'Stop!' Kate interrupted. 'Leah adored you. She loved the

28

very bones of you, and she knew that you felt the same about her. You did *everything* you could to support her. But until you open the letter, you will never know what she wanted to say.'

Kate held the envelope out, and cautiously, Olivia took it.

'I'm scared.'

'I know.'

'Opening it makes this whole thing real.'

'And not opening it doesn't bring her back either.'

Before she could stop herself, Olivia ripped open the letter and turned it upside down. Two pieces of paper fell to the floor, and she hastily plucked them from the carpet. The sight of her little sister's handwriting made her heart hurt.

> To my Liv, the best big sister in the world,
>   Surprise!
>   God, I wish I could see your face right now. I'm sorry for keeping this from you, but if you even had the slightest whiff of what I was planning, you'd have killed me before the cancer finally had a chance to. I've made sure the flight date is flexible (who knows at what point you've decided to open this!), but unfortunately it's non-refundable. You can't deny a dying girl her money or her wish, can you?
>   Go. Travel. Explore. Enjoy this thing called life!
>   Do it for me, my darling, brave sister.
>   I love you eternally.
>   Leah x

Olivia's mind was spinning but her eyes stayed fixed on the words in front of her.

She couldn't have.

She wouldn't have . . .

But realization began to dawn as she scanned the second piece of paper, her eyes competing with her mouth as to which could grow the widest.

'This is confirmation of your booking for flight BA46369 departing from London Heathrow to . . .' Olivia read out loud, her heart climbing higher and higher with each sound she made. '*Delhi, India* . . .'

'Shut up!' Kate burst into life, snatching the paper from Olivia's grip. 'No way!'

'This can't be real.'

'From what I can see, it's real all right.'

'I can't go to India.'

'Why not?'

'Because I can't! It's crazy.' The ringing in her ears grew louder and her stomach churned ominously. 'Why would she do this to me? *How* did she even do this? Surely she knew how much I'd hate this! I have never *ever* in my life wanted to go travelling.'

'You know, sometimes change is good. India is meant to be incredible.'

'So is climbing Mount Everest, but you don't see me signing up for that, do you?'

But Olivia knew Kate wasn't listening to her protests; she had that fantastical far-off look on her face whenever she was excited. And once Kate was in dreamland, it was extremely hard to bring her back down to earth.

'Ooh, maybe you could have a little *Eat Pray Love* moment?'

'An eat pray what?'

'You *know*, the Julia Roberts film, where she leaves everything behind and travels the world. You could be like her.'

'Don't you dare say it.'

'You could *find yourself*. Like Julia did!'

'The only thing I need to find is a way out of this stupid situation.'

'Why? You said it yourself: you didn't know how to fill your time off. This is it! It couldn't be more perfect.'

'Look, if you think it's such a great idea, why don't you take the ticket instead? I'm sure you can transfer the name or something. Especially if we explain the circumstances.'

Kate raised an eyebrow. 'You know full well I am not going to do that. This is for you. It was clearly important to Leah that you did this.'

'I know that. Don't you think I know that?' Olivia hissed. 'Urgh, how could Leah have been so stupid? She must have used half of her savings on this. It must have cost her a fortune!'

'I wonder who helped her book it,' Kate mused. 'Could she have done it all by herself?'

'Oh my god.'

Realization slapped Olivia hard in the face.

'I am going to *kill* Kyle when I next see him! I wondered why he was so obsessed with me opening the stupid letter. He was honestly harassing me over it! Why would Leah trust *him* with doing this? Nobody trusts Kyle with anything.'

'That's probably the exact reason. He could arrange the whole thing undetected because you all underestimate him.'

Guilt spiked in Olivia's chest.

'That's not entirely true.'

'Isn't it?' Kate looked at her knowingly.

'Regardless of whether or not it's true, it doesn't matter. Because either way, I'm not going.' She folded her arms decisively. 'There is no way in *hell* I am going to India.'

31

Olivia

'I can't believe you're going to India!' Kate took her hands off the steering wheel and clapped them together. 'This is so exciting. Are you excited?'

Olivia felt her stomach lurch as they turned off the motorway and followed the signs to the airport.

'Mmmm,' she mumbled, tightening her grip on her rucksack, which sat heavy on her lap.

'You're going to have the best time, I promise.' Kate reached over and squeezed Olivia's shoulder, as a large Departures sign directed them towards a looming glass building. '*And* I've got you here with plenty of time! So much for the rush-hour traffic, hey?'

Olivia looked down at her watch. Only two and a half hours until her plane departed. A plane that had a seat allocated just for her. A seat waiting to carry her away from her normal, organized, safe life to a world full of complete unknowns.

This is insane.

What are you doing?

You can't do this!

Olivia felt the blood rush to her head. Her entire body began to sear with pins and needles.

'Make sure you leave your coat with me in the car – you are *not* going to want to be carrying that all the way to India,' Kate babbled on.

I need to get out.

I need to get out right this second.

'Stop the car,' Olivia shouted.

'What?'

'I said, stop the car!' she repeated, louder and more urgently than before.

'We're nearly here, give me a second. I just need to park.'

Olivia's lungs felt tight, her throat narrowing so that not even a sip of air could find its way in.

'Kate, if you don't stop this car in the next ten seconds, I swear to God I'll open the door and jump out of it.'

In a state of panic, Olivia reached for the handle.

'OK, OK, I'm pulling in!' Kate dutifully swung the car into one of the taxi drop-off lanes and turned the hazard lights on.

Olivia closed her eyes and let her spinning head fall forwards.

'Are you all right?' Kate slumped down in her seat so that her face was almost level with Olivia's. 'Talk to me – what's going on?'

'I don't think I can do this. It's too much. It's all too much.'

'Olivia?' Kate whispered, leaning in closer.

'I can't. I can't go out there.'

'Olivia, I need you to look at me.'

Slowly but surely, Olivia raised her head, her knuckles white from gripping her bag so tightly.

'Now,' Kate began, sitting upright and rolling her shoulders back. 'First and foremost, let's be clear on one thing: it doesn't matter how scared you are, you are never *ever* going to threaten to jump out of the car while I'm driving again, OK?' Her auburn eyebrows knitted sternly together.

Olivia nodded slowly, allowing a small bubble of laughter to escape her mouth. 'OK.'

'And secondly,' Kate continued, 'you don't have to do anything you don't want to do. If you really want me to, I will turn this car around and drive you straight back home, but . . .' She placed a hand tentatively on top of Olivia's. 'Ask yourself, will you be able to live with yourself if I do?'

Olivia tore her eyes away from Kate's and stared out of the window. It had been hard enough to convince people she was going to go on this trip in the first place; could she face proving them all right? And then, of course, there was Leah. Her precious baby sister. What would she think? Olivia's heart swelled at the very thought of her and her final words.

Do it for me, my darling, brave sister.

'You're right,' she mumbled. 'You're totally right. I'm just scared.'

'Obviously you're scared, but that doesn't mean it isn't worth doing. You'll be fine, Olivia. If anyone can do this, it's you.'

Her racing heart slowed a little at Kate's comforting words.

'Now, have you got everything? I know it's a stupid question to ask you, but my mum always does this before I go anywhere and weirdly, it always calms me down.'

'Yes, I've got everything.'

'Passport?'

'Yes.'

'Boarding pass?'

'Yes.'

'Good.' Kate thought for a moment. 'Money?'

'Can't get that until I land.'

'Right.' She paused. 'What else, what else . . .' Her eyes flashed wide with excitement. 'God, how could I forget? Do you have your itinerary?'

Olivia peered inside the smaller backpack on her lap. There it was, in all its colour-printed, Excel-spreadsheeted glory. A twenty-two-page breakdown of every single move she was going to make over the next three months. How much she could spend. Where she would go. How she would get there. It was a meticulously planned schedule that left no room for imagination or diversion. It was the bible of her trip, and without it, her already sky-high anxiety would be stratospheric.

'I've got a digital version on my phone, a paper copy here in my hand luggage, and another spare copy in my big rucksack,' Olivia confirmed.

'Well then, according to me, you're all good to go!'

'Great.' Olivia unbuckled her seat belt slowly and began adjusting her top, desperately and not so subtly attempting to buy time. 'I guess this is goodbye, then?'

'Don't be so dramatic. I'll see you before you know it, and besides' – her friend leant over and planted a huge kiss on her cheek – 'I'll be on WhatsApp and FaceTime constantly. It will be like you've never left me.'

'Promise?' The old Olivia would cringe at her neediness, but at this point she'd take all the reassurance she could get. Her legs had turned to lead, and her hands were shaking.

'I promise. Now, as much as I love you and am going to miss you, I need you to get out of the car, because that security guard over there is looking pissed off that we've been sitting in the taxi zone.' Kate craned her neck to peer at a rather disgruntled-looking man in a high-vis jacket.

'OK.' Olivia took a deep breath and opened the car door. 'I'll message you when I'm on the plane.'

'You'd better.' Kate waggled a finger jokingly at her. 'Now, remember, go and be adventurous and have the most wonderful time.'

Despite the tears welling in her eyes, Olivia forced a smile and heaved her gigantic rucksack from the back seat on to her shoulders; the weight of it threatening to topple her over. She shut the car door and slowly turned towards the terminal entrance, her feet dragging as she began to walk across the pavement.

'Go and kick Julia Roberts's ass, and have the best time EVER!' Kate's voice bellowed out from behind.

Olivia turned and saw her friend waving frantically, like an overzealous mother, out of the car window, her wild, ginger hair blowing in the wind and her beaming smile stretching wide across her face. Olivia's cheeks burnt red with embarrassment, but her heart swelled for her friend, who was now unashamedly beeping her horn in a celebratory goodbye.

'*Stop it!*' Olivia called back, tears pouring down her cheeks.

'Why?' Another long sound of the horn blasted out. 'I'm sending you off in style.'

Olivia looked around and saw groups of travellers stopping to stare. Some of them were smiling kindly; others had a look of disapproval that she felt like a slap across the face. 'People are *staring*,' she mouthed, jerking her head back towards the flurry of people.

'And?'

Olivia should have known Kate wouldn't let her go quietly.

'And . . . I love you,' Olivia cried.

'I love you too,' Kate yelled back, pulling the little Fiat 500 out of the space and disappearing down the road with one last beep of the horn.

Olivia

Olivia scanned the crowd for what felt like the hundredth time. A thousand faces looked back at her, but none was holding a sign with her name on it. There were people everywhere, filling each tiny morsel of space with bags and fabrics and noisy children. Olivia knew how to handle busy places; she had lived and worked in London for the best part of seven years. It was a rite of passage to spend your afternoons being pinballed along Oxford Street by the swarms of manic shoppers. But this? This was a whole new level of chaos. Personal space seemed a non-existent concept here, and it did nothing to soothe Olivia's anxiety.

'Come on, come on, where *are* you?' She groaned, wiping her damp hair from her even damper face. The hotel had promised to provide an airport transfer. She had the email confirmation in her hand, and yet here she was, waiting at Arrivals with nobody here to collect her. What was the point in being organized if other people couldn't do their jobs?

She scanned the printed-out piece of paper once again,

checking and rechecking all the details. It was all there, no question about it. So where was her driver?

Exasperated, Olivia took another gulp of water and pulled her sweaty T-shirt away from her skin.

A large family barged past her, their luggage trolley piled so high with suitcases that Olivia was surprised they could even see where they were going. Two of the children stopped dead in their tracks and fixed Olivia with a look of complete and utter bewilderment. One of them, no taller than her knees, began to giggle uncontrollably.

'Girls, don't stare at the lady,' their mother barked, yanking the taller child's hand and pulling them away.

Olivia felt her already flushed face burn more intensely; she'd never felt more exposed in her entire life.

'Do you need a taxi, miss?' a man standing a few metres away shouted at her.

'No, no, I'm waiting for someone, thank you.'

'I'll take you. Where do you want to go?' He stepped closer to her.

'No, honestly, I'm fine.' Olivia felt her voice lift a few octaves.

She needed a moment to think. To catch some air. To make a new plan.

'Come.' He went to grab her rucksack, a dead weight lying on the ground.

'No!' she shouted, snatching the bag back. 'I said, I'm *fine*. Please leave me alone.'

The young man looked startled and held his hands up in apology. 'Sorry, miss, I was just trying to help.' He gave a small bow and disappeared into the throng of people buzzing around the Arrivals lounge.

Olivia narrowed her eyes once more in search of anyone holding a sign that bore even the slightest resemblance to her name. At this point, she was tempted to pretend that yes she was, in fact, Mr Bob Salsbury going to the Hilton Hotel. Anything to get her away from this overbearing heat and noise. Suddenly the world shifted, and everyone's faces began to swirl and merge into one. Olivia's head felt light, and her hands began to tingle.

Oh God, not again.

She sat down on her backpack and placed her head between her legs. Flashes of colour danced across her field of vision and her stomach rolled with nausea. How could she have failed this badly at the first hurdle?

Olivia continued to take deep, slow breaths. Soon the dizziness retreated, and her body began to solidify back into its skin. Although she still felt completely and utterly hopeless, Olivia knew that she needed to focus. There was only so long she could sit here waiting for her driver. If they didn't show in the next hour, she would get a taxi. In order to get a taxi, she'd need . . .

'Money,' she affirmed, standing with a newfound determination. She hoisted her bag on to her back and waddled over to the nearest cashpoint, carefully trying to avoid being knocked over by the unrelenting mass of travellers.

'Do you need help, miss?' an eager voice piped up from behind her. Olivia turned to find another smiling stranger staring at her expectantly. How desperate and hopeless did she look?

Do you really want to answer that?

'No, I'm fine thanks.' She nodded curtly, turning back to face the smeary, grease-stained cash machine screen. Thank God for the extra-large hand sanitizer she'd packed as a last-minute addition. Noticing that her new helpful stranger hadn't quite left her side, Olivia warily punched in her PIN and withdrew a sizeable wad of cash.

'Do you have everything you need now? Can I get you a taxi?' the man bleated, his hand twitching in readiness to relieve her of her backpack and carry it to his car.

Olivia paused for a second, rivers of sweat now pooling in the small of her back. Was she going to wait around for another hour in the vain hope that someone would magic-ally appear with a big white sign saying . . .

'JACKSON!' she shouted, her eyes clocking a weary-looking man lazily waving a placard in the air. 'THAT'S ME.' She pushed past the over-friendly stranger and made for her driver, who was standing on the other side of the Arrivals lounge.

'Excuse me,' she called, forcing her way through. 'Excuse me!' But the man didn't even blink; he simply continued to stand, slouched over, waving the sign at half-speed.

'HELLO?' she bellowed, her bag almost knocking an elderly lady to the floor as she darted between two reuniting families.

'Hi. It's me,' she panted, finally standing in front of the man with the card. 'I'm Miss Jackson.'

'Evergreen Hotel?' he asked half-heartedly, the sign still held aloft in front of him.

'Yes!'

'Come.' He jerked his head towards the exit and began to walk off.

'Wait, hold on,' she called. 'I need to get a SIM card for my phone. Could you help me?'

'There's no time,' he shot back over his shoulder, picking up his pace so that Olivia had to break into a light jog just to keep up.

No time?

You're the one that's nearly an hour late!

'Please,' she begged, the momentary bliss of relief disappearing as quickly as it came. If she didn't have a local SIM card, there was no way she was going to be able to keep in contact with people – not unless she was willing to fork out fifteen pounds a day.

'We'll get it later,' he replied, beckoning her to follow him.

'Are you sure? Is there a phone shop near the hotel?'

'Sure. Now come. The car is just down here.'

Olivia followed her driver through the double doors and nearly collapsed as the wall of heat hit her. If she'd thought the inside of the airport was a melting pot of chaos, it was nothing compared to the inferno waiting for her outside. Olivia had been following the weather reports for days before she'd arrived in Delhi. She knew full well what the temperature would be. But this heat was different. It was thick and heavy and clung to the skin like a coat of burning leeches, sucking you dry from the inside out. Even her eyeballs seemed to shrivel inside their sockets in response.

'How far away did you say the car was?' Olivia wasn't sure she could last another thirty seconds in the heat.

'Not far.' Her driver gestured to some vague spot in the distance.

It turned out that their versions of the word 'far' differed enormously. By the time they reached the car, Olivia didn't even bat an eyelid at its battered and bruised exterior. She barely registered the smashed front light and the scratched bonnet; all she cared about was clambering inside and whacking the air conditioning up to full blast.

'Excuse me?' Olivia asked, feeling the sweat-slicked skin

on her back sliding down the leather seats. 'Could we have the AC on, please?'

The driver gave her a toothy grin in the rear-view mirror. 'No AC. Just windows.'

Wherever you are, Leah, I hope you're bloody happy with yourself.

*

By the time Olivia arrived at her hotel she wasn't sure whether to be sick, cry or simply pass out. The journey had been one of the most traumatic of her life. There were cars and people and bikes and *cows* everywhere; lining the roads, pulling out with no warning, beeping their horns so loudly that the sharp sound was still reverberating in her eardrums. Yet despite the absolute pandemonium on the roads, her driver didn't even break a sweat. Not when a family on a moped cut them up and nearly sent them flying into another car. Not even when a group of begging children stuck their hands through the car window and began grabbing at Olivia's clothes. He simply blinked, changed gear and continued to drive.

Finally, the car pulled to a stop.

'Here we are,' the driver stated solemnly. 'Do you want help with your bags?'

'No, I think I'll be fine, thank you,' Olivia managed, her frayed nerves still sending waves of panic through her body.

'OK.' He opened the boot and waited for Olivia to drag her rucksack out.

'Before you go,' she said, heaving the solid weight up on to her shoulders, 'where was that phone shop you mentioned? I still need to sort my SIM card out.'

The driver, without uttering a word, turned around and

pointed over towards the end of the dirt track. Olivia could just about make out a small wooden shack with a big 3G Vodafone sign tacked up outside.

'*That?* You cannot seriously mean that?'

'Yes.' He shrugged, jumping back into the car. 'It looks closed though.'

'Well, where can I get one from the—' she called, but the driver had already slammed the door and started the engine. Olivia watched him drive away and felt the sticky sense of dread solidify in her stomach.

'Thank you very much for the help!' she bellowed to the clouds of dust the car had left in its wake.

Olivia looked up at the building in front of her. She had to admit she was a little taken aback by its shabbiness. In the travel guide, the photographs made it look a hell of a lot cleaner and newer and, in fact, quite different from the crumbling hotel presenting itself to her.

'You can do this,' she repeated under her breath, trying hard to reassure herself as she dragged her tired feet up the steps and into the rather deserted-looking hotel reception.

'Hello?' she called quietly.

Olivia dropped her bag to the floor and tried again.

'Hello! Is anyone here?'

An elderly man jolted into life from behind the front desk. He was unshaven and clearly half-asleep, with an unlit cigarette hanging out of his mouth.

'Hello,' he chirped brightly, as though being caught sleeping on the job by one of your customers was nothing to be sorry for. 'You have a reservation?'

'Yes.' Olivia tried to mirror his joyful expression, but she was finding it difficult in the dank interior. 'Olivia Jackson. Three nights.'

The receptionist pulled out a large leather book and began sifting through the stained pages. 'Miss Jackson . . . Miss Jackson,' he muttered. 'Ah yes. Here. Room twenty-two.'

'Great.' Olivia let out a sigh of relief. The last thing she needed right now was to be told there was a problem with her room booking.

'Let's go. I'll take your bag up after.' He beckoned, already striding out from behind the desk and towards the lifts at the end of the hallway.

'Are you sure? Will it be safe if I leave it here?'

'Yes, yes. All fine.' He waved nonchalantly. 'The lift is too small for all of us.'

Olivia nudged her bag behind the desk and followed the receptionist up the stairs towards the lifts. He jabbed the call button with a yellow, smoke-stained finger and began tucking his oversized, rather grey-looking shirt into his trousers. The old man wasn't wrong. The lift was the smallest thing she'd ever seen in her life. How the two of them were going to get inside, she had no idea.

'You first.' He gestured as the doors creaked open.

'OK.' Olivia sucked in her stomach, held her breath, and squeezed her body in as the man tucked himself in behind her.

'Very small.'

'Mhmm.' She nodded politely, the smell of stale cigarettes suddenly overwhelming her. She tried to ignore the rickety sounds the lift was making as it began its slow ascent.

Please don't break.

Please, whatever happens, do not break.

She closed her eyes until the lift shuddered to a standstill.

'Here we are.' The receptionist beamed, nearly falling out of the doors as they opened on to a very dark and dreary corridor. 'Your room is down there. Come.'

45

Olivia followed silently, unsure what was worse: the smell of stale tobacco breath in the lift or the damp, sweaty aroma that was now crawling up the inside of her nostrils. This couldn't be right, could it? This hotel had come recommended. It had four-star reviews, for Christ's sake.

'Room twenty-two.' The receptionist stopped abruptly and forced a rusted key into an even more rusted-looking lock. 'I'll bring your bag up now.' He turned on his heel and disappeared before Olivia even had a chance to reply. She placed her hand on the doorknob and noticed, with disgust, that it was sticky to the touch.

Here goes nothing.

She took a deep breath and stepped inside.

'Oh my god . . .' Her jaw nearly hit the dusty wooden floor.

Prison cell were the first words that sprang to mind. Depressing and dirty were fast followers.

'This can't be right.' She spun around, looking for any sign of the receptionist. 'Excuse me,' she called down the empty corridor. 'Hello?' But only the raucous sounds from the outside world echoed back to her.

'There's no way this can be right.' She shook her head, edging further inside the tiny little room. Panes of glass, acting as windows, were coated with such a thick layer of dirt that the sunlight could hardly find its way through. The walls were just about clothed in peeling, brown wallpaper, and the curtains were hanging on to their rails by a thread.

'Hello!' a loud cheery voice called from behind. 'Is everything OK?'

Olivia whipped her head round and stared aghast at the receptionist, whose beads of sweat were dripping from his skin on to her rucksack.

'No,' she cried. 'Everything is not OK. I need another room.'

'Why?' He put his head inside and peered around. 'Is there a problem?'

'Yes! This doesn't look anything like the pictures in the guidebook. Do you have any bigger ones? Any *newer* ones?'

Olivia hated how highly strung she sounded, but the emotions of the day were proving too much.

'Sorry, no. They are all the same as this one.'

'Oh.' Olivia felt her chest swell with emotion. 'I see.'

'Good.' The man nodded, clearly satisfied that he'd rectified the situation. 'Can I get you anything else?'

A litre of bleach and an air freshener?

Olivia was speechless. Her entire body was frozen in shock. What were her options?

Return to the airport and fly straight back to London?

Less than twenty-four hours after arriving?

Leave and find somewhere else?

Not without the ability to google a half-decent hotel.

'Actually' – Olivia's logical brain kicked into action – 'I need to buy a SIM card for my phone. Do you know where I can get one from?'

'Sure, come down to reception and I'll give you directions.'

'Thank you.' Olivia clenched her jaw and tentatively took her backpack from his grasp. 'I'll be down in a bit.'

'No worries. Enjoy!' the man trilled brightly, giving a small bow before scuttling off down the hallway.

Olivia willed back the tears that were stinging her eyes. She looked at the bed, with its faded, brown sheets and pink, knitted blanket. Who knew how many sweaty bodies had laid themselves down between those sheets? How many things other than their dreams had they left behind for the next person to sleep on? Olivia shuddered at the thought. She just needed to get her phone sorted and she could make a new plan from there. Simple.

Jacob

The second he'd stepped off the plane, India had welcomed him in the only way it knew how: with a blaze of heat, and a wave of pandemonium. It had taken him the briefest of seconds to acclimatize, before his body remembered how it felt to be here, to know the place as home, and to settle into the erratic rhythm that was the heartbeat of the country.

Jacob rarely allowed himself moments for reflection, but he couldn't help remembering how differently he had arrived each time he'd set foot in the country. The first time, way back when he had just begun his adventures, he had touched down with a bag the size of a small human. It was filled to bursting with clothes and toiletries and books and shoes. Everything he thought he needed. The bare minimum for survival. However, it didn't take long for those so-called necessities to become surplus. With each new place he roamed, he craved lightness and freedom, letting go of his past by relinquishing the *things* from his past. Now, upon his arrival for the third time, Jacob only carried with him a small backpack and a bum bag. Lighter, easier and far simpler. Not only to carry with him to new places, but also to leave behind old ones. Twelve hours after rolling his dice and finishing his birthday banana bread, Jacob had arrived in Delhi.

'I have to admit, kiddo, I never thought I'd see your scrawny ass again,' the large, gruff server chuckled, clearing Jacob's plate away. 'But I'm glad that you remembered us after all this time.'

As much as he loved exploring new places, Jacob had to admit that there were some benefits to revisiting old stomping grounds. Having been to Delhi multiple times, he knew exactly where to go for cheap accommodation that didn't involve risking your life every time you closed your eyes; he knew what areas to avoid, how best to travel around and, most importantly of all, where to go for the best chai and eggs.

'How could I forget this place? You do the best breakfast in town.'

'Psht' – the man kissed his teeth – 'we do the best breakfast in India, boy. Now, do you want anything else?'

Jacob rocked back on his chair and surveyed the little cafe. It was hot and dusty, hidden in one of the many side alleys that carved their way through the city like a network of veins. The table of local men next to him had drunk their chai hastily, mopped their furrowed brows and departed back to the streets. Outside in the chaotic alleyway, groups of women huddled over huge vats of steaming food. The reds, greens and golds of their saris flashed brilliantly in the light. The sun was scorching, and the dust gathered in thick clouds. Cows mooed lazily as children screamed and danced recklessly amongst them. He could stay here for hours, drinking tea and watching the world go by. But he knew that life was far too short to waste people watching.

'No, I'd better be off.' Jacob stretched his arms to the

ceiling. 'There's the whole world out there to explore! An entire day to seize. Am I right?'

The man's expression darkened in the face of Jacob's optimism.

'Sure, whatever you say, boy.'

'Hey now, don't look so upset, I'll be back soon.' Jacob reached into his pocket and pulled out a fistful of notes, stuffing them into the waiter's hand. 'And maybe . . . just maybe, that time I'll be lucky enough to catch you smiling.'

The man snorted, but squeezed Jacob's hand in gratitude. 'There's more chance of you finally staying put in one place than that happening.'

'You know me too well, Amir.'

'Unfortunately, that's very true. Now, go – you're putting off my other customers with your cheek.'

Jacob bit back the urge to point out that he was one of only three other people in the cafe. Instead, he gathered his stuff and walked out into the chaos, fuelled and ready to embrace the full might of the city. He closed his eyes, took a deep breath in, and stepped on to the street.

'Jesus Christ!' he yelped, as something hard slammed into his shoulder. He only just managed to steady himself when he noticed a girl lying in the dust at his feet.

'Oh my God, are you all right?'

But the girl's long, dark blonde hair was shielding her face, making it hard for him to tell if she was conscious or not.

'Hello, can you hear me?' He bent down next to her.

'Yes. I can hear you,' a curt voice snapped back. 'And I'm fine, I just need a second.'

'OK . . .' Jacob stayed crouched, waiting for the angry girl to rise from the earth. 'But I wouldn't stay down there too long, it's not the cleanest place to take a break.'

As if lightning had struck, she jolted upright, shooting him a look of utter contempt.

'Don't you think I know that? I was just checking to see if anything was broken.'

'And is it?'

'No.' The girl sniffed, brushing herself down. 'No thanks to you.'

'No thanks to *me*?' Jacob reeled. 'You were the one running through the streets of Delhi not looking where you were going.'

It was only now, when they were both standing upright, that Jacob could fully take in the overly aggressive stranger. She was tall, only a few inches shorter than him, with strikingly blue eyes. Her skin was so pale it practically glowed in the sunlight, and it was decorated with a mixture of dust and freckles. At his words, her deep scowl began to soften.

'Yes, well . . .' She shifted uncomfortably. 'I was lost and this tuk-tuk driver wouldn't leave me alone.'

'I see.' Jacob clocked the scrunched-up map in her right hand and the tour guide poking out of her left pocket. His frustration melted into sympathy. She was clearly new to this game, and it was not an easy one to play.

'Has he gone?'

'Who?' she bit back.

'The tuk-tuk driver.'

'Oh yes' – she checked over her shoulder – 'I think I lost him a while back.'

'Good, so let me guess . . . first time in India?'

'First day.'

'Ah, and dare I ask, how are you finding it?'

The strange girl raised an eyebrow, the scowl re-forming with greater intensity than before.

'Too hot. Too crowded. Insanely difficult to navigate. And now, thanks to our little run-in, I'm at risk of an infectious disease. So it's safe to say . . . not great.'

Jacob couldn't help but laugh.

'I'm glad you find it so amusing.' She bristled, brushing herself down once more and unfolding the crumpled map in her hand. 'Now, if you don't mind, I'd like to find this phone shop before the sepsis sets in.'

'Which one are you looking for?'

'Excuse me?'

'Phone shop,' he repeated. 'There are a few around here.'

'I was told to go to Airtel, but at this point I'll take anything.' Her gaze refocused on her map, eyebrows knitted in deep concentration. 'I think . . .' she mumbled, turning the paper 180 degrees, 'it's this way. Yes! It's this way!'

'I think you'll find it's that way.' Jacob pointed gingerly in the opposite direction.

'For God's *sake*,' the girl cried, the anger in her voice now joined by desperation. 'What's the point in being given a map if it's totally and utterly useless.'

'I'll take you.' The offer was out of his mouth before he knew what he was saying. 'If you'd like.'

Her expression morphed seamlessly between irritated, confused and relieved. It was quite mesmerizing to watch.

'Are you sure?' The act of accepting his help looked as though it was physically paining her.

Was he sure? This girl was rude and aggressive and clearly had very little patience for Jacob, and yet he knew deep down he wouldn't be able to leave her stranded, heading in the totally wrong direction.

'Why not! I don't have anything else planned for my day.' Guilt tapped its fingers at the edges of his conscience. Hadn't he promised himself that the second he landed in India he would email home? There was no doubt a message from his mother was waiting for him in his inbox, wishing him a happy birthday and asking for updates. But home was always there. This girl needed him now. 'Come on, we go this way!'

'Hold on! I don't even know your name.'

'A very sensible thing to ask,' he noted, lifting his sunglasses off his face and extending a hand to her. 'I'm Jacob.'

The girl gripped him firmly with her ghostly hand and shook hard.

'Hi Jacob, I'm Olivia.'

Olivia

When Olivia had left the hotel that afternoon, she couldn't have imagined things getting any worse. Now, here she was with two grazed knees, covered in God knows what, following a total stranger to a phone shop she had no hope even existed at this point.

'How far away is this place?' she asked, trying to match Jacob's long strides as best she could, whilst swerving through the crowded streets.

'Not far now, why?' He turned to look at her, his face suddenly dropping in realization. 'Wait, it's not painful to walk, is it? Do you want me to slow down? Do you need to rest?'

'No, I'm fine!' she barked back. 'I was just curious, that's all.'

'Well then, it's about ten minutes this way.' He nodded ahead.

'Good.'

She had no idea why she was being so unbelievably horrid to this man. Maybe it was the throbbing in her legs, the stinging of her palms, the intensifying heat that seemed to bore down through her skull into the very centre of her brain.

Or maybe you're embarrassed at being so useless.

The thought made her body tense instinctively in defence. It was bad enough feeling inadequate by herself, but in the presence of another person . . . well, that was her idea of hell.

'How long are you staying in Delhi for?' Jacob pressed on, apparently undeterred by her impoliteness.

'Three days.'

'Not too long, then. Where are you staying?'

'In a hotel.'

'Didn't fancy the full traveller experience, then?'

'What do you mean?'

'A cheap and cheerful hostel. Sharing a dorm with ten other people?'

'God, no.'

The image of her depressing room appeared before Olivia's eyes. Maybe a hostel would have been preferable.

'Which hotel are you in?'

'It's not far from the centre. You probably won't know it.'

'Try me.'

'Really?' She was exasperated enough as it was, without indulging in his silly game.

'Yeah.'

'Fine, it's called the Evergreen.'

'You're joking?' He winced.

'Why would I joke about that?'

'Because that place is a shithole.'

'Great. Say what you really think, why don't you?' Olivia snapped.

'Sorry, but it's the truth. Come on, you have to admit it's a dump.'

Olivia could feel her sense of inadequacy rearing its ugly head again.

'OK, I'll admit it's not the height of luxury, but how was I supposed to know that? I used a travel guide, and it came up as one of their recommendations.'

'A travel guide that was probably written about twenty years ago by someone who came to India once, for about two days. Things change around here by the minute. Sometimes it's better to turn up somewhere and feel out an area before booking anything,' he replied casually, his blasé attitude grating on Olivia's already wearing patience.

'And that's your expert advice, is it? Just turn up somewhere and "feel it out",' she scoffed, adopting a terrible impersonation of his cool nonchalance.

He steered them around another corner.

'Yeah, it is. It's always better to get to know a place through experience.' He raised his sunglasses and fixed his eyes on to hers. They were so dark, like pools of liquid liquorice. Olivia felt unnerved looking straight into them. 'Nice impression of me, by the way. Although I like to think I sound *slightly* less arrogant than that.'

Olivia's cheeks coloured with embarrassment.

'But in all seriousness, I wouldn't leave the hotel after dark, if I were you. You're not staying in the best part of town.'

'Thank you. Any other pearls of wisdom you'd like to bestow on this clearly inadequate traveller?'

'Erm . . .' He tapped his chin. 'Always look where you're going when running down the street. Stops you banging into people and hurting yourself.'

Olivia felt her blood boil under her already overheated skin.

'Come on, I'm only messing around.'

'Well, I'm not in the mood for jokes right now. I'm tired and hot and I want my phone sorted so I can get back to my shithole hotel, call my best friend who I haven't spoken to since I landed, clean up my open wounds, which are probably already a bacterial breeding ground, and not be judged by some random stranger who keeps taking the piss out of me.'

'Wow.' Jacob stopped and held his hands out in apology. 'Look, I'm sorry, I didn't mean to annoy you.'

Olivia wiped the sweaty strands of hair away from her face and gave a disdainful sort of sniff, desperately trying to calm her racing heart.

'It's fine, just get me to the phone shop in one piece and I won't care.'

'We're nearly there, I promise.'

Jacob started to walk again, falling in step with Olivia, who was feeling a lot better after her little outburst.

'How come you know India so well, then?'

Jacob looked a little startled at her attempt at conversation but quickly recovered. 'It's not my first time taming the beast.'

'You've been here before?'

'This will be visit number three.'

'No!'

'Yes.'

'You're telling me that after being here twice before, you decided to come back *again*? What for?'

'Oh well, you know.' He shrugged. 'The slow pace and tranquillity mainly.'

A small smile tugged at the corner of Jacob's lips, and Olivia couldn't help but return it.

'I thought London was bad, but this . . .' She waved at the long line of honking vehicles that rolled past them. 'This is another level.' A sudden longing gripped Olivia's chest as she let her mind wander to the damp, grey streets of her home city.

'London is child's play compared to this.'

'Is that where you're from?'

'Just outside. Although I'm not sure I would call it home any more.'

'Why, how often do you go back?'

'I don't.'

'Don't what?'

'Go home,' he replied indifferently, steering them round a corner.

'Wait a second.' Olivia recoiled. 'How long have you been travelling for?'

'About five years.' A flicker of emotion passed over his face, and before Olivia could try to decipher its meaning, Jacob grabbed her arm and jerked her sideways. 'We need to swing a left here.'

She just about managed to steady herself as they turned down a densely packed side street, questions firing like popping candy inside her brain. Before she had a moment to grasp one and ask it, Jacob stopped suddenly.

'Here we are!' He clapped his hands together in satisfaction. 'I told you we weren't far.'

Olivia looked up. They were standing outside a large white building with a gigantic red Airtel sign above the door.

'Safely delivered to the doorstep, madam. Now, is there anything else I can help you with? Half-decent hotel recommendations?'

'No, thank you.'

'Are you sure? I know some good ones.' He leant back against the white wall.

'As will Google, when I get my phone sorted.'

'Touché.' He ruffled his mop of hair and smiled. 'Well, Olivia, it was a pleasure to meet you.'

If only she could say the same.

'Just think,' he continued, 'who knows where you would have ended up if I hadn't bumped into you? Destiny is a funny thing at times.'

'Oh yeah, thank you, Destiny, for throwing me to the ground and leaving me battered and bruised.'

Jacob gave a deep laugh. 'The universe works in mysterious ways, Olivia. Sometimes you just have to trust it.'

'Sure, whatever you say.' She pushed open the door to the shop, releasing a blast of cold air on to the streets. 'Thank you for the help though.'

'Like I said, it was a pleasure. And hey' – he began to walk away, a look of childish mischief on his face – 'you never know. I might see you around some time.'

'I doubt it!' she called after him. 'India's a big place.'

'I know . . .' He was far enough away now that he had to shout to be heard, his sun-kissed figure slowly being swallowed up by the crowd. 'But who knows what fate has in store for us, hey?'

And before she had a chance to counter his stupidity, he was gone.

*

'Can you hear me?' Olivia shouted at the phone screen. Kate's face remained frozen; a blurred snapshot of familiarity.

'Kate?' She tried again, lifting the phone higher up into the air and swinging it from side to side. 'Are you still there?'

A small flicker of movement. 'I can h-he-hear you. Can y-yo-y-you hear m-m-me?' Her friend's voice crackled through the speaker.

'Kind of.' Olivia scowled, trying to keep her frustration at bay and resisting the urge to throw the stupid phone across the stupid, stuffy hotel room.

'How is it?' Kate asked, her face finally unfreezing.

'It's fine.'

'Just fine?'

'I won't say Delhi is my *favourite* place in the world.'

'How come? You've only been there a day.'

A day too long, in her opinion.

'It's pretty intense and quite overwhelming.' Olivia tried to keep her voice light. 'And you know how much I hate chaos.'

'True, that is very true.' Kate sighed, brushing a strand of her ginger hair out of her eyes. 'But I'm sure you'll get used to it soon.'

Olivia highly doubted that.

'By the way, where *are* you?' Kate's eyes squinted. 'It looks like some sort of prison cell in there.'

Jacob's arrogant voice rang out in her head.

That place is a shithole.

She felt the tension build in her body, as she tried to shake the thoughts of the smug stranger from her mind and concentrate fully on the screen in front of her.

'Not far off it.' The contempt in Olivia's voice was blatant. 'Turns out my hotel isn't quite the four-star accommodation I was promised.'

'Jesus Christ! *That's* supposed to be four-star? You should sue.'

'You think this is bad? You want to see the bathroom.'

'Ew, no!' Kate scrunched her nose. 'Why don't you leave and find somewhere else?'

'I don't know . . . it's a lot of hassle to move all my stuff, and I've already paid for the room. I'm sure I can survive a couple of nights here.'

It spoke to how much Olivia hated admitting defeat that she was willing to submit herself to two more nights sleeping in this hellhole.

'Hmm, rather you than me! But as long as you're safe, that's all I care about.'

Jacob's advice not to leave after dark reverberated around her brain.

'Eugh, stupid know-it-all,' she hissed out loud.

'Excuse me?'

Olivia's hand flew to her mouth. 'No, no, sorry. I wasn't talking to you; I was thinking about someone else.'

'Really?' Kate's eyes narrowed in suspicion. 'Who?'

Olivia knew that any mention of the opposite sex would throw her friend into a spin. Did she have the energy for this?

'Oi, Olivia. Can you hear me?' Kate's frowning face zoomed closer to the screen.

'Sorry, the signal went for a minute,' she lied.

'Well, don't leave me hanging. Who is the stupid know-it-all?'

Olivia steeled herself. 'Some guy I met today.'

'*Olivia Jackson*, you dark horse.'

'Trust me, it was *nothing* like that. I got lost on my way to the phone shop and he gave me directions. Turned out to be infuriatingly smug and rather annoying.'

'The best ones often are.' Kate sighed dreamily.

'In your opinion, yes. But in mine, they are exactly the kind of people who should be left well alone.'

'Well, I don't think you should write him off so quickly. It might be a good idea to make a friend or two out there. He clearly knows his way around.'

'And likes to show off about it! I have Google and guide-books for all my travelling needs.'

'Yeah, that guidebook has done you a solid so far, hasn't it?' Kate teased.

'All right! Enough about me, how are you? And more importantly, how are the attempts at making out with the guy at work going?'

'Terribly. Nothing's happened,' Kate grumbled.

'Well, have you tried my suggestion of asking him for coffee?'

'No, don't be stupid. I can't do that.'

Olivia rolled her eyes. For someone who took no prisoners in nearly all aspects of her life, Kate was painfully shy when it came to men. The number of hours they'd spent discussing the trials and tribulations of Kate's dating life didn't bear thinking about. Olivia was suddenly struck with an overwhelming wave of homesickness. What she wouldn't give to be in her flat, cup of tea in hand and her friend by her side.

'I miss you,' she whispered.

'Oh, my love.' Kate's face softened. 'I miss you too.'

Olivia could feel her bottom lip wobbling and the urge to cry rising up strongly inside her.

Don't do it. Don't let her see you break.

'I'm worried about you; you are having a good time, aren't you?'

She forced back the tears.

'I think it's going to take me some time to adjust, that's all.'

'And you know what the good thing about that is?'

'What?'

'If anyone can adapt to difficult situations, it's you. Nobody deals with that stuff better than Olivia Jackson.' Kate punched the air in triumph.

'Yeah . . . maybe.'

Olivia wrangled her self-pity back in the box where it lived and tried her best to muster a convincing smile. 'Anyway, I have loads to see and do tomorrow, so hopefully I'll be too distracted by all the wonderful tourist attractions to feel homesick.'

'You'll be what t-t-tomo-rr-ow?' Kate's voice began to cut out again.

'Distracted,' Olivia repeated loudly.

'W-w-hat?' The screen jarred once more. 'You've f-fro-fr-frozen.'

'For God's sake. This stupid room.' Olivia sprang up from the bed and began to wave the phone optimistically in the air. 'Can you hear me now?'

'O-liv-ia.' Kate's voice was getting harder and harder to understand. 'I-t's t-too crack-crackly.'

All at once, the screen went black and the call disconnected.

'I hate this. I *hate* this.'

Olivia threw herself on top of her bed and closed her eyes. She'd only been in the country for a day and already she felt exhausted.

Probably because you haven't eaten since the plane.

Right on cue, her stomach gave an almighty growl. She peered down at her scraped legs and grazed hands; there was no way she was going to risk venturing outside to find food. It was a bloody deathtrap out there, and she'd much rather stay cooped up in her miserable hotel room than put herself at the mercy of the Delhi nightlife.

'In that case . . .' She began rifling through her bag and pulled out three squashed granola bars. 'Emergency cereal bars it is!'

She took a bite and felt the dry grains stick to the roof of her mouth. She was a world away from her old life; her, usually, clean, organized flat with its fridge full of nutritious, safe food and Brita filtered water.

'Tomorrow is another day' – she held her crumbling bar aloft – 'and hopefully a much better one.'

Olivia

As it turned out, two hours' sleep and two cereal bars for dinner did nothing to help Olivia's mood the next day. When it wasn't the pack of dogs howling outside her window keeping her awake, it was the continuous spluttering from her air conditioning unit. That, along with the jetlag, the relentless honking of horns and the revving of car engines, had made for a very restless night. When her alarm sounded that morning, the urge to bury her head into the pillow and ignore the rest of the world was strong. However, the list of things she had to do that day was reason enough for her to drag herself up and into the basic excuse of a bathroom. Plus, the less time spent between those bed sheets, the better for her and her open wounds.

A measly dribble of a shower and a shoddy granola bar breakfast later, Olivia found herself at her first tourist stop of the day, the Red Fort. A gigantic, rust-coloured structure, it housed multiple different and equally incredible buildings in its grounds. If one had the luxury of time, the entire site could easily take the full day to absorb, but Olivia had two hours at best to make the most of it. She raced around, snapping pictures on her phone of every possible thing she thought Kate would want to see, barely pausing to take in the views herself before moving on to the next. For some reason, despite it only being mid-morning, the heat felt stronger than it did yesterday. The sun's fiery gaze seemed to sap her of any ounce of energy her diet of cereal bars may have afforded her, so that by the time she had finished her whistle-stop tour, she felt exhausted.

'Miss!' a frenetic man called to her, as she walked down the street in search of an available tuk-tuk. 'It's too hot to walk around – come in the shade and have a nice, cool drink, huh? Maybe some food?' He gestured vigorously towards the inside of his crowded-looking restaurant.

The prospect of a cold Coca-Cola and a big plate of delicious food was tempting. But as Olivia's stomach groaned in longing, she had to remind herself that temporary hunger was better than food poisoning from a dodgy masala any day of the week.

'No, thank you, I'm just looking for a tuk-tuk.'

'Where do you want to go?' the man continued. 'With this traffic, most places are quicker to walk to.'

Olivia eyed him with suspicion. Back home, it was rare you got a look of acknowledgement from people you passed in the street, let alone friendly help and support. Here, however, it seemed commonplace; it was a sentiment Olivia was still trying to get used to.

'I was hoping to go to Chandni Chowk. Is it far?'

'Maybe fifteen minutes that way.' He pointed ahead into a mass of crowds and vehicles.

Anxiety licked the inside of Olivia's stomach. How had her last attempt at navigating on foot gone? The cuts on her knees twinged in memory.

'I don't know . . . it looks a bit bus—' Suddenly, Olivia felt the ground pull beneath her feet. The world swam ominously in front of her, as flashes of light and streaks of colour danced across her field of vision. Her blood ran cold, and her stomach rolled with nausea. She closed her eyes and tried to steady herself. For a second, it was as though she was back in the boardroom, with Phil and his putrid breath.

'Miss?' The man's voice sounded like it was coming from deep underwater. 'Are you OK? Is everything all right?'

A hand on her shoulder grounded her instantly, and she opened her eyes to see the face of the stranger peering into hers. Thankfully, she was still upright.

'Yes, yes, I'm fine!' She tried to laugh, taking a small step backwards to create some distance between them. 'Just a bit too hot maybe.'

But the man was not convinced. 'I think a tuk-tuk might be best. And not to the market . . . straight home!'

'Yes' – she tried to bat away his help – 'good idea. Thank you.'

Olivia went to walk but the man stopped her, placing his fingers in his mouth and giving a piercing whistle. As if by magic, an empty rickshaw appeared at the kerbside.

'Where do you want to go?' the driver grunted.

'Take this lady home, please, and pronto,' the kind stranger instructed firmly, helping Olivia into the back and giving her arm a squeeze. 'Take care, and remember, rest. The sun takes no prisoners on a day like today.'

'Thank you so much.' She smiled, gripping on for dear life as the small vehicle pulled away abruptly.

'So, miss, what hotel am I going to?'

'No hotel,' she replied, trying to erase the concerned face of the generous stranger who had helped her. She felt fine now, and besides, she had no time to rest. Her twenty-two-page itinerary hadn't been created for nothing, after all. If there was a plan to complete, Olivia Jackson was going to complete it, come hell or high water. 'I'm going to Chandni Chowk, please.'

*

Twenty minutes in and Olivia was regretting her decision enormously. This wasn't a market. This was the centre of hell. People were everywhere, rushing this way and that, bags filled with treats and eyes scouting for more. Market sellers were shouting over one another, louder and louder with each new price they offered. Goods spilled out on to the street, the jewels and patterned fabrics sparkling in the sunlight. Scarves, each a different colour and ornately patterned in golds and silvers, were piled so high the stacks created small skyscrapers around the stalls. Barrels of spices stood like barricades, full to the brim with deep earth-coloured powders. The smell alone was enough to make Olivia's nose tickle. Her eyes had not been able to settle for a second, darting back and forth trying to take in as much as possible. The second she'd stepped inside the market, every single one of her senses had been kicked into overdrive. She was overstimulated, overwhelmed and overtired. And she needed to find a way out this very second.

'Excuse me.' She turned on the spot, trying her best to push against the tide of people dragging her in the opposite direction. 'Excuse me, I'm trying to get through.'

But her flustered cries were inaudible over the din of the market. Feebly she tried again, the panic making her voice even harder to hear.

'Please, can someone get me out of here?'

But Olivia, who in an act of self-protection had attempted

to make herself as small as possible, hunching her shoulders and folding her arms across her chest, seemed to be carried along with the crowd. A human pinball, she was shunted from side to side as the swell of people surged along the narrow lanes.

This was it, she thought. This was how she went. Too tired to fight the tide, she would be swept away, never to be seen again. Lost in the middle of Delhi without a clue how to find her way home. A single tear rolled down her cheek as her legs began to buckle. Her breath was growing shallower and her chest constricting, each rib folding in on itself, leaving no room for air. The surrounding sounds all blended into one, and her vision began to blur as the now all too familiar feeling of light-headedness kicked in.

I can't . . .

I don't know how to make it stop . . .

She tried to take a step, but her legs were too heavy, too full of tingling pins and needles. Panic began to thrum in her chest, the anxiety multiplying rapidly until it felt fit to burst from her.

'Help,' she whimpered. 'Somebody, help.'

But even her thoughts were getting lost, the endless roar of noise making it hard to distinguish what was coming from inside her and what belonged on the outside. Her name was being repeated over and over, louder and louder.

'Olivia?'

There it was again. But from where?

'Olivia!'

Was it her own consciousness calling for her? Or was there someone out there reaching for her?

But no, it couldn't be.

There was nobody here for her. She had nobody here for her.

Then, all at once, everything went black.

'Olivia? *Olivia*, can you hear me?'

The sweet, cooling darkness was being interrupted by a vigorous shaking. Why couldn't she just stay here?

'Olivia!'

But the shaking was getting rougher and the voice louder. It was harder and harder to ignore.

'OLIVIA!'

Reluctantly she opened her eyes.

Her insides froze and her heart plummeted.

No.

She blinked, praying that this time when she looked, her eyes would not be staring directly into pools of liquid liquorice.

No. No. Absolutely not.

'Aha, there you are! Thought we'd lost you for a moment.' The beetle-black eyes crinkled, and Jacob's face broke into a smile.

She turned her head to find that for some reason she was horizontal and . . . oh God, she was lying in his arms!

Immediately she tried to get up, but his firm, warm hands held her still.

'Woah there, easy does it.' Gently, he guided her upright.

'What the hell are you doing here?' she spluttered, noticing that a little ring of space had been cleared around them. If only her brain would stop being so goddam foggy, maybe then she could think straight. It didn't help that Jacob was looking at her with those abnormally dark eyes, and a cocky grin. Her skin was flushed, and her mouth was exceptionally dry.

'If you must know, I was stopping you from faceplanting the ground for the second time in two days.'

'But I don't understand.' Embarrassment and anger were

doing their familiar dance inside her, each one fighting to take the lead. 'Why are you even here?'

'I decided to take a walk through the market, and there I was minding my own business when I spotted you looking . . .' He hesitated, his brow furrowing. 'Well, not looking 100 per cent OK. So I called out for you, and when you didn't answer I came closer. I caught you just as you fainted. It was quite a save, if I say so myself.'

Olivia's cheeks blazed with shame.

'I see.'

'Yeah, you were as white as a sheet and stumbling all over the place. Lucky I was here, wasn't it?'

The horror seemed to penetrate new depths, robbing her of speech. Instead, she gave a feeble nod of her head.

'Anyway.' Jacob ran a hand through his mop of golden hair. 'How are you feeling? Are you still dizzy?'

'No. Just tired,' she mumbled, becoming aware of the leaden feeling in her bones. 'And thirsty. I'm *really* thirsty.'

'Hmm.' Jacob reached into his bag and pulled out a water bottle. 'I thought so. The classic case of not enough food, not enough water and way too much heat. Here, drink as much as you want.'

Olivia took the bottle and gulped the cool, fresh water, her body crying out in relief at the taste. Each sip brought her back to life a little more. How could she have got it so wrong? *Again?* This guy must think she was a total idiot.

'Now, when you're done drinking that, you should probably get something to eat. Anything you fancy?'

She could feel his eyes on her face, but she didn't dare meet them. Her humiliation was already too much to bear without his pity layered on top.

'Don't worry, you don't have to stay any longer.' She

straightened up, snapping her armour of invincibility back into place. 'I feel fine now.'

'I'm just asking if you want to get some food.'

'Look, you don't have to do this.' She sighed. Why couldn't he just take his hero moment and go?

'Do what?'

'Babysit me because you feel bad.'

'Jesus Christ!' He laughed.

'What?'

'Are you always this hard to make friends with?'

'No,' she bit back, hearing the true answer ring out loudly in her head.

'OK then, so how about some food?'

Olivia was about to find another way to dismiss the idea when her stomach lurched violently. Her cereal bar breakfast seemed like a distant dream. She was ravenous, and it didn't seem like Jacob was one to give up very easily. Was it worth the fight?

'Fine, but . . .' She grasped for some point to make, a show that she wasn't totally surrendering to his whims. 'I don't want to go too far from here.'

'As you wish.' He gave a little salute. 'Luckily, I know just the place, and it's only round the corner.'

'Is it clean?'

'Excuse me?'

'The place we're going, is it clean?'

The fact she sounded like an overly anxious mother didn't bother her; after all, how much lower could his perception of her get at this point?

'I would hope so – why?'

'Because, you know . . . all the awful stories you hear about India. I don't want to get sick.'

'I don't think anyone does.' He replied more seriously than she'd heard him before. 'But don't worry, this place is super clean. I've only ever seen one cockroach in there.'

'Jacob!' Olivia swiped him hard across the arm.

'I'm kidding.' He cocked his head to the side and raised an eyebrow. 'It's good, trust me.'

'How can I trust you? I don't even know you.'

'And yet . . . I've already saved your life today.' He gave a cheeky shrug, his charcoal eyes sparkling. 'Come on!' He turned and began to stride off into the densely packed crowd. 'The sooner we get going, the sooner we can eat. And the sooner we eat, the sooner you can find an excuse to ditch me! That is what you're planning on doing, right?'

'No!' Olivia baulked. 'Of course I'm not.'

Jacob grinned; a smile so wide it seemed to take up the whole of his face.

'I think you're many things, Olivia, but a good liar is not one of them. Now hurry, stuffed paratha await us!'

Olivia

Although the walk wasn't meant to be far, in the blistering heat Olivia felt like she was running a marathon with the weight of a small human on her back. Graciously, Jacob had given her all of his water to keep her hydrated. However, it seemed that every drop she took in evaporated straight back out a second later.

'So . . .' Jacob turned to her as they moved out of the market and into a slightly quieter street. 'Why India?'

Olivia's heart sank. This was one area of conversation that she didn't want to get into, not today and especially not with Jacob.

'You know . . .' she mumbled, a poor attempt at casual deflection.

'No, not really. That's why I asked.'

'Well, why does anyone come to India?'

'You like the hot weather?'

'Hot? This isn't hot, it's deadly,' she sniped.

'You like spicy food?'

'Nope.'

'You enjoy noisy, crowded places?' He raised an eyebrow.

'Not one bit.' Olivia dodged out of the way of a shrieking group of children.

Jacob threw his head back and laughed. 'Right, so I'll ask my question again. Why India?'

'*Because* . . .' Olivia felt herself getting flustered. 'I thought it looked like an interesting place to go.'

'OK . . .' He sounded unconvinced.

'And why did *you* pick India if you've already been twice before?' she cut in, leaving no space for him to press her further.

'That's a long story.'

'One that you're going to tell me?'

'Not now.'

'Why?'

'Because—' Jacob stopped suddenly. 'We're here,' he announced, pointing to a grubby-looking cafe on the corner.

'You can't mean . . .?'

'I do mean.'

'But it looks . . .' She paused, trying to find the most accurate yet least offensive word to describe what was in front of them. 'It looks so *basic*.'

'Now, now.' Jacob waggled his finger at her. 'Don't go judging a book by its cover. Look how busy it is! And how good it smells.' He lifted his nose to the sky and took a deep inhale. 'They do the best stuffed paratha in town.'

Olivia couldn't deny the tiny cafe was heaving, and she would be lying if she said the scent of rich butter and spices wasn't making her mouth water. But still, it didn't look the most sanitary place on earth.

'I'm not sure about this.' She reluctantly followed Jacob to join the back of the queue.

'You will be when you taste it. And don't worry, we won't be waiting long. The queue moves fast.'

'Trust me, that is the last thing I'm worried about right now.'

'You're funny.' He chuckled, edging closer to the counter.

'I'm not trying to be.'

'I gathered.'

Olivia rolled her eyes and folded her arms across her chest. 'So how long are you planning to be in India for, then? I imagine there's only so much to see when you've done it three times.'

'I'm not sure.'

'What do you mean?'

'I mean, I'm not sure,' he stated again. 'As in, I don't know yet.'

'But how can you not know?' Olivia frowned. 'Don't you have a job to get back to?'

'No.'

'But how do you survive? What do you live on?'

'Jesus, I didn't realize this was an interview.' He moved a few paces forward, so they were now standing inside the cafe.

'It's not. I'm just intrigued.'

'And as much as I'd love to answer you, it's our turn to order in a second. What do you want?' He pointed up at a faded chalkboard that hung over the counter.

Olivia tried to quickly scan the menu, but it was hard to read all the options whilst being shoved around by the other restless, hungry customers.

'I don't know, I can't see very well.' She craned her neck. 'I'll just have whatever you're having.'

'Great decision.' He turned to the man behind the counter.

'Two paneer paratha, please,' Jacob ordered. 'Oh, and two chai.'

The server nodded and held his hand out for payment.

'How much is it?' Olivia began rifling in her bag for some change.

'Don't worry about it, I've got this.'

'No, thank you. I'll pay my half.' She tried to pass over some coins, but Jacob pushed her hand away.

'It's fine, I've got this.'

'But I don't want you to.'

'Well, you can get the next round, how about that?' Jacob steered Olivia over to the side, before she could even process the fact that he was expecting a second round. 'Now, it's rammed in here – why don't you wait outside, and I'll bring it out for us, OK?'

Olivia was speechless. The way in which Jacob took control was unsettling. She wasn't used to it. Back home, it was her that took charge of things, and it was her who took care of the money. Her high salary afforded her the luxury to treat everyone else around her. On dates she always insisted on paying half, regardless of whether the guy was a total creep or not – which, more often than not, they were.

As Olivia reluctantly made her way outside, she caught her reflection in the cafe window; she'd be lucky to date one of those creeps now, judging by the look of her! Lank, dusty hair; sweaty face, blotchy from the heat. It was a far cry from the meticulously put-together person she was back home. In fact, it was possibly the least attractive she'd felt in her entire adult life. Not that it mattered. Rough and ready was part and parcel of the travelling life, wasn't it?

'Two paneer paratha and two chai!' Jacob burst from the door, holding a bag of food aloft.

Olivia hastily smoothed her hair away from her face and averted her gaze from her reflection in the window, taking from Jacob a warm, heavy parcel and a cup of steaming spiced liquid.

'Thank you for this.'

'My pleasure.' He raised his cup to hers. 'Now enjoy, madam, and let me know what you think.'

Olivia cautiously peeled back the greasy brown paper and took a bite. The buttery, flaky bread dissolved on her tongue, as the salty cheese and spices hit her taste buds.

Holy. Shit.

'And?' Jacob leant closer, his eyes wide and expectant.

'It's good.' She chewed hungrily. 'It's *really* good.'

'Aha!' He held his paratha to the air in victory. 'I knew it!'

Olivia shoved another bite into her mouth, not caring about anything other than devouring every last morsel of the insanely delicious food.

'Now, I forgot to ask.' Jacob swallowed, wiping away the dusting of crumbs that had accumulated on his chin. 'How's your hotel working out? Did you survive the night OK?'

Flashbacks of her dingy room rudely interrupted the blissful sensation of her chai and paratha.

'Erm . . . yeah . . . it was all right,' she replied vaguely, her eyes not meeting his.

'You hated it, didn't you?'

'No.'

'Yes, you did!' He grinned.

'No, I didn't!'

'I don't blame you, I told you that place was dodgy. Why don't you move?'

'It's not that bad.' She took another bite, playing for more time.

'Uh-huh.'

'And besides, moving feels like a lot of faff for a couple more nights. I'll be fine.'

Jacob eyed her suspiciously over the top of his chai.

'What's that look for?'

'Nothing.'

'Yes, it is. Come on.'

'I don't know.' He shrugged. 'It feels crazy to me that you'd stay somewhere you hate just because it's easier. You don't strike me as a person that takes the easy route.'

Whether it was intended as a compliment or not, Olivia felt a bristle of pride at his words.

'I don't. But I am also someone who prioritizes, and spending time moving when I have a list of things to do here feels counterproductive.'

'Oh yeah?' He raised an eyebrow curiously. 'Action-packed agenda, is it?'

'You could say that.'

'Come on, then, tell me.'

'What?'

'What's on the agenda?'

'You don't want to know.'

'Yes, I do! Or I wouldn't have asked.'

'Well' – she finished the final bite of her food, her stomach leaping in sheer joy to be full – 'today my plan was the Red Fort and Chandni Chowk. Tomorrow will be India Gate, Lodhi Gardens and the Raj Ghat. Then I have an early train to Agra the next morning.'

'Wow, so you weren't lying about the whole planning situation.'

'Nope.' Olivia smiled sheepishly. 'It's kind of my thing.'

'Your thing?'

'You know, the thing I'm known for. Like I'm sure you're known for your spontaneity and unrelenting humour,' she quipped.

'And don't forget my devastating good looks.'

'Ah, yes. That too, of course.'

'And yours is being organized?'

'Yes.'

'Well' – he shrugged – 'I guess there could be worse things.'

'Hey! I like being organized.'

'I'm sure you do.'

'It's better than being incredibly irritating.'

'Woah there, just a second ago I was devilishly handsome and hilarious.' He placed a hand over his heart.

'Those were your words, not mine.'

'True, very true.'

A comfortable silence fell between them as they finished their chai. The heat and the noise were becoming ever so slightly more bearable now that Olivia was properly fed and watered.

She stole a glance at Jacob, who seemed so perfectly at home amidst the mayhem. Serene, unfazed and totally grounded, it was as though he was made from the chaos itself. His eyes met hers and she felt a jolt of electricity radiate through her core.

Admit it, you've had a nice time.

'So, what's the plan now, then?' he asked. 'Fancy tackling the market again? It will be quieter, I reckon.'

'No,' she replied, more firmly than she intended. 'I think I ought to be heading back. It's getting late and I need to prepare for tomorrow.'

'Of course you do.' Jacob tucked his hands into his pockets, as something that Olivia could have easily mistaken for disappointment flickered across his face. 'The agenda waits for nobody!'

Had she been too harsh? After all, he'd been nothing but kind to her since they'd met. Cocky, and way too curious for his own good, but kind nonetheless.

'Exactly. But thank you for the food and, you know, saving my life and all that.'

'Yeah, I have been great, haven't I?'

Nope. She hadn't been too harsh.

'So great, in fact,' he continued, his eyes glittering mischievously, 'I wonder . . . what are you doing for dinner tomorrow?'

'I'm not sure yet, why?'

'There's this place I haven't been to before and I've been wanting to check it out for ages. I wondered whether you wanted to come too? We could celebrate me being the hero of today and you for making it through your Delhi experience alive and unscathed.'

Olivia looked down at the scab on her knee from where she'd fallen the previous day. Jacob's eyes followed.

'OK, mainly unscathed.' He laughed.

'I don't know . . .' Excuses flooded her brain. 'I have quite a lot to do tomorrow.'

'I know, and you're probably going to be tired when you get back and find a million and one reasons not to come, *but* how about this: I'll be at the Farzi Cafe at 7 p.m. There's no pressure, but if you fancy it, come and join me.' He held his palms open in front of him. 'Sound like a plan?'

'Yes, a ridiculous one.'

'Why?'

'Because what if I don't show up? Are you just going to sit there waiting for me?'

Jacob went to speak but Olivia cut him off. 'And how long are you going to wait for? What if I do want to come but get lost or delayed, and then by the time I arrive you've already eaten, and I'm sitting there starving and you have to wait for me to finish, or worse than that, I have to go somewhere else and eat by myself.'

Jacob's eyes grew larger with every word she spoke, examining her like a creature from another world. 'Was all that really just going on in that brain of yours?'

Olivia stiffened. 'I'm just saying, it seems like a foolish plan to me.'

'Obviously I won't be sitting there waiting for ever. If you're not there, you're not there and I'll eat,' he replied nonchalantly. 'And if you do turn up late, I'll order some more food and eat with you again. Trust me, I can *eat*.'

'Fine, I'll think about it.' She turned her head and attempted to flag down any potential mode of transport. 'But it would be much easier if we exchanged numbers, so I could text you if I'm coming.'

'Easier, but far less fun.' Jacob placed a hand on her shoulder and gave a shrill, ear-piercing wolf whistle. 'Here.' Dutifully, and seemingly out of nowhere, a yellow-and-green tuk-tuk appeared.

'I could have done that,' she muttered under her breath, clambering in.

'So, I'll see you tomorrow, then?' Jacob crouched so that his face was level with hers.

'Maybe.'

'Perfect.' He grinned, giving the top of the rickshaw a little tap, signalling for it to go. 'I'll take that.'

'It wasn't a yes, Jacob.' The tuk-tuk jerked forwards.

'But it wasn't a no.'

Olivia

Olivia fidgeted in her seat. The leather was sticking to the backs of her legs, and her skin felt too tight for her body.

This is a stupid idea.

A totally, utterly stupid idea.

The same words had been cycling through her mind for the entire taxi journey. In fact, the arguments against the idea had been growing louder and louder inside her head all day. She didn't have the time to spare. She was tired. She needed an early night. But despite the litany of reasons not to go, there was also a tiny voice in her head begging her to say yes. She was leaving tomorrow, and chances were, she would never see him again. What harm could one dinner do?

Suddenly the taxi stopped.

'Here we are, miss.'

Olivia peered out of the window and did a double take. They had pulled up outside a large, white building with an extremely posh exterior. Olivia watched in confusion as a stream of well-dressed people flowed in and out through the large, ornate entrance.

'Are you sure this is the right place?'

'Yes.' He nodded assuredly, pointing at a glowing sign that hung outside the front. 'Farzi Cafe.'

'I can see that, it just looks . . .'

Too nice? Too expensive? Too clean?

This had to be a mistake. Why hadn't she checked out the restaurant before she left?

Because you weren't planning on coming until twenty minutes ago.

'I just thought maybe there was another one somewhere,' she finished shyly.

'No, madam. This is the only one in the city centre.'

'Right then.' She began straightening out the creases in her white H&M T-shirt and inconspicuously wiping her dusty trainers on the mat beneath her feet. 'That's great, thank you.'

'Enjoy your evening.' He tipped his hat and unlocked the doors with a satisfying click.

'Thank you.' Olivia stepped outside and felt the familiar blanket of heat swallow her whole. Why on earth had Jacob not warned her that this was in fact a decent, well-established restaurant and not some side-street cafe like the one before?

A small yet terrifying thought struck her. Was this a set-up? Some sort of cruel joke that she had been gullible enough to fall for?

Her stomach sank.

'Good evening, madam.' A neatly starched waiter greeted her at the door. 'Do you have a reservation?'

'Erm . . . kind of.'

'Can I take a name?'

'His name is Jacob.' But Jacob what? She didn't even know his surname! Olivia looked up at the large, gilded clock hanging above them; it was nearly quarter past seven. 'He should already be here.'

'Ah.' The man smiled. 'Of course, Miss Olivia. He will be delighted you came. Follow me.'

The waiter turned and began to walk through the dining room. Olivia couldn't help but marvel at the dark wooden interior, the low lighting and luxurious green velvet seating. It felt more like a nightclub than a restaurant, but it looked gorgeous, and the smells coming from the kitchen were equally as sumptuous.

'Here we are. I will get someone to come and serve you shortly.' The man gestured to the table directly in front of them, where Jacob sat, cleanly dressed and already smirking.

'I cannot *believe* you did this.'

'And hello to you too.' Jacob raised his eyebrows as Olivia threw herself down into the seat opposite. 'Glad you could make it; I was going to give you another thirty seconds before I gave up and ordered.'

'Why didn't you tell me this place was so *fancy*?' She pulled at her T-shirt. 'I look like a . . . like . . .'

'Like a grubby, dishevelled traveller?'

'*Jacob!* Don't!'

'I'm kidding. You look great. A little casual maybe, but still great.' His eyes lingered on her face, sending a little jolt of electricity sparking through her. 'Besides, I thought you would have done some thorough research on the place before accepting my proposal.'

'Yes, well, my phone's been playing up.'

'Ah,' he smirked, 'and nothing to do with the fact you weren't going to come, until you changed your mind last minute and forgot to check before you left the hotel?'

'I don't know what you're talking about,' she muttered, turning her attention to the menu in front of her and praying her cheeks weren't as red as they felt. 'Do you know what you want to eat?'

'Yes, and I'm starving, so if you could hurry up and decide what you want, that would be great.'

Olivia's mouth began to water from just reading the words on the page. 'It all looks *so* good.'

'Right? And no cockroaches here. I asked them to check the kitchen myself.'

If it weren't such a posh place, Olivia would have been tempted to throw her napkin at his face. Instead, she settled for a deadly stare.

'You really are insufferable.'

'But you still came for dinner with me, didn't you?'

'Only because I felt bad at the thought of you sitting here on your own waiting for me.'

'Is that so?' The edges of his mouth curled into a smile.

'Yes. It's more of a good deed, act of charity kind of thing.'

'The only charitable deed I want from you right now is to pick your food! I have been waiting all day for this!'

'OK, OK.' Luckily, the strong ache in Olivia's stomach was forcing her brain to choose quickly. 'Right, I think I know what I want.'

'Good, let's get this show on the road, then.'

All it took was a look for one of the poised-to-pounce waiters to come over and take their order. Olivia tried not to look too surprised as Jacob reeled off two starters, a main and three side dishes. He hadn't been lying when he said he could eat.

'Now, tell me,' Jacob said, the second the waiter disappeared, 'how was your ridiculously busy day?'

'It was good!' Satisfaction swelled in her chest. 'I saw everything I wanted to see, I'm packed ready to leave tomorrow, *and* I didn't fall over or faint.'

'Sounds like a roaring success to me.'

'It was.'

'How are you finding the craziness?'

'Still crazy,' Olivia scoffed. 'I don't think I'll ever get used to it.'

'You will, in time.'

'I'm not so sure.' She fiddled with the napkin in front of her. 'I don't know how you do it.'

'Do what?'

'Live out of a backpack for months at a time. Never go back home!' His admission the other day still blew her mind. 'I am dreaming of the day I get back, have a bath and put a wash on.'

'Wow, don't go too wild.'

'It's true! It's always the little things you miss. You know, the home comforts.'

'Enlighten me.' He took a sip of water. 'Like what else?'

'I don't know. Seeing friends, going back to work.'

'I'm sorry . . . did you say "going back to work"?'

'Yes.'

'You are looking *forward* to going back to work?'

'Yes, what's wrong with that? I like my job.'

'No, you don't.'

'Yes, I do!'

'I'm sorry, but I won't accept that as an answer.'

'Why not?'

'Because you're a young, attractive woman living in London . . . *surely* you have more fun things in your life than work?'

Olivia sat up a little taller, trying to ignore the warmth she felt at his compliment.

'Work is important to me. It always has been and I'm not ashamed to admit it.'

'Let me guess.' Jacob narrowed his eyes. 'You're an only child?'

'No.' Her body tensed.

'Right, well, the oldest child then?'

'Maybe,' she replied, praying the waiter would arrive imminently with their food.

'Of how many?'

Two.

Now only two.

'Three.'

'Cool. That must be fun.'

Oh yeah, it's been a real hoot.

'How about you?' she deflected, spotting a man carrying what looked like their food order heading towards them.

'How about me what?'

'How many brothers and sisters do you have?'

'We're not asking questions about me yet, Olivia.'

'Why not?'

'Because *you* are way more interesting.'

'As if! I'm a single, almost thirty-year-old girl living and working in London. I don't think you can get more typical than that. *You*, on the other hand, are a travelling free spirit with seemingly no care in the world.'

'Is that what you think of me?'

'Yes. And if you don't tell me anything else about you, how will I know any different?'

Jacob seemed to chew on his answer, but just as he was about to speak, the server appeared by their table.

'The paneer and mushroom masala?' the waiter announced.

'That's mine.' Olivia smiled, annoyed at the interruption but grateful for the food.

'And the rest' – Jacob rubbed his hands together – 'is all mine.'

'Very good.' The waiter placed the food down in front of them. 'If there's anything more I can do, please let me know. Otherwise, enjoy your meal.'

'Thank you!' they both replied in unison.

The server turned on his heel and left.

'So come on . . .' Olivia pressed. 'Tell me why I can't know any information about you.'

Jacob spooned some thick black dhal on to his plate. 'It's not that you can't.'

'What then?'

'I just don't want to make it too easy for you.'

'Easy?' She pierced a cube of paneer rather aggressively. 'Surely conversation should be easy? Isn't that the whole point?'

'Yes, but like I said before, you don't strike me as someone who enjoys taking the easy route.' His face lit up in delight. 'I know – let's make a deal.'

'What kind of deal?'

'Firstly, you let me pay for this meal, and *then*,' Jacob continued over Olivia's attempted protest, 'if you agree to come for a walk and get some dessert with me, I'll let you ask me some questions.'

'Absolutely not.'

'Why?'

'Because that's a stupid deal.'

Olivia sat back in her seat, fully taking in the strange creature opposite her. His wild hair looked like it had seen a brief kiss from a comb, and his white shirt glowed pristine under the lights. The dark eyes remained the same: searching, curious and intense in their gaze.

'All right, then.' He licked his fork wickedly. 'No questions for you.'

'Jacob! I can't let you pay *again*.'

'Who says?'

'I do! And besides, why does everything have to be some sort of bargain with you? Why is nothing straightforward?'

'Because what in life ever is?'

He extended his hand across the table.

'Do we have a deal?'

Olivia folded her arms across her chest. There was no way she was going to let him do this. No way . . .

'Look.' He leant forwards. Olivia could smell the scent of his soap and see the freshly shaved stubble on his chin. 'It's your last night here. I know it's expensive. I know you are an independent woman who can afford to buy her own meals and look after herself. I just . . .' He dropped his gaze momentarily. 'I just would like to treat you, if that's all right?'

Olivia felt her guard lower a little.

'And this way, you get something out of it too. All the information about me that you want.' He grinned, edging his outstretched hand an inch closer to hers. 'Please?'

As much as she hated to admit it, there was something deep inside her that needed to know more about this man, with his beetle-black eyes and his irritatingly attractive smile.

Slowly, she brought her hand up to meet his and shook it firmly.

'Fine. We have a deal.'

*

'I swear we've already been down this street,' Olivia huffed, a sense of déjà vu settling over her as they wandered aimlessly along yet another dusty side road.

Jacob turned around and looked behind him. 'Hmm, I don't think so. I don't remember seeing that cat before.' He pointed at a scrawny tortoiseshell across the street.

'*Please* don't tell me you've been using stray animals as landmarks, or I'll lose my mind.'

'No, that would be ridiculous!' He laughed. 'And "landmarks" suggests there's a final destination in mind.'

'And you're only telling me *now* that there isn't?'

'There sort of is and there sort of isn't, you know?'

'Not really, seeing as *you* said we were going to get dessert, therefore implying *you* knew where to take us.'

Jacob crossed the road, looking back at Olivia over his shoulder. 'Does it make you uncomfortable not having a plan?'

'No.'

'Really?'

'Not uncomfortable, I think it's just a completely inefficient use of everyone's time.'

'That's fair enough.' Jacob stopped still and looked around. Olivia watched as the scrawny cat, their only hope of direction, scarpered off down an alleyway.

'So, no more time shall we waste!' he declared suddenly. 'Follow me, I know where to go.'

'Are you sure?'

'Completely.'

'Wouldn't it be easier to look it up on your phone?' she asked, reaching into her pocket for her own.

'I don't have one.'

Olivia stopped still. 'Oh, come on.'

'What? I don't have a phone.'

'You're joking?' She remained frozen on the spot. 'You have to be joking, right?'

'Nope.' His face was deadly serious.

'But . . . that's *insane*.'

'Is it?' Jacob placed a hand on Olivia's arm, pulling her from the spot she'd been rooted to.

'Yes! Of course it is.' Realization dawned on her. No wonder he hadn't wanted to exchange numbers about tonight's dinner; he couldn't! How reckless could one person be? 'How long have you not had a phone for?'

Jacob shrugged. 'I don't know, maybe six months or so.'

'*Six months!*'

'More or less.'

His nonchalance bewildered her.

'Did someone steal it?'

'No.'

'Did you lose it?'

'Nope. I gave it to a family I was staying with. It was a present for their kid; he needed it more than I did.'

The fact that the story was very sweet and generous did not detract from the absurdity of it.

'And it never crossed your mind to buy another one?'

'Not really. I found I was relying on it way too much, and soon it started to defeat the whole point of me travelling. I wasn't being present because I could so easily lose myself in what was happening on my screen.' He steered them down a little side alley. 'I know it's mind-blowing, but things can be organized without a mobile phone.'

'I know that,' Olivia replied spikily, shaking her arm free from Jacob's grip. 'I was thinking more about how you speak to people back home.'

'I email them. There's an internet cafe every ten metres out here.'

'But don't your family mind?' Olivia asked, suddenly realizing she hadn't yet rung her own parents.

'No,' he replied sharply. 'They're fine.'

'I think my best friend would call out a search party if I didn't reply to her in a couple of days, let alone weeks.'

'Who's your best friend?'

'Hey, I'm meant to be the one asking the questions, remember?'

'Oh yeah.' He slapped his hand against his forehead. 'How could I forget?'

'So where do your family live?'

'Hold on.' Jacob held up his hand. 'First we need dessert.'

'Come *on*,' Olivia whined, 'that wasn't part of the deal.'

'Yes, it was. I said let's go for a walk and get dessert, and *then* you can ask me a few questions.'

'A few?' she scoffed. 'It's now been limited to a *few*.'

'I can't give you everything on a plate, Olivia, I need to at least maintain some air of mystery.' He waved his hands around like a magician mid-conjure. 'Come on. The longer we stand around here chatting, the less time we have for Q and A.'

'Are you sure you know where you're going?' she groaned.

'I see bright lights and I smell sugar.' He pointed towards the end of the street. 'There's got to be something sweet down there!'

Olivia squinted just past where Jacob's finger was pointing. 'Fine, but let's hurry up. I have an early train tomorrow morning, so I can't be out late.'

Jacob

The stark lights of the cafe were blinding. It was noisy and crowded, and the smell of syrup and fried batter laced the air.

'Do you really think we need all of this?' Olivia was eyeing the bowls of desserts laid out in front of them.

There were many mantras that Jacob chose to live by, but none more so than 'there's always room for pudding'. In hindsight, he may have gone a little over the top, but he wanted to make sure Olivia had a chance to taste all the good ones before they left. He had a feeling she wouldn't step into a place like this by herself.

'Why not?' Jacob picked up a ball of fried dough and popped it into his mouth. 'You only live once.'

'And we'll die much sooner if we eat all this sugar-coated fat.'

'Aha! I like it when you get all feisty.'

Olivia rolled her eyes, but Jacob couldn't help but notice the smile that pulled at the corner of her mouth. She prodded suspiciously at another bowl of syrupy dessert.

'Can I ask you some questions now? Or do I have to wait until after you've sent your sugar levels through the roof?'

'About that . . .'

'Here we go,' she huffed, leaning back in her seat and folding her arms, reminding Jacob simultaneously of a disgruntled old woman and a petulant toddler.

'You still get to ask me questions, it's just I thought we could spice it up a bit . . .'

He cringed at his turn of phrase. Who said 'spice it up' these days? The sugar must have gone to his head already.

'And how do you propose we do that?'

'I thought we could play a game.'

Olivia's brow furrowed. 'A game?'

'Yes, using these.' Jacob reached into his pocket and pulled out his two very worn-looking dice. 'Basically, you roll the dice like so.' He let the two wooden cubes fall out of his palm and on to the table. 'If it's an even number, you get to ask me a question; if it's odd, I get to ask you one.'

'Why can't we have a normal conversation like normal people, where I ask you a question and you answer it?'

'Because normal people don't exist. And this way is much more fun.'

'For you, maybe.'

'Come *on*, at least give it a go.'

'Jacob, are you ever serious?' She sighed.

'Roll the dice, and if you get the right number, *maybe* I'll give you an answer.'

He popped another syrup-soaked ball into his mouth and watched the myriad of emotions unfolding on her face. He knew that deep down, under all the layers of control and organization, lived a playful version of Olivia. There was one in everybody, if you looked hard enough.

'*Fine*,' she conceded eventually, picking up the dice and shaking them in her hands. 'But I get to add in a rule.'

'Go on . . .'

'If we don't want to answer a question, we can use a pass. We have three each.'

He had to hand it to her, an escape clause was a fantastic idea. Jacob knew that there were a lot of questions he would rather not answer, parts of himself that even he was loath to talk about, but it was interesting to learn she felt the same.

'Hmm, that sounds fair enough,' he agreed. 'Let's play!'

Olivia let the dice roll.

'Two threes,' he announced. 'The floor is yours; ask away.'

His heartbeat quickened underneath his shirt as he watched her searching for a starting point. Her eyes looked suddenly brighter with the power the dice had afforded her.

'OK, let's start nice and easy. Where did you grow up?'

Oh, Olivia, you're going to have to do better than that.

'Surrey,' he replied swiftly, gathering the dice and handing them to her. 'Roll again.'

'Excuse me! I wanted a bit more detail than just Surrey.'

'Ask more specific questions, then.' He sat forward in his seat. 'You get as good as you give in this game.'

Olivia snatched the dice and rolled once more, her expression darkening a little in frustration.

'Look at that' – Jacob pointed – 'a four and a five. My turn!' He leant further across the table, his fingers drumming a mindless rhythm on the surface, his question already fully formed in his mind. 'Now tell me, what's the real reason you decided to come to India?'

Olivia recoiled ever so slightly, her face remaining impassive but her body revealing the impact of his words. He knew there was more to her trip than she was letting on.

After years of keeping his own secrets, it was easy to see when someone else was doing the same.

'My sister bought me the ticket as a present,' she eventually said. 'I came because she wanted me to.'

'Aha!' he cheered, banging his fist down on the Formica table. 'I knew it wasn't your idea!'

'No, I can safely say it was not.'

'Your sister must be awesome – that's one hell of a gift!'

'Yeah. She is.'

Jacob wanted to probe further into why Olivia looked so desperately unhappy in that moment, but he knew better than anyone that the rules of the game must be followed. If he wanted another question, he had to earn it.

'Go on, roll again.'

And she did, relief washing over her as a four and a two lay face up on the table.

'Your turn, Olivia . . . ask away.'

'Yesterday, when I asked you why you came back to India if you've been here before, you said it was a long story. I want to know why. Why did you decide to come back?'

Jacob ran his tongue across his teeth. 'I'm impressed, well remembered.'

'Why, thank you.' She took a sip of her chai with satisfaction. 'Please proceed to answer whenever you're ready.'

The temptation to pass was strong, but he knew there were better things to save his passes for. As Olivia herself had said, prioritization was key.

'The thing is' – he took in a deep breath – 'I didn't decide to come back.'

'Well, you obviously did, because here you are.'

'Yes, but *I* don't decide where to go.' He gestured to the dice staring at them both from the table. 'These do.'

'I don't get it.'

'Every week I roll the dice. If it's an odd number, I stay where I am; if it's even, I move on. I have a list of possible places to go, all decided by the number on the dice.'

Jacob knew she'd think he was crazy, that his way of life would be totally alien to her. But the reality of seeing Olivia's eyes as wide as her mouth, staring blankly at him in total horror, was harder to take than he thought.

'You don't,' she said at last. 'You don't seriously do that.'

'Yes, I do.'

'But . . . but that's *crazy*.'

'More crazy than not having a phone?' He dipped his finger in a bowl of cooling syrup and licked it.

'Yes, obviously!'

'Why?'

'*Because*. What if you're somewhere awful and you hate it? What if there's an emergency and you have to get out of a place? You can't just stay because some random number says so.'

'If there was an emergency, I'd leave. But touch wood' – he tapped two fingers to the top of his head – 'that doesn't happen.'

Olivia sat there, her mouth opening and closing, without so much as a whisper of sound escaping.

'I wish you could see your face right now; you look horrified!'

'I am.'

'Why?'

'Because it's totally *outrageous*! I mean, it's a logistical nightmare. How many places do you have written down? How often do you change them?'

'*Technically* I should make you roll again before I answer.'

Don't push her, she's already set to head into a meltdown.

'Fine.' She picked up the dice and put them back down on exactly the same numbers. 'Oh wow, look, another four and a two.'

'I'm seeing another side to you, Olivia,' Jacob replied in admiration. He reached into his pocket and pulled out his precious, ragged-looking notebook. 'I make lists. I roll for the country and then a place within that country. Whatever number I get will correspond to a destination I've written down. Wherever it says, I go to next.'

'And you're being totally, 100 per cent serious?' Olivia stared dumbfounded at the notebook. 'You're not making this up?'

Jacob flipped open the book and pushed it towards her, tapping the page that contained his list of scribbled place names. 'This is one of those rare moments when I am being deadly serious.'

'I don't know what to say.'

'I'm guessing it's a little different from how you travel, then?' Jacob closed the book and tucked it back into his pocket.

'Just a little! I like to plan things.'

'You said that before.'

'But, like . . . everything. In an extraordinary amount of detail.'

He noticed her cheeks colouring at the edges. 'Christ, don't tell me you have a spreadsheet,' he joked, and then, seeing Olivia's reaction, dropped his jaw in horror. 'You do, don't you?'

'Maybe . . .'

'More than one?'

'*Maybe.*'

'Jesus, I bet it's all colour coordinated with little code words, isn't it?' he marvelled. 'Can I see it?'

'No!'

Her embarrassment was endearing.

'Why not? I showed you my list.'

'Yes, but you'll just make fun of mine. And besides, I don't want you to know where I'm heading to next.' She regained her composure, shooting him a sarcastic look. 'You might follow me again, like you did at the market.'

'Hey, I was not following you. And even if I wanted to, I couldn't, could I?' He picked up the dice and shook them at Olivia. 'The universe decides where I go, not me.'

'The universe isn't a *thing*, Jacob.'

Well, why is it that we're sitting here? Why did I come back to Delhi? Why did we run into each other, not once but twice?

'If you say so.' He drained the dregs of his tea and shrugged. 'Now, do you want to roll again, or do you need to get back home?'

He didn't want to give her any more reasons to dislike him, and he sensed making her late would be a deal-breaker.

'Holy shit.' She pulled out her phone and gave a jolt. 'It's nearly midnight!'

'Well, you know they say time flies when you're having fun.'

Olivia gave him a scathing look as she gathered her things and made her way towards the exit.

'You want to share a tuk-tuk home? I can drop you off en route?'

As they stepped on to the street it was clear that, although the air may have become a little cooler, the madness and mayhem of the daytime had not relented at all.

'Sure, are we going in the same direction?'

'Kind of . . .' He spotted a sleeping man in an empty rickshaw across the road. 'Hey!' Jacob ran over and woke him from his slumber. 'You free, buddy?'

'Well, I *was* sleeping, but I guess now you've woken me up, I'm free. Where are you going?'

'The Evergreen Hotel and then on to the Red Town hostel.'

'I'll do Red Town hostel first as it's closest, and then Evergreen.'

Jacob could feel Olivia's eyes boring into him from across the street. He lowered his voice, making sure it couldn't be carried on the breeze.

'No. Can you do Evergreen first? I want to drop off my friend before me.'

'It will cost you double.'

'Double!' he cried, at which point he heard Olivia's footsteps racing up behind him.

'Is everything OK?'

'Yes, it's fine, I'm just trying to negotiate.'

'Negotiate?' The driver snorted, still horizontal in his seat. 'He's trying to get me to go out of my way and not pay for the inconvenience.'

'Jacob, if your hotel is near by, I'll go by myself.'

He went to protest, but she cut him off. 'Honestly. It's fine.'

'Are you sure?'

But before he'd even finished the sentence, Olivia had climbed inside the back of the rickshaw.

'I'm sure. I let you pay for dinner; I'm not letting you do this too. I can look after myself you know.'

And we don't have time to look after anyone else . . .

The thought tugged on his conscience.

'All right, fine.'

'Good.' She adjusted herself in her seat. 'Just one stop – to the Evergreen Hotel, please.'

'At last, someone talking sense.' The driver kicked the tuk-tuk into life, arranging himself into a slightly more upright position.

'Well, Miss Olivia, thank you for a wonderful evening.'

'Thank *you* again for dinner.'

'My pleasure.' The tuk-tuk was about to pull away when Jacob was struck with a thought. 'Wait!'

'What now?' the driver grunted.

Jacob crouched down so that he was at eye level with Olivia. 'You don't happen to have a pen on you, do you?'

'I think so.' She looked at him in confusion. 'Why?'

'Can I borrow it?'

'Are we going or not?' the grumpy driver shot back. 'You woke me up and now you don't want to go?'

'Hold on, buddy, two seconds.' Jacob held his hand out. 'Pen?'

Olivia rifled through her backpack and presented a biro from its depths.

'Thank you.' He took the pen and then grabbed Olivia's hand and began to write on it.

'Hey!' She tried to pull her hand away. 'What are you doing?'

'Hold on . . . one more second . . .' He stuck his tongue out in concentration, hoping that he wasn't pressing too hard on her freckled skin. 'There we go!'

Olivia looked down. The letters were just about visible in the dark.

'Is that—?'

'My email address. I thought you might like it – you know, just in case.'

Olivia brought her hand close to her chest, cradling it as though it might break. 'Thank you,' she breathed, their faces so close that he could feel it tickle his cheeks.

The air suddenly felt heavy and dense. Olivia's lips, so delicately pink, parted slightly. Jacob's insides twisted, his lungs struggling to draw breath, his entire being prickling in anticipation. There was a moment, the briefest of moments when the world felt easy. When his life was his own, and he could simply reach out to the girl in front of him and kiss her. When the consequences of his decision didn't matter.

But they do.

They always do.

And just like that, reality knocked him back down to earth with a brutal blow.

'Right then.' Jacob stood, hitting the top of the tuk-tuk decisively. 'I'll say goodnight.' He prayed she hadn't heard the quiver in his voice as he tried to scoop his emotions back up inside himself.

'Oh.' Olivia dropped her head. 'Goodnight, then.'

The rickshaw began to pull away. Jacob balled his fists and stood still, forcing his body to remain where it was. Fighting the urge to ignore his logic. Fighting the urge to run after her. To feel the silk of her skin and to look, one last time, into those big ocean eyes.

Let her go.

For her sake, you have to let her go.

And he did. Although it took all of his might, he did it. Because ultimately, what other choice did he have?

II

Sometimes we can only find our true direction
when we let the wind of change carry us.
Mimi Novic

Olivia

Everyone said to take the train. That travelling by rail was the best way to see the country. In fact, one of the guidebooks had gone so far as to say that not journeying by train would be deeply regrettable, even criminal. Olivia wondered whether those same people would have maintained their level of enthusiasm if their journey had been as stressful as hers; an hour spent stuck in traffic on the way to the station, two cancelled trains, and a five-hour delay whilst running on about three hours' sleep did not make for a positive review. The train itself, whether due to the delays or simply because it was Delhi's default state, was rammed full. People were squashed three to a seat, luggage stuffed into every spare space like a game of Tetris. Families scrambled over one another, babies howled above the screeching of the rails, and further down the carriages, groups of men were forced to hang out of the doors, clinging to the handles of the train as it sped through the country.

By the time Olivia reached Agra, it was already late; she was hungry, overstimulated and, worse than all of that, she'd been forced to miss an entire afternoon of activities due to the delays. Her mind was buzzing as the taxi dropped her off outside her homestay. How was she possibly going to manage to fit everything in now? There simply weren't enough hours in the day and, judging by the exhaustion weighing heavily in her bones, missing sleep was not a clever plan. Her restless night had been caused in part by the noise outside her window, but mainly by the racket inside her own head. Her thoughts had thrashed around, as slippery as eels, in between and over one another. Too many to catch and too many to count, but all coming back to just one thing.

Jacob.

The way he had looked at her. The sudden change in his expression. The short, sharp, almost cold goodbye. And then Olivia looked down at her hand; there was his email address, the faded outline still visible on her skin.

To message him or not to message him? To message him or . . .

The internal argument looped around her brain as she plodded down the dusty path to her homestay. She was so distracted that she barely noticed the yellowing, parched grass growing greener and lusher as she rounded the corner. The sounds of tooting horns interspersed with the swell of laughing voices, and the smell of exhaust fumes blended into rich, spiced cooking. It was only when Olivia was standing right outside the bright, sky-blue building that she registered her arrival.

The Blue Paradise Homestay certainly seemed, on the outside, to live up to its name. It was an injection of tranquillity and colour in the seemingly endless landscape of dust. The building stood tall and proud in the centre of a quaint little courtyard; stone water features tinkled merrily in the corners whilst red, pink and orange flowers broke through the rich green foliage that bordered the edges, like cheerful waving hands. It was a far and distant cry from the misery of her Delhi hotel room.

Olivia had barely set her bag down when a warm, doughy-faced woman came hurrying out of the house to greet her.

'Hello!' she cried, her jewellery jangling and her smile beaming. 'You must be Olivia. I'm Suki – welcome, welcome!'

Olivia's reply was lost amongst the folds of Suki's skin, as she was unexpectedly engulfed in a firm hug.

'You look so tired! Come, let's get this big lump of a bag of yours up those stairs and I'll show you to your room.'

'Oh no, please don't,' Olivia cried, as Suki hoisted the backpack off the ground in one fell swoop. 'It's really heavy!'

'Heavy?' She let out a deep, rumbling laugh. 'You want to try raising three children and carrying their chubby butts around all day, then you'll know heavy! Come, let's get you settled in.'

Without waiting for a response, Suki turned and strode off inside the house. Olivia trotted behind, noticing how the scent of spices seemed to strengthen with every step they took.

'Was your journey OK? Where did you travel from?' Suki chattered, as she led Olivia down an egg-yolk-yellow corridor.

'I came from Delhi, and if I'm honest, the journey was awful.'

'Let me guess, train delays?'

'Delays, cancellations, traffic jams . . . I was meant to be here with the whole afternoon to spare and now it's practically evening.' Olivia's bitterness felt out of place in the sunny interior of the house.

'Ah, but at least you're here now, hey?' Suki's comment

was as bright and breezy as the violet-coloured staircase they had begun to climb.

'Yes, but I've wasted a whole day travelling and I have to replan *everything*.'

'Now, see, that's the problem.'

'What is?'

'Trying to plan!' Suki turned to her as they stopped outside a lurid green door. 'In this country, you can plan and plan all you like, but things will happen as and when they want to. All we can do is relax and go with it.'

Suki's laissez-faire attitude reminded Olivia instantly of Jacob and his tales of universal powers. Her frustration doubled on the spot.

'I see. Well, unfortunately I don't have time to relax. I need to adjust my schedule and do some prioritizing.'

Suki looked Olivia up and down, a smile dancing at the edges of her lips. Without saying another word, she unlocked the door and pushed it open to reveal a charmingly decorated and wonderfully clean-looking bedroom.

Olivia's entire body melted in relief at the sight.

'Hopefully this will be a comfortable enough place for you to do all your planning?'

'This is *perfect*, thank you!'

'My pleasure. Now, why don't I bring you up some tea whilst you sort yourself out. And then you can come and have some dinner with us all.'

'Thank you, but I don't have time.'

'To eat? Or for tea?' Suki chuckled. 'Because in this country, they are the most important activities in life. So, you'd better get used to that!' She put the bag on the floor and gave Olivia's shoulder a squeeze. 'I'll leave the tray outside so I don't disturb you, and I'll call when dinner is ready, OK?'

Olivia didn't even wait for Suki to close the door before diving into her bag and digging out her thick, bound itinerary. Suki could bring her all the tea she wanted, she thought, but there was no way she was going to give up on her plan yet. She had to regain some semblance of control. Too many things had gone wrong so far, and she was barely a week in.

She needed to organize herself.

And . . . she looked down at her hand, the black ink almost illegible in the dying light. She needed to stop thinking about Jacob. Life out here was hard enough without anything more to distract her, especially when it came to an idiot boy with no sense of responsibility.

Press on, push forward.

We have a job to do.

*

Thankfully, by the time Suki had sounded the dinner gong, Olivia had managed to salvage an agenda for her only day in Agra. True, cuts had to be made, but overall she felt satisfied. Tomorrow was a new day, and maybe, at last, she could relax just a little bit for the evening.

As she descended the stairs, Olivia was instantly hit with the most delicious and intoxicating smell of food. It was potent and rich, with a kick of chilli that she could feel at the back of her throat. Her stomach growled in anticipation and her mouth began to water. As she approached the kitchen door, she could hear the same hum of chatter that had greeted her when she'd first arrived at the homestay.

How many people were staying here?

Suddenly the anxiety that had quietened to a low simmer reared up and gave an almighty kick. The thought of sitting in a room full of strangers with their questions and curiosity turned her stomach. Could she ask to eat in her room alone? She knew Suki would object, and besides, Olivia was many things but blatantly rude was not one of them.

With a deep inhale she pushed the door open to reveal an egg-yolk yellow room, filled with steam and laughter and the sound of very content and very full people.

'Ah, Olivia!' Suki stood in the centre of the kitchen, her bulky frame wrapped in a glittering sari that hung like a dark green snakeskin over her body. 'Come, sit down here next to me.' She beckoned her over to the other side of the table. Everywhere Olivia looked there were bowls of food, almost as vivid as the paint on the walls.

'This looks incredible!' she gasped.

'And all of it must be eaten, so come.' She grabbed Olivia's hand and pulled her round to the empty chair next to hers. Olivia's cheeks flushed as she noticed the eyes that were following her to her seat. There were two sets of couples, one old and one young, both rosy-faced and freckled from the sun. Sitting in between them was a ruddy-faced, short-haired woman who, despite being fifty plus, was wearing an ensemble fit for a toddler. The effect of the orange dungarees with the lime-green T-shirt and polka-dot socks pulled up to her knees, was quite something for the eyes.

'Hey, why didn't you put old Liv next to me, Sooks? Us solo travellers have to stick together, am I right?' the woman barked across the table. Her voice was abrasive, like stones rubbing against the inside of Olivia's ears.

'Because she didn't want her running for the hills on her first night,' the elderly man whispered to his wife, just loud enough for everybody to hear.

'Now, now, let Olivia sit down before we descend into total chaos,' Suki artfully interrupted, piling food high on a plate and placing it in front of Olivia. 'Shall I do introductions?'

The group nodded, mouths too full to object.

'Right, well then. Everybody, this is Olivia.'

'Hi, Olivia,' they chorused cheerfully.

'And we have Andrea and Alison.' The two women sitting in the corner waved. 'Betty and Peter.' Suki gestured to the oldest pair of guests, who were seated to Olivia's right-hand side. 'And, last but not least—'

'Tracey Warwick, a pleasure to meet you,' the brash lady interrupted, reaching her thick hand across for Olivia to take. 'I have to say, it's nice to see a young woman braving it by herself out here. Single women travellers. We are a rare old breed, you and I!'

'That's because you're both off your rockers.' Peter snorted, stuffing a piece of roti into his mouth. 'Who on earth would try and tackle this place by themselves?'

'*Peter.*' Betty swiped at his hand. 'Don't be so rude.' She turned her wrinkled face to Olivia. 'I'm sorry about him. He doesn't know how to behave sometimes.'

'Feels like all the bloody time with the amount you tell me off,' he grumbled, reaching for a bowl of thick, red curry.

'No!' She moved the dish away from her husband's reach. 'Remember what the doctor said, less saucy stuff. It's not good for your arteries.' Ignoring Peter's angry mumblings, Betty turned her attention back to Olivia, her blue eyes so light in colour they looked like they were made from glass. 'So, how long have you been in India then, dear?'

'This is my fourth day,' Olivia replied, trying her best to resist the urge to shovel all the food into her mouth in one go.

'Ooh, it all must still feel so new and exciting! Are you away for a long time?'

'It's about three months in total.' To even say it out loud felt like a life sentence. 'How about you?'

'Well, this is our last stop before flying home. We've been here two weeks.' A flicker of sadness rippled through the lines of her crepe-paper face. 'And if I'm being honest, I'm rather jealous of your adventure. Oh, what it must be like to be young and have time on your side!'

'You're not dead in the grave yet,' Peter grouched.

Olivia nearly choked on her spinach curry as she tried to stifle a laugh.

'I think three months is a good amount of time.' Alison tried to wrestle the conversation back on track. 'Are you in between jobs or do you have an incredibly awesome boss letting you take that much holiday?'

Olivia shifted uncomfortably in her seat. She hated the thought of lying, but at the same time, she wasn't sure talking about her mental breakdown with this group of complete strangers on her first night was appropriate.

'I had a lot of holiday saved up.' She smiled falsely. 'And yes, a very nice boss.'

Piggy Phil and his dirty shirts.

'Good! That's what I like to hear.' Tracey raised her fist jubilantly. 'I'm sick of all these young people being forced to work all the hours God sends with zero rewards. *Especially* young women.' She shook her head in dismay. 'Life's too short to be spending it at a desk.'

'Hear hear!' Andrea cheered.

'And what made you decide to come to India?' Alison asked. 'Sorry, you must feel like you're being interviewed. It's just that you're new and exciting.'

'And what? We're all old and boring?' Andrea teased.

'Speak for yourselves, girls. There's plenty of life in this dog yet,' Tracey announced proudly, causing Peter to mutter something derogatory under his breath, earning him yet another swift slap from Betty.

'Anyway, Olivia' – Alison took the reins once again – 'why did you choose India? Have you always wanted to visit?'

'Not really,' she mumbled.

'Is it part of a bigger tour or something?'

Olivia was reminded of the back-and-forth she'd had with Jacob. Why did everyone always ask so many questions? Sweat started to glisten across her forehead, and suddenly her stomach felt far too full and extremely uncomfortable.

'Nope.'

Alison's brow furrowed. 'Surely it wasn't a spur-of-the-moment decision? I don't imagine India is a place you wake up one morning and suddenly decide to visit.'

Olivia felt the pressure mounting behind her forehead. How could she tell the truth without *actually* telling the truth?

'It was a present.'

'A present?' Peter barked. 'Who on earth gives someone a trip to India as a present?'

'*Peter!*' Betty struck him again, but to no avail.

'What? Back in my day you'd be lucky if you got a slap round the ear, let alone a holiday to the other side of the world.' He crunched down hard on a samosa. 'This world is going crazy, I tell you. Absolutely bloody crazy.'

'Who was the present from, dear?' Betty cooed, now switching to the technique of ignoring her husband completely. 'It must be a very special someone.' Her eyes twinkled and Olivia's heart dropped an inch in her chest.

'It was from my sister.'

'Goodness me.' Betty's hand flew to her chest. 'How wonderful is that!'

Olivia felt the tears prick her eyes, hot and salty. She tried to swallow the lump in her throat, but it seemed to be growing larger with every passing second.

'Uh-huh,' she managed, her throat tightening around the words.

'Jesus, the best thing I got from my sister was a freaking BHS voucher. Two months later they went into administration, so I couldn't even use it.' Alison laughed, her tight blonde curls shaking with the force.

'And what do you plan to do while you're in Agra?' Betty continued the interrogation, extending her bony elbows across the table so that her husband was all but blocked from view.

Olivia's mind drifted upstairs to the reorganized agenda that lay on her bedside table.

'I've decided to visit the red stone town tomorrow morning.'

'Ah, Fatehpur Sikri.' Suki surreptitiously placed two samosas on to Olivia's plate. 'It's breathtaking.'

'That's the one.' Olivia placed her hand over her food in an attempt to stop any more being added. 'And then I was going to try and squeeze in the Agra Fort and the Tomb of Akbar, then a quick stop at the Taj Mahal in the afternoon before my train in the evening.'

'Jesus Christ, kid, are you trying to kill yourself? I'm exhausted even listening to that,' Peter groaned.

'That's probably because you're old and decrepit.' Tracey grinned, leaning back in her chair and patting her swollen stomach. 'You don't have the stamina of a young buck like Livvo.'

'I'll give you old and decrepit in a minute—'

'Hey! Hold on a second . . .' Andrea interrupted. 'Did you say you're seeing the Taj in the afternoon?'

'That's the plan, yes . . .'

'Because I would recommend seeing it at sunrise if you can.'

'Ooh yes, you've *got* to see it at sunrise,' Angela chimed in. 'It was amazing!'

'They say it's the only way to see it,' Suki added.

'I did read that.' Olivia fiddled with her fork, trying to push away her building irritation. Didn't they know how much time had gone into meticulously scheduling every detail of her day to perfection? 'But I also wanted to do the furthest thing first and work backwards. Logistically, it made more sense.'

'Screw logic, it's a Wonder of the World!' Tracey threw her hands in the air.

'We're heading there first thing tomorrow morning if you'd like to join us?' Betty chirped.

'No, no, don't be silly. I don't want to hijack your plans.' Olivia tried to hide the mounting tension in her voice, but she could feel the words straining as they came out.

'Honestly, you'd be doing me a favour, dear.' Betty jerked her head towards Peter, who was still troughing his way through more servings of food. 'Company would be a welcome addition at this stage. Helps dilute his moaning.'

'I may be old, but I'm not deaf.'

'No, that much is clear,' she sniped back. 'Come on! It will be fun. Besides, you don't want to be looking around by yourself, surely?'

Olivia felt the entire table's eyes on her face and the flush of heat creep up the back of her neck.

Betty gave her hand a little squeeze. 'It really is the best way to see it, dear. That's what everyone says.'

Before she knew what she was doing, Olivia's head gave a small but definite nod. Her resolve buckled under the weight of their stares.

'Oh hell, why not.' Tracey slammed her fists on the table. 'I'll come too! We can make a real adventure of it.'

'Wonderful!' Betty cheered, before Peter could even think about uttering a retort. His face, however, said exactly what Olivia was feeling. 'Shall we all meet down here at half past five?'

'Sure.' Olivia nodded, her mouth suddenly very dry and her stomach extremely tight. 'That sounds good.'

'Good? It sounds better than good, Livvy.' Tracey raised a piece of paratha in the air triumphantly. 'It sounds *great*!'

Olivia

Despite her entire body aching with exhaustion, Olivia found herself tossing and turning for most of the night. Her brain was too full of thoughts and her stomach too full of food to settle. For the first couple of hours, she'd managed to convince herself that it was the change in schedule causing her restlessness, but soon even she had to admit a large proportion of her brain was still being consumed by Jacob and his infuriatingly arrogant smile. She'd tried everything to help her sleep, but in the end, she decided the only way to silence her brain was to take action.

To: jpgreen@gmail.com
Subject: Hello
Hi Jacob, it's me Olivia. How are you? I wanted to let you know that I arrived in Agra safely, if not a little delayed. I hope you're keeping well?

Olivia stared down at her phone screen, anxiety spiking as she reread her pathetic attempt at a message. Why was she being so formal?

This isn't a work client you're emailing.
She rolled on to her front and started again.

Hey Jacob, I thought it was only fair to make use of the address you so kindly scribbled on my hand and drop you an email.

OK, that's a bit better.

I've arrived in Agra safely, and from what I've seen so far . . .

From inside the taxi.

It looks as crazy and chaotic as Delhi! The train was delayed so I only got here last night.

And nearly had a panic attack because my schedule got messed up.

But I'm here and it's really nice. No more shitholes for me . . . Anyway, I hope you're OK and let me know where you end up rolling next!

AKA please write back to me.

Olivia x

'Hmm.' She reread the message. 'Kiss or no kiss, kiss or no kiss.'
Does it matter?
She hovered over the send button, the kiss staring back at

her like a loaded gun, when suddenly her phone started to vibrate violently in her hand.

'Jesus Christ!' she yelped, as the sound of her alarm rang out harshly against the cool silence of the morning. How was it time to get up already? It felt like five minutes ago that she'd started writing her message to Jacob.

Fumbling to quiet the piercing sound, Olivia hurriedly hit the send button on the email and turned off the alarm, stuffing the phone down under the covers. Now it was done, she didn't even want to look at it, let alone hold it in her hands. Thank God today was busy; at least she'd be distracted.

Yeah, by Tracey . . .

The thought sent a groan of regret rippling through her body. Could she stay in bed and pretend to oversleep? No. She was certain that someone from the group, probably Tracey herself, would come up and rouse her. Why did she agree to the stupid idea in the first place? Why couldn't she have stuck to the original plan?

'This had better be worth it.' She yawned, dragging herself up out of bed and throwing on some clothes.

Slowly, and a little reluctantly, Olivia grabbed her pre-packed rucksack and headed down the stairs. The sky was lightening from jet black to a deep, inky blue, and the chill in the air sent shivers down her spine.

'Good morning,' came a croak from the dark hallway.

'Oh my god!' she yelped, jumping out of her skin and practically tumbling into Peter, who was hunched over against the front door.

'Sorry, I didn't mean to frighten you there.' He came forward into the half-light. 'But at least the adrenaline will wake you up a bit. It's an ungodly hour to be up.'

'Where is everyone?' Olivia scanned the space for any other sign of life.

'I left Tracey outside doing who knows what, and Betty is still upstairs deciding which scarf to wear. Apparently it's important for the photographs.'

'Will it be cold out? Do you think I should get another jumper?' Olivia asked anxiously.

'No, no, it will warm up soon enough. But if that woman doesn't hurry up, I swear I'll leave without her.'

'Excuse me!' a sharp voice interjected from the top of the stairs. '*That woman* is here and ready to accompany her perpetually miserable husband to the Taj Mahal.'

Betty descended into the hallway, immersed in a cloud of jasmine perfume and Elnett hairspray.

'Good morning, Olivia dear. I hope you haven't had to wait too long with this bundle of joy. He can kill a mood quicker than a turd through a letter box.'

Olivia choked on her laugh as the old lady linked her arm.

'All right, enough childish talk; we've got Tracey for that. Now, let's get a move on,' Peter grunted, making his way unsteadily out of the front door and into the courtyard. 'It takes me an age to walk anywhere these days.'

'Hello, fellow explorers,' Tracey bellowed as they all stepped outside, her outfit just as shockingly bright and mismatched as before. 'Are we ready to rumble?'

'We certainly are,' Betty bleated brightly. 'Isn't this exciting! I have waited all my life to see this building, and today is the day.'

'Not unless we get a *move* on,' Peter huffed.

'You're right, Petey.' Tracey clapped her hands together. 'We'd better get cracking – the sun don't wait for no one.'

The pair began to stride ahead, leaving Betty and Olivia following in their wake.

'Do you know why the Taj was built, dear?' Betty turned her orb-like eyes to Olivia.

'Not really.' She knew she'd read something about it in one of her guidebooks, but at this time in the morning after little sleep, her brain was in no mood to function properly.

'Ah! Well . . .' It was instantly clear how excited Betty was to be the one to tell Olivia the tale. 'The story of the Taj Mahal is one of love. It was built by the Mughal emperor as a mausoleum for his wife, who died in childbirth. It is probably the biggest labour of love the world has ever seen.' She sighed wistfully. 'And to think, it took Peter six months to even put up a new clock in our kitchen.'

'Because I'm eighty-five years old and have better things to be doing with my day,' he shot back over his shoulder. 'Now, hurry *up*, you two. You're dawdling.'

'Good God.' Betty squeezed Olivia's arm tighter, picking up her pace just a fraction. 'That man drives me bonkers, and yet I love him more now than the day I met him. Funny that, isn't it?'

'How long have you been together?' Olivia asked, noticing that the road they were walking down seemed to have filled rapidly with groups of other rather excited-looking tourists.

'We'll have been married sixty years in November.'

'That's amazing!'

'I have to say, it has been worth every second.' She leant in closer to Olivia and dropped her voice. 'I don't suppose you have anyone special, do you, dear? A beautiful young thing like yourself must have them queueing round the corner.'

A little pang of longing pulled at Olivia's chest. Back in London she rarely felt lonely; there was simply too much to do and no time to think about her lack of relationship. Besides, it wasn't in her plan for at least another three years. But somehow, out here, where everyone seemed to be travelling in pairs or large groups, and people filled every inch of space available, being alone felt like quite a statement.

'Nobody special for me yet,' she answered. 'The plan is to focus on my career first and then find a relationship after.'

'Gosh, you young ones and your obsession with planning.' Betty chuckled. 'My youngest granddaughter is the same. She's got her whole life mapped out, and she's only in her twenties. When she wants to get this job, and have this house, and the year she wants to get married and have children . . .' She paused and looked Olivia square in the face. 'But I always tell her, you can't plan when you fall in love. Heck, look at me!'

'What do you mean?' Olivia asked, trying to resist making a case for why Betty's granddaughter sounded like she had, in fact, got a very sensible and admirable approach to life.

'You think I wanted to fall in love with this one?' She pointed at Peter, who was mopping his brow with the sleeve of his jumper. 'Heavens, no! I had a whole plan in my mind to marry Jasper Cartwright. He was head boy at our school, exceptionally handsome and from an incredibly well-off family. But one summer spent at my auntie's in Portsmouth changed it all. I met Peter, fell in love and never looked back.' She sighed, placing a hand on Olivia's arm. 'We like to think we have complete control of everything in our lives, but if there's one thing I've learnt, my dear, it's that death is the only guarantee we have.'

Olivia bit down hard on her lip as the image of Leah sprung to her mind.

'I don't mean to be morbid; I only mean to say how important it is to celebrate life every single day we get to live it.'

Olivia lifted her eyes to meet Betty's. She went to speak but found all she could do was let the air fall in and out of her open mouth.

'Right, people!' Tracey's brash voice interrupted the moment like a slap across the face. 'We have arrived! Who needs tickets? Because if you haven't got one, you'd better get in that queue over there. Time is marching on and we have a Wonder of the World to see!'

Peter rolled his eyes and grimaced, shuffling his way to join the end of the line. 'The only wonder I want to see is her being quiet for five minutes.'

*

It took longer than anticipated to get the tickets, and by the time the group got inside the grounds the sun was already peeping its golden face over the horizon.

'Come *on*, we need to get closer. I want to get a good picture of this.'

'Peter! You can't just barge past people,' Betty called after her husband, as he pushed his way through the middle of a group of rather bewildered German tourists. 'So sorry. I'm really sorry,' she apologized as they trotted behind. 'It's quite miraculous how quickly he can move when he wants to. Back home, dragging him round Asda for the weekly shop is like hauling a dead weight.'

'And *that* is the amazing thing about men: they always manage to produce miracles when it's something *they* want to do,' Tracey bellowed, the volume of her voice never seeming to drop below a shout. 'That's why us women are better off doing things by ourselves most of the time – am I right, Livvy?'

The use of the nickname felt like a rake across Olivia's skin; she was about to politely object when Peter stopped dead in front of them and threw his arms open wide.

'Aha!' he cried. 'Perfect. Isn't it just perfect?'

Olivia followed his gaze and nearly gasped out loud at the sight before her. As much as she was loath to admit it, the other guests had been right. The building in itself was impressive, but seeing the sun rise over the glistening white marble, throwing its pink-and-orange light like rivers of silk until the entire building was drowned in a rosy glow, was simply breathtaking. The sounds around them seemed to have been muted; the cries of bored and restless children, the 'oohs' and 'aahs' and clicking cameras of the other tourists, were all silenced. All Olivia could sense was the magic of the moment, the wonder that lay before her. It truly was the greatest labour of love the world had ever seen, and she found a tiny part of herself thanking Leah for giving her the chance to witness it.

'I'll bet you want a picture of this to show your sister when you get home,' Betty trilled in her ear, as if Olivia had spoken her thoughts of Leah out loud. 'Do you want me to take one for you?'

Olivia, who was still mesmerized by the view in front of her, was caught off guard by the offer, and before she had a chance to fully register what was happening, Betty had somehow manoeuvred her into position and was reaching for her camera.

'No,' Olivia yelped, realization dawning. 'No, honestly, it's fine. I don't want a pi—'

'Nonsense!' Betty grinned, her finger already happily clicking away. 'You have to remember this moment. It's a once-in-a-lifetime experience.'

Olivia tried to force her tense jaw into some sort of smile, but all she could think about was Betty's haunting words.

To show your sister when you get home.

A deep well of grief opened up inside her, carving a hole right through her centre. It should be Leah standing here, having her photo taken. It should be Leah dancing under the magenta sky and drinking in the incredible views. Except it wasn't, and it never would be.

'Are you OK, dear?' Betty dropped the camera and cocked her head. 'You look a little off all of a sudden. Did you eat anything before we left? I don't even have a snack with me.' She began digging her hands in her pockets, in search of sustenance.

'The poor lass is probably overwhelmed by you forcing her into a bloody photoshoot,' Peter quipped, pulling his wife towards him. 'Leave her be, woman, and come and get into a picture with me. I think I've finally mastered this selfie thing our Annie was telling us about.'

Olivia watched as the elderly couple strained to fit themselves and the gigantic Taj Mahal into the tiny phone screen Peter was holding aloft.

'Betty love, just move your head a bit to the left,' he instructed through gritted teeth, his smile fixed and unwavering.

'I can't, your blasted shoulder is there,' she replied, through the same frozen grin.

'Ah, to be old and so in love.' Tracey sighed next to her. 'You fancy taking a walk together and letting those love birds be?'

'Erm . . .' Olivia's entire body screamed no. 'Yeah, OK. Sure.'

'Great, let's head this way.' Tracey nodded to the left.

The pair began to weave their way through the grounds, closer towards the imposing white building.

'I meant what I said, by the way: it's great to see a young girl adventuring on her own. Not enough of us do it.'

'Mmmm.' Olivia wondered how great Tracey would think it was if she knew the true reason why she'd come, and that she was hating every second of it.

'Do you know where you're heading next, or is it more of a . . . see where the wind takes you kind of trip? Wake up in the morning and say, hell yeah, today I feel like going to Mumbai!'

Even the thought of such recklessness made Olivia's stomach churn.

'No. I've got a fixed plan.'

'I see.' Tracey's disappointment at Olivia's apparent lack of spontaneity was clear. 'So, the next stop on the agenda is?'

'Tonight, I head to Jaipur for five days. Then to Jodhpur, Udaipur, Hyderabad, Mumbai, and finally three weeks in Goa.' Olivia recited her itinerary as easily as if it were written out in front of her. 'I'll head back to Delhi and fly home from there.'

'No!'

'Erm . . . yes?'

'No way!'

Olivia looked around her to check if Tracey's disbelief was aimed at something other than her.

'Yes. That's my plan. Why?'

'Because I'm going to Jaipur tonight too.'

If insides could crash and burn, Olivia's would have instantly turned to ashes.

'Oh, really?'

'Yes!'

'Tonight?' Olivia pressed, praying that there was some miscommunication occurring between the two.

'Yes, Livvy, tonight!' Tracey whooped, sending a group of pigeons near by fleeing for their lives. 'Would you look at that? The solo travellers can become a duo!'

No, they can't.

They 100 per cent can't.

'The thing is, I'm on quite a tight schedule.'

'Great, I need someone to kick me into touch. Otherwise, knowing me, I won't get there until midnight.'

'I have a very specific train I need to catch.'

'Brilliant. I love travelling by train. It's the best way to see the country. What time are you heading?'

Olivia was desperate now, clinging to every possible excuse and escape route. 'I don't know – it depends how quickly I finish at the other tourist sites this afternoon. I have a lot to see.'

'Hold on.' Tracey's face crumpled in confusion. 'I thought you said you had a specific time to leave?'

'I do, but also, you know what it's like out here . . .' Olivia felt the heat prickle along the back of her neck. 'Things never go to plan.'

'You're damn right about that, kid! But hey, you just tell me where to be and when, and I'll do it. Travelling by yourself is great, but if the offer of company is there, I am not going to say no.'

Olivia swallowed hard, her mouth dry and her body temperature rising rapidly. There must be a way out of this. Could she lose Tracey after the Taj and sneak off without being noticed? Tell her to meet her at the station and then jump on an earlier train? She knew it was cruel, but surely there had to be a way to escape being lumbered with this woman for any longer than she had to.

'Shall we keep walking, Livvo?' Tracey placed a solid

hand on her shoulder, pulling Olivia out of her spiralling thoughts. 'You want to make sure you've got plenty of time for the rest of your activities if we are going to make that train later, hey?'

'Yeah . . .' Olivia bit down hard on her tongue, her jaw clenching almost as tightly as her fists. 'Yeah, we do.'

'Blimey, what a turn-up for the books! Jaipur, watch out, because here we come!'

Jacob

Jacob made his way back to his hostel after yet another long day. He'd been spending his time wandering the streets of the city, taking the opportunity to revisit all of his favourite haunts. The dusty cafes tucked away, saturated with the smells of spices and cigarette smoke; the little market stalls overflowing with trinkets and talismans; and, of course, the masterfully built palaces that stood tall and, proud, watching over the city with a composed knowingness, rare sanctuaries of calm amidst the labyrinth of madness that unfolded around them. He walked morning to night, never stopping to rest, the unrelenting energy of the city pulsing through his veins, pushing him forward on his quest of discovery. What else could he do? What else could he see? But no matter what he sought out or where he went, he couldn't help but notice how different it felt doing it by himself.

All alone.

Normally his solitude was his one constant comfort. However, over the past few days he had to admit that his solo pursuit had, at times, felt a little lonely. Had it only taken three days for him to get accustomed to company? To enjoy having another pair of eyes to view things with, and another brain to share ideas with. He was annoyed at himself for thinking it could be any other way. Hadn't he learnt, from doing this for five years, that the moment you open yourself up, you immediately invite in the fall?

And the last thing we can afford to do is fall . . .

Jacob could feel his swollen feet throbbing against the seams of his ragged trainers. His legs were so heavy with exhaustion that the last few steps towards his hostel felt like an impossible task. Today he had outdone himself, covering miles and miles in a vain attempt to settle his mind. All day it had been racing with thoughts, flitting erratically from one thing to the next. A thousand insects were trapped inside his skull, whispering her name over and over. And then, like clockwork she would appear. The same face with the same blue eyes. So close to his, and yet so completely and utterly out of reach.

Yes, and for good reason.

At last, Jacob reached the front door, and with all the remaining effort he had, pushed it open and stepped inside the brightly lit reception. His weary heart lifted a little when he saw the oversized teenager hunched behind the front desk. Jacob selfishly had to admit he was glad that Kushal was still working in his father's hostel; it was always nice to start the day with a friendly, albeit often exasperated, face.

'Jesus, Kushal, are you still here? I thought you only worked the day shifts?'

The boy turned his drooping eyes to Jacob. He had the expression of an old man, but the facial hair of a teenage boy. 'Someone called in sick, so I said I'd help out.' His fine moustache fluttered as he sighed.

132

'Very admirable of you.'

'Not really. My dad said if I didn't help he wouldn't pay me for the month, so what was I meant to do?'

'Say no? Demand a raise?'

The boy barked out a laugh, sending his chins wobbling. 'You haven't met my dad.'

'No, but I've met mine and, trust me, I'm sure yours is a welcome gift in comparison.' Jacob leant against the wooden counter.

'I don't know. Your parents must be cool to let you go travelling by yourself.'

'They didn't have a choice. I was an adult – what could they do?'

'Lock the doors and tell you that you weren't going? I reckon that's what my mum would do. She won't even let me go down the road without worrying I'll burst into flames and die. It's so *annoying*.'

The whine in Kushal's voice sent Jacob straight back to his teenage days of raging hormones and sprouting body hair. Of stuffy bedrooms that smelt like guinea pig hutches, and uncontrollable urges to break things. To kiss girls. To run away from home and never come back . . .

'Come on, that's only because she loves you.'

'Too much, if you ask me.'

'That's just mums for you, I think.'

Guilt prickled the back of Jacob's throat. He'd forgotten how quickly even the most innocent talk of families could take him back to places he didn't want to go.

Thankfully, Kushal seemed just as reluctant to continue the topic, reaching for one of three chocolate bars sitting in front of him.

'You want one?'

'Nah, you're OK, buddy. I reckon you deserve that sugar hit after the day you've had.'

'Tell me about it.' He ungracefully shoved half of the first bar into his mouth. 'Anyway, how was your day?'

'It was good. I stayed local, just wandered around a bit.'

'A bit? You've been gone all day.'

'I know, but there's just so much to see and I am only one man.'

'True. How long are you staying here for, again?'

'Not sure yet.' The dice felt heavy in his pocket. 'Going to play it by ear. See where the wind takes me and all that.'

'Don't you . . .' the young boy began to ask, before stopping himself and taking another sizeable bite from his chocolate.

'Go on. Don't I . . .?'

'Well, I suppose I was thinking.' He shuffled awkwardly in his already too-small seat. 'You've been travelling a while now, right?'

'Five years, give or take.'

'So, do you ever get lonely? Without your friends and stuff.'

From the vaults of his memory, a flood of old faces surfaced. Ghosts from a past life reaching him all the way from sleepy Surrey. Ties that he had severed, purposefully . . . intentionally. He had been too young to fully know the pain of a lonely life, but it was one that he had chosen gladly over the alternative.

'Sorry, that's probably a bit personal,' Kushal backtracked.

'No, it's fine!' Jacob forced himself back to the present, blinking away the visions of his childhood. 'I just don't think anyone could feel lonely in a place like this. There's never a dull moment!' His laugh was empty and flat. 'And you can always make friends as you go.'

'That's true. Have you met anyone cool so far in Delhi?'

The china-blue eyes appeared in a flash.

'I have, actually.' The honesty felt refreshing after his collection of lies. 'In fact, you don't know any good internet cafes around here, do you?'

'Sure, but if you want to check something, just use our computer.'

'Won't your dad mind?'

'He'll probably be glad that someone is stopping me from playing video games on it for a bit.' He laughed, sending his moustache rippling once again. 'You need to check something?'

'It's only an email.'

'You want to do it now?'

No.

'Yes.' He was taken aback by the eagerness of his own response. 'If that's OK?'

'Sure. It's slow as hell, but it will do the job.' Kushal hoisted himself up and pulled out the chair for Jacob to take. 'I'll go grab a chai while you do your thing.'

'OK, cool, I won't be long.'

Nervous energy tingled across Jacob's skin, and his fingers felt as though they couldn't move quick enough as he began typing in his login details. When was the last time he'd checked his inbox? How many messages would be waiting for him? How many of those would he ever even open? As the page loaded, guilt raked over him. Ten unread emails. Fifty unread emails. One hundred . . .

Focus on the task. Look for her name. Only her name.

As he scanned the list, he noticed that although the majority were junk, there were a few familiar names that caught his attention. His mother would appear every ten messages or so, her emails as constant as the 'looking for love?' and 'you've won a million pounds' promotional crap that flooded the screen. And then, sprinkled in between, like sharp spikes of nostalgia, were other names, their jubilant subject lines aggressively screaming at him.

Jamie's Engagement Party!!!
Join Connor and Izzy in welcoming their beautiful baby girl Elsie.
Sara is turning 30 – let's celebrate!

Why were they there? And why were there so many?

Hadn't he done that thing where all non-essential messages were filed away automatically? Hadn't he specifically blocked their email addresses?

He knew it sounded cold, and at first it was quite nice to hear the news from back home, to see the way everybody else's lives were unfolding in the way he had expected his to. But then there came a point when it didn't feel relevant any more. In fact, it felt painful. He was away from that world and unlikely to ever rejoin it.

He was here now.

And here was all that mattered.

Quickly and efficiently, he moved the messages to junk and then, at last, he spotted it.

An email from Olivia Jackson herself.

A wave of joy erupted from within, extinguishing the heaviness in his chest. Without hesitation, he clicked on the message and began to read, trying as hard as he could to ignore the voice in his head screaming at him to stop.

'Wow, it must be somebody special.' Kushal snorted,

making Jacob jump in his seat. 'Your face is practically touching the screen.'

'Jesus! When did you sneak in?' Jacob shifted an inch back, suddenly conscious of how much he had crept forward in his seat.

'You were probably too engrossed in your message to notice.'

'My eyesight is bad, what can I say? Another perk of getting older.'

Kushal clicked his tongue and went back to munching on his chocolate bar.

'So, who is it from?'

'Just a friend.'

'I see. And are you going to reply?'

No.

Yes.

Maybe?

Jacob's hands instinctively flew to the dice in his pocket. There was only one way to solve this.

'Not sure.' He plucked them free and held them in the air. 'Let's see, shall we?'

'You're going to roll a pair of dice to decide this?'

'Why not?'

The young boy huffed, slouching his weight over the front of the counter. 'You're a weird man – you know that, don't you?'

'Yes, but with very good reason to be.'

Jacob shook the wooden dice and screwed his eyes shut tight.

Evens is yes. Odds is no . . .

He opened his palm and let them free, unable to hide his joy at the two sixes staring up at him.

'What's the result then, numbers boy?' Kushal peered over. 'Is it good or bad?'

'Well, my friend . . .' Jacob began to type his response, refocusing his attention on the screen in front of him. 'I think you'll find it's a bit of both.'

Olivia

It turned out that, despite Olivia's best efforts to escape, Tracey was unshakeable. At one point she was convinced Tracey was going to accompany her to the toilet to make sure they stayed together. Olivia felt like a marked woman, and no matter what tactics of diversion she tried, it was clear that come hell or high water, there were two of them travelling to Jaipur that night. And it was just as bad as she'd imagined. Because for Olivia, whose opinion of India's railway system was already low, travelling five hours in cramped conditions with no obvious escape routes, with a woman who talked solidly for twenty minutes about her underwear rotation technique without taking breath, was a real-life version of hell.

Fortunately, the gods decided to show a little mercy and place Tracey's hotel in Jaipur as far away from Olivia's as you could get, ensuring there would be enough distance between them that the chances of crossing paths over the next few days would be minimal. This fact, whilst a relief to Olivia, meant Tracey had insisted they exchange numbers when the tuk-tuk dropped her off.

Two days and five unanswered messages later, Olivia had started to see Tracey's face around every corner. Many excuses had been concocted as to why they couldn't meet up, each one less convincing than the last. And yet the guilt never came because, as harsh as it sounded, Olivia didn't have time for friends, especially loud, overbearing ones. She had a list as long as her arm of places to see, and she was determined to visit them all by the time she left. And so far, it seemed to be going quite well.

'Remind me' – Kate flitted in and out of the screen, as she hurried to get herself ready to go out – 'how many days have you got left there again?'

'You have my entire itinerary; you don't need to ask me!'

'I know, but there are *so* many pages, and it gets confusing.'

'I have three more days here and then I move on.'

'Three days, gotcha. And how is it?' Her friend's face popped into view, her eyes full of hope. 'Are you starting to like it yet?'

'Erm . . .' Olivia thought for a second. It was true that she wasn't hating it as much, or praying every minute of every day to be back home, but *like* it? The jury was out on that one. 'Yeah, it's getting better.'

'That's good! And have you heard any more from the hot mystery guy?'

The thought of Jacob triggered in Olivia equal parts annoyance and affection. She hadn't heard a peep from him since she'd sent the email back in Agra, and she'd now taken it upon herself to limit the number of times she checked her inbox. What had started as impatience at his lack of response had quickly begun to morph into rejection, hurt and confusion. Confusion at the silence, but also confusion as to why she cared so much about a message from a guy she barely knew.

'Hello? Can you hear me?' Kate's face came so close to the screen it was practically all forehead. 'Olivia, are you there?'

'Yes, sorry. I was trying to work out who you meant, because I don't think I've ever mentioned a hot mystery guy before.'

'Come on! You know who I mean.'

'If you are referring to Jacob then no, I haven't heard from him. Why would I? He's all the way in Delhi.'

'That's a shame.'

'Is it?' Her attempt at nonchalance was pitiful, but thankfully Kate was too absorbed in her flurry of activity to notice. Sometimes her friend's inability to multitask was a godsend.

'Don't worry, I reckon you'll see him again.'

'Really?'

'Yes!'

'Why?'

'Come *on*. What are the chances that you run into someone *twice* in a place like Delhi? That's not coincidence. That's . . .'

'Don't you dare. Whatever you're about to say, don't!'

'*Fate!*' She grinned. 'It must be.'

The irony of her statement was not lost on Olivia, who could picture Jacob now, having a field day listening to Kate.

'Right, well, when you have something more concrete than a mystical power governing everybody on earth's movements to back up your argument, then please let me know. Until then, let's agree to disagree.'

'Hmm, luckily for you, I have to go, otherwise I would have made you stay and argue with me.'

'What a *shame*. Where are you off to? A hot date?'

If Olivia had blinked at that very moment, she might have missed the flicker of fear passing over Kate's face. Within half a second it had vanished, but it was too late; Olivia had spotted it.

'You *are*, aren't you!' She gasped, wishing she could reach through the screen and shake her friend into honesty.

'No!'

'I can tell you're lying, Kate. Who are you meeting?'

'No one! It's a work thing. Forced fun and free drinks, you know the drill.'

'Hmm.' Olivia narrowed her eyes, looking for any more tell-tale signs of deceit in her friend's face. 'I think you have a crush on someone going.'

'And you're entitled to think what you like, but you're wrong.'

'I'm never wrong. Surely you must know that by now.'

Kate threw her head back and laughed, her mane of ginger hair rippling from the force. 'You're an idiot sometimes.'

'As are you.'

'But I love you all the more for it.' Kate brought the screen close to her face and blew Olivia a huge kiss. 'Now, I miss you. Stay safe. And I'll speak to you soon, OK?'

'OK, see you later!'

Olivia hung up the phone and closed her eyes. Just like that, she was alone again.

The silence always felt more profound after a phone call with Kate, who, despite being thousands of miles away, always managed to make her feel like she was sitting right next to her. What Olivia wouldn't give for that to be true right now. For her friend to be by her side in India. She could imagine the pair of them holed up in their homestay, stuffing bags of crisps into their mouths whilst Kate sampled every local sweet treat she could get her hands on. If anyone was going to be able to tackle India head-on, it would be Kate. Why hadn't she come with her? Leah wouldn't have minded. Leah loved Kate. Why did she have to do this all by herself? Why did she have to do *everything* by herself?

Olivia gripped her phone tighter, knowing the promise she'd made not to check again for another day. To not even think about going near her inbox for at least twenty-four hours. Before she knew it, she was opening her emails and watching as the messages loaded.

One after the other after the other until . . .

From: jpgreen@gmail.com
Re: Hello

There it sat, as inconspicuous as all the other messages, yet the sight of it sent her nervous system sparking. She clicked on it, her heart in her mouth.

Surprise . . . it's me! I know you probably thought I'd disappeared off the face of the earth, but no. I'm here. Just extremely bad at replying to people (it's not personal, I promise). I'm still very much in Delhi, enjoying revisiting my favourite places, and putting the world to rights with my friend Kushal. He works behind reception at my hostel, is always miserable and always eating chocolate bars. What can you expect from a teenage boy?

How was the Taj? As magical as you thought? I'm guessing you've left Agra now and are on to Jaipur (I think!). If so, just FYI there are some amazing places to get stuffed paratha from, if one so desires.

For now, I'll stop rambling and say goodbye.

Yours, ever so apologetically for taking ages to reply, Jacob x

She had to read it three times for the words to properly sink in. Olivia's eyes were darting back and forth so quickly that she kept skipping parts and missing sentences. It was as if someone had injected a high dose of energy directly into her veins, her body fizzing with excitement.

There was so much she wanted to say back, so many stories to tell and questions to ask, but from somewhere deep within she managed to find the restraint to hold off replying. She did not want to become the kind of girl who loses her head over a boy, especially one she barely knew. He'd taken his time to respond to her, so why shouldn't she do the same to him? Wasn't it enough that she'd got a response?

FYI there are some amazing places to get stuffed paratha from, if one so desires.

His words triggered a rumbling from deep within her stomach. It was getting late and she was hungry.

Since her arrival in Jaipur, Olivia had taken to eating dinner at her homestay; a clean, spacious and comfortable place that might not have been a patch on Suki's multicoloured masterpiece but gave Olivia no reason to complain. Tonight, however, whether it was the thrill of Jacob's message or simply the mention of a stuffed paratha, Olivia found she was tempted by something different. There was an unfamiliar urge to explore outside her comfort zone, to go a little further afield and take a walk beyond her four walls. And so, with the voice of Jacob cheering her on in her head, she grabbed her bag and left the room.

Besides, she thought to herself as she hurried down the stairs towards the front door, how hard could it be to find a decent plate of food?

*

Forty minutes of wandering and Olivia still couldn't decide where to go. It wasn't for the lack of options; in fact, there were far too many for her brain to handle. Down every street she walked, she passed restaurant after restaurant, cafe after cafe, and handfuls of market stalls, to boot. There was an endless supply of fried, spiced and deliciously scented food, all of which *looked* good enough to eat – but looks, as Olivia was well aware, could be deceiving.

The city itself didn't help matters, with its writhing crowds and glaring lights. The cacophony of noises, which by day felt overwhelming, was even more of an assault at night. It was as though the darkness brought everything closer, made it more oppressive and harder to escape.

She turned down another street, which frustratingly looked exactly the same as the one before, and the one before that. Her hunger and impatience were now joined by a jolt of panic. The longer she walked for, the further she was from home. And the further she was from home, the greater the chances of her getting lost.

Should she call Tracey?

And say what?

Hi, I'm by myself and can't even find a place to have dinner, please save me.

The thought alone made her cringe with shame.

No.

She could do this.

She was a capable young woman, who simply needed to make a decision.

'Excuse me.'

Olivia stopped abruptly as a man appeared out of thin air in front of her. For someone so large he seemed to have moved with surprising ease, his protruding stomach almost closing the gap between them. 'You look a little lost.'

'Erm . . . not *lost* per se. Just . . .' Olivia took a step back, introducing some space between her and the man's pot belly. 'Just looking for somewhere good to eat.'

At her words the man jumped into the air, his entire body quivering in the aftermath.

'Oh wow, do I have the place for you! My restaurant here does the best curry in Jaipur.' He nodded towards a white-painted building to his left. It was brightly lit, and the interior was simple but modern-looking. 'Come, you look starving.'

Olivia peered through the window; there were only two men sitting inside, neither of whom had any food in front of them yet for her to inspect. It did look clean, she supposed – empty, but at least clean.

'I'll do you a good price,' the man coaxed gently, sensing Olivia's resistance waning.

'I don't know.' She tried to get a better view, craning her neck to see if she could catch a glimpse of the kitchen, but it was hidden out of sight.

'Do you like spice?'

'Not really, no.'

'Great!' The man seemed thrilled. 'We can make anything you like with only a little spice. We will cater to all your needs. In fact, we can cook omelette, chips, cheese sandwich. We can do it all!'

His desperation should probably have been a red flag for Olivia, but her curiosity got the better of her.

'I don't suppose you do stuffed paratha with your curries?'

If the man could have burst with excitement, Olivia was

sure he would have. 'Yes! Oh yes, it's one of our top specialities.'

Olivia tried to find another excuse, another reason to question her choice, but she had nothing. She was so hungry that her brain had all but given up rational thought.

'OK, fine.' She nodded. 'I'll have a table for one.'

'Fantastic!' The man was so overjoyed Olivia thought he was about to hug her; instead, he opened the door and ushered her inside. 'Great choice, madam, you will not regret it. I promise you will not regret it.'

Olivia

Olivia woke suddenly. Her body felt as though it had been doused in ice-cold water. Her sheets were soaking and clinging to her shivering skin.

'Oh God,' she moaned, feeling the bitter taste of bile rise up in the back of her throat. 'Oh God, please no.' She clutched her stomach. It writhed and rolled at her touch, the contents swirling. She needed to move, but the thought of standing made her queasiness triple in intensity. Her head was swimming, and the room began to spin.

You're not going to be sick.

It will pass.

Just lie still and breathe.

Olivia's entire body contracted.

'I'm going to be sick,' she whimpered, hauling herself out of bed and into the bathroom.

Fortunately, she made it in time for the best curry in Jaipur to make its way back up and out into the toilet. Olivia sobbed as her body ejected every last morsel and more. Her stomach ached with the effort and her throat burnt from the

148

acid. How could she have been so stupid? She'd known the moment her plate of greying, insipid food arrived that something wasn't right. But had she left? No. Anger flooded her, causing her chilled skin to burn red hot and her palms to drip with sweat.

Thankfully the ordeal was over in moments, but Olivia, who had now cried herself into exhaustion, couldn't bear to move. Instead, she curled herself around the toilet and laid her head on the floor, her knees tucked up to her chin, her body folding in on itself. As she closed her eyes and willed herself to sleep, she felt her mind fill with thoughts of her baby sister. The nights she'd found her in this very same position, whimpering into piles of towels she'd fashioned around herself in a little cocoon. The poison that was being pumped into her veins killing not just the cancer but every bit of goodness inside her too.

'You need to tell someone when you feel this bad, Leah,' Olivia would say, dropping to her sister's side and placing a cooling hand on her forehead.

'Why? There's nothing anyone can do. It's just part and parcel of the cancer life.' She'd sigh, trying her best to joke even in the darkest of times, with sick in her wispy hair and tears streaming down her face.

'Well, you don't have to do it alone.' Olivia would grab a blanket from her bedroom and coil herself around her sister, throwing the cover over them both and holding her tight until their mum would discover them in the morning.

'Oh, Leah,' Olivia cried, the reality of her sister's absence cutting through her. The pain flooded her, pushing any remaining swirls of nausea aside.

My darling, brave baby sister . . .

After an hour on the floor, Olivia's body had accepted that

there was nothing left inside her to give. Her head was pounding, and her mouth tasted faintly of spices and strongly of bile. She needed water and she needed proper rest.

Slowly, and very carefully, she made her way back to bed, wrapping her tender body in her still-damp sheets. Olivia glanced down at her hair; it lay in dirty tangles, clumped together with sweat and sick. What a mess she was. The infallible Olivia Jackson reduced to this.

I want to go home. I need to go home.

But it wasn't her home in London that she craved. It wasn't the pocket of solitude and tranquillity she'd so carefully crafted for herself that her body longed for. No, it was her childhood home. The place she hadn't yearned for ever since she left it at eighteen. It was such an unexpected urge that, before she knew what was happening, Olivia's chest had started to heave and a deep, guttural howl ripped from her mouth.

Oh, how it hurt to want to be held. To see the images of her parents flash before her, reaching out to her but unable to grasp hold. She buried her head deeper into the soaked pillows and bawled, allowing her feelings to fully take over. Not since she was young had she cried like this. Leah's diagnosis had put a stopper in any thought or desire to do so; Olivia knew full well that whatever she was experiencing was nothing in comparison to her sister. But now . . . now it was just her.

Call them.

The thought was so small, yet powerful enough for Olivia to reach for her phone and turn it over in her clammy palms.

And say what?

Reality sobered her. As much as her childish longing wanted to, she knew she wouldn't be able to speak to her parents in this state. Pride was a powerful armour that was hard to remove after decades of wearing. Instead, she wiped her tears and took a deep breath in, allowing her fingers to find the only other number she could think of calling.

After three rings he answered.

'Big Sis! I was wondering if I was ever going to hear from you . . .'

'Kyle?' Her voice cracked immediately, its pitch too high and too constricted to pass as normal.

'Jesus Christ, are you OK? You sound . . . I don't know.' He paused, as though unable to compute the words Olivia knew he was going to say. 'You sound like you're crying.'

'That's because . . .' Her throat tightened and her breath grew shallow. 'That's because I am.'

'Holy shit. Hold on, I'm going outside and I'll FaceTime you, OK? Do not go anywhere.' Notes of fear were audible underneath his serious tone. 'Do you hear me, Liv? Do not go anywhere.'

*

After an hour on FaceTime with her brother, Olivia felt much more herself. Her body was still sore and her hair rancid with vomit, but her mood had lifted significantly. Hearing Kyle's updates on life back home, and the drama that seemed to occur daily at his work, was respite for her sorry self.

'Now, what are you going to do with yourself for the rest of the day? Apart from shower – because let's face it, you look like you stink.'

'Of course I'll be showering, thank you very much, and then . . .' She shrugged. What was she meant to be doing today? Probably looking round a thousand and one tourist sites. 'Not sure.'

'Why don't you meet a friend and grab some food?'

Because I don't have any friends.

151

The thought stung a little more than she expected.

'Hmm no, I'm not hungry.'

'Not now you're not, but you'll have to eat at some point.'

'Maybe.'

'No, not maybe. You need to eat something.'

'Wow, OK. Since when did you become so sensible?'

'Maybe since I stopped being a little boy and grew up.'

'That's news to me,' she joked, but she soon saw that Kyle wasn't laughing. 'Oh, come on, I'm only messing around.'

'I know you all find it so hard to believe, but I'm not a totally incapable idiot. I can look after myself.'

'I know you can. Of course you can!'

An awkward silence wedged itself between them, and Olivia knew she was going to have to be the one to break it.

'Speaking of food, I was thinking: do you remember when Leah used to get sick, how she would always want mashed banana and milk to soothe her stomach?'

'Yeah,' Kyle replied reluctantly, his scowl softening ever so slightly at the mention of Leah.

'And Mum used to refuse, and make her drink litres of electrolytes and eat dry toast.'

'God, those drinks used to make me want to gag just looking at them.' He softened even more.

'I know! I felt so bad for her, until I found out that *you* would sneak upstairs afterwards and bring her a bowl of the banana stuff!'

'What can I say? I was always the rule breaker.' Another flicker of sadness darkened Kyle's expression. 'And I couldn't stand to see her so unhappy. I just wanted to make her smile.'

Olivia's heart grew heavy. The void that had carved itself into the very centre of her being after Leah passed seemed to grow wider and emptier. It was the absence of something, a missing part, a hole through her very core. An endless chasm of nothing, which she knew would never be filled by anything again.

'Kyle?'

'Olivia.'

'Do you . . .' She dropped her gaze from the screen. 'Do you think I was ever too hard on you both growing up?'

The question had been lingering on the fringes of her mind for a while, and now, in her moment of weakness, it had made its bid for freedom from her brain and out of her mouth.

'What do you mean?'

'I don't know. I sometimes worry that maybe we didn't have a lot of fun together.'

A lump in her throat and a throbbing in the absent space made Olivia's eyes brim with tears.

'Hey, don't you worry about that. I brought enough fun for all of us.'

Normally she would have welcomed Kyle's attempt at distraction, but not today.

'You know what I mean.'

He looked at her hard; his big, brown eyes were a complete contrast to hers, but still as piercing in their gaze.

'I do know what you mean, and yeah, if I'm honest, sometimes it felt like I had three parents at home instead of two. *But* now I know that you were just trying to take care of everyone, because nobody seemed to be able to take care of themselves. Leah became the priority, and you filled in the gaps.' He looked away from the screen, a slight colour in his cheeks. 'And in all honesty, I don't know what we'd have done without you, Liv.'

She let the nickname slide as her own cheeks blushed with affection.

'Saying all that' – Kyle returned his focus to her – 'I do think you're too hard on Mum and Dad.'

The affection vanished and she felt herself prickle defensively.

'How?'

'Firstly, you never speak to them! The number of messages I've got since you've been away, asking where you are and how you're doing. I've had to promise to give them a weekly update for the rest of your trip.'

Olivia scoffed at the ridiculousness of this statement.

'They don't want to know that much about me.'

'They do! And when you do talk to them, you're fussing or telling them off or treating them like they're kids.'

'Because they aren't doing anything to help themselves.'

'No, they're grieving. And trying to make sense of a world without their baby daughter.'

His words were like punches to the gut, each landing harder than the last.

'I know it's not my job to tell you how to live your life, but maybe . . .' He shrugged, clearly choosing his words with care. 'Maybe try and be a little kinder to them in the future. It's not their fault they aren't as put together or as brilliant as you are.'

Olivia, once again, was rendered speechless by her brother. Since when had he become so wise? So emotionally attuned? And so . . . *right*.

'Anyway, Kate tells me you've met some annoying guy out there, who you hated but he's kind of your friend now? Why don't you message him?'

Kyle had changed the subject so fast that Olivia felt a little whiplashed.

'Excuse me?'

'She said his name was . . . John something? Or James maybe?'

'His name is beside the point. What the *hell* are you doing talking to Kate?'

And why the hell is she telling you about Jacob?

'I needed an update for the parents, and I was worried about you and wanted to see if she'd heard anything. I know you like to be left alone and I didn't want to keep bothering you, so I messaged her. No big deal.'

Except it felt like a big deal. A very big deal. The fact that her brother and her best friend were exchanging messages about her behind her back went against the most basic and fundamental of friendship codes.

'Right, well in future just WhatsApp me, OK?'

'Fine, but stop deflecting.' Kyle's eyes narrowed. 'Who is he?'

Nobody. Let's face it, he's nobody.

'His name is Jacob, and he isn't in Jaipur.'

'That's annoying. And there isn't anyone else?'

'Not really, unless you count a fifty-plus northern woman called Tracey, who is about as graceful as a lump of coal.'

'She sounds great.' Kyle brightened. 'Why don't you call her?'

'Maybe.'

'Look, Liv, she may not be your ideal person, and on the surface she may seem a little rough around the edges—'

'A *little*,' she murmured cruelly, under her breath.

'But right now, you need some company. So, if I were you, I'd stop being so judgemental and give the woman a call.'

'I'm not being judgemental. She's probably busy.'

'But you won't know until you try, will you?'

Olivia scowled; maybe this new version of Kyle was less

155

desirable than she first thought. Sweet and emotionally intelligent she could deal with, but righteous and highly annoying? Those were characteristics she could do without.

'Fine, but if I'm going to do that, I need to get off the phone and shower.'

'That's the spirit! Now, I'll speak to you in a couple of days and see how you're doing, all right? And if you need anything in the meantime, call me.'

A little warmth bloomed in her chest.

'All right. I'll speak to you soon.'

'Bye, Sis! And remember . . . Call. Your. Friend!'

'FINE!' she shouted at a blank screen. Kyle had hung up and all she could see was her sorry reflection mirrored back at her. 'Fine . . .' She scrolled through to her contacts and found the name she had been so keenly avoiding for the past few days.

One click, three rings and the loudest hello she'd ever experienced.

'Livvo! My girl! How are you doing? Jesus, you don't know how great it is to hear from you, I was starting to worry. Thought something might have happened to you.'

'Ah, that's the thing—'

'You know, maybe you'd eaten something dodgy and got sick, but then I remembered, not our Liv. She's a sensible one. She wouldn't risk anything more exciting than a cheese omelette! Then I thought maybe you were just ignoring me. Giving me the old silent treatment,' Tracey continued, Olivia's input apparently surplus to requirements. 'What is it they call it these days? Ghouling? Or ghosting, is it? But then I didn't think you were the type.' She paused and took a long inhale. 'So, what's been going on? Where have you been hiding?'

'Well, funnily enough . . .' Olivia winced. 'I did get sick, from some *very* dodgy food.'

'Get away with you. You're joking?'

'Unfortunately, I'm not.'

'Jesus, I knew I was many things, but psychic was not one of them. Are you OK now? How long were you out for? Have you seen a doctor?'

'It was last night, but I'm fine. I feel fine now.'

'You sound tired. Have you eaten anything since?'

Tracey and her twenty questions were suddenly making Olivia feel rather nauseous again.

'No, not yet. It's why I called, actually.'

And now wish I hadn't.

'I was wondering if you were around for a tea or a walk or to grab something to eat.'

'Hell no!' Tracey roared. 'There's no way you're going anywhere, my girl. Not after a Delhi belly situation. You do need food, but also fluids and a whole lot of rest. What's the name of your hotel? I'll come over right away.'

'You don't have to do that.'

'I know, but I'm going to.'

'Are you sure? You really don't need to.'

'I know. What's your hotel called?'

'But honestly, Trac—'

'*Liv.*' Tracey dropped her voice. 'Quit arguing with me, and just give me the name of your bloody hotel!'

Olivia knew she had two choices. Hang up and run, or admit defeat.

'It's the All Seasons homestay.'

'Thank you. Now, sit tight and I'll be with you in two shakes of a lamb's tail.'

Olivia

Olivia had only just managed to get out of the shower and open a few windows by the time Tracey arrived, dressed head to toe in every shade of yellow, arms full of shopping bags.

'Just a couple of essentials,' she'd proclaimed, bursting into the bedroom and ordering Olivia to sit in the corner. 'Now, don't move. I'll be back.'

Olivia barely had time to process how one person could own so many garish items of clothing, before Tracey returned with a rather unsettled-looking lady from reception and a bundle of clean bed linen.

'We can't have you sleeping in that, it will only make you feel worse,' she huffed, stripping the sweaty sheets and handing them to the woman. 'I'd wash these on a *very* high temperature, if I were you. Oh, and is there a kitchen I can use to make tea?'

The lady nodded and pointed down the long corridor outside Olivia's bedroom.

'Great!' Tracey turned back to face Olivia as the shell-shocked woman disappeared. 'You've showered, yes?'

'Uh-huh.'

'Good, now get into bed. I'm going to put the kettle on, and while it's boiling, I'm going to clean that bathroom of yours.'

Olivia's stomach dropped in horror. 'No! Surely one of the cleaners could do that?'

'They could, yes, but they work hard enough as it is. And besides, it won't take me two seconds.'

'Tracey, please don't.'

'Why not? You think, as a mother of four daughters, I haven't dealt with my fair share of bodily fluids?' She stood, hands on hips, glaring at Olivia like a custard-covered bulldog. 'Jesus, when they were all under six, there wasn't a piece of me that wasn't covered in some form of excrement.'

Olivia tried not to gag at the very disturbing image now planted in her head.

'Not that that's a thought you want to be having with an iffy stomach, but you get my drift.' Tracey patted the edge of the mattress. 'Now, bed, please, or I'll have to use brute force, and we both know I'd crush you like a flea.'

Maybe it was delirium setting in, or the idea of Tracey wrestling Olivia dressed as a human banana, but Olivia did as she was told and nestled down under the covers.

'Fine, but I'm not happy about this,' she grunted petulantly, breathing in the clean smell of the freshly laundered sheets.

'I'm sure you're not' – Tracey rummaged in one of the shopping bags and pulled out a pair of rubber gloves and a bottle of bleach – 'but you're going to have to deal with it.

So buckle up and get comfy, kid, because it's time you got a little TWC.'

'Don't you mean TLC?'

'Nope, I mean TWC.' She snapped the gloves over her hands and grinned. 'You're getting yourself some extra special Tracey Warwick Care.'

And care it certainly was. After cleaning the bathroom, Tracey had appeared with a tray full of goodies from the kitchen. There was fresh mint and ginger tea, some porridge, a pile of dry toast and . . .

'Oh my god,' Olivia gasped, looking down at the little bowl of mush.

'What's up, kiddo?'

'Nothing, it's just . . .' She pulled it towards her. 'Is this mashed-up banana?'

'With milk and a bit of sugar, you got it! My girls used to go mad for this stuff.'

'My sister did too.'

'Oh, really?'

'Yeah.' The memory struck deep, and Olivia gripped the bowl harder.

'Well then, I'm glad it wasn't just my family who were a bunch of weirdos when it came to food.' Tracey came to perch on the edge of the bed. 'Oh, you should have seen some of the concoctions they would make. Harry always said I indulged them too much, let them play with their food rather than eat it. Silly bastard – always got so worked up over things. But I guess you can't blame the guy for being on edge, living with five women. It takes a certain type of person to do that, I can tell you.'

'Is Harry your husband?'

'Was.' Tracey paused, paying a bit too much attention to the corner of Olivia's duvet cover. 'Until he went and died on me last year.'

Olivia stopped with her spoon halfway to her mouth.

'I'm so sorry.' And she genuinely was. 'How long were you together?'

'Thirty-five years. We survived four kids, five house moves and one triple bypass, and then he goes and chokes on a cashew nut and pops his clogs. What an idiot! Couldn't believe it when I got the phone call.'

'A cashew nut?' Olivia tried not to let her disbelief detract from the seriousness of the conversation.

'I know! Who would have thought such a tiny thing could kill a big old slab of meat like my Harry. But life is full of surprises, isn't it?'

'That must have been quite a shock,' Olivia whispered. 'Again, I'm so sorry.'

'Nah, you're all right, kid. He had a good life. I mean, he was married to me, so some would say he was the luckiest man in the world!' She chuckled, a note of sadness breaking through the bravado. 'But yeah, after he passed, I told my girls . . . I said, I need to get away. I need to explore, clear my head, be somewhere nobody knows me. Where I don't have to act a certain way or be a certain person.'

Olivia stared at the bowl of banana.

Is that what you wanted for me, Leah?

Is that why you sent me here?

'So I came here, and guess what, it's worked a treat!'

Olivia eyed Tracey as she slurped loudly on her tea. This woman, for all her rough edges and brash swagger, was just as wounded as she was.

161

Grief, it seemed, spared no one.

'But weren't you nervous? About coming out here on your own?' Olivia asked.

'Too right I bloody was. Weren't you?'

'I don't think I've been anything *but* nervous since I arrived here.' The honesty tasted refreshing on Olivia's lips.

'Don't blame you, kid, but I thought you young'uns were meant to be resilient and up for adventure. An old bag like me can't stand it if I have to change my washing powder, let alone countries. But the change has been good – kicked me right up the arse, so to speak.'

'It's impressive. I can't imagine my mum getting on a train to Liverpool, let alone a plane to India.'

'Ah, you say that, but I bet she's a dark horse at heart.'

'Hmm. You don't know my mother.'

The weeping, fearful, closed-off woman Olivia had grown up with sprung to life in her mind's eye, followed swiftly by the echoing words of her brother.

You're too hard on Mum and Dad.

'No, I don't know her, but I reckon' – Tracey leant in closer – 'if she raised a daughter like you, she can't be anything less than a firecracker.'

Appreciation and, dare Olivia say it, affection began to unfurl at the compliment. She noted how much lighter her heart felt, and how soothed her soul was from the afternoon with Tracey. Yes, she was still audacious and brazen, and she wore the most horrific combination of clothing that Olivia had ever seen, but her heart was bigger than all of that, and Olivia felt a tide of gratitude swell in her chest for her new friend.

'Thank you. Your girls are lucky to have you.'

'You see, that's what I've been telling them all for years,

but they never listen!' Tracey threw her head back, letting out an almighty laugh. 'I'm glad at least someone appreciates my efforts.'

'I really do,' she replied earnestly. 'I didn't realize how much I needed today, but it's been lovely, so thank you.'

The edges of Tracey's cheeks blushed. 'Ah, get away with you, kid. It was the least I could do.' She cocked her head and focused her gaze even more intensely on Olivia. 'You see, I've learnt that it's usually the ones that never ask for help who need it the most. The ones always giving, who need a little giving back to. The ones who are always fine' – she gave a sly smile – 'that are often those most in need of the TWC. Do you know what I mean?'

'Yeah . . .' Olivia felt her heart twist in angst and her eyes prickle with tears. 'Yeah, I think I do.'

'Good, because we have to get you fighting fit for the rest of your trip, don't we?'

Olivia's eyes found the large, bound itinerary on her bedside. A flicker of panic. A knot in her throat. There was still so much to *do*.

'I think I'm going to need all the strength I can get.'

'Remind me, what's on the agenda?'

'Two more days here and then I go to Jodhpur.'

'And remind me, where to after that?'

Olivia brought to mind the map of her trip. 'Udaipur, Hyderabad, Mumbai, then Goa.'

'Jeez, that's an action-packed schedule. You're going to get back to the UK more tired than when you left. At least you have some time down south to relax at the end.'

Relax.

Even the thought of the word triggered prickles of anxiety to erupt across Olivia's skin.

'Well, I have quite a few things planned for when I'm there. Lots of churches to see and temples to visit.'

'I knew it.' Tracey slapped her hands down on the bed. 'I knew you were one of those.'

'One of what?'

'The doers.' She smiled as though uncovering a great mystery. 'Knew it the second I saw you. My Jen is the same. Can't sit still for love nor money. Always on the go, planning this, controlling that, organizing someone to do something. Non-stop, she is.'

'You say it like it's a bad thing.'

'Not bad, just exhausting. Don't you get tired of trying to hold everything together all of the time?'

'Rather than what? Going around letting things just *happen*?' Olivia could feel her defences locking into position, armouring her ready for battle. 'No direction. No decisions. No responsibility to do anything.'

Like Jacob and his silly dice.

'Woah there, kid, there's no need to get yourself worked up. I didn't mean to cause offence.'

'I'm not offended.'

'You sound offended.'

'I'm *not*. I'm just sick of people thinking life works like we're in some kind of fairy tale or movie.' The agitation instantly switched to sadness. Tears filled her eyes and her voice began to quiver. 'It's all well and good saying everyone should just go with the flow, but some things . . . some *situations*' – her throat was constricting with every sound she made – '*need* someone to take control.'

Tracey fixed her with a curious expression, and after a brief silence nodded in recognition.

'I see.'

'You see what?'

'I see where it comes from now.'

Olivia was about to snap back when Tracey continued, her words silencing her immediately.

'Because when my Harry passed away, I sort of fell apart a bit. It didn't happen overnight, of course. It was more of a gradual thing. But soon I became obsessed with controlling everything around me. His death was such a surprise that I couldn't handle the thought of anything unknown. I'd drive my kids mental, calling them, checking what they were doing. Making sure everything was in the same place in my house, eating the same thing every day. I thought, ain't no bloody rogue nut going to kill me off too!'

Olivia's chest ached for the woman sitting opposite her. It ached for her pain, but it also ached in understanding.

'It was bonkers and it was unbearable, but it was how I coped. When life begins to unravel before your eyes, you grab on to anything to keep steady, don't you?' She fixed Olivia with a look that seemed to burrow beneath her layers and into the very centre of her soul. 'What made you try and hold on to it all then, love?'

Don't answer that.

Do not go there.

But the words came rushing out before she had a chance to hold them back.

'My sister.' Her voice was so small.

'Ah.' Tracey nodded. 'The mashed bananas.'

'Yeah, she used to ask for them when the chemo would make her sick.'

'I see. How old was she when she got diagnosed?'

'Four.' Olivia's shoulders slumped under the heaviness of it. 'I was twelve and my brother Kyle was nine.'

'Jesus, that's tough. It's tough at any age but especially when you're a kid.'

'It wasn't ideal.'

Tracey dropped her voice. 'And let me take a wild guess here: as the oldest, you did what you could to help out while everyone around you, including the adults, were losing their minds?'

Her words were like a blunt instrument hitting Olivia's heart.

'Pretty much.'

'Hmm, you see that's the thing about parents. At the end of the day, they are just as messed up and raw and emotionally clueless as the rest of the world. They can't protect you from everything. They aren't the big heroes you want them to be. In fact, sometimes they are the complete opposite. The moment your child sees that, it's like the spell is broken.'

The memory of Olivia's mum and dad holding one another, crumpled on the floor in tears whilst she watched on, holding Kyle's hand and telling him it would all be OK, made her heart stop momentarily and her body run ice cold.

'Yeah, you can say that again.'

'But trust me when I say this, it hurts just as much for them to know you've seen them like that, as it does you seeing it for yourself.' A shadow of anguish flittered across Tracey's face. 'How is your sister now?'

Dead.

'She's . . .' Olivia lifted her head and saw the hope in Tracey's eyes.

Dead. Say it. She's dead.

'She's good. She's really good.'

'Great!' Tracey reached for her hand and squeezed it hard.

166

'That's brilliant, that is. She's OK and you're OK, and now you can start getting back to relaxing and *enjoying* your life! Letting go a bit more, not getting so het up about everything.'

'I guess . . .'

'You guess?'

'I don't know.' She sighed in frustration. 'It sometimes feels hard to do that, you know? It's not like I can just flick a switch and chill out all of a sudden.'

Because nothing would get done.

Nothing would be achieved.

'No, it takes time and patience. God knows it took me long enough. Time, a lot of therapy and a ton of yoga, but eventually I found my way.'

'Yoga?' Olivia couldn't keep the surprise from her voice.

'Hey, just because I'm built like a brick shithouse does not mean I can't bend over and touch my toes.'

'I didn't mean it like that!'

'Ahh, I'm only messing with you, Livvy. I've been doing yoga every day for nine months and I still can't reach past my ankles, but that's not the point. It's about the breathing and the focus and presence. Being purely in that moment, in your body, and feeling everything as it is. Powerful stuff, that is. *Healing* stuff.'

Olivia let the words sink in past her scepticism. 'Really?'

'Really. The biggest thing I learnt is that when you're in the darkness and you feel like there's no escape, find one thing that brings you joy. One little thing, and do it every day. Soon those small things add up to the big things, and without you even realizing, that fog will clear and life will feel a little lighter.' Tracey took a long, slow sip of her tea. 'Joy is all we've got in this messed-up, crazy world, kid. We

167

all die some day, no matter how hard we try and fight it. So, we might as well make the most of the ride while we're still on the bike.'

Olivia laughed. 'Sounds like something Jacob would say.'

'And who the ruddy hell is Jacob?' Tracey jerked her head so quickly that Olivia was worried she was about to fall off the bed.

'He's a friend I met out here.'

'A friend, hey?' Tracey winked. 'I raised four daughters, remember; I know what you girls mean when you say that word.'

'Trust me, he's just a friend,' she stated adamantly, 'although I'm not even sure you could call him that.'

'How come?'

'I don't know.' Olivia sighed. 'He's travelling all over the place, and we've started emailing a bit, but sometimes I think, what's the point?'

'Does there have to be a point?'

'Obviously, otherwise it's a waste of time and effort for everyone. We probably won't ever see each other again.' The words made her sadder than she expected.

'So? What if the point is simply getting to know someone? Speaking to another person with a different perspective? Having a connection with someone you like? Not every-thing always has to *be* something.'

Olivia picked at the corner of her toast. There was undeni-able truth in what Tracey had said, even if she wasn't willing to admit it just yet.

'Maybe.'

Tracey stood and lifted the tray from Olivia's lap.

'How about this: I'll go and make us another pot of tea while you email your *friend*.' She gave an overly dramatic wink. 'And then we can finally make a start on the pack of doughnuts I brought with me. What do you say?'

Olivia reached for her phone, cool from being untouched for so long, and heavy in her hand.

'Sure . . .' She hesitated. 'Why not? Let's do it.'

'That's my girl!'

Jacob

From: Olivia_Jackson@gmail.com
Re:Re: Hello

Wow, sounds like a thrilling time. Do you think he's miserable because he eats so much chocolate or he eats so much chocolate because he's miserable? Either way, sounds like you two are having a ball. I, on the other hand, have been laid up in bed after an extremely dodgy dinner including what can only be described as the worst stuffed paratha and curry in the world. Am I blaming you for encouraging me to find one? No. But am I ever touching one again . . . also no! The Taj was incredible – honestly, more magical than I could have ever imagined. Have you been?

I hope you're doing well over there and maintaining your blood sugars in spite of Kushal and his candy.

Yours, rather queasily, Olivia x

To: Olivia_Jackson@gmail.com
Re:Re:Re: Hello

No!!!! I am so sorry to hear you got sick, although in the same breath I will also say congratulations – you've gone through the rite of passage all good travellers experience. You're lucky yours was fairly tame – my first (yes, there have been multiple) was during an eleven-hour train journey. I'll say no more. Is the lady still in Jaipur or has she ticked that off the list and moved on?

I am STILL in Delhi, much to my increasing frustration, but what can I do? I roll again soon, so keep all those fingers crossed we get some movement. I've been working hard with Kushal to swap at least one chocolate bar for a piece of fruit . . . it's not gone down well. Alas, we try!

Yours, most ready to move on already, Jacob x

From: Olivia_Jackson@gmail.com
Re:Re:Re:Re: Hello
I have indeed moved on and am coming to you all the way from Jodhpur (not to make you jealous or anything!). The rest of Jaipur was great. Even though I had to take it a little slower, I got to see everything I wanted to and even made a new friend (I think you would love her!), so we did a lot of it together. Now I'm solo again and trying to enjoy the desert life. Have you been before? If so, any recommendations for places to eat? I am clearly not a very good judge of restaurant character.

I'm sorry 'the universe' is keeping you stuck, but maybe you're being held there to support Kushal on his path to a nutritious and wholesome life. If so, maybe hurry up and do better so you can get out of Delhi and on to somewhere new!

Yours, still haunted by the thought of your eleven-hour train journey, Olivia x

To: Olivia_Jackson@gmail.com
Subject: Eleven hours in toilet hell!

Hey! (Hope you like the new subject title — I thought I'd make sure you never forget about my rite of passage!) I can't tell you how jealous I am that you're in Jodhpur — I've never been, but it's always intrigued me. Mainly to see what camels are like up close and personal. I hear they smell and they spit? Is this true? Can you confirm for me, please?

I'm glad you made a friend, although I am 100 per cent certain that they aren't as incredibly humble, endearing and enjoyable to hang out with as me. We can't all be perfect, I guess.

The Kushal Project is going much better, as I've now taken to eating at least two of the bars myself — short term it's great, long term maybe not so much. Anyway, after the desert, where to, my intrepid explorer?

Yours, very much on a sugar high, Jacob x

From: Olivia_Jackson@gmail.com
Subject: Camels suck

I think you can infer my thoughts on camels as a species from my subject title, but for clarity — yes, they smell and spit, sometimes directly into your eye (and no, I don't want to talk about it). I'll just say I was quite glad to be rid of them and find myself in Udaipur, which so far is my favourite city. The lake is beautiful!

I have to say, I am concerned by your tactics when it comes to the Kushal Project — it wouldn't be my approach, but then again, what were the chances of you and me being aligned in our thinking? Just don't make me re-route my plan to come and wean you both off the stuff; it's not a sacrifice I'm willing to make. On that note, any news on if you'll be leaving soon?

Yours, slightly worriedly, Olivia x

P.S. I totally forgot how incredibly self-deprecating you are, and your last email was a stark reminder of that, so thank you!

Jacob leant back in the creaking office chair and stretched his arms above his head. He was filled with the same feeling he always had after reading one of Olivia's emails: a silly, boyish playfulness and a strange sense of hope. It flooded his entire body, right to the very tips of his fingers. And sometimes it felt nice to just bask in it for a moment, before hurrying to reply.

'You've got that stupid look on your face again,' Kushal grunted, lifting his sleepy head from the desk, where it had been laid for the past fifteen minutes. 'Let me guess, your girlfriend replied?'

'For the fiftieth time' – Jacob sat forward, the glorious feeling he had just been experiencing disappearing in a flash – 'she's not my girlfriend. But yes, she's replied.'

'I don't know why you don't just ask her to be.'

'Oh Kushal, so young and so innocent, with so much to learn.'

The boy scowled, shooting Jacob a look of annoyance. 'I hate it when you say stuff like that.'

'I'm sorry.'

'No, you're not.'

Jacob laughed, patting his friend's thick shoulder affectionately. 'I know, but sometimes you have to say it regardless.'

He turned his attention back to the screen, scrolling up through the messages he'd exchanged with Olivia over the past couple of weeks. At first his replies were unintentionally staggered, but now, as time had gone on and the excitement of their conversation had built, he had to make a concerted effort to restrain himself. The fact that he was even having a back-and-forth with someone should have been a red flag, but he'd managed to convince himself that it was harmless. Deep down, they both knew their connection would fizzle out in about a month and turn to nothing. Her world was completely different from his, and there was nothing that would change that, especially not a couple of innocuous emails.

It was fine.

Everything was fine.

'Are you going to reply, or can I have the computer back?' Kushal asked. 'I want to finish my game.'

Jacob's fingers hesitated over the keyboard. He could respond now – there were enough things he wanted to share – or he could wait until he'd rolled his dice tomorrow and found out if he was staying or going.

'You need to get out more – you know that, don't you?'

'Oi, can I have the computer back or not?'

'Yes, yes, you can have it back – give me one second.' Jacob clicked out of the conversation and back to his inbox.

He froze instantly.

'Good, because honestly, if I lose another round against this idiot I'm playing, I'm going to go crazy!' Kushal sighed, reaching into his pocket and retrieving a half-eaten chocolate bar. 'I'm off my game and I don't like it. You don't fancy doing a two-on-one, do you? Me and you team up together?'

Jacob remained still, his eyes staring directly ahead.

'Oi, Jacob?' Kushal waved a hand in front of his face. 'Are you there?'

'Yeah . . .' He spoke without paying attention to the words coming out. 'Yeah, I'm here. I just . . .' He leant forward in his seat. 'I just need a bit longer.'

'Man, you said you were done!' The boy looked from the computer to Jacob and back again. 'Is everything all right? You look like you've seen a ghost.'

Jacob inched the mouse forward and clicked, ever so cautiously, on the new message that had appeared so innocently and inconspicuously at the top of his mailbox.

From: Andrew_Green@STPinvestor.com
Subject: Response required ASAP

'Something like that, yeah,' he murmured, trying to focus on the words on the screen.

Jacob, I'll get straight to the point. It's been three months since your mother received a phone call from you, and quite frankly it's not good enough. I don't need her harassing me for an update because you are too irresponsible to bother to call. I got over my disappointment in you years ago, but apparently your mother is still clinging on to some hope you're not the utterly selfish and careless human being that I know you to be. Get in touch and make both our lives easier.

It took five painstaking read-throughs for the words to land fully, each one like a tiny grenade thrown at his soul.

'Jacob, what's happened?'

'Let's go out,' he announced suddenly, exiting the browser and standing up so fast he practically knocked Kushal off his chair.

'What?'

'Come on, let's go somewhere and get a drink,' he insisted, the urgency in his voice verging on anger.

'I can't!'

'Why not? All you're planning to do is play your dumb video game!' Jacob slammed his hand down hard on the desk. 'Let's do something fun for once, hey?'

'I know, but technically I'm working.' Kushal looked distressed, like a puppy whose owner had suddenly turned on him. 'I can't leave here. My dad would kill me.'

Jacob bit down hard on the side of his cheek, the rage burning wildly inside him.

'Yeah, well' – he pushed past his empty chair and made his way towards the exit – 'dads can go fuck themselves, if you ask me.'

*

It had been a long time since he'd visited a place like this. A place where the lights were so low you could barely see a foot in front of you. Where the drinks were always 70 per cent water, and a thick layer of dirt carpeted the surfaces. It was a place where the lost and lonely came to drown their sorrows, and Jacob was already three beers in.

'I'll have another, please.' He nodded at the barman, pushing his empty glass away.

Already his head felt a little woozy. When was the last time he'd had an alcoholic drink? He tried to cast his mind back, his brain struggling to sift through the years of discarded and disjointed memories. Fragments of a past he never revisited. A jumble of places and faces that swirled around without rhyme or reason.

Maybe he was drunker than he thought.

'Here you go.' The barman switched his empty for a full glass, and Jacob downed half of it straight away. The tepid fizz tickled his nose, and the warm, sweet taste of hops coated the back of his throat.

'Jesus, that's disgusting.' He winced, slamming the glass down and staring around the room. For a relatively crap bar, it was full. A mixture of locals and tourists milled about on the makeshift dance floor, whilst groups of tired old men gathered in the corners and along the bar. It wouldn't have been his top choice of venue, but it was the first one he'd stumbled upon after storming from the hostel.

Two girls shrieked ecstatically as their accompanying group of young men made their way through a tray of suspicious-looking shots, each one trying to outdrink and outshine the next.

Oh, to be young.

Jacob took another swig of his drink, catching his reflection in the dusty mirror that hung in front of him. To the untrained eye, all that stared back was a youthful, sun-bleached, run-of-the-mill traveller. But Jacob could see the signs: the weariness in his eyes and the weight growing heavy on his shoulders. Back in the day, he too would have been grabbing the shots and laughing wildly in the centre of the group, trying to be one of the guys. One of the gang. A collection of lone wolves, huddling together to try and belong to a pack for a night. Making friends within seconds, promising to stay in touch for more than the twenty-four hours you got wasted with them. It was fun for a bit and, at least for a while, it had helped him to pretend that he wasn't totally by himself in this world.

But you can't run from the truth for ever. And over time it had become too hard to lie any more. To find excuses not to meet up with people again, to sit with the guilt he felt at ignoring them, to have to leave people behind over and over again. It was easier, in the end, not to try in the first place.

'Hey, you.' One of the squealing girls had sidled up beside him, her long, blonde hair draping over both their shoulders. 'You look a little lonely over here.' She placed a cool hand on his shoulder, her breath sharp with liquor.

'Oh no, I'm fine.' He remained as still as possible, knowing that one infinitesimal engagement with her and he was done for. 'You don't need to worry about me.'

'Come *on*' – she leant in closer – 'you're too cute to be drinking by yourself.'

Whether it was the hand moving on to his, the heat radiating from her skin, or simply a momentary lapse in control, Jacob turned to face her. She was pretty. Very pretty, in fact, with a sparkling smile and amber eyes. She was staring at him hard, her body inching towards his ever so slightly.

God, how long had it been?

If you're asking that question, it's been too long.

Would one night matter? It wouldn't mean anything, and nobody would get hurt.

Just like that, the orange eyes of the strange girl became a dazzling blue. The tanned skin faded to a pearly white and Olivia's face stared back at him.

'Shit.' He jerked backwards, knocking his glass and spilling beer over both of their hands. 'I'm sorry. I didn't mean to do that.'

'That's OK.' She wiped her hand on his shorts in a clear act of seduction, but unfortunately for Jacob, the moment had well and truly gone. 'Let me buy you another,' she whispered.

'No. I'm fine.'

'Come *on*,' she purred again, pressing herself into him hard.

'I said no!' he shouted, all at once feeling stifled by the sickly-sweet smell of her perfume. 'I've had enough already. I just want to be left alone.'

'Jesus.' She removed her hand and straightened up, only allowing the disappointment of rejection to mark her perfectly made-up face for a second. 'There's no need to be like that. I was only trying to be friendly . . .'

As she flicked her hair over her shoulder and walked away, Jacob could have sworn he heard her mutter the word 'arsehole' under her breath. She may be pissed off now, but he knew deep down he was doing her a favour. After all, wasn't he just a *selfish and careless human being*? One that his dad had given up on years ago, it seemed.

'Bastard.' Jacob grimaced, gripping the glass so tightly in his hand it was at risk of breaking. 'Hypocritical *bastard*.'

As he recalled his dad's words, Jacob was overcome with a whole new series of memories. He was five years old; his dad had been away on business for six weeks and he was due home that day. Within an hour of arriving, he'd already left again, with his bags packed for yet another work trip. All Jacob got was a gruff hello and a pat on the head.

He was now six; his mother had been crying for days on end, unable to get out of bed, let alone take care of him. When he'd asked her what was wrong, she cried, 'Your father, it's always your father.'

Then he was eight, and his dad had cleared his things from the house. No trace of him remained, except the anger and betrayal that poured from every cell of his mother. Jacob had been sat down by his dad and, in a sixty-second conversation, been told that he needed to go and live with his new family now, but that Jacob would always be his first-born son, and that would always mean something.

And I'm the selfish one, hey?

The torrent of flashbacks was too much, the music suddenly too loud and the darkness too enveloping. Jacob had to leave. He had to get out into the fresh air and away from all the noise and drunken chaos. As he stood, he stumbled backwards, his head pounding and a shooting pain ripping through the back of his skull. Panic flooded him immediately.

You're OK. It's just the drink.

He managed to steady himself just enough to find the exit, practically bursting out on to the street. The anxiety lessened a little from the instant hit of air and the fading sound of the drum and bass, but the sensation in his head was still very present and very painful.

You're fine.

He made his way back to the hostel, each step slow and deliberate, whilst his body throbbed in hurt.

Everything is fine.

*

The next morning, Jacob woke up in a world of pain. His head was still aching, and his body felt exhausted. It took him much longer than usual to rouse from sleep, and even longer to finally get up and out of bed. Dread spread through his body, covering him like a second skin. Surely he couldn't be this hungover from a few beers?

At the thought his stomach gurgled, the taste of hops still lingering on his tongue despite cleaning his teeth three times. God, this wasn't how he wanted this day to start. It was, after all, a rolling day: the most exciting and hopeful day of every week. After a month stuck in Delhi, the anticipation of a potential move should have had him leaping from the sheets and sprinting down the stairs. Kushal had become almost as invested as him in his weekly ritual, captivated by the bizarre rigmarole that Jacob undertook with his dice and his lists.

Kushal.

Jacob's face burnt in shame. The way he'd snapped at his

friend last night, pushed him to come out with him, and stormed away like a toddler when he didn't get what he wanted. What must the boy think of him?

'Only one way to find out,' he mumbled under his stale breath, pushing the door to reception open and dragging his leaden feet through.

'Wow.' Kushal winced. 'You look rough.'

'I feel it.'

'Went a bit heavy last night?'

'Hmm.' Jacob came and sat beside him, aware that the smell of alcohol may still be strong enough to detect. 'Not really, I'm just not used to drinking any more.'

'Well, you were very insistent on doing it.'

'I know, and I'm sorry about the way I acted. I just . . .' He didn't want to recall the email from his dad, but he also knew he owed his friend an explanation.

'You don't have to say anything. It's cool.' Kushal smiled, reaching into his desk drawer and pulling out two chocolate bars. 'You want one?'

Relief swept over Jacob; his kind, pure, overly sugared friend wasn't mad at him, and that was something.

'Hell yes.' He grabbed one. 'Thank you.'

The pair sat in silence, munching down hard on their bars. It was only when Kushal had polished off his in record time that he turned to Jacob and spoke.

'So, are you going to leave me hanging any longer, or are you going to get on with the rolling?'

Jacob swallowed, trying not to choke with laughter.

'Sorry, we're running a little behind schedule today.' He reached into his pockets and retrieved the goods: dice, notebook and a handful of hope.

'I can see that, but I need to know if I'm going to have to

clean your room today or not. I'm already very busy.' A sly smirk pulled at the corners of Kushal's mouth.

'Sure you are, buddy.' Jacob laid the notebook in front of him, clasping the dice and squeezing them tight in his fist.

He closed his eyes and, with a deep breath in, began to shake the dice in his hand.

Two shakes and a roll. Show me, Universe, where I should go . . .

As the two cubes spilled out across the wooden table, Jacob scrunched his eyes tighter. Was he ready to see an odd number staring back up at him? Could he stand the disappointment when he was already feeling so fragile?

'NO WAY!' Kushal yelped, causing Jacob's eyes to snap open and his heart to fill with expectation. 'It's evens . . . evens is good, right?'

A three and a five.

Permission to go.

'Yes, it's good!' Jacob roared, snatching up the dice and holding them close to his chest. 'I mean, not good because I won't get to sit here and give myself type two diabetes every day with you, but yes, it's good.'

'OK, now what? What happens now?' The joy in the boy's eyes was almost enough to bring Jacob to tears. He was really going to miss his friend.

'Now I roll again and the number will correspond to a list of countries in the back of my book. Then I roll again to find out where in that country I'll end up.'

'What if you roll the same country, and roll the same number as before?'

'Then I stay where I am.'

'This feels quite complicated for something that's meant to be random.' Kushal scowled, scratching his baby-haired chin.

'Oi, don't question the process, please. We've got a job to do.' Jacob released the dice once more and let them fall.

A six and a four.

'India is not done with you yet, apparently!' Kushal cheered. 'Go again: let's see where you end up!'

Though he normally undertook this activity by himself, Jacob found he was quite enjoying sharing the magic of his weird and wonderful world with someone.

'All right, let me get the list ready.' He flipped through his tattered notebook until he found the India page. 'OK ... come on, Universe, take me somewhere good, please!'

Another shake, another roll, another prayer to the gods of fate, and then he released them.

'It's six,' Kushal announced. 'Two threes is six!' He practically grabbed the book from under Jacob's nose. 'What's six?'

But Jacob had already seen it. His mind was piecing together the hundreds of thoughts that were racing through his sluggish brain. His heart was pounding and his breath was growing shallow. Olivia's face, which had thrown him so off kilter when it appeared yesterday, now flooded him with elation.

'It's Udaipur. I'm going to Udaipur!'

Olivia

Olivia had nearly dropped the phone on the floor when his email came through. She was fresh out of the shower after a brutal day of sightseeing, ready to settle into bed and FaceTime Kate when she saw it. Waiting for her, as innocent as anything. She wasn't even going to open it straight away – nobody could craft a witty and interesting reply when half-comatose – but thankfully she did. It didn't bear thinking about if she hadn't.

From: jpgreen@gmail.com
Subject: . . .
Guess where the universe is sending me next? If you fancy doing the honours of tour guide, I'll be outside the station at 9 a.m. Udaipur, here I come . . .

Her first thought was that it had to be a joke.

Surely it was a joke?

What were the odds that out of everywhere in India – everywhere in the *world* – Jacob would end up in the same city as her? *And* on her final day as well.

What kind of almighty universal force did that to someone?

One that doesn't exist!

Olivia had read the email repeatedly, each time swinging between excitement at the possibility of seeing him again and scorning herself for even believing it was true.

And yet, despite her continued scepticism, she still woke the next day full of nervous energy. She still showered extra thoroughly, making sure that every strand of her now much lighter hair was cleaned and conditioned, and she still dressed with more care than she'd ever done in the past month.

Just in case.

Luckily, her homestay wasn't far from the station – a comforting thought, she told herself, because if all else failed and he didn't show, then at least the walk of shame wouldn't take too long.

Way to go on the positive thinking.

Olivia fiddled with the hem of her top, pulling the already sticky T-shirt away from her skin. It was only 8.55 a.m. and yet the sun felt as though it was beaming down on her through a magnifying glass, focusing all of its power and attention on the very top of her head.

She looked around, scanning the crowds for a hint of a bleached curl or a pair of raven eyes. It was getting busier by the second. The area outside the station was swollen with people. Claustrophobia began to creep in, a tightness coiling around her throat, closing it off so that she could only take tiny sips of air. People pushed and jostled past her; a thousand faces belonging to a thousand strangers blurred before her eyes.

He's not coming.

You're a totally foolish idiot. He's not co—

'Olivia!'

The sound of her name was like a bullet through her thoughts. Every cell in her body stood to attention, waiting to hear it again.

'Olivia, over here!'

She turned on the spot, her eyes darting left and right in search of him, but nobody she saw matched the man she'd been unable to stop thinking about. Should she move towards the sound of his voice? But then what if she lost him? What if he was moving towards her and she was only making it harder for him? Her brain whirred as the intensity of the situation pressed down on her.

'Hey!' A single hand broke through the crowd, and then, all at once, there he was.

A mass of golden hair, a red bandana and a pair of jet-black eyes.

'There you are.' He smirked, the smell of burnt wood and spices lingering at his edges. 'I didn't think we'd ever find each other in that. How are you doing?'

Suddenly the whole situation felt very real and very overwhelming.

'Uh-huh.' Her mouth was bone dry, and she could feel her forehead dripping with sweat. 'I'm OK.'

'It's a bit mental out here, isn't it?' Jacob placed his hand on her shoulder, its weight and warmth a jolt to her system. 'Shall we move over there; I can barely hear you.'

That's probably because I'm not saying anything . . .

Olivia didn't even look at where 'there' was before nodding and following closely behind, as they dodged and weaved their way through the masses. The only thing she could focus on was the screaming voice inside her head, berating her for her complete lack of social skills.

'That's better.' Jacob grinned, as they positioned themselves on the outskirts of the swarming commuters. 'How crazy is it that I'm here? I can't believe it!'

'I know,' she mumbled, averting her gaze to anywhere other than Jacob's face, which, since the last time they met, seemed to have only grown in attractiveness. 'If I'm honest, I wasn't sure if you were going to show up.'

'How come?'

'I don't know.' She shrugged. 'I thought it might have been a joke.'

'A joke?'

She sneaked a glance at his expression, which seemed surprisingly hurt by her suggestion.

'That would have been a cruel joke.'

'No, I know, I just mean . . . I don't know. I guess I can't believe you're here, that's all.'

'Me neither.' A smile swiftly returned to his face. 'But the universe likes to play her wicked games, Olivia. I've told you this before.'

Whether it was the shock of his arrival wearing off, or maybe his infuriating talk of fate, but Olivia felt herself snap back into life.

'And I've told you before that I don't believe in that nonsense.'

'Well, even the best of friends can disagree sometimes.'

She hated herself for it, but she couldn't ignore the twist of disappointment in her stomach at his words. *Friends*.

'So, when did you get here?' she managed, recovering.

'Last night. I rolled in the morning and was on a train that very afternoon.'

'A quick turnaround.'

'There was no time to waste! My tour guide was only

187

going to be here for one more day, so I had to act fast. The perks of being a light traveller, I suppose.'

'About that tour guide point . . .'

'I know – good idea, right? I thought it might be fun for you to show me around this time. I can pay handsomely in snacks and good company.' Jacob plucked a half-eaten packet of sweets from his pocket and waggled them at her. 'And this is only the beginning. I have plenty more where that came from.'

Olivia pursed her lips in careful consideration. 'As extremely tempting as that offer is, I fear that I have already seen the main attractions of interest to you and would only bore you with my plans today.'

'You've seen everything there is to see in Udaipur already?'

'Pretty much.' She pouted, rather proud of the truth in her statement.

'I get it.' Jacob drew himself up to full height. 'I see what's happening here.'

'What?'

'You're trying to get rid of me, aren't you? Not even one day together and you're already palming me off.'

'No, I'm not! I'm simply saying that I have a plan and you might not like what it involves.'

'I think that any plan that involves you is good enough for me.'

Olivia cursed herself for being so easily flattered as her face flushed with colour.

'Your charm will get you nowhere.'

Jacob threw his head back and laughed. 'God, I forgot how funny you can be.'

'And what's that supposed to mean?'

'It means . . .' He took a step towards her, closing the

already small gap between them. 'That you are a very hard nut to crack, Miss Jackson. But I will not give up. I want to come and explore with you.'

Olivia wouldn't have been surprised if her face was beetroot at this point.

'Well' – she tried to compose herself – 'if you really want to tag along with me, we need to get a move on. We have a lot to do today and there is no time to waste.'

'Yes!' Jacob punched the air in victory. 'I am ready and raring to go whenever you are.'

'Great. We need to find a taxi or a tuk-tuk.'

'No problem.' Jacob put two fingers in his mouth and let out a shrill, piercing whistle. Three men in rickshaws snapped their heads up at the rallying cry. 'Which one do you fancy? You've got your pick of the men today.'

If only.

'I don't mind,' she shrugged, 'you choose.'

'OK, let's go with this guy here, he looks the most awake.' Jacob strode over to the last tuk-tuk in the line. 'Where are we heading, fair maiden?'

'The Monsoon Palace.'

'Right you are.' Jacob began to bargain with the driver, and after a couple of minutes waved at her to join him.

'Our friend Mitesh here will be glad to take us. Hop in.'

'Thank you.' Olivia clambered inside, the backs of her legs already sticking to the leather seats. As Jacob settled down next to her, she became very aware of his thigh touching hers. Her damp skin brushed up against his, lunar white against walnut brown.

'Right, buddy.' Jacob leant forward to the driver, breaking the contact between them. 'Take us to the palace, please!'

The little tuk-tuk pulled away sharply, the jerking

movement catapulting Olivia forwards. She would have gone flying if Jacob's arm hadn't flung itself across her and held her in place, a physical barrier keeping her seated.

'Woah there!' He smirked. 'Be careful, Olivia. I can't be losing you already.'

She let out a shy half-laugh and gripped the sides of the rickshaw tightly, unable to shake the feeling of his skin on hers, burning as though she'd been imprinted by his touch.

Friends, remember.

You're just friends.

*

'Wow, Udaipur *is* nice!' Jacob marvelled, sticking his head out of the tuk-tuk like an overzealous puppy. 'Look at that' – he pointed far into the distance – 'we have to go and visit that later!'

Olivia sat as still as she possibly could, bracing herself as the little vehicle jerked violently left and right.

'Do you have to lean so far out?' She cringed as two motorbikes flew past, uncomfortably close to Jacob's nose. 'Someone might hit you as they go by.'

'Ah, don't worry. Either they'll move or I will, no big deal.'

'It will be a big deal when a ten-ton lorry knocks your head clean off and I have to mop up the mess,' she snarked, shrinking as far back into the seat as possible. There was no way she was risking life and limb for a blurry view of the city.

'Charming!' Jacob snorted, drawing his head back inside the rickshaw. 'At least it's nice to know you'd mop me up; I don't think I fancy my remains being left out to dry on the road.'

Olivia shuddered at the thought.

'Are you hungry, by the way?'

'Seriously?' She gawped. 'Two seconds ago, you were talking about splaying your guts on the tarmac, and now you want food?'

'Exactly! Did you already eat?'

Olivia took a second to simply appreciate the absurdity of the man who sat next to her. It was safe to say she had never, and probably would never again, meet anyone like him in her life.

'Yes, I ate.'

'Hmm, well then, looks like it will be a little snack for one, doesn't it?'

'What about the sweets you so generously offered to bribe me with earlier?'

'These!' Jacob pulled the dried-out, half-eaten packet from his shorts. 'They won't sustain a man long enough to fully embark on the Olivia Jackson twenty-four-hour tour.'

'We're not pulling an all-nighter, so you'll get at least eight hours back.'

'A midnight excursion isn't on the cards, then?' He raised an eyebrow, making Olivia's entire body radiate with heat. 'Good to know.'

Before she could try and fumble some form of reply, Jacob had leant forward in his seat and tapped the driver on the shoulder.

'Hey buddy, know anywhere en route for a good bit of breakfast?'

'I know a great place, but it's not en route.'

Olivia's insides contracted in angst. Not only at the fact the driver had turned fully in his seat and was not looking at the road, but also because of the potential interruption to their plan.

'How far are we talking?' Jacob continued, clearly not bothered at all that their driver's eyes were anywhere but on the traffic in front of them.

'An extra fifteen-minute drive.'

'That's not bad. And how good are we talking?'

'The best dosa I've ever had' – he flashed them a toothy grin – 'but don't tell my wife that, she'll kill me!'

'Awesome.' Jacob looked back at Olivia for support. 'What do you reckon – shall we give it a go?'

Her first instinct was a hard no. Fifteen minutes was never fifteen minutes out here, what with the traffic and the general chaos that seemed to instantly add another half hour to any simple task. Plus, the last time she'd heard the word 'best' when it came to street food, it had ended badly. Very badly.

But when faced with Jacob's overt enthusiasm, she decided to take a slightly softer approach.

'I'm not sure. Is there nothing else a bit closer?'

'There are lots of things closer' – the driver shrugged – 'but nowhere near as tasty.'

'Ah!' Jacob slapped the back of the driver's seat affectionately. 'Spoken like a true salesman.'

Olivia felt her neck prickle with a heat that had nothing to do with the morning sun.

'It's just, there's lots to see and not much time. I want to make sure we get it all done.'

The explanation sounded feeble and uptight even to Olivia. She didn't want to be difficult, but at the same time they had a plan to stick to. A plan that he'd *said* he wanted to be a part of. Except now, two minutes in, he was already veering off course.

'Oh, come *on*, we deserve the best! Don't we?' Jacob pleaded. 'We only have one day together, after all . . .'

192

Whether it was his sobering reminder of how little time they had together or the annoyingly endearing look on Jacob's face, before she knew it, Olivia found herself saying a reluctant yes.

'You heard the woman!' Jacob cried, practically bouncing up and down in his seat. 'Take us to the best dosa in town! And then . . .' He nestled in close, lowering his voice and fixing Olivia with a serious expression. 'We'll head straight to the palace, OK?' His hand was now on her arm, sending a ripple of electricity down her spine. 'You won't miss a thing on your list. I promise.'

'Sure,' she mumbled, unable to concentrate on anything other than his touch. 'Whatever you say.'

Olivia

As Olivia had predicted, the 'quick detour' had taken over an hour to complete. The traffic didn't help, but neither did Jacob offering to buy the tuk-tuk driver food, and then going back in for second helpings. By the time they arrived at the Monsoon Palace it was already lunchtime, almost three hours behind schedule. Not even its magnificence could soothe Olivia's edgy and now – ironically, after rejecting any offer of food herself at the cafe – hungry disposition.

'Woah, you can see everything from up here.' Jacob gasped, moving closer to the edge of the cliff. 'Cool, huh?'

'Please don't do that.'

He shuffled an inch further forward. 'Do what?'

'*That!*' she shouted, sounding scarily like her mother. 'You're too close to the edge, it's making me nervous.'

'Sorry, but it just looks so awesome. You're missing out.' He peered over.

'I can see perfectly fine from here, thank you very much.'

And she wasn't lying. The palace was set atop an enormous hill, with unbroken views of the city. Thousands of buildings and countless trees shrunk to tiny dots, clustered together in a patchwork quilt of green and grey; mountains rose and fell like the tide, undulating in waves across the landscape. It was truly breathtaking, and with the sun tucked neatly behind a blanket of clouds and a cool breeze on her face, Olivia felt that, if she had all the time in the world, she could sit here for hours, simply watching the world unfold around her. It was something she and Leah would often do together, whether in their local coffee shop or lying out in the park: they would simply sit and let the world pass them by. Leah often made up the stories of passing strangers' lives, weaving intricate and often dramatic details together to form complex and impressively realistic fantasies.

The thought of her sister made her breath catch in her throat. Everything had been so full-on in the past few days that, although Leah was never far from her mind, the anguish and longing for her sister had lessened. The volume had been turned down on her grief, so that instead of being a cymbal crashing inside her skull twenty-four hours a day, it played like a soft snare in the background; present and continuous, but not so overwhelming.

'Are you *sure* you don't want to have a little look?' Jacob teased, beckoning her over to join him.

'I couldn't be surer.'

'*Fine.*' He hurried over to sit next to her, lifting his face to the sky and letting out a long, slow sigh. 'I have to say, this was a great idea. Sometimes it can get a bit seen-one-palace-seen-them-all, you know?'

'Maybe, but then again, it's all still relatively new for me. I'm not a worn and weary old-timer like you are.'

'Oi!' He elbowed her gently. 'Worn and weary? I don't look a day over twenty-three.'

'Well, your delusional personality isn't a day over twelve.'

This time Jacob stood up, affronted.

'Excuse me, Miss Jackson, I will not be insulted in such a manner.'

'I'm sorry. Of course, you are mature and wise, yet incredibly youthful and handsome.' She smirked. 'Better?'

'Yes.' He pouted, coming to sit back down once more. 'A bit.'

'Good. Now, are you done here? Because we should probably be heading to the next place.'

'Lead on, fair lady, I am ready for the next adventure.' He gave a little salute. 'Where to?'

'Well, we were supposed to take a walk around the Badi Lake, which isn't too far from here, but . . .' She checked the time and felt a stab of panic. How had it got so late?

'But what?'

'I don't think there's enough time to do it all. We still have to see the temples and head back to the city in time for the sunset on the lake.'

'How behind are we? Surely it can't be by that much.'

'You say that, but somehow we are.'

'This is my fault, isn't it? All because I wanted a stupid dosa.' He kicked the ground hard, sending clouds of dust flying.

'I won't say it helped things, no.'

'I'm sorry.' His face became solemn. 'And you're sure there's no way to get us back on track? Surely you can come up with something. If anyone can do it, it's you.'

Olivia brought the agenda for the day to her mind, locating each place on the map she'd imprinted to memory. Unfortunately, this was going to be one problem not even her finest logic could solve.

'I can't. But it's OK, we can prioritize. Like you said, seen one temple, seen them all. Now, the best way to do this is to group things by proximity, therefore reducing the travel time and ticking more off the list. So, it makes the most sense to stay up here and do the lake and the temples. We'll have to skip the boat ride and sunset.'

A pang of sadness struck her. The boat ride was the thing she had been looking forward to most. The one thing she had specifically saved for her last night.

Jacob shot her a look of intrigue.

'*Or* you could prioritize based on what you want to see most? Surely there are some things you'd like to do more than others?'

'Yes.' Was her disappointment that obvious? Olivia needed to get her poker face back, and fast.

'Right then!'

'Except, emotion doesn't have a part to play when it comes to efficiency.'

The statement, although very simple and obvious to Olivia, looked as though it had physically assaulted Jacob, whose jaw was nearly on the floor.

'Jesus Christ! You are brutal.'

'I'm thoroughly organized; there's a difference.'

He ran his hand through his mess of hair and let out a slow, long whistle. 'I don't know. I think deep down you'd rather sack everything off and just go and do the boat ride.'

'Do you now?'

'I do.'

They were in a standoff, but the intensity of his gaze threatened to disarm her resolve at any moment.

'I vote the boat ride,' he shouted.

'I vote the temples,' she replied, a little less convincingly.

'Alas, we find ourselves at an impasse, then, don't we?' He took a purposeful step towards her.

'Yes.' She tried not to let his sudden closeness unnerve her. 'I suppose we do.'

'You know the only way I think we're going to solve it?' Another step.

'How?' Olivia cursed the quiver in her voice.

One more step.

They were practically toe to toe.

'With these.' He reached into his pocket and produced the same pair of dice that she'd seen all those weeks ago in Delhi.

'Oh, come on.' She snorted, breaking the tension of the moment instantly.

'It's simple. If it's odds we do the temples, and if it's evens we do the lake.'

'*Or*' – even as she prepared to say it, her heart sank a little – 'we could go our separate ways and do what we both want to do by ourselves.'

'I'm not going anywhere without you, so that's not an option.'

His words sent her heart soaring right back up from where it had fallen.

'Fine, but make it quick; we need to get going.'

'No problem.' He began to shake the dice, his victorious expression painful for Olivia to watch. 'Come on, Universe, where should we go next? Lakes or temples . . . lakes or temples . . .'

His hand opened.

The dice fell.

Both pairs of eyes, blue and black, stared in anticipation.

'Yes!' Jacob punched the air. 'Two fours. Lucky number eight.'

Olivia knew she had to pretend to be disappointed, to arrange her face into some sort of put-out expression, but deep down, she was relieved. More than that, she was excited.

'Fine. You win. Let's grab a tuk-tuk and head back to the city,' she announced. 'There's at least one temple we can squeeze in en route, and I can find somewhere to eat too.'

'Sounds like a plan to me,' Jacob replied.

Olivia

'What did you think?' Jacob asked. 'Not the best temple I've seen.'

'No, but it was charming, I guess, in a rustic sort of way,' Olivia mused.

Unfortunately, the temple en route turned out to be nothing more than a crumbling structure on the side of the road, with a few stone carvings and a tiny, neglected altar. It took them less than fifteen minutes to walk the entire perimeter before bundling themselves back in the tuk-tuk and heading into the city. This did mean, however, that they had regained some time, which fortunately for Olivia meant there was a strong possibility she could eat something before the boat ride. Low sugar levels out on open water were a sure-fire recipe for disaster.

'Spoken very diplomatically, considering it was nothing more than a destitute wreck.' He reached for her arm and tipped her watch towards him, his hand around her wrist a welcome shock to the system. 'Now, do we have time to get you some food? You must be starving.'

'Yes, please! I just don't know where's good.'

And clean.

And safe.

And not going to give me food poisoning again.

'That's all right, we can ask some of the locals. No big deal.' Jacob made to flag down another tuk-tuk, catching the eye of its driver as it sped past.

'The thing is . . .' Olivia hesitated.

'Go on?'

'Since I got sick, I haven't been eating anywhere other than my homestays.'

'I see.' Jacob nodded in understanding.

'And there definitely isn't time to go back there and have food before the boat ride.'

'No, I don't think there is.' He shook his head in dismay. 'What a devastating blow to the stuffed paratha business. I thought I'd made one of their best customers out of you.'

His gentle tease was enough to ease Olivia's embarrassment.

'I know, but at least I got to sample a very good one before abstaining.'

'It *was* tasty, wasn't it?' He smiled dreamily.

'Don't! I'm still hungry, remember.'

'Sorry, I'll keep that sacred memory to myself from now on.'

'Thank you.'

Jacob chewed the corner of his mouth in deep contemplation.

'What to do . . . what to do . . .'

Olivia was thinking the exact same thing. Why hadn't she at least packed some emergency snacks?

'I know!' Jacob exclaimed.

'You do?'

'Yes. You don't think you're the only one with a brain for planning, do you?'

'No,' she lied.

'Good, because I have come up with an ingenious, efficient and extremely creative answer to your problem.'

'Really?'

'Really! The only question is . . .' Jacob turned, their knees knocking together as the tuk-tuk trundled along the bumpy roads. 'Do you trust me?'

No.

'Yes,' she replied, unable to take her eyes off his. 'But only because I am starving.'

'Don't worry, my lady, you won't be for much longer!' He leant forward and whispered something into the ear of the driver, who nodded in acknowledgement and jerked the little tuk-tuk off to the left. 'Hold tight, we're making a pit stop.'

*

Twenty minutes, a supermarket visit and one chai stop later, Olivia found herself sitting by the lake with what could only be described as a tourist's dream picnic laid out in front of her. Multipacks of crisps, bags of peanuts, granola bars, packets of cakes and biscuits, and, of course, large slabs of melting chocolate spilled out from the grocery bag next to them. It was a junk food addict's heaven, and despite her initial disgust, Olivia found that it hit the spot.

'Pass me the rest of the chocolate – it's got to go before it becomes too liquid.'

Olivia pushed the sticky packet in his direction. 'You haven't totally weaned yourself off the hard stuff since leaving Kushal, then?'

Jacob dipped his finger in the mush and scooped it up into his mouth.

'Absolutely not – I'm too far gone. There's no coming back from it now.'

'You were only with him for a few weeks!'

'Some people only take a day to change your life, Olivia.' He smacked his lips together. 'It's not about time, it's about impact.'

The weight of his words struck her. Hadn't she experienced that first-hand? Not just with Jacob, but also with Tracey, and Betty and Suki . . . all the wonderful, kind souls she'd met on her travels so far. Fleeting flashes of joy, of comfort and of friendship.

'And anyway, there's worse things in life than being addicted to chocolate.'

Olivia went to comment but thought better of it.

Unfortunately, it hadn't gone unnoticed.

'Go on.' Jacob cocked his head. 'What were you about to say?'

'Nothing.'

'Come on, say it!'

'It was honestly nothing.'

'Olivia.' He wiped his hand on the front of his shorts and shifted himself to face her. The way he said her name made the hairs on her neck stand to attention. 'You are many things, but a good liar is not one of them. Tell me!'

'Fine. I was only going to ask if you are always so optimistic? But then, I think I know the answer without having to ask.'

'Well, nobody is *always* optimistic.' He grinned, clearly a little flattered by her comment. 'But I'd say, 99 per cent of the time I am. Life's too short to be any other way. You either dwell on your problems or you do something about them. Joy can be found even in the darkest of places. That's my opinion anyway.'

'Hmm.'

Olivia bit down hard on the inside of her cheek, the flippancy of his answer igniting a burst of anger. Clearly his problems had never run so deep that they nearly broke you in two. Clearly his life had been untouched by the darkness of loss and grief and excruciating, earth-shattering heartbreak. Clearly, he'd never lived in the real world.

'You don't agree?'

'Not entirely.' The tension in her jaw was building as she tried to hold back the words that were piling up, rushing to be spoken out loud. But it wasn't his fault. How was he to know what she'd gone through? What she'd lost? *Who* she'd lost?

'Care to expand?'

'Not really.' She managed to push the rage back down and out of sight. 'And anyway, like you said before, even the best of friends can disagree.'

'Touché, Miss Jackson.' He began to chuckle. 'Now, any more food? Because it looks like our boat is coming in.'

Olivia lifted her head, scanning the shimmering expanse of water that rippled like silk before her. People were crowded at the edges of the lake, adults admiring the view whilst children desperately tried to dip their toes in. The grand hotel floated majestically in the centre, as though it had simply been plucked from the sky and placed there as a gift to the city. It was a hive of activity and yet still managed to remain incredibly peaceful, a feat quite rare in the midst of an Indian city.

'Where? I can't see it.' She squinted, unable to make out any sign of a touring boat on the water.

'You won't by looking out there. It's already in the dock!'

She followed the direction of his pointed finger, where, just as he'd said, their touring boat was sitting, its deck filling up with a line of eager visitors.

'We're going to miss it!'

'No, we won't.'

'Yes, we will.' She jumped up, kicking over the bag of peanuts and sending them flying. 'We haven't even got tickets.'

The panic of unpreparedness whipped her like a lasso around the chest, squeezing the air from her lungs and flushing blood to her face.

'We'll make it if we run. It's only down there.' Jacob nodded calmly to the little jetty about a kilometre down the road.

Olivia began to flap, looking from her watch to the jetty and back down again. They needed to clean up first. They couldn't leave the food here. Then what about the tickets; could they even get them so late? And even if they did make it, would there be room for them? They should have been first in the queue. They should have been there waiting, not lounging around stuffing fake food in their mouths.

'I don't know what to do!' She was paralysed by her own thoughts.

'Come on.' Jacob grabbed her hand and pulled hard. 'Let's go.'

'We can't!' she squealed. 'What about the food?'

In one move, he swept the floor and shoved everything back into the bag. 'There we are, now let's go!'

'Jacob, this is stupid,' she cried, as he dragged her along behind him. 'We're never going to make it . . . look!'

He followed her finger to where the little boat floated, now nearly full. Instead of slowing, he simply tightened his grip on her hand and picked up his pace. At first, Olivia resisted, dragging her heels in resignation at their inevitable defeat, but still Jacob pulled, his hand like a vice on hers.

'Come on, Olivia, we can do this!' he bellowed.

Maybe it was a delayed rush of sugar hitting her system, or maybe the fact that suddenly the jetty seemed within reaching distance, or maybe . . . just maybe it was the reckless thrill of it all, but soon Olivia found herself running just as hard and just as fast as Jacob down the street.

'Wait!' he shouted. 'Wait for us!'

They were almost there. She could see the man ushering people on give a nod to the skipper.

No.

Not yet. Please, not yet.

'WAIT.' A loud, piercing screech erupted from Olivia's mouth. 'Hold that boat!'

They closed the final few metres in seconds and Jacob tried, in between deep, heaving breaths, to persuade the man to let them on.

'We'll pay double!' Jacob begged. 'And we're only small. Look, we can fit right in the back, nobody will even notice.'

The other customers were staring in blatant disapproval at their holding up the boat.

'Please . . .' he tried again. 'We really want to make this trip. It's our last night together and I promised my friend here we'd do this. It's the only thing she's been desperate to do since she got to India and—'

'All right, all right, get on!' The man cut Jacob's rambling short, shoving them on to the boat and giving the final command to the skipper to go.

'I can't believe we just did that,' Olivia panted, wiping her brow self-consciously. 'Everyone must think we're crazy.'

'Nah, they just think we're typical Brits abroad. You want to sit?'

'Yeah, I think my legs are in shock.'

Jacob led them to two empty seats near the back of the boat. It was a full deck and they had to squeeze their way in between a pair of rather sullen-looking men and a very sunburnt middle-aged couple, who were already glued behind the lenses of their cameras.

'This'd better be worth it.' He lowered his voice to a whisper. 'I don't run like that for just anything, you know.'

'It will be.' Olivia shuffled closer, the entire length of their bodies touching now, beads of her sweat mixing with his. 'Trust me, it will be.'

Jacob

He wasn't often lost for words, but as the little boat made its way around the lake, Jacob found himself rendered speechless. There was something so comforting about the gentle rocking motion, the lapping of the water and the spray of cool breeze on his face. He'd often thought, in the early days of his travels, that maybe he should just buy himself a boat. Nothing fancy, maybe a little doer-upper, so he could learn to sail and spend his life on the ocean. Then he really would be alone. No one but the mighty waters to answer to, and no one to let down or disappoint. But for all his best intentions, he found that the reality of his idea was simply a step too far. Just because he would never have a fixed home again, it didn't mean he should shun himself completely from society. Besides, after a while he always got seasick, and there was no place for that when living on a boat.

Jacob lifted his face to catch the final rays of the sun before it began its descent and clocked off for the night. Its farewell was greeted with appreciative 'ooohs' and 'aaahs' from the other passengers, who began clicking their cameras and waving their phones in the direction of the skyline. Who could blame them? Seeing the magnificence of the palace floating on the water was one thing, but set against the backdrop of the ruby-red and deep ochre sunset, it was breathtaking. It looked as though the entire sky was set ablaze, a beautiful inferno; a fittingly dramatic exit for the majesty of the sun.

'So.' He leant in closer to Olivia, who had been equally as quiet. 'Was it worth skipping those boring temples to come and see this?'

'Definitely,' she whispered, the smell of peanuts and sweet vanilla cake still heavy on her breath. 'Was it worth doing all that running for?'

'I don't know. You've seen one sunset, you've seen them all, am I right?'

The joke came out before he could stop it, his humorous reflex kicking in automatically. If only he could take back his stupid comment and tell her honestly that it had been one of the best things he'd done for a very long time.

Olivia simply tutted and rolled her eyes, shifting her gaze back out on to the water, and Jacob knew the moment had passed.

For the rest of the journey the pair remained silent, Jacob watching Olivia, mesmerized at the sights before them. Her eyes, so deeply blue in the daytime, had now become almost haunting in the darkness, and her skin glowed milky white in the moonlight. He wasn't sure which view was more beautiful, and for the briefest of seconds he had the overwhelming urge to reach out his hand to hers.

... the utterly selfish and careless human being that I know you to be.

His dad's words came out of nowhere, a sucker punch to

the gut. Jacob snatched his hand into his lap and held it close to his body. What the hell was he doing? Who did he think he was? Some loveable rogue from a romance novel, sailing around at sunset with a pretty girl he could just reach for?

'Are you all right?' Olivia's voice dragged him back to reality. 'You look strange all of a sudden.'

'Do I?' He feigned surprise, slightly embarrassed that she'd been looking at him. 'Probably just a little bit of sea-sickness, that's all.' He shuffled away from her, hoping physical space would help settle him.

'Well, don't worry, we're nearly back on dry land.'

'Good.' He shifted another inch, his mind still spinning with thoughts. 'That's good.'

Less than ten minutes later, the boat pulled up at the jetty. The moon was now at its full height in the sky, bringing with it a chorus of blinking stars and making the lake look even more enchanting. With the last few flashes of cameras, the passengers began to disembark, both Olivia and Jacob moving in silence, maintaining a good distance between them.

'Are you feeling any better?' Olivia asked, as the pair finally touched down on solid ground.

'A little.'

'Whenever we felt nauseous growing up, my dad would give us ginger beer. I don't know if it did anything, but it tasted good all the same!'

'My dad would have probably given me a slap and told me to get on with it.' The words tumbled out of his mouth, much to Olivia's horror.

'Would he really?' She stopped walking.

Jacob tried to force a laugh but found he was too weary to muster it. 'Yeah, he isn't a very nice guy.'

'I'm sorry.' And the look on her face told him she was.

'Thanks, but it's OK. I'm just happy I didn't turn out too badly, given he contributed to 50 per cent of my make-up.'

Olivia reached for him, her hand landing softly on the top of his arm.

'I think you turned out great.'

The smile on her face made his stomach flip.

'I mean, annoying and arrogant at times, but still great.' She shrugged, releasing her hand and continuing to walk.

'I think my charm must be rubbing off on you. That's probably the nicest thing you've ever said to me.'

'That's not true!'

'It is!' He grinned. 'But I'm not complaining, I'll take any compliment I can get. I don't imagine you give them out lightly.'

'Too right.' She looked away shyly, as she so often did.

Silence fell over them again as they made their way through the slightly quieter streets. He didn't know where they were headed, and he was sure she didn't either, but the thought of bringing the evening to a close made a terrible sadness come over him.

'You fancy getting some dinner? I think we could both do with a little more than a supermarket picnic for sustenance?'

Olivia looked at her watch, and instantly he knew what her answer would be.

'I would love to, but I should be heading back. I have an early train tomorrow and I still need to pack.'

'Ah, I see.'

Ask her to stay.

Just one more day.

No! You know you can't.

'And I couldn't possibly persuade you to miss the train

211

and stay a couple of extra days?' His inner world was screaming out in protest at his offer, but somehow, he managed to ignore the voices just a little longer. 'You're the best tour guide I've had. It would be a shame to have to explore the city without you.'

Even in the dark, he could see the depths of her blue eyes finding his. She opened her mouth and then closed it, a pained expression on her face. The seconds of quiet felt like they stretched out into days. He knew she was tempted, a battle raging on in her head, as much as it was in his own.

'I can't. I have to go.'

The flicker of hope in his heart snuffed itself out immediately as his voice of reason cheered in victory.

'But I can send you my recommendations if you'd like?' she added.

'Sure.' He couldn't help but be touched by her offer. 'It's a poor substitute for your presence, but it will have to do.'

The pair remained frozen; neither one, it seemed, was quite ready to be the first to leave.

It's over. Just say goodbye and go.

'Well then.' He clenched and unclenched his fists, swinging his arms by his side. 'Until next time, Miss Jackson, I guess this is goodbye.'

'I don't know if we'll be so lucky as to have another next time.' Her voice was small and full of sorrow. It made his heart hurt to hear it.

'You never know . . .'

He took a step towards her, closing the space so that they were toe to toe.

'If you dare finish that sentence with anything about the universe, I will kill you,' she teased.

They were so close now; he could feel her breath on his face, the heat from her skin pouring into his.

'I don't doubt that you would.'

'I'm glad you take me seriously.'

'I would be a fool not to.'

Stop! You have to stop right this second.

One more inch, that's all it would take.

She deserves more.

Remember why she deserves more.

And with that, a switch was flicked, sending a series of images rushing through his brain. Engulfing him in memories, clouding his vision to the point where, for the briefest of moments, he thought he'd gone blind.

'Jacob?' Olivia's voice centred him. 'Is everything all right?'

'I'm sorry.' He pulled away, the moment shattering with one simple move. 'I think I'm just tired.' The excuse was feeble and flat, and it felt shameful to speak it out loud. 'You should be getting back.'

He closed his eyes, unable to stand to see the look on her face as he bent down and planted the lightest of kisses on her cheek.

'Goodnight, Olivia.' He walked away without even so much as a backwards glance. His heart begged to turn, but his body marched onwards.

III

The best and most beautiful things in this world cannot be seen or even heard, but must be felt with the heart.
Helen Keller

Olivia

It had been another busy morning in Goa for Olivia. Even here, where most people preferred to spend their days lying on the beach, she had made sure her action-packed agenda continued. Culturally, it felt important to continue to explore the delights of what this new place had to offer, but also, selfishly, it helped her mentally. The more Olivia had to do, the less time she had to think about Jacob and the fact it had been two weeks since she'd last heard from him. It was true that ever since she'd left Udaipur their communication had dwindled – his replies growing less and less frequent as time passed. But this was the longest they'd gone without talking and it was, quite frankly, driving her mad. The unanswered email did laps around her brain, until the words barely made sense to her any more.

To: jpgreen@gmail.com
Subject: Might have found the new best dosa in India . . .
I know it's a bold statement but really, truly, it was the most delicious thing I've ever experienced in my life. I wish you

could have sampled it yourself, and I did think about saving you a piece, but I wasn't sure it would travel well via mail. How is Udaipur treating you, if you're still there?! Where else have you explored? I'm off to Goa in a few days – can you believe it? My final stop! Tracey keeps hounding me to try yoga while I'm there, but let's see. Maybe next time you speak to me I'll be a fully enlightened being.

Yours, about to enter full spiritual awakening, Olivia x

'Argh, stop looking,' she cursed under her breath, shoving her phone back into her bag and forcing herself to concentrate on the horizon. She had been sitting by the water for a good twenty minutes yet had barely looked at it. This was supposed to be a moment of calm, a little slice of peace in the chaos, and she was wasting time thinking about someone who was clearly not thinking about her at all.

She closed her eyes and tried to let the crackling electricity in her brain settle. Olivia had never been one for the ocean. In fact, she was the only person in her family that wasn't excited when their annual trip to the beach came around. The sand irritated her skin, the salt stung her eyes, and she would always – no matter how meticulously she applied her sun cream – get burnt. The whole thing felt like more effort than it was worth. Which is why, when she arrived in Goa and saw the stretch of crystal-blue water only moments from her homestay, it was a surprise that the sight nearly moved her to tears. The sound alone was a balm for her soul. The inhale and exhale of the waves as they lapped at the shore. The cool, salted breath that danced across her skin and soothed the burning glare of the sun. The force, the depth, the sheer expanse of it, was incredibly humbling, and yet at the same time wonderfully empowering. And so, she promised herself that at least once a day she would sit on the sand and simply allow herself to be.

'Hi there!'

Olivia practically jumped from her skin at the sound of the voice to her left. Snapping her eyes open, she turned to see a rather tall, incredibly beautiful woman standing next to her on the beach. Any thought of exchanging terse words disappeared from Olivia's brain the second she laid eyes on the stranger. Long, jet-black hair flowed down her back, making the orange of her eyes glow even brighter. Her skin, the colour of honey, was almost completely covered in tattoos. The intricate patterns were like a living, breathing sketchbook. She was breathtakingly striking, and Olivia suddenly felt very plain and very boring-looking.

'Oh my god, I'm so sorry! Were you meditating?' The girl looked horrified, her deep voice lifting a little in fear.

'Meditating? No, I was just . . .' What was she doing? Trying to pull herself back from sending a panicked email to a guy she barely knew? 'Having a second to myself.'

'I didn't realize you had your eyes closed or I would have come back another time.'

'Is everything OK?' Olivia was quite unsure why this gorgeous human being was trying to talk to her.

'Don't worry, everything's fine. I just wanted to say hi and introduce myself. I'm staying in the hut opposite yours and I've been meaning to catch you ever since you arrived, but each time I've been home you've been out. I thought I'd seize the moment while I saw you sitting here.' She presented one of her finely decorated hands. 'I'm Cece.'

'Nice to meet you, I'm Olivia.' She took Cece's hand with her own very plain and very pale one, and gave it a firm shake.

'It's a nice little group we've got at the moment.' She

nodded back towards the rustic wooden huts that lay beyond the sand. 'Although, past 8 p.m.' – she came and sat down next to Olivia – 'maybe steer clear of Patricia and Tania in number seven. They often get a bit rowdy after their fourth fishbowl.'

'Gotcha.' Olivia nodded, recalling the two deep-fried, bleached-blonde women she'd seen lying outside the hut across the way, slurring their words and cackling long into the night. Their bodies were so dehydrated that with a touch, Olivia imagined they would crumble to dust.

'While I have you, I wanted to ask you about your washing line.'

'I have a washing line?'

'Yeah, that's the thing, it's currently living at my place. I borrowed it when no one was staying here and I haven't had a chance to speak to you about it. Do you mind if I use it for one more day then return it?'

'Sure, just give it back whenever you're done with it.'

'Amazing, thank you!' Cece squeezed Olivia's arm affectionately. 'I teach yoga and there is no way you can get away with wearing the same stuff twice out here. The sweat is *real*.'

'You're a yoga teacher? That's cool.'

Flashbacks of her conversation with Tracey whirred through her brain.

Powerful stuff, that is. Healing stuff.

'I am indeed. Six days a week, right here on the beach. Do you practise?'

'God no! I can barely balance on two legs, let alone do all that other fancy stuff.'

'I see.' Cece's face darkened. 'Let me guess, you've done the type of yoga where they make you plank for eight minutes then stand on your head?'

Olivia brought to mind the two classes she'd forced herself to go to, where the only pose she could master was the one at the end where everyone lay down on the floor and closed their eyes. Even then her brain was racing and her body itching to move.

'Something like that.'

'*Urgh*, that is *not* the type of yoga I teach. Stupid, westernized, commercial crap.' She folded her arms across her chest.

'I'm sorry.' Olivia could feel the prickles of tension emanating from Cece. 'I didn't mean to offend you.'

'Oh, God no, of course you didn't!' She laughed, a warm smile returning to her face. 'It's the industry that offends me. I love my job so much, but at times I get frustrated by it all.'

'I can imagine.'

Except she couldn't. Cece should try a day with Phil the pig, and then she'd know frustration.

'It's the exact reason every time I think about going back home to London, I change my mind.'

'You're from London too?'

'Uh-huh, although that feels like another lifetime now. I haven't been back in forever.'

Olivia's thoughts immediately turned to Jacob.

'Hey!' Cece clapped her hands together. 'Why don't you come along to one of my classes some time? See what true yoga is all about. I'm confident you'll be a convert by the end.'

'Oh gosh.' Olivia felt her stomach contract. 'I would love to, really I would, but I have so many things left to do while I'm here, I'm not sure I have the time. And besides, I'd be totally rubbish anyway, you wouldn't want me there.'

Cece narrowed her eyes. 'Time I'll just about accept as an excuse, but the other crap I don't buy. There is nobody on this earth who is bad at yoga. You can't be. It's impossible.'

'Well, expect to see someone defy all possibility then!' Olivia joked, her attempt at deflection making Cece grow even more stoic.

'Come to class tomorrow and prove me wrong. You can be my guest!'

'Tomorrow?' Olivia's face began to burn. 'I can't. I have to be up early for this tour I've booked on to. It starts at like 8 a.m.'

'Great, my class is at seven – you'll be done by seven forty-five.'

God, that is just great, isn't it.

'The thing is, I'm quite tired so I'm not sure I'll be up in time.'

'Hey' – Cece held her hands up in surrender – 'the offer's there. I'd love you to come, but if you don't want to, then of course that's totally fine too. It's 7 a.m., just a little bit further along by that patch of trees. You can't miss it, just follow the signs.' She reached for Olivia's arm and gently touched it. 'Anyway, I've intruded enough. It was lovely to meet you, and hopefully' – Cece grinned, calling over her shoulder as she strode away down the beach – 'I will see you bright and early for some *real* yoga!'

Olivia nodded and smiled, knowing that even if a single part of her did want to try it, there was no way she could risk embarrassing herself in front of a group of people like Cece. Did everyone who did yoga out here look like a goddess? Because if so, then quite frankly, she could kiss her spiritual awakening goodbye.

*

'Come *on*, why don't you just go?' Kate asked for the third time in a row. 'What's the worst that could happen? You can't be the only beginner; it's a tourist spot. Every man, woman and their grandma will be wanting to try out some traditional yoga! In fact, it's probably the best place to do it.'

Olivia rolled over on to her side, regretting ever mentioning her conversation with Cece to her best friend. It was their weekly FaceTime, and what she thought would simply be a passing comment about her day had turned into a ten-minute debate.

'Because . . .' She was running low on excuses now. 'It's too hot to exercise.'

Her friend pulled the phone screen closer and scowled.

'Yet miraculously you manage to go and visit about a hundred boring churches every day.'

'That's different,' Olivia grunted.

'How?'

'Because most churches are dark and sheltered and cool inside. Plus, it's a cultural experience. This would just be physical hell.'

'You don't know that.'

'Kate . . . do I need to remind you of the last yoga class we took together?' Olivia knew full well that any mention of said experience was banned by Kate due to the unfortunate incident when she ripped her leggings whilst not wearing any underwear, during a rather overambitious splits attempt.

'No, you don't need to remind me, as the shame will be imprinted on my memory until the second I take my last breath. But didn't your friend say it wasn't that type of class?'

'She's not my friend.'

'Well, if you actually made an effort and went to class, maybe she could become one.'

'Urgh, why are you so insistent on this?'

Kate's face, which had been scrunched up so tightly she

resembled a ball of freckled paper, suddenly softened. 'Because I don't want you to spend all your time looking around boring monuments by yourself. It's your final two weeks! Go have some fun.'

Perhaps it was the sombre look on her friend's face, or the truth of her words landing heavily on her heart, but Olivia felt her resolve begin to shake.

'I don't think putting your legs behind your head is technically classed as fun,' she sniffed, 'but maybe I'll go and have a look at the studio, see what the vibe is.'

'What the *vibe* is, hey? Look at you with all your traveller lingo.'

'Shut up.'

'That Jacob must be rubbing off on you.'

The mention of his name was unexpected, and Olivia bit down hard on her tongue to stop herself from reacting.

'Are you two still talking?' Kate took her moment of silence to poke a little deeper.

'Erm, a bit.'

'What does that mean?'

'We've emailed back and forth but, you know, I've been busy so it's a little quieter than before.'

Quieter? Try radio bloody silence.

'I see, and are you OK with that?'

'Why wouldn't I be?'

'I don't know, I'm only checking.'

'Well, I'm fine.' She grimaced, praying her tone was enough to make Kate well and truly back off. 'Now . . . how are things with you? You never tell me anything any more.'

Olivia saw the smallest flicker of something pass across Kate's face, but before she could catch and assess it, it disappeared.

'Because there's nothing to tell! Everything is same old, same old this side.'

'Work?'

'Same boring as ever, looking for a new job as we speak.'

'Family?'

'Boring as ever, looking for a new one as we speak.' She winked, the lightness returning to her expression.

'Dating life?' Olivia continued, noticing the same flicker of emotion flash across her friend's face.

'Don't even go there.' She sighed, her eyes everywhere but on Olivia's face. 'We don't need to depress ourselves with that subject.'

'Hmm, if you're sure.'

'I am.' Kate nodded, closing down any further questioning. 'Now, I have to finish my lunch and get back to work. But promise me you'll go and check out the yoga tomorrow? I want a full report on the *vibe*, please.'

'If you don't stop making fun of me, you'll get nothing!'

'Hey, you know it's only because I love you.'

Olivia hesitated, touching a finger to the screen. 'I love you too.'

Olivia

The yoga studio wasn't too hard to find. Although she wasn't quite sure the word *studio* was the correct term for what she found, tucked away in the sheltered crop of palm trees. In front of a big welcome sign sat a rustic wooden platform, constructed on small stilts. It had no solid walls, only swathes of coloured material that hung partially draped around the outside. It was a nice touch aesthetically, but in practice it meant that Olivia's woeful incompetence would not only be seen by the class, but also any passing stranger that cared to watch.

Immediately she wanted to run.

'Hey!' a familiar, soulful voice called out.

Could she run?

'Hey, Olivia!'

No, it was too late. She was trapped.

Cece had spotted her and was now weaving her way across the platform towards Olivia, stepping gracefully in between a dozen or so mats that had been neatly lined up in rows. Nearly every one of them was occupied with a student poised and ready for action, like obedient puppies. Olivia's heart sank when she saw two vacant mats near the front.

'I'm so glad you made it.' Cece pulled one of the flimsy pieces of cloth aside and poked her head out. 'Come in, we're just about to begin.'

'Are you sure? I'm not too late?'

A pathetic final attempt to escape.

'Of course not. Just leave your shoes there and grab any mat that's free.'

Olivia kicked off her sandals and placed them neatly alongside the other pairs lined up outside, a mixture of worn-out espadrilles, cheap and cheerful flip-flops and sand-smeared trainers. From the footwear, at least, it looked like there would be a mixture of people in the class, offering Olivia only the smallest slice of relief as the anxiety began to spike in her chest.

'Right, everyone.' Cece disappeared inside, her voice loud and low, rumbling through the space. 'Let's get started.'

Olivia scrambled up the stairs and made her way towards one of the free mats, avoiding making eye contact with any of the other students.

'This morning's class is going to get a bit fiery. I want you to stay open-minded and receptive to whatever comes up. Because whatever comes up . . .'

'Is asking to come out!' the room replied in unison.

'Exactly!' Cece beamed proudly as Olivia's heart sank to the floor. Everyone seemed far too awake and far too keen for a 7 a.m. yoga class. Her mood sat like an unwanted black cloud amongst a sea of sunshine smiles.

'Now, if everyone could start by closing their eyes, we are going to begin with some breathing exercises . . .'

Olivia shuffled on her mat, crossing and uncrossing her

legs in an attempt to find a comfortable seat. Breathing was OK. She could do breathing.

'When you're ready, let's all take a nice big deep inhale together . . .' Cece instructed.

The whole room sucked in air like a vacuum.

'And now exhale . . .'

The group sighed out in a collective groan.

'And inhale . . .'

Olivia closed her eyes and did as she was told, breathing in and out in time with the room. Everybody filled themselves up with the warm, salt-tinged air that came blowing off the sea, the sound of the ocean mirroring the rhythm of their breath, the waves pounding out a steady beat upon the sand.

Inhale, exhale. Inhale, exhale.

'Whatever happens over the next forty-five minutes' – Cece's voice rose over unified sighs and expulsions of air – 'I want you to come back to your breath.'

Come back to the breath.

'Focus on the expansion with the inhale, and contraction on the exhale . . .'

Inhale expand.

Exhale contract.

'And whatever you do, try to surrender.'

Surrender?

This was a yoga class, not some sort of battleground. A few stretches and she'd be done. Just a few more breaths and it would all be over, wouldn't it? Olivia tried to refocus her attention on the breath.

'If everybody could finish their next exhale, we're going to move straight into our sun salutations,' Cece announced, turning to look straight at Olivia, her eyes glinting with mischief. 'And prepare yourselves, because here is where the work really starts.'

*

Olivia was covered in sweat. Every inch of her skin was slick with a salty layer of the stuff. Even her toes felt damp.

She looked at the old man next to her, who seemed to be mastering the one-legged posture that Olivia had been wobbling her way into for the past ten minutes.

'Remember to *focus*,' Cece urged firmly, staring straight at Olivia, who had become so engrossed in the talents of the acrobatic grandad next to her that she was practically on the mat with him. 'Remember to *breathe*.'

How the hell was Olivia supposed to breathe when all she was concentrating on was not falling on her arse?

'Keep your gaze fixed on a point straight ahead. Relax your shoulders and try not to tense so much.'

Tense? I'll give you tense . . .

Olivia clamped her jaw shut and tried again, silent frustration coursing through her body. If there was one thing she was going to do before she left this class, it was to get her bloody foot on the inside of her bloody thigh and stay there!

Olivia tried again to lift her right leg, only just managing to get it halfway before Cece interrupted.

'Beautiful, everyone. Now release the foot and place it on to the ground. Take a deep breath in and reach your arms up to the sky . . .'

Olivia ignored the instruction, grabbing her foot and forcing it into place. She was not going to be upstaged by a wrinkled OAP with flatulence and shorts that were way too short to be worn in public. With one final hoick, Olivia found the pose, standing tall and proud in her victory.

229

'Yes!' she hissed under her breath, only slightly offended that the class hadn't erupted into raucous applause at her mastery.

'For our next move,' Cece continued, oblivious to Olivia and her achievement, 'we are going to come into our goddess pose. But this time we are going to have a bit of fun with it.' She moved to the front of the platform and began to demonstrate the posture. 'You are going to move into a wide-legged stance, feet wider than hip-distance apart, facing the ocean.'

Olivia grudgingly untangled herself and moved into position, trying not to focus on the pools of sweat gathered around the edges of her mat. How did everyone else look so composed? Was this the definition of enlightenment? Never perspiring even when you were trying to contort your body like it was a piece of elastic?

'Once you're there' – Cece scanned the students – 'you're going to place your hands in front of your chest like so. And then take a deep breath in.'

The class perfectly mirrored Cece's actions. Olivia just stood and watched.

'Then, on an exhale, you are going to push your hands away from you and bend your knees, almost like a squat – forcing the breath out through the mouth and pushing the space away. At this point, I encourage you to make noise. This is a wonderful releasing posture, so anything that comes up, I invite you to let it go.'

Olivia glanced around for any other confused faces. But to her amazement, the rest of the class seemed to be nodding.

'OK, hands in front of the chest, inhale . . . and exhale, push away.'

The space filled with noise: grunts and groans and fiery exhales.

'Good. And inhale, straighten the legs, bring the hands to the chest . . . and exhale *release*.' Cece's voice rose loudly, spurring the others on to make even more noise.

Olivia stood silently, watching the strange phenomenon around her.

This is stupid.

This is ridiculous.

'Now I want you to close your eyes and repeat it, over and over, falling into the rhythm.' Cece began to walk between the mats. 'Let this become a moving meditation.'

Olivia knew exactly where Cece was heading. Quickly, she closed her eyes and tried to blend in with the rhythmic chanting of the others. Her breathing was light and silent, her hands mimicking the motions half-heartedly.

'Let go of the ego. Don't worry about what it looks like.' Cece's voice grew stronger. 'Tap into what it feels like. *Feel* into the movement. *Feel* into the body. If you want to stamp your feet, do it. If you want to scream and shout, *do it*! You deserve to be heard. You deserve to take up space!'

Olivia sensed someone standing behind her.

'Keep going, Olivia,' Cece whispered. 'Let the thoughts come, let the emotions come. Just keep moving and keep breathing. Feel what needs to be felt.'

Ridiculous – was that a valid emotion to feel? Olivia wondered.

'Inhale . . . exhale . . . inhale . . . exhale . . .'

The platform pulsated with breath, the noises getting louder and louder, the stamping more insistent and almost threatening.

'Let go,' Cece demanded.

Olivia scrunched her eyes tighter.

'Let go of thinking . . .'

231

But all I do is think.

'Let. Go!' Cece shouted, as the noise of the class rose to meet her command.

The stamping of feet was so heavy, so full of anger, that the entire platform shook from the impact. The roaring wails that tore through the air, the cries of anguish, the screams of jubilation, one after the other, pressed in on Olivia like a series of physical blows. It was too much. It was all too much.

Olivia wanted to run, to push her way through the sea of crazy people and back into the safety of her little hut. To run from everything and everyone. But each time she made to move, to open her eyes, to do something other than stand frozen on her mat, she couldn't.

This trip is stupid.

I hate it.

I hate this whole fucking thing.

She didn't think it was possible, but the sound from the class had reached an even higher volume. And yet, despite the deafening racket, she could hear Cece right behind her.

'Inhale . . . exhale . . .' She quietly repeated the words, like a mantra in her ear. 'Inhale, bring the hands in, exhale, push them away . . . You can do this, Olivia.'

No, I can't.

I want to go home.

I want to go home and see my sister.

Tears began to pour down Olivia's cheeks, merging with the sweat that was glistening across her skin.

Leah.

Oh God, Leah.

Boiling rage, thick like lava, rolled around in the pit of her stomach, rising up into her chest. Wave upon wave of red-hot energy, each one more deadly than the next. The pain of it threatened to destroy her right there and then, unless . . .

Olivia began to move her body. Slowly at first, a soft hand to the chest and a gentle release. The breath was still shallow and the fire inside her still burning.

'That's it,' Cece encouraged. 'Now deepen the breath, go all the way in and all the way out.'

Olivia did as she was told, drawing in deep and desperate breaths as her movement became stronger and more intentional.

'Yes! Now, can you allow yourself to release? Scream. Shout. Stamp your feet,' Cece hollered.

In and out she moved, over and over, allowing the molten anger to build from her chest up into her throat. A swirling mass of liquid rage, it pressed against her windpipe, clawing up the sides of her neck, until all at once it was too much to contain.

Olivia opened her mouth and screamed, a lifetime of hurt ripping through her.

It's not fair.

It's just not fair.

The sobs racked her heaving chest.

Olivia's heart felt fit to burst, her breath growing erratic and laboured in her chest. She bent over and let the tears stream down into puddles on the floor beneath her.

'Take deep breaths, Olivia,' the calming, reassuring voice from Cece whispered next to her.

'I can't. I can't breathe.'

'Yes, you can,' Cece stated firmly, crouching down next to her. 'Come sit with me.'

Olivia let herself be guided to the floor, Cece's firm grip anchoring her through every movement.

'Try to stop all the resistance, if you can,' she encouraged. 'Stop trying to fight what you're feeling. Allow it.' Cece took one of Olivia's hands and placed it over her heart, then took the other and placed it on her stomach. 'Ground yourself, feel your breath.'

Olivia let her hands settle on her body, and instantly felt the panic's sharpness soften.

'Sit here for a moment and just be. OK?' Cece whispered.

Olivia nodded in response, unable to muster words.

'Everyone, if you could start to slow the movement until you come to a standing position, hands on body, eyes remain closed,' Cece called out loudly.

The stamping and the grunting ceased as the entire class seemed to extinguish itself of sound.

'Now, very slowly, I want you all to make your way down to Savasana. Lying on your back, arms out by your side and legs slightly apart.'

Olivia could hear the shifting of people as they lowered themselves down into the position. Slowly and very gently she followed suit, allowing her hot back to rest fully on the cool floor.

Her heart was thumping furiously in her chest and, as everyone fell into silence, she was certain it could be heard echoing around the platform.

'Clear your mind and allow every part of your body to relax.' Cece's voice reverberated around the space. 'Feel yourself sinking deeper and deeper into the ground beneath you . . .'

Olivia's body continued to vibrate with the echoes of her crying. Her internal world was still a flurry of activity, a tornado of emotion and conflict.

Had she just done that? Had she really just sobbed in front of a room full of strangers?

'Let the thoughts come and go,' Cece implored, as if she could sense Olivia's mind kicking into action. 'Watch them as they pass . . .'

You can't ever look Cece in the eye again.

'. . . witnessing and accepting them, but not holding on . . .' Cece's voice was getting quieter and quieter.

You can't look anyone here in the eye again!

Olivia's body grew heavy, and the thoughts, whilst still whirring ominously through her mind, seemed to grow fainter and fainter.

'Allow this moment to be one of complete surrender . . .'

What was Cece saying? It was becoming harder and harder to hear.

'Just total and complete . . . surrender . . .'

*

Olivia blinked her eyes open and stared up at the sky.

'If everyone could quietly roll up their mats and leave anyone who is still resting to come round in their own time,' Cece instructed softly, triggering a wave of rustling and shuffling amongst the students.

Reluctantly, Olivia turned over on to her side and pushed herself upright, stretching her arms above her head and scrunching her toes together tightly. The movement made her head swirl.

'Hey, how are you doing down there?'

Olivia turned her head to find Cece crouched down beside her. How was she doing? Confused? Totally and utterly embarrassed? Sad . . .

'Yeah, I'm OK. Tired, but OK.'

'I'm not surprised you're tired, that was a big release.'
Cece eyed Olivia with concern. 'You want me to help you
up?'

'No, no, I'm good,' Olivia replied, ungracefully making
her way to standing; her legs felt like they were made of lead
and jelly all at the same time. She looked around the platform; everyone else had disappeared. 'Please don't tell me I
was the only one who fell asleep?'

Cece placed a warm hand on her arm. 'Of course you
weren't. Simon at the back there dozed off towards the end,
and Jane goes from awake to snoring in less than twenty
seconds. And like I said' – her face softened further – 'you
had a big release.'

'I just wish my releases didn't have to be so *public*.'

'Ah, the emotional hangover?' Cece chuckled. 'I've had
my fair few of those in my time.'

'I'd take fifty tequila shots over this any day.'

'Really? I think if people had the courage to express their
feelings more openly, this world would be a much better and
healthier place.'

Of course Cece thought that way. Of course she'd have
everyone go around spewing their deepest, darkest emotional secrets out into the world. Have everyone wallow in
their self-pity and sorrow, sitting around drinking green
juices and burning incense. But what about real life? Where
was the time for that in real life?

'Maybe,' Olivia grunted.

'You don't believe me?' Cece smirked, flicking her hair
over her shoulder. 'Let me ask you, how are you feeling?
Beneath the tiredness and the embarrassment. How do you
feel in your body now?'

Olivia took a moment to check in. She *was* tired, there

was no doubt about that, and her legs felt like they'd run a marathon. But as she let herself drop down below those sensations, she found that, strangely, there was a spaciousness within her that wasn't there before. Almost as though her soul had let out a long, deep sigh.

'I feel . . . lighter? Maybe?'

'See!' Cece tidied the last few mats away and ushered Olivia to follow her outside. 'When we express, we no longer suppress. And when we no longer suppress, we create *space*. We give ourselves more freedom on the inside. Does that make sense?'

'Kind of,' Olivia lied, her brain still foggy from exhaustion.

'Good. Now, make sure you eat something hearty for breakfast. It's important to ground down after practices like that.'

'OK.' Olivia wasn't quite sure what 'grounding down' was, but she nodded obediently anyway. 'By the way, before I forget . . .'

Olivia reached into her pocket and began to count out the money she owed.

'Don't.' Cece placed a hand over hers.

'But I need to pay for the class.'

'I told you; you were my guest.'

'Are you sure?'

'Yes! You can repay me by coming back tomorrow.'

Olivia laughed awkwardly, yet Cece's face remained impassive.

'You are joking, aren't you?'

'Nope.'

'You want me to go through *that* all over again?'

'Yes!' A cackle of laughter broke Cece's stern expression. 'I just think it would be good for you, that's all. You're carrying a lot of weight on your shoulders that I sense you're ready to put down.' Cece took a step towards her, the space between them so small that the rich, smoky perfume of her tattooed skin filled Olivia's nostrils in an instant.

It was a smell so reminiscent of Jacob that, for a second, Olivia felt she was right there with him. Back in Udaipur. Saying goodbye. Faces so close to touching.

Her heart ached at the memory.

'Hey' – Cece broke the spell – 'all I ask is that you think about it. I'm here at the same time every day. The offer's there.'

'Thank you.' Olivia nodded, her mind a blur of emotions and a whirlwind of thoughts, each one clambering over another in a bid to be chosen from the pile.

'My pleasure.' Cece smiled, giving Olivia's arm one final squeeze, before reaching down and grabbing the only pair of weather-beaten flip-flops left. 'Now, I have to go – I have another client to teach – but take care of yourself, drink lots of water, and make sure you eat!'

'I will, I promise.'

'Good!' Cece grinned, turning to stroll the opposite way down the beach. 'And maybe see you tomorrow?'

'Yeah.' Olivia watched as Cece was absorbed into the crowd of persistent beach dwellers, who seemed so at peace with wasting entire days lying prostrate on the sand. 'Maybe see you tomorrow.'

Jacob

Jacob's nose was so close to the screen that he could practically feel the years of other people's grime seeping into his skin. Dirty fingerprints smeared across the glass and bits of old food and drink crusted on like a second skin were enough to turn anyone's stomach, but Jacob was too distracted to notice. He had been staring at the same message for the past ten minutes, unable to tear himself away, yet still unable to bring himself to reply.

From: Olivia_Jackson@gmail.com
Subject: Might have found the new best dosa in India . . .

Jacob read Olivia's message again. The pull of her words was so strong that he wanted to fall through the computer screen and transport himself right to where she was. Yet every time his fingers so much as twitched in response, he pulled away.

'Urgh!' He slammed his fists down on to the table, sending the keyboard into the air and startling the middle-aged man next to him. The internet cafe he'd found in Udaipur wasn't the most glamorous of establishments, but it served a purpose. It was dark, private and extremely cheap, which was lucky for Jacob, as for the past two weeks he'd spent all of his time simply staring at that one unanswered email.

Indecision was not a feeling Jacob was used to experiencing. If he wanted to do something, he did it, and when he wasn't sure, he handed the question over to the universe. But now . . . now things felt different. Now there was a new voice inside of him. A voice of desire, of yearning, of wanting to be closer to someone, that the rest of him wanted to pull away from. There was a full-scale battle raging in his head and it was adding a whole new palette of colours to his black-and-white way of thinking. Nothing was simple any more. Nothing felt clear cut. And everything was starting to feel a little bit out of control.

He let his head fall into his hands, his temples burning white hot under the mounting pressure gathering across the surface of his skull. Last night his migraine had got so bad that he'd been sick from the pain, his body buckling under the weight of his brain, the sheer volume of sensation overloading his system to the point of breaking.

He sneaked another glimpse at the screen, the bright light automatically sending a shooting pain through the back of his eyes. His stomach rolled with nausea and his body ran ice cold.

Just make a decision and stick to it . . .

Jacob took a long, slow inhale and, with his eyes half closed, raised his head and allowed his fingers to land on the keyboard. He couldn't ignore Olivia for ever, and if sending an email would lighten even a tenth of the load in his head, he was willing to accept the consequences.

240

To: Olivia_Jackson@gmail.com

Re: Might have found the new best dosa in India . . .

Surprise! It's me! I'm alive!

Really? That's how you're going to kick things off?
He deleted the sentence and tried to start again.

Guess who's back?

Delete.

Hey there, you.

Delete.

Hi.

He stared at the screen. Five minutes and only one word written.

I'm so sorry I've not replied sooner. I picked up a nasty bug and have been laid up in bed for a while. It wasn't pretty, so I'll save you the details.

That wasn't a total lie; he had technically been sick, after all . . .

I don't want to believe you've found a better-tasting dosa, but I trust you enough to take your word for it. I hope you got to Goa safely, and your career as a yogi is going fantastically. Say hi to the ocean for me.
Jacob x

He looked at the message. The measly output of fifteen minutes' carefully considered and overly edited work. He hated it. It was cold and formal, and quite frankly it said nothing, but without wasting another second, he clicked send, unable to stare at his pathetic words any longer. Off it went, out into the ether – straight to Olivia, with her blue eyes and freckled skin.

A wave of guilt struck him, followed by a stronger wave of sickness.

His eyes were almost totally closed now, only the tiniest slit of light allowed through between the lids. His head felt so heavy that it was almost too much to keep it upright. He needed to get out of here, away from the sounds of other people typing, and the whirring of machines. He needed the silence and solitude of his bedroom. He needed . . .

Mum.

The thought took him by such surprise that he snapped his eyes wide open, flooding his system with unwanted sensations. His body screamed in protest as flashes of light swarmed across his field of vision. He tried to stand but found that his right leg had gone so numb it might as well not have been there. And as he fought to stay upright, with the swirling colours now totally blinding him, all he could think to say was her name. Over and over.

'Mum. I want *Mum.*'

Olivia

Olivia woke with a start.

Once again, she was the only member of the class still laid out on the floor, dribble crusting her cheeks and limbs splayed out to the sides. How, after three mornings in a row, was she *still* falling asleep during Savasana? It was as though the second she hit the ground, everything switched off. Her aching body, cooled by the hard, wooden floor, the sound of Cece's low, lyrical voice, and the beating waves of the ocean made it impossible for her to fight the pull of sleep.

'You need any help, Olivia, or are you all right down there?' Cece peered over. Her dark, satin hair was twisted into a plait that swung over her shoulder like a piece of glossy rope, begging Olivia to reach out and grab it. Resisting the temptation, Olivia forced herself to sit up, blinking away the flashing lights that darted across her eyes. The same spacious, slightly delirious feeling she'd experienced after the previous two classes made her head spin, and it took her a couple of moments to steady herself.

'I'm good. Just takes me a little while to come back to earth, I think.'

Cece offered a hand, which Olivia willingly took, pulling her up to standing and drawing them to eye level. Deepest blue staring into brightest orange. Water into fire.

'It was another intense one today, huh?'

'Yeah.' Olivia flushed with embarrassment. 'When does that ever stop? *Please* tell me it stops.'

Cece cracked a smile, but Olivia couldn't join in with the amusement. It had been another session of deep, heartbreaking, soul-shattering crying. How much more grief existed inside her? It felt like more than a lifetime's worth and yet it continued, wave after wave, pouring from the centre of her being, out into the space around her.

'Eventually.' Cece slung her arm over Olivia's shoulders and pulled her closer. 'We just have to give it time.'

'We? You're not the one having the public emotional meltdown.'

'No, but I have been that one, and so you can trust me when I say it does get better.'

Olivia looked Cece up and down. Had this incredibly fierce, insanely beautiful, calm and composed woman really found herself with snot all down her face, sobbing her heart out during a simple yoga class?

'If you say so.'

'I do! And do you know what else I say?'

Cece had begun to walk the pair towards the exit, the swathes of material blowing wide open in the strong ocean breeze.

'Go on . . .' Olivia shoved her feet into her shoes.

'I say we get some breakfast. I know a *great* little place that does the most amazing pancakes. Can I tempt you?'

Olivia's mind flew to a thousand excuses she could make, a hundred reasons why a relaxing morning breakfast would not be conducive to her schedule, but something inside her answered before her default 'no' could come out of her mouth.

'Sure. That sounds nice.'

'Great!' Cece flung her braid over her shoulder and nodded in the direction of the road. 'We go this way.'

They left the yoga space and headed away from the ocean, walking along a dirt path that ran parallel to the busy main road. Although the traffic was far from light, the rush of mopeds and the honking of tuk-tuks didn't affect Olivia as it had in the bigger cities. Maybe the yoga was doing something to her inner world after all.

It wasn't long before they arrived at a little whitewashed cafe, hidden amongst a nest of palms.

'This is so *cute*,' Olivia gasped, as they stepped inside.

The space was filled with a mishmash of colours and materials; the walls were covered with abstract paintings and fabric hangings. Squashy sofas and wicker chairs gathered in small groups, decorated with throws and woven pillows. In every corner stood a collection of plants, their burst of green leaves singing brightly against the white stone and mosaic floor.

'Isn't it?' Cece guided them over to a free table.

'Yeah, I would never have found this place by myself.'

'Most people don't like to wander too far away from the seafront.' Cece shrugged. 'But when you've been here a while, it's nice to mix it up.'

'I can imagine.' Olivia picked up the menu and began to scan it hungrily. 'How long did you say you've been out here for?'

'Nearly six months now.' Cece leant back in her chair and hooked one long leg over the other, flashing Olivia with works of tattooed art that she had yet to see. 'I can't believe it. I only planned to come out for two weeks.'

'What made you stay?'

Cece rested her chin on her hand. 'I guess I sort of fell in love with the place. There was an opportunity to teach yoga; I could swim in the ocean every day, surf, lie on the beach, eat good food. It felt stupid to leave.'

Olivia was trying hard to hide her scepticism. 'But don't you miss home? Living out of a suitcase and being away from your family must be hard, no?'

'Yes and no.' Cece let out a long exhale. 'My family is very small – it's literally only me and my mum. And of course I miss her all the time, but she had big dreams for me. She wanted me to see the world, to go and explore and have adventures. She practically packed my bags for me when I told her I wanted to go abroad!'

Olivia couldn't help but wonder if her mum would have done the same for her, if Leah hadn't got sick. If their whole world hadn't become about doctors' appointments and hospital visits. What would her mum have dreamt for her? For all of them? A pang of sadness twinged in her chest.

'And in terms of living out of a suitcase,' Cece continued, 'there's a strange type of freedom when all your possessions can be carried on your back. I feel so much lighter than I did back home. Don't you?'

Olivia chewed over Cece's words carefully. Although the weight of her backpack had left near permanent red marks on her shoulders, there was something freeing about it. The ease that came with only having a select few items of clothes to choose from each day. All the hundreds of pounds she'd spent on perfumes and beauty creams, the toiletries that she swore she could *never* live without, now reduced to a face wash and sun cream.

'In a way.' She pulled at her once white T-shirt. 'Although I can't pretend I'm not dying to get back to using a proper washing machine when I'm home.'

'I'll give you that.' Cece nodded at a passing waiter. 'Are you ready to order?'

'No! There's so much to choose from!' Olivia glanced at the menu once more. 'Is there anything you'd recommend?'

'The smoothie bowls are incredible. And the pancakes are always good.'

'OK.' Olivia looked up into the eager face of the young waiter. 'I'll have the tropical smoothie bowl and a latte, please.'

'Good choice.' He nodded. 'And for you?' He looked at Cece. 'The usual?'

'You bet!' She grinned, passing him the menus and pouring them both a glass of water. 'It's so funny how much I used to judge people who came back to the same place on holiday every single year. They'd stay in the same hotels and eat in the same restaurants, year in, year out. I used to think it was such a waste, but now . . .' She took a sip from her drink. 'Now I can see why they do it! It's so nice having people who know you and what you like.'

'Back home, there's this cute little coffee shop at the end of my street; I only need to step one foot inside the door and the guy is making my order for me. Every day, like clockwork, he's waiting for me.' Olivia laughed sadly. 'I think if I were to go missing, he'd be the first person to alert the police.'

'So, you like a routine, then?'

'I don't know how anyone can survive without one!'

Cece arched one of her perfectly sculpted eyebrows. 'You'd be surprised. Sometimes a little spontaneity does wonders for the soul.'

'Soul maybe; productivity less so.'

'And that's the most important thing for you?'

Olivia knew there was no malice in Cece's question, but she couldn't help but feel a little judged.

'It's one of them, yes.' She felt her face flush. 'Otherwise, how would anything get done? I have a lot of responsibility, in my job and in my family. If I'm not productive or organized, or on top of everything, things fall apart. And that just can't happen.'

'I get it.' Cece flashed her a small, rather sad-looking smile. 'You like to be in control because you have been put in that position your whole life.'

'It's not control.' Olivia clenched her jaw. 'I don't like controlling people. I'm not like that.'

'I don't mean you intentionally manipulate people. It's that you feel safe when you know what's going on. When there is order and process and certainty.'

'Well, doesn't everyone?' Olivia snapped, her voice louder than she intended. 'Don't you?'

'Not really – to me it feels kind of pointless. We like to think we can control things, but the truth is, we can't. The more we try to hold on to things and keep them a certain way, the more painful it is when it all tips on its head and changes direction,' Cece replied calmly. 'We can't make people love us, no matter how much we do for them; we can't stop ourselves ageing, no matter how much Botox we pump into our faces; and we can't stop people dying, no matter how fiercely we try to protect them from the world. Ultimately, it's all out of our control.'

Thankfully, the food arrived just as Cece finished speaking. Olivia could feel the tears stinging her eyes and the thoughts of Leah floating up to the surface. She'd already exceeded her emotional breakdown quota for the day, and she supposed it wouldn't be quite as acceptable to wail and scream whilst people sipped their coffees and tucked into their morning eggs.

'I'm sorry, I don't mean to preach.' Cece began carving into her towering stack of pillowy pancakes. 'It's something I've had to learn the hard way, that's all.' She held out her arm, presenting the deeply tanned skin to Olivia.

'My dad died when I was four.' Cece pressed a finger lightly to the incredibly detailed image of a man that sat hidden amongst the lines and dots snaking around the contours of her forearm.

Grief clamped down hard on Olivia's heart, so intensely she felt she might crack in two right there in the cafe.

'God, I'm sorry.'

Olivia berated herself for not noticing the tattoo sooner. For assuming, once again, that because someone looked a certain way, they carried no heartbreak or war wounds. That they bore no scars from life's cruelty. She should know better than anyone that looks can be deceiving. Hadn't she been pretending her whole life that she was fine?

'That's OK. It was a long time ago now.' Cece folded her arm back into herself, still cradling the place where the image sat. 'But what about you?'

Olivia drew in a deep breath, nervous but no longer afraid to share her story. Not with Cece, anyway: a woman who had held her in her most vulnerable pain, and understood the depths in which she found herself drowning every day.

'It was my little sister.'

My beautiful, precious, baby sister.

'She died four months ago.'

Olivia

By the time they left the cafe, it was nearly midday. The streets were busier, the sun was hotter, and Olivia's heart felt a little lighter.

'Now, is this or is this not the best banana milkshake you've ever had in your life?' Cece grinned, proudly raising her cup in the air as they made their way back to the beach.

'It's delicious' – Olivia sucked the cold, sweet liquid in satisfaction – 'but I'm surprised; I thought you yogis were all green juice and kale salads.'

'Hell no!' Cece looked horrified. 'Life is way too short not to eat sugar.'

'I can get on board with that.' Olivia polished off her drink with one final slurp. 'Although I'll probably crash in about an hour.'

'Ah, always the risk with a morning shake.' Cece shrugged. 'Have you got much to do today?'

'I have a couple of churches to visit and, if there's time, a small temple to the north.' Olivia could feel her blood fizzing with sweetness – under the heat of the sun, it was making her feel a little drunk.

'Are you religious?'

'No.' Olivia steadied herself as a stray dog hurtled past her on the sand. 'Definitely not.'

Her mind began to swim with images. Walking into the living room and seeing her mum and dad on their knees, eyes closed, fervently whispering prayer after prayer for Leah. The local priest visiting the house to bless the entire family, whilst her baby sister lay in the bed next to them, unable to even open her eyes from the pain. The funeral, with the same priest praising God for taking Leah into his arms and welcoming her to heaven.

'But you love visiting churches?'

'Let's just say, I'm not very good at lying on a beach all day and reading books.' Olivia nodded towards the swarms of tourists that had descended upon the beach, loaded with towels and not enough sun cream. The patchwork quilt of red and white skin was stark against the golden sand. 'I needed something a bit more cultural to do while I was here.'

'Ah, well that blows my offer of sitting by the ocean out of the window.' Cece winked. 'I have an hour until my next client.'

'Hey, there's always room for negotiation.'

'Go on . . .'

'I'll sit for a bit, as long as it's in the shade. I'll roast in this heat otherwise.'

'Deal!' Cece gestured to a patch of palm trees a little to their left. 'Over here looks perfect.'

Annoyingly, they had no towels or deckchairs to protect them from the searing hot sand, which, even in the shade of the trees, had risen to quite a temperature. Olivia hovered above the ground, switching her weight every so often between bum cheeks so as to avoid crisping one more than the other. As she rested her back against the rough bark of a tree, she took a moment to absorb the view. The ocean and sky bleeding their blues into one another like halves of the same whole. Children throwing themselves into the oncoming waves, tossing their bodies around as though they were easily replaceable. Fishermen hauling their catch up the beach, their boats standing to attention like neat wooden toys, each painted a mixture of reds and greens and yellows. It was beautiful. So beautiful, in fact, that Olivia couldn't help but reach for her phone to take a picture.

'I know, I know, it's super touristy.' She laughed as Cece watched her snap away. 'But my friend Kate will kill me if I don't show her this.'

'Hey, no judgement here. I have about a hundred pictures of this beach on my phone. It's idyllic.'

'It is.' She took a couple more for good measure and fired off the best ones to Kate, her brother and then, as a quick afterthought, her mum and dad.

'I've been to many places in my life, but I don't think anywhere beats this.' Cece sighed, shuffling further down into the sand. 'Where's your favourite place?'

But Olivia couldn't answer. In fact, she'd barely heard the question. Her whole being had become focused on the little notification that sat at the top of her screen. She hadn't seen it before, the glare from the sun obscuring it from view. But there it was, almost yelling the words at her.

One new email from jpgreen@gmail.com

'Olivia?' Cece peered over at her. 'Is everything OK?'

How could she even think about answering that without

reading Jacob's email? The fact that he was alive was a huge relief, but now the sting of his two-week delay pierced her heart. What was he playing at?

'Uh-huh,' she replied distractedly, clicking on to the message and watching as it loaded. Her eyes plucked words at random from the short paragraph on screen.

Was that it?

She tried to scroll further down the screen.

That's it!

She read the email again. It was so concise. So cold. Where were the stories? Where was the teasing and the joking? And – she felt a hairline splinter through her heart – where was their usual sign-off?

Say hi to the ocean for me.
Jacob x

Just Jacob.

'Olivia!' Cece gave her a firm nudge. 'What's wrong?'

'Sorry. It's just an unexpected message, that's all.'

'Unexpected in a good way or a bad way?'

'Both, I guess,' she answered honestly, staring at the message once more. 'It's from a friend I met out here. I hadn't heard from him in two weeks, and he's just replied but it feels . . . I don't know.' She wanted to shove the phone under Cece's nose as evidence, and at the same time toss it straight into the ocean and never look at it again. 'He said he's been sick – that's why he didn't reply – but the whole message feels a little cold.'

'Can I take a look?'

'Sure.' Olivia passed the phone, too consumed by her own

thoughts to care about Cece reading her previous messages to Jacob.

'And you two are just friends?'

'Yeah.' The truth hurt to say out loud but, based on that message, there could be no denying it now.

'Well' – Cece handed the phone back to Olivia – 'I think it's a boy being his usual emotionally unaware self, and we shouldn't read too much into these things. Plus, he said he'd been sick, which, as a seasoned traveller myself, I know can knock you for six.'

'That's true.' The toilet in Jaipur came flooding back to mind.

'I say reply as though nothing's wrong, talk to him exactly how you usually would, and if he carries on being weird then ask him directly. Life's too short not to eat sugar, and it's too short to play games.'

Olivia was direct in many aspects of her life, but somehow asking Jacob why he wasn't being his usual self with her felt terrifying.

'Maybe.' She shoved the phone into her pocket.

'Actually, you know what you *should* do?'

'What?'

'You should invite him out here for a few days. Get him doing some yoga by the ocean with the sun on his face. It's the cure for almost anything.'

'I can't do that!'

'Why not?'

'Because . . .' Olivia ran through the litany of reasons why that would be an incredibly foolish idea. Number one, she could be rejected. Number two, those godforsaken dice. 'He doesn't like to plan anything. It's all very spur of the moment.'

'I think booking a random trip to Goa because a friend asks you to come is pretty spur of the moment.'

'I know, but it's a bit more complicated than that.'

'If you say so.' Cece shrugged, stretching out her body so the ends of her toes broke the boundary of shade and peeped out into the sun. 'Ah, this feels so nice, but if I don't move now, chances are I'll be stuck here all day, and I don't think my client will appreciate sunbathing as an excuse for missing class.'

'No, probably not.'

'You coming?'

Olivia knew she should head back, get herself ready to tour some more churches, but something was keeping her seated, and for once in her life, she decided to go with the urge. 'I think I'll stay here a little longer.'

'No problem. I'll see you tomorrow for class?'

'Of course.'

'Great!' She gave Olivia's shoulder a little squeeze, lowering her voice to a half-whisper. 'You do whatever you feel is right with your friend, but just remember . . . life is too short for games. Say it with me. Life is too short for what?'

'Games.'

'Exactly!' Cece beamed.

Life may be too short for games, Olivia thought, watching her friend disappear, but what happens when someone's whole life is based on one?

Jacob

It took three days of total bedrest for Jacob to feel like a human being again. Everyone in the internet cafe had been extremely concerned after his rather dramatic fainting episode. So much so that it took a good fifteen minutes to convince the owner that he didn't need to call an ambulance, and he was fine to leave unaccompanied. Luckily, his hostel wasn't far, and he just about managed to crawl back to his room before passing out once more, sleeping solidly for twelve hours straight.

Thankfully, he had curated a little stash of snacks in his room, so in between bouts of sleep, he forced himself to eat a packet of nuts or munch on a dry cereal bar, his stomach still rolling with nausea and his body so weak that, even if he wanted to, he didn't think he could manage anything more substantial. All he was good for was rest.

By the morning of day four, the fog finally began to lift. The shooting pains across his forehead had lessened to a pulsating ache, and the flashing lights in front of his eyes had almost cleared completely. He was feeling fragile, but only from lack of food, something he knew could easily be rectified as soon as he dragged his sorry self out of bed and into the shower. In fact, on the whole, he felt good. The only thing he couldn't shake quite yet were the final thoughts he'd had before he'd fallen unconscious.

Mum.

I want Mum.

The urge for her was still as strong. Her face interrupted both his sleeping and waking thoughts, the image so clear it was as though she were standing right in front of him, close enough for him to reach out and touch her, to feel her soft, powdery skin against his and smell the heavy, floral scent of her perfume. The woman who was there for him every single day of his life, until he left her behind without a second glance. How on earth could he face speaking to her now? After all this time, out of the blue, simply because he was sick and needed comfort? Maybe his dad was right; maybe he really was that selfish.

The thought of his dad was enough to drive him from his bed. He couldn't spend another day wallowing in self-pity. He had to get up and he had to eat. And if he happened to swing by the internet cafe on his travels and ended up sending a few emails, so what?

Excitement gathered in the base of his throat. Maybe, just maybe, Olivia would have replied to him by now. Not that he should want that. Not that he should even deserve that. But there was no denying it: a part of him was still hopeful. And he knew, more than anyone, that hope was the most dangerous emotion of them all.

*

'For my time the other day' – Jacob slapped down a handful of coins on the sticky counter and placed a cup of steaming chai by the pile of money – 'and a thank you for looking after me.'

The owner of the cafe looked at him, and then, without so much as a word, pushed both gifts back towards Jacob. 'I won't let you pay for being sick.' He offered a fatherly smile. 'And, my friend, I think you need the chai more than I do.'

'Do I still look that rough?'

'I've seen worse.' The man twiddled his thick, bushy moustache. 'Now, are you staying or going? I have only one free space left.'

Jacob cast his eyes around the little space. It was surprisingly busy for a midweek morning; rows of hunched bodies were crammed in next to each other, eyes glued to screens and fingers flying across keyboards. It was strange, he thought, how this had become the new way to connect with people. In a dark, soulless room, hidden behind a machine. It didn't make any sense, and yet here he was, about to do the very same thing.

'Yeah, I might as well since I'm already here.' Jacob shoved a few of his coins back across the counter and picked his way through to the one empty desk in the corner.

His fingers were filled with nervous energy, almost tripping over themselves in anticipation.

He logged on to his emails and found the last message she'd sent him, dated on his birthday and still unread.

From: Helen.K.Green@btinternet.com
Subject: Another year older and hopefully a little wiser . . .
Hi darling, it's me, Mum.

He couldn't help but laugh at her opening sentence. Why did parents insist on announcing their identity in every form of communication they had with their children?

I just wanted to send a quick message to wish you a happy birthday! I've sent quite a few texts, but they don't seem to be getting through any more – perhaps you've lost your phone or changed numbers? Either way, just let me know you're safe.

Guilt pulled his heart down into his stomach.

In my head I like to picture you on a beautiful beach somewhere, sunning yourself by the ocean. I'll never forget what you said to me once – life's too short to be anywhere but by the sea! You always were my little water baby. But wherever you are, my darling boy, know that I love you. I think about you every day, and even though it breaks my heart you're not here, I am so proud of the life you chose to make for yourself.

Here's to another year of you.

Mum x

It was all he could do not to burst into tears right there and then. Quickly, he began to type out a reply, allowing the emotion of her words to spur on his own. It was surprisingly easy once he got going: updating her on his phone situation, where he was in the world and how he was doing; all of which contained about a hundred white lies, but still, there was truth nestled in there somewhere. He wondered if his mum would even believe it was him writing; he hadn't shared so much in so long that he wouldn't be surprised if she mistook it as a fraudulent attempt to scam her into sending money abroad. Either way, he'd done his bit, and now it was a matter of time before he saw her reaction.

As he pressed send, the tears began to fall, blurring the screen so much that he almost missed her name.

From: Olivia_Jackson@gmail.com

Re:Re: Might have found the new best dosa in India . . .

His heart immediately rose from the pit of his stomach to the top of his throat.

> Hey! I'm so sorry to hear you got sick – are you feeling better now? I did wonder if a rogue street food vendor had been the cause of your absence, and it appeared my intuition was right. Must be what happens when you become spiritually enlightened. Because yes, I am an official yogi master now. Three sessions in and I still can't stand on one leg! I do it in this little shack on the beach, with an amazing teacher called Cece – you'd like her, she's a universe convert too. I think Agonda is my favourite place on earth – the sand and the ocean are stunning. Only a few days left for me, and then back home I go. So, if you need some R&R for your health, and if the gods of fate allow it, of course, I would highly recommend you come here. The ocean wants to say hi to you back.
>
> Yours, relieved you're alive, Olivia x

An entire landslide of emotions cascaded through him. Shame at the cold and callous message he'd sent to her. Joy and pure euphoria at reading hers. Relief that she'd even bothered to reply. And then, buried beneath all of that, a deep and powerful longing. To go to her. To feel the sand between his toes and the salty sweet breath of the water on his face.

Life's too short to be anywhere but by the sea.

He *had* said that as a little boy! He could remember it so clearly now. He was trying to convince his mum to take him out of school for the day, so that they could run away to the beach together after his dad had left. It was the only place that made him happy, that brought him peace. The only place he ever wanted to be.

Jacob looked around him. The cafe was suddenly too dark and too tightly packed. The pollution of the city air clogged his lungs with each forced breath he tried to take. What was he doing staying here? Wasn't his whole reason for leaving home to live a life he wanted? A life of freedom?

An irrational urge to run took over his body. He went to stand; the motion was so abrupt that out of his pocket fell his notebook and dice. Their presence was a sobering reminder of why he did what he did. Why he gave himself up to the mercy of fate.

He felt his body tense under the pressure, his entire being wrestling with itself as to which step to take next. He scooped up his belongings and slammed them down hard on the desk. Maybe he should ask his friend the Universe what she thought of all this. Wasn't it her that had brought Olivia into his life in the first place, thrusting her into his path not once, but twice? If she didn't want him to feel these things, if she didn't want him to find connection, why the hell did she insist on bringing it to him?

He snatched up the dice and squeezed them tightly in his hand.

Two shakes and a roll. Show me, Universe, do I stay or do I go?

He threw the dice hard, scattering them across the desk. One flew out of sight, the other coming to a stop in front of him.

A five.

'A five and a what, though . . .' he hissed, peering down at the floor in search of the missing die. He tried not to think about what his hands were touching as he fumbled around, reaching into the corners and along the back walls. There was hair, empty sweet wrappers and some very hard and very used chewing gum, but no die.

Jacob stood up and pulled the bulky computer away from the wall. The die had to be somewhere. He *needed* it to be somewhere. Reams of wires tangled in on themselves like knotted veins, gathering dust and debris. He prised them apart like pieces of spaghetti, trying hard to ignore the dirty looks from the woman next to him as he worked.

'Excuse me,' she finally interrupted, 'but may I ask what the hell you're doing?'

'I'm looking for my dice,' he replied, not bothering to look up from his excavation project.

'Well, it's right there.'

His head snapped up so quickly he felt his neck crack from the force. The haughty-looking lady was pointing at the desk behind them. Jacob launched himself to the floor. There it was: the second die. Nestled in the corner, stuck on its side. Halfway between two numbers.

A three and a six.

An odd and an even.

A burst of laughter erupted from him.

The answer to his question was suddenly extremely clear.

This time, it was his turn to decide.

Olivia

It took a full week of morning yoga for Olivia to finally remain awake during Savasana. The odd tear was still shed here and there, but overall, she felt incredible. She had energy now, and not the frenetic caffeine high that she had spent so long believing was normal. From the moment she woke up until the second she laid her head on the pillow at night, she felt invigorated. However, it wasn't just a physical transformation. The niggling, gnawing, continuous angst that had made itself at home in the back of Olivia's heart had eased somewhat. Tracey had been right: yoga really was healing stuff.

And so, life had settled into a steady and comfortable routine. Yoga in the morning, breakfast or a coffee with Cece afterwards, followed by sunbathing, reading and, of course, the odd excursion to a church. Yoga may be powerful, but it couldn't erase thirty years of incessant organization and activity overnight. At the end of the day, she was still Olivia Jackson, and a few downward dogs and cleansing breaths weren't going to change that.

Not entirely, anyway.

She checked the time and felt her stomach plummet.

'Shit.' She jumped out of bed. 'Cece is going to *kill* me.'

Grabbing her T-shirt from the previous day and shoving it over her head, Olivia slipped on her sandals and made a dash for the studio. Thankfully it was close by, and nobody cared what anyone looked like, because a fleeting glance in the mirror before she left told her that her hair needed a brush, and her clothes needed a wash. However, she was praying that Cece still lived by her mantra 'it's not about what it looks like, it's about what it feels like'.

As she approached the little shack, she could see her friend waiting for her on the steps.

'Sorry! I am so sorry,' she called, stumbling across the warming sand.

'That's OK' – Cece waved her in – 'I thought you might have overslept.'

'No, I had plenty of time and then suddenly, I didn't!' She kicked off her shoes and ran inside. 'I don't know what happened.'

'What happened was, you finally adjusted to Goa time.' Cece laughed, closing the drapes behind them and following Olivia into the space.

The class was quite full, with only two spare mats available. Olivia knew Cece would make a comment if she didn't choose the one in the front, so she picked her way across the platform, smiling and whispering hurried hellos to familiar faces.

'Good. Now that everybody is here' – Cece smirked – 'I think we're ready to begin.'

Olivia took a few deep breaths and tried to calm her

racing heart. Running to yoga probably wasn't the best idea she'd ever had. Beads of sweat gathered along her hairline, as she desperately tried to cool her body temperature. How was it already roasting in here?

As ever, the chorus of thoughts chattered inside her head, and it took Olivia a moment to realize Cece had stopped midway through her routine introduction.

'Hello? Can I help you?' she asked, walking past Olivia to the back of the studio.

On cue, everyone turned their heads, eliciting a synchronized rustle of bodies. Olivia kept her gaze forward; she was having enough trouble willing her armpits to stop gushing water, without any further distraction.

'Hey.' A man's voice drifted through the studio, causing every cell in Olivia's body to contract. 'I didn't mean to interrupt.'

If Olivia's body was hot before, it was now on fire.

'That's OK – are you here for the class?' Cece's voice was quieter now, but Olivia could still pick out every word.

'If that's all right?' the man spoke again, louder now. 'I know I'm a bit late.'

It can't be.

But Olivia knew that sound. A sound that made the hairs on the back of her neck prickle, and the ends of her fingers tingle. A sound that sent a rush of shooting stars flying through her centre. A sound that she never thought she'd hear again.

'That's fine. Come in and take that mat at the back – we were just about to get started.' The padding of Cece's footsteps grew louder. 'What's your name, by the way?'

Olivia didn't dare breathe.

'I'm Jacob.'

At that, she finally caved, whipping her head round to lock eyes with his, liquid liquorice piercing through her.

'Hey,' he mouthed at her.

But she couldn't respond. Her brain had gone into full meltdown, the world pulled like a rug beneath her feet, throwing her off kilter completely. There were now so many thoughts in her head that it was simply white noise.

'So, back to what I was saying . . .' Cece restarted her speech, forcing Olivia to finally tear her eyes away from Jacob and turn back to the front, one thought now breaking through the blur of the others, growing louder and more prominent with every beat of her heart.

He's here.

He's really and truly here.

*

It had been hard to concentrate on anything Cece was saying for the rest of the class, when she knew that Jacob was less than ten metres away from her. There was so much adrenaline coursing through her veins that she was anxious to get out of every pose the second they moved into it. She knew there was no chance in hell she'd be able to relax in Savasana. Even Cece had noticed something was up, coming to check on her repeatedly and asking if she was all right. Olivia did not want to draw even more attention to herself, so she blithely nodded and carried on trying to balance on one leg, feeling Jacob's eyes following her every move. By the time class was over, she was exhausted.

'Thank you, everyone. Please be respectful to those around you still coming back to the space. If you could fold your mats away and tidy your area. I'll hopefully see you again tomorrow morning.'

Olivia, normally the last to leave, was on her feet before Cece had even finished speaking.

'Are you all right? You seemed distracted today.' Cece eyed her as though an answer would reveal itself with a look.

'He's here.' Olivia dropped her voice to a whisper.

'Who's here?'

Murmurs and chatter began to swell as the students came and replaced their mats, acknowledging Cece with thumbs ups and whispered thank yous.

Olivia kept her back to the room.

'Do you remember I told you about that guy I met in Delhi? The one I've been emailing, who got sick – you told me to invite him out here.'

Cece's face practically exploded with glee.

'No *way*! Where? Where is he?' She began to crane her neck in all directions. 'Did you do it? Did you ask him to come and visit?'

'Stop it,' Olivia begged. 'Please!'

'Wait . . . was he the one that came in late? Tall, very tanned, sun-kissed hair with a cute bandana and ridiculously dark, sexy eyes?'

'Yes, that's him.'

'Great, because he's heading straight over here.'

'No!' Olivia jerked her head back. 'I don't know what to do.' She was full-scale panicking now. 'What do I *do*?'

'You take a deep breath and calm down,' Cece muttered out of the corner of her mouth. 'Hey!' She switched instantly back to teacher mode as Jacob placed his neatly rolled mat down on the pile next to them. 'How did you find class?'

'Really good.' He ran his hand through his already

mussed-up hair. 'Although I'm sorry for being late, not a great first start.'

'That's all right.' Cece's smile could not have got any bigger if she tried. It was practically hanging from each ear-lobe. Olivia remained silent, her social ability reduced to nothing.

'Hi, Olivia.'

She felt him shift towards her, but Olivia remained where she was. It was odd; she'd played out this moment a hundred times in her head and it was always accompanied by an overwhelming sense of joy and excitement. Yet, as she stood here, the reality felt quite different.

'Hi,' she uttered, a little coldly.

'How are you doing?'

'Good. And you?' The formality was jarring; even Cece looked uncomfortable.

'Starving! Who knew yoga could make you so hungry?'

Olivia didn't reply, instead remaining tight-lipped and tense. The air between the three of them seemed to crackle under the strain.

'I was wondering if you wanted to get a chai or maybe some food?' Jacob continued, his timid tone eliciting a strong feeling of guilt. Olivia knew she was acting unfairly, but what did he expect? A celebration after ghosting her for weeks? Not likely.

'I'm actually going for breakfast with Cece.'

'Oh God,' Cece cried, slapping her hand to her forehead melodramatically. 'I totally forgot to tell you. I can't get food today; I have a clash.'

'What?' Olivia snapped.

'Yeah, I've got a new client . . . a private client.'

'Really? Who?'

'It's a friend . . . you wouldn't know them.'

The lie was so blatant that it was almost painful to listen to, and whilst Olivia knew Cece had the best intentions for her, the betrayal still hurt. What the hell was she supposed to do now?

'So, it looks like you're free, then?' Jacob piped up, forcing Olivia to turn at last and face him fully. The sight of him was even better than she'd imagined.

'Yes.' She stiffened. 'It looks like I am.'

'Awesome! You lead the way; I don't know anywhere around here.'

'Fine.' She shot Cece a final look of disappointment, which was returned with an infuriatingly exaggerated smile and a wink, before making her way out of the studio.

Was this real? Was this truly happening? The thoughts pounded her brain with every step she took. How could he be so casual? Appear out of thin air with no warning, no heads-up, nothing, and pretend this wasn't a big deal?

The moment they stepped outside, she found she couldn't hold back.

'Jacob.'

'Yes, Olivia?'

'Why didn't you tell me you were coming? You've been off with me for weeks and then you just decide to show up?'

He opened his mouth to speak but quickly closed it again. Butterflies stirred in her stomach.

Say it.

Say you came for me.

He reached into his pockets and pulled out the two wooden dice.

'I'm here because of these.' He shook them at her. 'You know that.'

'Right.' Olivia felt the butterflies die instantly. 'Of course.'

'But' – he took a step closer – 'I didn't tell you because I wanted to surprise you! I thought it might be a nice leaving present for your final days.'

Some of the butterflies sprang alive from the ashes, but Olivia still felt confused. Something felt off about the whole situation, but she couldn't pinpoint exactly why.

'How did you know where I was?'

'You told me you were doing yoga on Agonda Beach every morning; it wasn't hard to track you down.'

'I see.' So he had read her emails: he just didn't think it necessary to respond.

'I knew if I was coming to Goa, I had to make sure to do it in style. And hopefully . . .' He shuffled a little self-consciously, the slightest tinge of pink colouring his cheeks. 'Hopefully it was a good surprise?'

It wasn't often that Jacob appeared so unsure of himself, and the sight made Olivia's steely resolve soften a touch.

'It was certainly a surprise. And one of the better ones I've had.'

'Good.' He straightened up, his confidence fully back in place. 'Because that was my plan.'

'I thought you hated plans.'

'Hate is a very strong word, Miss Jackson. Just because I might not indulge in them often, doesn't mean I'm incapable of making them.'

'Really?'

'Yes. For example, after we've had some breakfast, I was *planning* to see if you wanted to hang out with me for the day?'

More of the butterflies came back to life.

'But you still haven't answered my other question.'

'What other question?'

'Why you've been so quiet lately. I've barely heard from you, and now you just show up here out of the blue.'

Jacob dropped his head and scuffed the sand with his shoe.

'I'm sorry about that.' He kept his head hung low. 'I got sick and it took me longer to recover than I thought, and . . . I don't know . . . maybe . . .'

'Maybe what?' She could feel the answer on the tip of his tongue. She wanted the truth. She deserved the truth.

'I guess a part of me freaked out a little bit.'

'About what?'

'I'm not sure.' He shrugged. 'I suppose I'm not used to speaking to someone so regularly. I told you that I got rid of my phone so I didn't have to be connected to the world outside my very small bubble. At times it felt like I was going against my own rules. And those rules were set for a reason.'

Olivia could see his jaw tighten. His honesty was refreshing; upsetting, but refreshing. And in an odd way, Olivia understood. Didn't she also find it uncomfortable going against the rules she set for herself, the principles she adopted for her life?

'I get it.'

'You do?'

'Yeah, it's annoying when someone comes along and disrupts the plans you'd made for yourself, isn't it?' she teased, noting the relief wash over him.

'Touché, Miss Jackson.' Jacob took a step closer, licking the front of his teeth and sending unnerving levels of adrenaline through Olivia's body. 'Now, will you allow me to make it up to you with breakfast and an afternoon of fun?'

Olivia folded her arms across her chest, resisting the urge to make a host of very inappropriate comments about what an afternoon of fun may consist of.

'I'm very busy.'

'I didn't expect anything less.' He inched towards her. 'But I was hoping you could make an exception for me?'

'I'm not sure – maybe we should consult your trusty dice.'

'Oh, I already have.' He pushed a stray piece of hair from his face. 'They say yes. I even rolled three times to make sure.'

Whether it was the absurdity of the situation or the yoga high setting in, Olivia found she could no longer pretend to fight.

'Fine. I'll hang out with you this afternoon.'

'Yes!'

'But first, before we do any of that, we need to eat.'

'As you wish.' Jacob gave a solemn nod and a short, sharp salute. 'Where shall we dine?'

Olivia began to tread the familiar path around the back of the studio and away from the beach.

'You like pancakes?'

Jacob followed closely behind. 'Are you for real? Obviously I like pancakes.'

'Good, then come with me. I know just the place.'

*

The whole morning had felt like a dream. Even as Jacob sat opposite her, stuffing forkfuls of food into his mouth, breathing, laughing, talking, she'd still had to pinch herself. It didn't feel real. None of it felt real. Not even when Jacob dropped her home and hugged her so tight she felt her ribs push against each other. Not even when he promised to be back in three hours to collect her for an afternoon adventure. It was as though Olivia were existing in a mild state of delirium. So much so that, when she woke from her nap, she was certain she'd made the whole thing up, only to realize that she had about ten minutes until Jacob arrived. Ten minutes to get ready for something she had no idea how to prepare for. In true Jacob style, he had kept his cards close to his chest, waving off her questions with vagueness and changes in conversation. Olivia had been too full of sugar and too giddy at the time to push it, but now, as she sat cluelessly trying to plan what she needed, she felt frustrated with herself.

After much deliberation, she decided to adopt a rudimentary and rather unsophisticated approach; if in doubt, pack everything. She now had six minutes remaining, and she wanted to at least run a comb through her hair before he turned up.

'Towel, yes ... bikini, yes ... sun cream, 100 per cent yes ...' She flung items on top of each other, trying not to dwell on the idea of Jacob seeing her in a bikini, the thought alone igniting equal parts excitement and nausea inside her.

'OK, right ... snacks.' She grabbed a few granola bars and an unopened packet of Oreos. 'Change of clothes, sunglasses, book, portable phone charger ...'

Olivia scanned the room and found her eyes settling on a small green plastic box on the dresser.

She opened the lid and peered inside. Bandages, antiseptic wipes and pain relief were all packed neatly in their little compartments alongside safety pins, scissors and some plastic gloves. Growing up, it had become second nature to bring medical supplies on any venture outside the house; with Leah around, you couldn't afford to take chances. Except – the thought was sharp and piercing – she wasn't with Leah any more. And she never would be.

Olivia swallowed down the ball of grief that had formed in her throat, hastily grabbing some plasters and paracetamol from the box and shoving them into her rucksack. She was about to run to the bathroom and attempt to perform some sort of miracle work on her face, when a shrill laugh and a deafening rumble stopped her in her tracks.

She ran over to the door and pulled the curtain aside.

'What the hell . . .'

The two women, Patricia and Tania, who Olivia had only ever seen horizontal in their deckchairs outside their little cabin, were now very much upright standing on their porch, clapping and cheering.

'You got room on that bike for me, sweetheart?' the taller of the two rasped, twiddling a piece of frazzled blonde hair through her fingers.

'I bet you could show me what a good ride looks like, couldn't you?' the other barked gleefully.

Olivia followed the direction of their gaze and felt her stomach drop to the floor.

'Oh God, no!' she squealed.

There was Jacob, grinning from ear to ear, sitting astride one very large and very loud motorbike.

'This has to be a *joke*?' she screeched, opening the door and storming over to him.

'Hello to you too.'

'You can't be serious, Jacob.'

'Why not?'

'*Because* . . . look at that thing!' Olivia pointed at the

growling hunk of metal and fumes. 'There is no way I am getting on that motorbike.'

'If you won't, darling, then I will!' The short, barrel-shaped woman chuckled. 'You don't know how lucky you are, pet! Not every day you get the chance to have something like *that* between your legs.'

The pair of women collapsed into raucous laughter.

'*Technically* it's not a motorbike,' Jacob remarked, 'it's a moped. Smaller, and far less dangerous.'

'It looks just as lethal and terrifying to me.'

'I promise I'll drive slowly.' Jacob held out a helmet for her to take.

'No.'

'Come *on*,' he whined, 'it's the only way we can get to where we're going. Unless you want to walk for five hours?'

'Obviously I don't want to do that.'

'Well then' – he gestured to the bike – 'I promise it will be worth it.'

Olivia stared at Jacob. The glint in his eye and the grin on his face were doing nothing to help her defences, but she remained standing, feet planted wide, hands on her hips. There was no way in hell she was getting on that bike.

'Come *on*, Olivia,' Jacob urged, throwing his hands to the sky. 'Be reckless! Be bold! Be *brave*!'

Leah's words hit her square in the chest.

Go. Travel. Explore. Enjoy this thing called life!

What would her sister say if she could see her now? Rejecting the offer to ride off with a gorgeous man to a mysterious location in a foreign land? It was the stuff of any young girl's dreams, and Olivia knew that, if Leah were here right now, she would already be on that bike and halfway down the road.

'*Fine*,' Olivia caved, 'but there are rules.'

'Go on . . .'

She hardened her stare, which was extremely difficult when Jacob was looking at her so intently. 'If I ask you to stop, then you have to stop. If you try to be clever and go too fast, I'll get off and come home. Do you understand?'

Jacob held his hands up in front of him. 'Completely. Your wish is my command.'

'Good. Now let me get my stuff and we can go.'

Olivia turned her nose to the sky and stomped back into her hut, her heart racing and her palms sweating. Was she really going to do this? Ride on the back of a motorbike with a stranger?

It's technically a moped and he's not a stranger.

She cursed her own thoughts, hauled her bag over her shoulder, and made her way back outside.

'Christ, how much stuff are you taking?' Jacob baulked as she dumped the bag on the back of the bike. 'It's an afternoon trip, not a week away.'

'Don't look at me like that. I had to prepare for all eventualities, didn't I? I have no idea where we're going, remember!' She tentatively seated herself on the bike, her feet barely touching the ground.

'True, but trust me, the surprise will be worth it.' He passed her a helmet. 'Here, put this on and hold on to me tightly.'

Olivia did as she was told, looping her arms around Jacob's waist, feeling the warmth of his skin seep into hers.

'Now, sometimes I'm going to ask you to lean in the opposite direction than the one you're going to want to, but just trust me and follow my lead, OK?'

'I'm not very good at trusting people.' She adjusted herself, her legs already suctioning themselves to the leather.

'Well, this will be a great lesson, won't it?' Jacob shoved his helmet on and turned the key in the ignition. The bike roared into life and Olivia felt the engine vibrate through her entire body. 'Are you ready?' he shouted over the noise.

'Kind of . . .' She squeezed him tighter and closed her eyes.

'Let's do it then!' he yelled, turning the bike around and speeding off down the path towards the ocean.

Olivia

'Stop!' Olivia screamed, her hair lashing her cheeks as it whipped around in the wind. 'Jacob, I feel sick, we need to stop.'

'Again? But we're so close.'

'You said that ten minutes ago.' Olivia's stomach heaved as they rounded yet another corner. She knew Jacob was getting frustrated with her. They'd already stopped six times and the first three were within five minutes of them leaving, but it wasn't her fault she was a nervous passenger.

'Honestly, it's just up there.' He pointed in the distance.

'BOTH hands on the handlebars, please!'

'Sorry, my bad.' He turned and flashed her an apologetic grin.

'And keep your eyes ON the road.'

She dropped her head and rested the top of the helmet against his back, trying her best to follow the movement of Jacob's body as it leant left and right.

'Look!' Jacob shouted excitedly. 'You can see it now.'

With caution, Olivia lifted her head. Where moments ago

there had been a wall of dense vegetation, there now lay a glistening stretch of ocean, as though it had simply dropped from the sky and appeared before them. She had to admit it was spectacular.

'See, didn't I tell you it was a good surprise?' Jacob chuckled, steering the bike down a rocky dirt track. The smell of salt and the sound of waves hit them as they slowed to a halt, parking at the edge of a deserted enclave of golden sand.

'Cool, huh?' Jacob took off his helmet and admired the view.

'It's *amazing*.' Olivia felt the anxiety drain from her immediately. 'How did you even find this place?'

'What can I say? I got talking to some locals, asked for some recommendations, said I had a *very* important person to impress, and . . . voila.' He gestured to the secluded beach. 'Here we are.'

'Yeah.' She smiled shyly. 'Here we are.'

Olivia took a moment to absorb the view, before rifling in her bag for her phone. She knew that Kate would want to hear about every single detail of the trip – therefore making photographic evidence mandatory – but also, Olivia had a sneaking suspicion that this would be a day she'd want to look back on.

'You ready?' Jacob asked.

'I'm just trying to find my phone.' She dug deeper into the depths of her rucksack. 'But I can't see . . . one second.'

'I'm not surprised – even Mary Poppins would struggle with that thing.'

'It's not funny, Jacob, I need my phone.' Her searching grew increasingly frantic as her anxiety spiked. 'I would never have left without it.'

'Maybe you left it on charge and forgot,' he offered casually, her mild hysteria having no effect whatsoever on his mood. 'I used to do it all the time.'

'*Shit.*' Through the thick fog of panic came a vision. Olivia plugging her phone in to charge. A last-minute decision to attempt to get as much battery as possible. To be as prepared as possible. And then what? How had it slipped her mind?

The bike.

Jacob and his ridiculous bike appeared.

She swallowed the angry accusation building in her throat, knowing deep down she couldn't blame him for her mistake.

'How could I have been so stupid?'

'Hey.' Jacob bent down next to her as she began to repack her bag. 'It's going to be fine. We have everything we need right here.'

'But what if there's a problem?'

'There won't be.'

Olivia looked up into Jacob's calm face and felt her worry ease a little.

'There'd better not be.'

'I promise you. We're in paradise, remember? Nothing goes wrong in paradise.' Jacob stood up and flung his arms out ahead of him. 'Now, shall we go and enjoy the delights of having a beach to ourselves?'

'Fine,' she conceded, 'if we have to.'

The cove was completely empty, except for a few stray dogs seeking refuge in the slivers of shade, and so the pair settled themselves right in the very centre. Olivia could feel the sand scorching her through the denim of her shorts. Sweat began to bead across her forehead as the sun bore down on them.

'Tell me you have a bikini packed in this freaking suitcase of yours?' Jacob nudged Olivia's bag with his toe. 'And some sun cream. Even I think I'm at risk of frying today.'

'Who do you think I am?' She fished out a bottle of factor fifty and handed it to Jacob. 'Some kind of novice?'

'Nope, you're a lifesaver.' He whipped off his T-shirt and turned himself away from her. 'Will you do my back?'

A pang of longing struck her hard at the sight of his mahogany skin.

'Sure.' She took the bottle and began to spray the cream liberally, trying not to laugh as he squirmed.

'God, that's cold.'

'Sit still, or it will be patchy!'

Olivia ran her hands up and down the length of him, the muscles in his back firm beneath her touch, the tugging in her stomach growing sharper and more intense.

'There we go. All done.'

He craned his neck over his shoulder. 'Promise me you haven't drawn something rude in the cream so I'll wake up with a beautifully artistic burn on my back?'

'Really?'

'What! It's good to check.'

'Not everyone is as immature as you, Jacob. The thought of doing that wouldn't even have crossed my mind.'

'You never know – you're already quite different from the Olivia I met in Delhi.'

'Am I?'

'Definitely.' He looked her up and down, her skin tingling wherever his eyes touched. 'You seem, I don't know . . .' He dropped his head to the side. 'You just look different.'

Olivia held out her freckled arms. 'Less ghostly white?'

'Maybe, although still at risk of becoming a lobster if you don't cream up.' He reached out his hand. 'Shall I do your back?'

The thought of Jacob's hands on her body made her want to scream in ecstasy and die from embarrassment all at once.

'Yes, but I need to change into my swimsuit first.'

'Good point.'

'Do you ... erm ... do you mind maybe ...?' She gestured in the opposite direction to where he was facing.

'Oh! Of course. I'll look over here.'

'Thanks.'

Jacob dutifully turned away from her, as Olivia awkwardly removed her clothes and tried to put on her bikini as quickly as possible. Why had she not done this at home? Everybody knew it was impossible to change into a swimming costume without accidentally flashing a boob or worse ...

'You OK back there?'

'Uh-huh,' she replied, squirming her way into her bikini bottoms, hoisting them up along with a bucketload of sand. 'Although I have to say, that seemed much easier when I was thirteen.'

'Isn't everything?'

'Maybe ...' Olivia's thoughts drifted to her younger self at her thirteenth birthday party, her sister so sick she was in the hospital with both her parents, her grandma trying her best to pretend nothing was wrong.

'Is it safe for me to look?' Jacob's question cut short her trip down memory lane.

'Oh, right.' She brushed the sand from her legs. 'Yes, I'm done.'

He shifted to face her, taking the cream from her lap and

holding it proudly aloft. 'Turn around then, and let me do your back.'

'I swear, if I feel even a hint of you drawing something . . .'

'Come *on*. Do you think I'm stupid enough to mess with you? My life wouldn't be worth living.'

Olivia was glad that Jacob couldn't see the little smile that had appeared on her face.

'Now, it's going to be a bit cold . . .'

'Jesus!' she yelped, as his hands made contact with her skin.

'I told you.' He carried on, sweeping the cream up and down her shoulders. 'Cute freckles, by the way.'

She peered over at the sprinkling of spots that were dusted over her skin. 'Thanks. My brother always used to tease me about them, said they were dirt marks.'

'How charming of him.'

'That's Kyle for you.' She shuddered as Jacob's fingers tickled the sides of her. 'When we were young, he convinced my sister that they meant I had an incurable disease and was going to die. Which wasn't very funny at all, considering . . .'

Jacob's hands stopped still. 'Considering?'

Shit.

'What?'

'You said "considering" . . . I was asking what you meant?'

'Well.' She sat up, angling herself to face the sea in front of them. 'Considering she was like five years old! She didn't know it was a joke, you know? She got upset, and it took ages for my parents to convince her I was fine.' Olivia's voice was growing louder and more forceful as she continued with the lie.

'Sounds like your brother is a bit of a joker.'

'You can say that again.' Olivia felt Jacob's hands slow their movement.

'There we are, madam, you are well and truly sun-creamed. The penis on your back should be burnt on in around an hour or so, but I'll check back in and see how it's cooking in a few minutes.'

'Jacob!' She slapped him hard on the arm. 'Don't you get tired of being such an arse all the time?'

'Surprisingly . . .' He flipped on to his stomach and lay down next to her. 'No.'

'I didn't think so.' Olivia raked her fingers through the warm sand. 'Although there will be times in life when you're going to have to.'

'Like?'

'I don't know. When you're at work. When you're buying a house. When you've got kids who depend on you.'

'Yeah, but that's for adults.'

'Right, and you don't count yourself as one of those, then?'

'Nope! I'm Peter Pan. Travelling this earth and having adventures until the end of my days.'

'That's your grand life plan?'

'It is indeed. Why? Do you have a problem with my plan?'

Where should she start?

'I mean' – she was trying to be as tactful as possible – 'it's all well and good now, but what happens when you get to eighty and you aren't able to hop around from place to place so easily?'

'And why do you care what I'll be doing at eighty?' He lowered his sunglasses and smirked.

'I don't care about *you* specifically. I'm just curious as to the logistics.'

'Oh.' He nodded smugly. 'I see, the logistics.'

Olivia turned away and stared ahead at the ocean.

'Why? What's your big plan?' He nudged her gently.

'In life or work?'

'Aren't they one and the same?'

'Not really. Not to me.'

'OK then.' Jacob turned on to his side. 'Give me your high-level plan for the next ten years.'

'You really want to know?'

'I wouldn't ask if I didn't.'

Olivia closed her eyes and brought to mind the handwritten plan she kept stuck to her mirror in her bedroom. It was something for her to look at every day. A constant reminder of the direction she was heading, and the hurdles she had to conquer.

'Well, in the next three years I want to get promoted to be a director at work. Then I want to stay for a year before leaving to set up my own business. After that's turning a profit, ideally within two years, I'll get married and have my first child, followed swiftly by my second and third.'

Jacob let out a long, slow whistle. 'Jeez.'

'You asked!'

'I know, and it's my foolish mistake for underestimating your organizational powers,' he replied kindly, softening Olivia's defensive edges. 'And I know you've thought these things through very, *very* carefully, but I have a question . . .'

Olivia prickled once again. 'What?'

'Where's the fun?'

'Oi!' She kicked him hard this time, causing sand to fly in every direction.

'I'm serious. What about seeing the world? Or following a passion? Writing a book maybe? Don't you want to do any of those things?'

'My work is my fun; I've told you that.'

'And yet you seem to have managed very well without it for the past couple of months.'

'Only because I've had to.'

'You know what I think we need to do?' He started to draw a rectangular box in the sand. 'I think we need to make you a living list.'

'A what?'

'A list of things to do that make you feel alive, that *aren't* work related.'

'If you want to do that, you go ahead, but you're wasting your time.' She folded her arms and turned her attention back to the horizon.

'Number one,' Jacob mused. 'Go to at least one new country a year.'

'Not going to happen.'

'Number two . . . climb a mountain.'

'Absolutely not!'

'Number three—'

'Stop!' Olivia scribbled out the markings he'd made in the sand. 'This is stupid. I'm not a kid – I don't need some fantasy list about becoming an actress or eating chocolate cake every day. You asked for my plan, and I gave it to you.'

'Fair enough.' Jacob sat up, clearly unbothered by Olivia's little tantrum. 'Can I ask a serious question about the plan?'

'If you have to.'

'Why do you have to wait so long to set up your own business? Why don't you do it now?'

'I don't have enough experience yet. I'll need funding and a client base, and right now I'm too young to do it alone.'

'Hmm, those seem like excuses. Not real reasons.'

Olivia tried hard to keep her voice measured.

'No offence, but I think I know my industry a little better than you do.'

'I don't doubt that you do, but sometimes those on the outside have a better perspective than those on the inside.'

'How very profound of you.'

'I'm just offering my opinion.' He flicked a grain of sand in Olivia's direction. 'Do you have a name for your business?'

'No.'

'Come on! You're telling me you haven't already pictured the name, the little slogan that will go at the bottom of all your emails and company stationery?'

'I haven't.' Olivia saw the mock-up she'd drawn on a Post-it at home, the different fonts she'd played with and the logos she'd sketched. 'I have other, more important things to do than play pretend. When the time is right and I need the name, then I'll think of it.'

'How about . . .' He scrunched up his face in thought. 'Wait, what do you do again?'

'I'm a business consultant.'

'OK, I'll ask the question again.' He laughed. 'What do you actually *do*?'

'I help companies become more efficient and improve their output. Ideally by motivating the existing workforce and inspiring people to do better.'

And not firing people as though they mean nothing.

'OK, I've got it,' he announced proudly. 'Jackson Green Consulting. Putting people first . . . *always*.'

'No.'

'Why not?'

'Because—'

'OK, how about Jackson Green Consulting,' he cut her off. 'Making people our priority.'

288

'It wasn't the tag line I had a problem with. It was the fact your name was featuring in my company.'

'Yes, because *obviously* I will be your ideas man.'

'You're finally going to hang up your nomadic lifestyle and come join us mortals in the real world?'

Jacob shot her a look of disgust. 'Not a chance! Haven't you heard of remote working? I can just email you.'

'Oh yes, because you always reply so quickly and efficiently.' Her comment made him wince. 'I need my ideas guy in the office at my beck and call.'

'Aha! Here she is. The corporate, ball-busting, bad-ass boss. I knew she was hiding in there somewhere.' He poked her ribs gently.

'Hey, I'm not a ball-buster. I'm just strong-minded. There's a difference, you know.'

'I see. Let me guess, you were a red personality type in all those leadership tests they made you do?'

'I was a mix of red and yellow, actually.' Olivia narrowed her eyes. 'And how do you know about those personality tests?'

'I did have a job once, you know.'

'Oh yes, the corporate Jacob that nobody knows about. I wonder what he was like,' she teased playfully.

'He was just as handsome.' Jacob winked. 'But apart from that, completely different.'

'Tell me more.'

'Why?'

'Because I'm curious. You know so much about me and I know hardly anything about you.'

'You know loads about me.'

'Not really. I know you grew up in Surrey, and that's about it.'

'And that's probably the most exciting part.'

'Hey, stop deflecting.'

'Look, I don't like to talk about my life back home.' His voice dropped. It wasn't harsh or angry, but the tone had changed. There was a firmness to it, a steeliness that wasn't there before. 'It's so long ago that it doesn't even feel like it belongs to me any more. I'm not the same person I was, so to me, it's irrelevant.'

Olivia's brain was overrun with questions, but she knew that asking them would push Jacob further than he was willing to go.

'And in all honesty,' he continued, drawing patterns in the sand with his toes, 'there's nothing much to say. I'm an only child, my mum and dad are divorced. I don't speak to my dad. My mum and I stay in basic contact. I was bored of living the same old life that everyone else did, so I left and never looked back.'

'I see.' She sat up, brushing the sand from her arms. A few moments of silence passed before Jacob lifted his head and smiled. A simple gesture, but one that eased the building tension instantly.

'Anyway, how are you feeling about coming to the end of your trip? I bet you're looking forward to seeing your family again, right? Are you close to them?'

'Erm . . .'

Don't go back to me, don't go back to me.

'Kind of. My brother and I have a strange relationship. We don't see or speak to each other a lot, but we're still close.'

'And your sister?'

Olivia's heart contracted.

'Yeah . . . she's . . .' The words were rushing up her throat. 'She's . . .'

Tears pricked her eyes and her chest ached with the weight of the grief. She had allowed it too much freedom lately, and now it believed it could come out whenever it pleased. But not with him. She couldn't let it, with him.

'Olivia?' Jacob moved closer to her.

'My sister . . .' She faltered, her voice so small it was barely audible over the crashing waves. 'My sister's . . . well, she's . . .' Olivia took a deep breath and closed her eyes. 'She's dead.'

The words landed like bullets on the ground between them.

'Shit, Olivia. I didn't realize. I'm so sorry.'

'It's OK.' She smiled through the stream of tears that were flowing freely down her face. Olivia lifted her chin to the sky and felt the sea air chill the salty tracks on her skin. 'She passed away a few months ago but she'd been sick for years. She got diagnosed with cancer when she was four.'

'She was a fighter, then?'

'Just a bit! If there was one thing Leah loved, it was living.'

'That's why she bought you this trip?'

He remembered.

'Yeah, she bought me a ticket as a farewell gift, wrote me this beautiful letter about how she wanted me to go and explore, and live my life . . .'

Olivia lowered her face and looked at Jacob. The cheeky bravado that seemed to permanently cloak him had softened to a gentle sweetness.

'Wow. That's special.'

'I mean, let's be honest, it had to take something special to get me to come and travel round India.' She dug her toe deep into the baking sand. 'I'm not sure if you've noticed, but it's not exactly my natural habitat.'

Jacob lifted up her gigantic bag. 'I have no idea what you mean!'

The pair burst out laughing.

'I could never say no to Leah. Nobody could.'

'It sounds like she was an amazing person.'

'She was.' Olivia raised her eyes to the ocean. 'God, she would have loved this.'

'What do you think she would be doing right now if she was here with us?'

Olivia didn't have to think twice. The moment she'd seen the water she'd thought of Leah, running straight towards it and diving in.

'She would have been in there, headfirst.'

'The ocean?'

'Uh-huh. I swear that girl was part fish.'

Jacob took her hand.

'You want to do it?'

'What? Go in there?' She nodded at the swirling mass of blue.

He squeezed her tighter and grinned. 'Exactly!'

Olivia closed her eyes and brought her sister's face to mind. A face that hadn't been ravaged by the drugs and the slow eating away of her body. A face that had years to live, a face that had a future, a world to inhabit and dreams to fulfil.

'Fuck it.' She snapped open her eyes and stood suddenly. 'Let's do it!'

'Hell yes.' Jacob jumped up and pulled Olivia towards the ocean. The pair ran so fast, mouths wide open, screaming at the top of their lungs as the cold water lapped at their feet.

'It's *freezing*,' she screeched, as the salty waves broke against her thighs.

'You can't think about it. You just have to jump in.'

Jacob let go of her hand and dived into the water, emerging moments later like a baby seal, his hair and skin shining wet. 'Trust me! Just go for it.'

Olivia clenched her fists and tightened her jaw.

One . . .

'The longer you stand there, the colder you're going to get.'

Two . . .

'Come on, Olivia! You can do this.'

Thr—

With a deafening scream, she lowered herself under the water. Her entire body went rigid as the cold engulfed her, the strength of the current sweeping her feet from the sand and tossing her upside down like a piece of paper on the wind.

'Oh my god!' she cried, finally breaking through the surface.

'Are you OK?' Jacob swam closer to her. His face was speckled with drops of the ocean, glittering in the sun.

There was water up her nose and in her ears, the salt stung her eyes, and her hair was splayed all over her face, yet Olivia couldn't do anything but smile.

'I'm great.' She beamed, flinging her arms up in the air. 'In fact, I've never felt better!'

Olivia

It was gone seven by the time they decided to admit defeat and head for home. Olivia had insisted she was fine to stay longer, but when her teeth started chattering and her body shivering, Jacob demanded that they leave.

'Hey!' she called, trying to keep her head low and out of the biting wind. 'How much further is it?' It felt as though they'd been driving for hours, the darkness an impenetrable tunnel that swallowed up everything beyond the road two feet ahead of them.

The bike veered slightly to the left.

'*Jacob.*' She leant in closer. 'I'm freezing back here. Do you know how far we've got to go?'

'Notlongbetheresoon,' came the jumbled response.

'You said that last time!' She squeezed him hard in frustration.

The bike jerked violently to the right, sending a jolt of fear up her spine.

'OK, I'm sorry,' she joked. 'I get grumpy when I'm cold.'

The bike continued to veer to the right, pulling them to the centre of the road.

'Jacob, that's not funny.'

Olivia tightened her grip around his waist as the handlebars spun off to the left erratically.

'*Jacob.*'

But there was no response. The bike was now drifting dangerously close to the edge of the road.

In fact, it was heading dangerously close to a very large and very solid tree.

'Jacob, stop it now!'

Why isn't he saying anything?

Olivia started to shake him hard, his body growing oddly limp in her hands and his head rolling back.

Oh my god, he's unconscious.

'HELP!' she screamed, the wind snatching the words from her lips and carrying them off in its grasp. Olivia reached her hands forward and on to the handlebars; she could just about get her fingertips to touch it. How the hell was she supposed to steer this thing from back here? Adrenaline surged through her as her grip tightened on the bars.

'JACOB,' she tried one last time, attempting to use her body to shake him awake, whilst simultaneously steadying the bike.

His head lolled forward and then, as though someone had flicked on a switch, he came back to life.

'Holy shit.' He slammed hard on the brakes, twisting the bike away from the tree they were veering directly towards. They hit the trunk sideways on with a sickening crash.

Olivia screamed, half falling, half jumping off the bike.

'Oh my god.' Jacob took off his helmet and looked around,

eyes wide and face full of terror. 'Are you all right? What the hell happened?'

'You tell me!' she roared, fear and anger searing through her. 'You were the one driving the bloody thing.'

'I . . . I don't understand.' He climbed off the bike and ran his hands through his damp curls. 'One minute you were talking to me and the next we were heading straight for the tree.' He staggered back.

'Woah, hold on.' Olivia ran to his side and took the weight of his body on to hers. 'Sit down for a second, will you, I think you lost consciousness.'

Jacob lowered himself to the ground and rested his head in his hands.

'I don't know,' he murmured over and over, 'I just don't know what happened.'

'You must have had some warning sign! You didn't feel faint or anything?' She tried to place a hand on his forehead, but Jacob shook her off. 'How do you feel now?'

'I'm fine. I felt fine, and I feel fine now.' He lifted his head up suddenly. 'Are you hurt?'

Olivia checked herself over; there were no cuts or bruises, only a deep sense of anxiety brewing in the pit of her stomach. 'I'm OK, but we need to find a way to get you home and to a doctor.'

'I'll drive us, I just need a minute.'

'No, you won't.'

'I'm *fine*,' he growled. 'It's probably dehydration; too much sun and not enough water.'

She couldn't help but remember the same reason he'd attributed to her little incident in the market back in Delhi.

'I'm sorry, but you are not driving us back.' She passed him her bottle of water. 'Not in this state.'

296

'Well, what do you suggest?'

She looked around for a moment, as if the answer would spontaneously erupt from the dusty ground and the mounds of frazzled vegetation. 'We'll call a taxi.'

'With what? I don't have a phone and you left yours at home.'

Dread seeped through her skin.

'Argh!' She kicked the floor hard. 'This is ridiculous. We can't sit here all night. You need to go and see a doctor.'

'No.' Jacob's voice was cutting. 'I'm not seeing a doctor. I told you, I'm *fine*.'

'Oh yes!' Olivia threw her hands up in the air. 'Because every fit and healthy person simply loses consciousness whilst riding a motorbike, don't they?'

'It's a moped.'

'I don't care what it fucking *is*, Jacob. All I care about right now is getting us home.' She stood and began pacing up and down, trying to search for a solution amongst the tangled mess of her thoughts. 'Maybe someone will drive past and help us.'

'Uh-huh, because how many cars did we pass on our way here?'

One.

'Could have been a quiet time of day.'

'And how many have we passed on our way back so far?'

None.

'Well, what the *hell* are we going to do, Jacob? What do you suggest? We sit here by the side of the road in the middle of fucking *nowhere* and slowly dehydrate or get ravaged by wild animals?'

'The way I see it, we only have one option.'

'And that is . . .?'

'You drive us home.'

Olivia's jaw dropped.

'You are joking, aren't you?'

'No. What other choice do we have? You won't let me ride the bike, so . . . who else can?'

'Erm, not *me*.' She laughed. 'I've never driven a motorbike. In fact, I haven't ridden a normal bike since I was about thirteen.'

'Olivia.' He rubbed his forehead. 'How many times do I have to tell you, it's not a motorbike.'

'And how many times do I have to tell *you*, I don't *care* what it is. I'm. Not. Driving. It.'

'Fine, let's sit here in the dark and pray that someone comes past and saves us before some wild animal appears and decides it fancies us for dinner. We could play I spy to pass the time. I'll go first, shall I?'

Olivia whipped her head round so fast her neck spasmed in pain.

'You think this is funny?'

'No, of course not.'

'Good, because if it wasn't for you and your stupid spontaneous trip and your irresponsible ideas about living life without any communication with the real world, then we wouldn't be in this mess.' The words spilled out of her, taking their aim directly at Jacob's chest. She saw him flinch a little at their assault. 'If you had just been a bit more *sensible* for once in your life, then maybe we wouldn't be in this mess.'

Jacob's face crumpled and his head fell into his hands.

'I'm sorry.' He peered up at Olivia with a look that made her heart ache. 'I didn't mean for this to happen.'

The sight of him sitting in the dust, head hung low and shoulders slumped, was too much to bear. She needed to take control of the situation and, as much as she was loath to admit it, it did seem like they had only one viable option left . . .

'You'll have to teach me.'

'Huh?'

'How to drive that thing.' She nodded to the bike, which was now lying on its side. 'And I won't be going fast. In fact, I'll be going so slowly that it'll probably be quicker for us to walk back.'

'Really?'

'Yes.'

'Thank you, Olivia.' Relief visibly washed over him. 'I promise I'll be with you every step of the way.'

'Good. Now, hurry up before I change my mind.'

*

'You're doing great,' Jacob reassured her, his grip tight around her waist, his body solid against her back. 'Keep the handlebars steady.'

Breathe, Olivia.

Remember to breathe.

She tried to straighten up, but instead sent the bike off to the left.

'Oh my god. I can't do it,' she squeaked.

'Yes, you can.' He spoke calmly in her ear. 'You've got this, Olivia.'

The bike was bumbling along at a steady pace. For the first ten minutes it had been very stop and start, with Olivia spending more time stationary than moving. But to his credit, Jacob had been patient and encouraging, giving her as much time as she needed to get going again. Not that he had much choice; she was their only ticket home.

'Now, we've got a straight bit of road coming up with no twists or turns. It might be the perfect opportunity to try going a bit faster? If you wanted.'

'I'm going quite fast enough, thank you.'

'Your choice; I was only saying.'

'Well, don't.' She straightened up a little, feeling the bike shift under her weight.

'I'm proud of you for doing this.'

'Thank you, but you can save your patronizing praise for when I've delivered us home safely. We're not there quite yet.'

'As you wish.' Jacob chuckled, readjusting his arms so that they wrapped tighter around her. 'What do you think your sister would say if she saw you driving a motorbike then, hey?'

Olivia relaxed her shoulders and tried to calm her mind.

'I think . . .' She smiled, knowing exactly what Leah would have thought. 'I think she'd be impressed. Shocked, but impressed.'

'Me too.'

The pair sat in silence as Olivia drove the bike steadily on, through the dense vegetation and out into the open. The wind was cold in her face, but she was concentrating so hard that she barely felt its bite.

'Woah,' Jacob gasped from behind.

'What? What's going on?'

'The sky,' he marvelled. 'You have to look up at the sky right now.'

'I can't, Jacob, I'm driving.'

'I know you are, but seriously . . .' He gave her a gentle squeeze. 'Trust me.'

Olivia flicked her eyes upward.

'Holy shit!'

It was the clearest night sky she'd ever seen in her life. Thousands of stars poked their silver heads through the blanket of indigo, clustering around one another in intricate, dazzling patterns. It was magical. It was intoxicating. And the more Olivia tried to take it in, the more it seemed to grow, expanding outwards and upwards like a glittering ocean. The tides of the heavens, painted in such spectacular detail that they didn't look real.

'It's amazing.'

'Hell yes, it's amazing!' Jacob whooped in appreciation, releasing his hands from her waist and throwing them up to the sky.

Olivia stole another glance, letting tears of joy stream out of the corners of her eyes. Exhilaration flooded every cell of her body. Was this what it was all about? Was this how it felt to be alive?

'Thank you, Leah,' she whispered, turning up the gas and picking up speed. 'Thank you.'

*

By the time they arrived back at Olivia's hut, every part of her body was frozen, but she couldn't wipe the grin from her face.

'Maybe I need to get me one of these in London.'

'They're fun, right? When you finally decide to go over ten miles per hour.'

Olivia gave Jacob's arm a sharp slap and suddenly noticed how tired he looked.

'How are you going to get home?'

'I'm guessing riding the bike is still not an option?'

Olivia took the keys from the ignition and held them tightly in her hand. 'Nope.'

'Then I guess I'll walk.'

'Are you sure?'

'What other choice do I have?'

Olivia stared into Jacob's weary face. There was another option.

'You can stay with me, if you like.' The words were out of her mouth before her logical brain had a chance to stop them. 'Obviously, I can sleep on the floor.'

'Don't be silly, you don't want me to do that.'

Her cheeks blazed. God, if only he knew just how badly she wanted it.

'I don't necessarily *want* you to, it's just . . .' She started fiddling with the bike keys, shifting her weight back and forth. 'I don't think I'll sleep properly tonight if you're by yourself. What if something happens again?'

'Nothing's going to happen, Olivia, I'm fine.'

'But what if it does?' She took a small step towards him. 'I know it sounds crazy but, after Leah . . . I don't know . . .'

She let her feeble excuse trail off; how foolish and immature she must sound. This was a fully grown man – a capable, independent adult.

'Will you be that worried if I don't?'

'Annoyingly, yes,' she admitted.

'In that case' – he lifted her chin with his finger – 'I'll stay. Only if it makes you feel better.'

'Thank you!'

'On one condition though.' He raised an eyebrow.

'Go on . . .'

Their eyes locked for a fraction too long. Olivia felt the skin on her face tingle from his touch and her face burn a deep scarlet. How the hell was she going to cope sleeping in the same room as this man?

'You promise me you don't snore.'

'As if I would snore!' Olivia welcomed the lightness of his joke and began to walk towards her front door. 'However, I do have earplugs in case you need them.'

'Now, why does that not surprise me. Oh, and let me guess, a full-blown first-aid kit on hand, in case of emergencies?'

Olivia unlocked the door and stepped inside, knowing exactly what Jacob was about to see when she turned on the light.

'Aha!' he cried, pointing at the green plastic box across the room. 'I *knew* it.'

She rolled her eyes and began to tidy away her piles of clothes, deliberately hiding her printed itinerary under a stack of T-shirts. If he thought she was a crazed organization freak from a first-aid kit, seeing that masterpiece would surely seal her fate.

'So . . .' Olivia hovered by the bathroom door, the space suddenly feeling very confined. 'I'm going to get ready for bed. Do you need the bathroom or anything?'

'Nope, all good.' He sat down on the edge of the bed and began to take off his shoes. 'You do you.'

Does he need pyjamas?

Well, he can't sleep naked, can he?

Oh God, do not think about him naked.

Olivia shook the unhelpful thoughts from her head and concentrated fully on cleaning her teeth and washing her face.

Throughout her life, she'd never much cared for the way she looked. Next to Leah she was always 'the plain one' and besides, good looks and fancy make-up didn't make you any more efficient or productive. But seeing herself in the mirror now, Olivia couldn't help but admire the reflection. Her cheeks looked a little scorched from the sun and her freckles seemed to be multiplying by the second, but there was a spark in her eyes and a glow on her face that she'd never seen before.

'You don't happen to have a spare toothbrush, do you?' Jacob's voice called out. 'Miss Prepared For All Eventualities?'

'Sorry.' She dried her face on the towel and walked back to her room. 'Only paracetamol and blister plasters.'

'Damn it.' He stood and walked past her to the sink, plucking the toothpaste from the side and squeezing a line on to his finger. 'I guess I'll have to use my finger, then, won't I?'

'Ew, that's gross.'

'It will be more gross if I don't.' He aggressively rubbed his finger back and forth along the front of his teeth.

'Right. While you're doing that, I'll sort the bedding out.'

Olivia looked around the room for anything that could aid her in her makeshift bed construction. She rolled up her large rucksack to use as a pillow and found a couple of spare blankets in the wardrobe.

'You're not seriously going to sleep on that, are you?' Jacob stood in the doorway, watching her feeble attempts. 'Get into bed, you idiot.'

'No, honestly, I don't mind.' She rolled up a couple of T-shirts for extra padding. 'You need your rest.'

'And so do you. I won't sleep knowing you're down there on the floor like a little dormouse. Come on. Get in.'

She eyed the pathetic heap and then reluctantly clambered into the bed.

'Fine.' She wiggled all the way across to the edge. 'But if it gets too cramped, wake me up and I'll move.'

'I think we'll manage.'

He lifted up the covers and climbed inside. Olivia stiffened her body so that she took up as little room as possible;

even breathing felt like an invasion of his space. Her whole body was rigid and on alert. The perfect conditions for a relaxed night's sleep.

'Are you feeling OK?' she whispered.

'Yes.'

'Are you sure?'

'Olivia.' He turned on to his side to face her. 'Stop asking me that. And please' – he placed a cool hand on her arm – 'relax, will you?'

'Sorry.' She softened a little. 'I think I go into default carer mode whenever someone is sick.'

'I'm not sick.'

'I know, but . . . you know.' She turned ever so slowly to face him. She could feel the warmth from his body through her cotton pyjamas.

'I know,' he whispered back, his eyes wide and lips so close to hers. Too close.

Olivia went to move her face away when she felt his hand on her cheek.

'Please don't.'

'What?'

'Don't do that. Don't look away.'

Every inch of her skin started to tingle, her whole body lighting up like a switchboard.

'Olivia?'

'Yes?'

'Can I . . .' He dropped his gaze momentarily.

Her heart was in her mouth.

'Yes?'

'Can I kiss you?'

Before he'd even finished the sentence, Olivia had pulled him to her, wrapped her arms around him tightly and kissed him. Jacob groaned in response, running his hands through her hair and down along her spine. Her back arched in response, her kisses becoming harder and hungrier.

'Olivia.' He spoke her name into her mouth. 'Oh, Olivia.'

She kept her eyes closed, allowing her other senses to experience him. The feel of his hands tracing every curve of her body. The scent of his skin as it grew hotter and flushed; deep, smoky wood and a rich, warming spice. The cold taste of mint and salt on his lips. Every part of her wanted to feel every single part of him, until there was nothing left to separate them. She deepened her kisses, the longing inside her building to an unbearable level. After all this time, after everything they'd been through, here they were at last.

'Look at you,' he whispered, pulling her on top of him.

'Don't,' she begged shyly, trying to cover her face with her hands.

'Why?' He reached up to meet her. 'You're the most beautiful thing I've ever seen.'

Olivia pushed him back down, unable to take the intensity of his stare.

'Thank you,' she whispered, feeling his hand grip her thighs hard.

'For what?'

'Surprising me here.'

'It's been my pleasure.'

'But not just that,' she continued, babbling away as the intensity of the moment started to overwhelm her. 'Taking me to the beach . . . getting me to go in the sea.'

Why was she talking? Why had she not stopped talking?

'Even the bike was kind of fun in the end – apart from, you know . . .' Her brain was screaming at her to stop, to immediately close her mouth and focus on the kisses Jacob was planting delicately along her jaw line. Tiny, soft, incredibly tender kisses. 'I guess I spend so much time in my head that sometimes I find it hard not to overthink things.'

'Olivia.' He stopped what he was doing immediately.

'Yes?'

She'd ruined it. Her stream of nonsense and nervous chatter had killed the moment.

'Will you do something for me?'

'Sure?' She felt her body close in on itself ever so slightly, preparing itself for rejection. 'Is everything all right?'

In one fluid motion, he switched their positions, pulling her underneath him. The full weight of his body was now pressing into hers, one hand on her lower back, lifting her up to meet him. Instinctively, she wrapped her legs around him and felt an entirely new world of desire open up inside her.

'I want you to promise me,' he whispered into her ear, 'that whatever you do, you won't overthink this.'

'I won't.' She sighed, finally surrendering as his mouth trailed down her chest, his hands clawing at her skin. 'I promise I won't.

'Good. Because for the rest of the night, I don't want you to be thinking at all . . .'

Olivia

Olivia had been staring at him for the past three minutes. At first it was simply to make sure he was real and not a figment of her imagination, then it was to check he was breathing, and now . . . now it was simply because . . .

Her mind flashed back to last night. The way he held her. His eyes never leaving hers as they moved over one another. Wave after wave rising up inside her, filling every inch until she couldn't hold back any longer. Her body ached with the memory of it: the most raw and messy yet perfect night of her life.

Jacob took a deep breath in and turned over. The side of his face fell directly into the stream of honeyed sunshine that bathed the entire room. How beautiful he looked. How peaceful. She couldn't help but steal another glance at his sleeping face.

'If you're checking to see if I'm alive, don't worry.' He began to stir. 'You may have exhausted me last night, but you didn't kill me.'

Olivia, mortified at being caught staring, tried to turn her face away. But it was too late. Before she had the chance, Jacob was wide-eyed and awake, staring right back at her.

'You look so cute when you blush.'

'I'm not blushing.'

'Must be the light then.' He took a finger and stroked her cheek gently. 'Did you sleep OK? I wasn't keeping you awake with my snoring, was I?'

Only for an hour and a half.

'No, you didn't make a sound.'

'That's good. And how many times did you wake up to check I was still breathing?'

'Once . . .' She snuggled down deeper into the covers. 'Or maybe three times.'

'Ha! I knew it.' He smirked, casually throwing his arm across her side. 'Hoping that you wouldn't have to wake up and do the whole awkward, "I'm sorry, Jacob. I had such a nice time last night, but if you ever come near me again, I'll kill you" conversation? I guess it *would* be easier if I was dead.'

'Of course not.' She tentatively reached her hand to his. 'And please don't say that.'

'Sorry.' He tilted his head closer to hers, the memory of his kisses making her lips tingle with anticipation. 'I didn't mean it like that.'

Olivia's heart grew larger in her chest, as he tucked a stray piece of hair behind her ear.

'So, you wouldn't be totally repulsed if I asked to kiss you again? Even though I haven't done my very thorough and hygienic teeth-cleaning-with-the-finger routine?'

Olivia rolled her eyes, whilst pushing her hips forward into him. The combination of exasperation and desire was a totally new sensation for her. 'I guess I'll allow it.'

'How kind of you.' He smiled and then kissed her very gently on the mouth.

Her insides instantly liquified, and she was surprised when they finally pulled apart that she was still, in fact, a solid object.

'Now, tell me, what's on the agenda for today, Miss Jackson? Because I'd be foolish to think that you don't already have a plan that I'm going to have to try and squeeze myself into.'

'Funny you should say that . . .' She began to play nervously with the edge of the sheet. 'But I realized this morning—'

'When you were subtly checking me out.'

'Stop that.'

'Sorry.' He wound his fingers through hers. 'Carry on. You realized this morning that . . .?'

'That today is my last full day. I leave tomorrow morning.'

A look passed across Jacob's face, so quickly that Olivia was unable to catch it before it disappeared.

'Tomorrow? What time?'

'Early.'

He turned over on to his back, his expression still unreadable.

'Wow, that's gone quickly.'

'I know.' For someone who had been counting down the days until she left, the imminent prospect of going home suddenly felt wrong. 'I can't believe it.'

'How's that for timing, hey?' He gave a small, slightly sad laugh.

'Yeah . . .' A weight seemed to pull on her. 'Thanks, Universe.'

Neither spoke for a while, both content to lie next to each other, hands intertwined, swimming in their own thoughts. It wasn't until Olivia's faithful alarm sounded that both seemed to jolt back into action.

'Look.' Jacob twisted to face her. 'I imagine there's quite a lot you want to get done today, and having someone as incredibly enthusiastic and distracting as myself around probably isn't the best idea.'

'You are very distracting.'

Especially when half-naked.

She decided to keep that last thought to herself.

'I don't have much to do. I said I'd see Cece, maybe go and explore a market for the afternoon, and then I need to pack.'

'Sounds busy to me.' Jacob brought their hands to his lips and kissed her knuckles softly. 'How about you spend the day doing your thing, and then you meet me for dinner later on the beach? A little farewell celebration?'

His words took her by surprise. A celebration? Why would he want to *celebrate* her leaving?

'I could do dinner.'

'Perfect! In that case' – he dropped her hand and pulled back the covers – 'I'd better get myself together.'

He sprang out of the bed and began dressing hastily. Olivia stayed where she was, trying desperately not to beg him to hide away in the little cabin with her for ever. There was crazy and then there was downright insane.

'OK, but you don't need to leave straight away. Cece doesn't finish teaching for ages.'

'Yes, but' – he leant across the bed and planted a kiss on her cheek – 'I've got to plan! Because if there's one thing I know about you, Olivia Jackson, it's that you appreciate a plan.'

311

She went to kiss his lips but was too late. He'd already pulled away.

'Shall we say seven o'clock on the beach?'

'Uh-huh.' She tried not to let the rejection sting too much. 'I'll be there.'

He opened the front door, the sun drenching him in golden light. He looked otherworldly, almost angelic, except for the mischievous grin that had appeared on his face. 'Good, because I promise you, you will not want to miss this.'

'No.' She smiled, her heart fluttering at the sight of him. 'I don't think I will.'

*

How had twelve hours passed so quickly? One minute Olivia was leisurely making her way to meet Cece, enjoying the thought of a slow, delicious breakfast where she knew, of course, that her friend would demand to hear about every single second of her day with Jacob. And the next, she was only half packed, face half done, rushing to the beach to meet Jacob for dinner.

Maybe time did operate differently out here. Because there was no way on earth she would have let this happen back home.

Home.

The word sat heavy on her chest. The thought of leaving and the mixed emotions it brought with it had been haunting her all day. Was she ready to leave? Most definitely. But was she happy about it? Not entirely.

'Wow. You look . . .' Jacob faltered as Olivia hurried towards him.

Overdone?

Ridiculous?

She pulled at the dress she'd bought from the market earlier that afternoon. It wasn't anything fancy, just your standard floral-patterned summer dress, but Cece had insisted that frayed denim shorts and an old white T-shirt were not going to cut it for the evening's events. Because of the time, she'd only managed to apply a little bit of make-up, quickly twisting her hair so that it fell in loose waves down her back. It wasn't much, but apparently the transformation was shocking.

'. . . you look lovely,' he finished, pulling her in for a hug.

'Thank you.'

Olivia turned her head as Jacob leant in for a kiss. Their faces knocked together clumsily.

'God, I'm sorry,' she bumbled.

'No, it was my fault, I went in without warning.'

The verbose, confident Jacob seemed to have been replaced by a rather shy, unsure version.

'It's OK.'

Jacob clenched his fists and gave a long exhale, shuddering, as though shaking himself from his thoughts. 'I guess I'm just not very good at being nervous.'

His admission made her tummy flip.

'*The* Jacob Green, nervous? Surely not.'

'Apparently so.' He brought his face down to hers and kissed her in the most deliciously delicate way. 'Doing that helps though.'

Olivia felt herself relax as he held her tighter, the sudden confidence reflected in their kisses; faster, hungrier, with greater intensity.

'Woah there.' She pulled away. 'We can't do that here.'

His dark eyes bored into hers. 'Why not?'

'Because if we carry on any longer, I'm not sure I'll be able to stop at just kissing.'

Olivia heard the soft moan escape under his breath, which did nothing to quell the desire that was rising up inside her.

'Come on.' She took his hand in hers. 'Let's go eat.'

'Do we have to?'

'Yes!' She gripped him tightly. 'But you have to lead the way because I don't know where we're going, remember?'

'OK, OK.' He steadied himself, rolling his shoulders back and leading them down the beach.

'No mopeds in sight.' She grinned. 'This is a good start.'

'Yeah, I thought it was best we left that as a one-time experience.'

A little boy sped past them on a push bike, quickly followed by his rather exhausted-looking dad.

'Because let's be honest, even that kid is going faster than you were.'

'Hey!' Olivia gasped. 'In my *defence*, that was my first time ever on a moped, and I had a sick patient with me. I had to drive carefully.'

Jacob's jaw fell wide open. 'Don't you dare use me as an excuse. If anything, the adrenaline rush would have helped keep me alert. Riding with you was like being rocked to sleep in a pram.'

'You are such a shit, you know that?' Olivia tried to free her hand from his, but Jacob held on tighter, lifting it to his mouth and kissing it.

'It's so sweet when you compliment me like that.'

'What can I say? I'm too kind.'

The further they walked along the beach, the quieter it became. Save for a few dedicated sun worshippers, they seemed to be the only people not crowded into a restaurant or a bar. Olivia's stomach rumbled impatiently.

'Can I ask where we're going for dinner yet, or are you still keeping it under wraps?'

Jacob stopped still. 'Well, Miss Jackson, funny you should say that, because if you'd care to look right there' – he pointed ahead – 'then you'll find our table for the evening.'

Olivia followed the direction of his finger.

'You're joking, right?'

She looked back to Jacob.

He couldn't be serious.

'Nope.'

'That? That right there?'

She was looking at a large white-cloth table positioned in the sand, midway between the ocean and a bustling seaside restaurant. Hundreds of tea lights had been placed around it, twinkling like hidden jewels in the sand. Rose petals, scarlet red and mother of pearl pink, lay scattered in between.

'The very one.'

'But—'

'Come on, I'm getting hungry.' Jacob pulled them closer. 'Ah look, there's my guy now!'

A rather compact-looking man, with a shining bald head and a beaming face, came rushing out to greet them.

'Mr and Mrs Jackson!' he called eagerly.

Olivia snapped her head around so quickly her neck jarred. 'What did he just call us?'

'About that . . .' Jacob kept his eyes forward, face fixed with a smile, 'I *may* have told them we were celebrating our first week as a married couple.'

'You told them *what*?'

'That we're newlyweds. Hence all the fancy decorations.'

'Jacob!'

'What? I wanted it to be special.'

'So you lied?'

'I used my imagination.'

'You are unbelievable.'

'Look, I understand you being annoyed at me, but don't take it out on poor Vish.' Jacob gestured to the jolly man standing by the table. 'He's made a real effort for us.'

'Yes, I can see that,' she growled.

'Mr and Mrs Jackson!' the man greeted them again. 'So lovely to see you, and congratulations again on getting married.'

'Thank you, Vish.' Jacob shook the man's hand firmly. 'The table looks stunning, thank you so much.'

'Only the best for our happy couple.'

Olivia blushed at the lie.

'Now please, please, take a seat, and one of our waiters will be over to take your drinks order.'

'Perfect.' Jacob held out a chair for Olivia. 'After you, madam.'

'Don't you mean, my darling *wife*?'

'Yes, that too.' He sat down opposite her, the twinkle in his treacle eyes shining especially bright. 'Did you like the fact I used your surname? Very progressive of me.'

Jacob's audacity was mind-blowing but, as Olivia took in the view, the ocean only metres ahead of them, the flames of the candles winking at them in the breeze, she had to admit it was a special set-up.

'I *cannot* believe you did this.'

'Are you happy I did though?'

'Maybe . . . just a little bit.'

'Good, because I get the impression that you're a very difficult woman to please.'

'That's not true.'

'Really?'

'Having high standards is not a bad thing.' She bristled.

'I never said it was.'

'Excuse me, sir, madam.' A younger but dourer-looking waiter appeared at their side. 'Can I get you anything to drink? Some wine, perhaps?'

'We'll have two bottles of water.' Jacob looked at Olivia. 'One still and one sparkling?'

'Please,' she confirmed.

'And . . .' He paused, eyeing the thick, leather-bound drinks menu. 'A bottle of champagne.'

'*What?*' Olivia hissed.

'You're right.' He nodded, turning back to the waiter. 'Make that two. Thank you very much.'

'Excellent. I'll be back shortly with your drinks.'

'Jacob, what are you doing? You can't do that.'

'Why not?' He leant forward. 'This is a celebration, right? And I only accept the *highest of standards* when it comes to my celebrations . . .'

Olivia shook her head in disbelief. Once again, she felt as though she was dreaming, as if at any moment someone would shake her awake and pop the beautiful bubble she'd found herself in. With him. Her dark-eyed Peter Pan.

Except he wasn't make-believe.

He was real.

And Olivia wasn't sure she was ready to let him go just yet.

Jacob

'You're drunk.' Olivia snorted.

'No, I am not.' Jacob swayed a little. '*You're* drunk.'

'Can we not both be drunk at the same time?' Olivia's scowling face reminded him of a wrinkled baby. He was about to tell her so when he decided otherwise. A comment like that could ruin a perfectly brilliant evening.

'You do make a lot of sense, a lot of the time.'

'A lot of the time? You mean, *all* of the time.' Olivia wrapped her arms around herself, unsuccessfully hiding her shivering body.

'For the fifteenth time, woman, do you want my top? Because I'll let you have it.' He began unbuttoning his shirt, his fingers struggling to coordinate properly. 'Olivia Jackson, you can have the shirt off my very back if you want!'

A young couple walking past them began to laugh.

'Jacob, for Christ's sake, will you please keep your clothes on.'

'You've changed your tune.' He raised his eyebrows and

stopped dead in his tracks. 'Because that is not what you were saying last night.'

'Oh my god.' The horror on her face made his heart stumble over itself. 'Will you be *quiet*.'

'Never! You can never silence me.'

Olivia pulled at his hand and tried to drag him along, but he was too heavy, and she was unsteady on her feet.

'Come sit with me for a second.' He plonked himself down on the damp sand. 'I love watching the ocean, especially at night.'

He could see the 'no' making its bid for freedom from her mouth.

'I know you have to be up early for your flight tomorrow; I just want a couple of minutes. That's all. I promise.'

'OK, fine.' She came and sat next to him, snuggling her body close to him.

Her hair shone white in the moonlight; her skin prickled with goosebumps. She looked ethereal, almost ghostly. Like she belonged to a world other than his, which deep down he'd known all along to be true.

Sorrow pooled in his stomach, and his breath caught in his throat.

'What time do you fly tomorrow?'

'Around nine thirty, I think.'

'You *think*?' He nudged her softly.

'Fine. I leave Goa at nine forty and then fly from Delhi to Heathrow at one twenty.'

'There we go, planned to a tee.'

'What can I say? It's my superpower.'

'And are you ready to go back? To unleash your powers of organization on the miserable, soul-destroying western world?'

'Kind of. It will be nice to see everyone and get into a

routine again, but I reckon it's going to feel strange for a while.' She dropped her gaze to the floor. 'Stranger than I thought, anyway.'

'That's because you're used to the beach and yoga life now. In a few days, though, this will all feel like a distant memory.'

And so will I.

The thought brought with it a deep sadness, but also an element of relief. Who had he been kidding the past couple of days? This wasn't his life. It was never supposed to be his life.

'I don't think so.' She rested her head on his shoulder. 'How could I ever forget this?'

'It was a pretty good dinner, if I say so myself.'

'You know what I mean.'

'I suppose they do have yoga back in London.'

'*Jacob* . . .'

'I know.' His voice was small, his body contracting. If he folded in on himself enough, would he be able to disappear, to avoid dealing with the question he knew was coming? He could feel it waiting to jump from her lips: the question that would ruin everything.

'Why don't you come back with me?'

The words were out; the bomb had been dropped.

'I mean, I'm not going to say no to a sleepover.' He laughed loudly. Falsely. 'But I thought you had to be up early tomorrow?'

'Not *tonight*, Jacob.' Her deep blue eyes locked on to his. 'I mean to London. Come back to London with me.'

Silence. Deadly, crushing silence that seemed to suck the very air from his lungs. This was his fault. This was all his fault.

'I can't.' He spoke at last. 'You know I can't do that.'

Her face crumbled. 'Why not?'

Jacob dropped his head to his hands and clawed his fingers against his skull. He didn't know what was worse: the disappointment in her words, or the devastation that was raging like a wild beast inside him.

'I mean, it doesn't have to be for long,' she continued. 'You could come and stay for a few days, catch up with people from home, and then go back on your adventures again?'

The hope in her voice was unbearable. It reminded him of how foolish he'd been. How he too had allowed himself to be caught up in the dangerous clutches of dreaming. The fantasy he had been playing out in his mind, the fairy-tale ending that felt so close and so very real, was crumbling down around him. He had to face the consequences; there was no other choice.

'Jacob? Say something, please.'

End it.

End it now.

His thoughts pulled him back to earth so fast he felt whiplashed.

'Because that's not what I *do* any more, Olivia.' His voice was firm and strong. 'I don't go back. Not for anything.' He paused, waiting just a moment longer before delivering the final blow. 'And not for anyone.'

The finality of his words punctured both of their hearts.

'I see.'

'I'm sorry.' He ran his hands through his hair. 'I really am.'

How had he created such a mess? This was supposed to be a nice evening. A *fun* evening.

'Oh God no, I'm the one that should be sorry,' she spat,

her voice sharp and venomous. 'I was the one who forgot that you're going to play pretend for the rest of your life, avoiding everything and *everyone* who takes you back to reality.'

'Please don't be like that.'

'Like what? Like a normal person living in the real world? Like an adult taking responsibility for their life instead of letting a pair of dice decide their every move?' She shifted away from him, the swell of emotion carving a divide between them. 'Should I buy a house? Should I get married? Oh, how many kids should I have? I know, let me roll the dice and see. Woops, it's an even number so, sorry, not going to happen this time.'

The sarcasm was cutting, the contorted look of disgust on her face heartbreaking, but he held firm. She was angry, and she had every right to be. After all, he had brought this upon himself.

'Can't you see it's *pathetic*, Jacob? It's pathetic and childish. When are you going to wake up and become an adult?' Her fists were clenched so tightly that the veins on her hands were popping out. 'God, I don't know how I let you convince me that you were anything other than idiotic, inconsiderate and completely and utterly *selfish*.'

Selfish.

He knew he shouldn't react, that he didn't *deserve* to react, but something inside him snapped, and before he knew what was happening, he started to laugh. Quietly at first, then gradually louder and louder, until his whole body was shaking with the force.

'What?' She slammed her hands down on to the sand. 'What is so fucking *funny*?'

'You!' he cried, unable to hold it in any longer. 'You and

322

your notion of what everyone else should be doing with their lives, when you're barely living your own.'

'Excuse me?'

'You sit there and preach to me about growing up and being responsible, but who says having a house and kids, and a marriage where two people never speak and probably end up divorcing and hating the sight of each other, makes you responsible? You live your life based on what society thinks you should do. What other people say is the right way to be. What's wrong with doing it differently? What's wrong with doing what *I* want to do with the time *I* have left on this planet?'

'Time left?' She looked incandescent, his words pouring oil on an already raging fire. 'Don't you dare talk to me about time left. My sister had no time. She had no *time*.'

'Yeah, and I bet she tried to live more than you ever will with how much time you have left.'

He was in dangerous territory now, but even if he wanted to, he knew he couldn't stop.

'It's only because of her that you're even here. If she hadn't died, I reckon you would have happily just spent your days clocking up more hours sitting in your office, working yourself to the bone. Earning money that you have no time to spend, unless it's to buy heaps of shit that you never get to enjoy, giving half of it away to a government that quite frankly doesn't care about you in the slightest – as long as you're paying for them to live their wonderful lives – until you finally retire and realize you don't have anything else to talk about except how much you miss work, or how your body is breaking down because you've put it through so much stress it's forgotten how to function. Am I right?'

Olivia's face was mutinous.

'Fuck you, Jacob. Fuck you and your simplistic view of the world.'

She practically jumped from the ground.

'You sit there passing comment on my life. *Judging* my life so harshly. And yeah, maybe I do spend too much time at work, and maybe I do earn more money than I need but those taxes that I give away so foolishly? The money I *naively* hand over to the government? That money goes towards paying nurses and doctors, and running the hospitals that tried to save my sister's life. In fact' – she pointed her finger in his face – 'they *did* save her life, over and over again. So yes, I may be boring and a sheep, but at least I have family and friends and people who are there for me when I need them. People who stay around long enough to care about me and my life.'

Tears were streaming down her face, her tiny frame physically shaking with anger.

At him.

All because of him.

'I'm sorry.' He went to reach for her, to take his cruel words and stuff them back inside his mouth. 'I didn't mean anything about your sister, you know I would never—'

'Save it,' she hissed. 'I don't need your apologies and take-backs now. In fact, I don't need anything from you, ever again. Have a nice life, Jacob, wherever the hell you end up.'

And without even a backwards glance, she left him, running off down the beach, swallowed by the darkness.

'Fuck!' He screamed, tensing his entire body and allowing the pain that had been building inside him to surge to the surface. '*Fuck!*'

He shouted until his throat was hoarse and the sound no

longer came, emptied of everything except the sickening vortex of guilt and rage that swirled inside him.

Jacob reached into his pocket and felt for the dice. He wanted to throw them, hurl them into the ocean and never see them again. His two trusted companions were supposed to keep him safe. To keep *everyone* safe – from him. What good had they done?

He raised his hand in the air.

One simple move and they would be gone.

But he wouldn't. He knew he couldn't.

He laid his weary body back down on the sand. The sky was achingly beautiful with its canvas of stars.

'I'm sorry, Olivia.' He began to sob. 'I'm so, *so* sorry.'

IV

An end is only a beginning in disguise.
Craig D. Lounsbrough

Olivia

'Good evening, ladies and gentlemen. We will shortly be starting our descent into London Heathrow. If you could please remain in your seats, with your seat belts fastened, tray tables stowed away, and your seat in the upright position.'

Olivia switched off the screen she'd been pretending to stare at for the past four hours. No matter how hard she'd tried, how many films she'd attempted to watch, how many times she'd willed herself to sleep, all Olivia could focus on was the argument with Jacob. Their angry words played over and over on a loop inside her brain.

You and your notion of what everyone else should be doing with their lives, when you're barely living your own.

Her hands balled into fists.

I bet she tried to live more than you ever will with how much time you have left.

Her stomach twisted itself into tighter knots.

'Stupid idiot,' she spat under her breath, leaning her forehead on the plastic window. She felt the stare of the man next to her; the stranger who, for nearly nine hours, had had to endure Olivia's incessant and restless shuffling, mumbling and, most embarrassingly, crying.

She pressed her head harder against the window, enjoying the pain that shot through her skull.

Stupid, selfish, totally irresponsible idiot.

Doesn't have a clue about real life.

Doesn't have a clue about being a decent human being.

Harder and harder she pressed, the sensations on the outside not strong enough to mute the hurt on the inside.

He didn't even say goodbye.

The childlike voice emerged from deep within the angry depths. A tear escaped down Olivia's cheek as her heart sank lower in her chest.

He'll message. Just give it time.

Instinctively, she grabbed her phone and clutched it to her. There had been nothing when she'd woken up that morning, her body beaten from the battle. Nothing when she'd arrived at the airport, tired and overemotional. Nothing when she'd boarded the plane to Delhi. Nothing when she'd landed and transferred to her flight for London.

No email.

Nothing.

Not a single word from Jacob before she left him for ever.

What were you expecting?

She swallowed a sob that was forming in her throat. Something, she admitted to herself. She was at least expecting *something*.

The plane smacked down hard as it made contact with the tarmac. Olivia was thrown upwards from her seat, her forehead banging against the window.

'Ladies and gentlemen, we have now arrived at London Heathrow, where the local time is 5.35 p.m. The use of electronic devices is now permitted, but the seat belt sign is still on, so please remain seated until the aircraft has come to a complete stop. Thank you.'

A series of beeps and vibrations echoed around the plane, people turning on their phones and switching back to reality.

Olivia tentatively pressed the on button and watched as her phone lit up in response.

Message from Kate BFF
Message from Mum
2 messages from Kyle Brother

Her eyes were glued to the screen, watching as the notifications piled up, one after the other. Friends and family wishing her safe travels and welcoming her home. Companies spamming her, hounding her to buy their products. But nothing, not a word, from Jacob.

She stuffed her phone into her bag and bit back the urge to scream.

'Ladies and gentlemen, the seat belt sign is now off and we are ready to disembark from the aircraft. We wish you a pleasant onward journey, and from everyone here at Virgin Atlantic, thank you for travelling with us and we hope to see you again soon.'

'Not bloody likely,' Olivia spat, standing up and pushing herself out of the narrow row of seats.

'Never say never.' A jolly man behind her laughed as they walked down the aisle.

'Yeah?' She whipped her head around as the exit came closer. 'And what the hell do you know?'

*

It had to be said, it was slightly awkward standing opposite the man she'd been so rude to as they waited for their bags to arrive. He kept looking over at her as though, at any moment, she was going to shout her apologies across the conveyor belt. Instead, she kept her eyes glued to the revolving train of luggage that snaked in front of them at a painfully slow pace.

Why was everything taking so long?

The lack of sleep was starting to kick in now, exhaustion weighing her down, burning through the final reserves of her patience, and leaving her prickly and frazzled.

'Excuse me!' She elbowed her way forwards, spotting her lumpy backpack emerge on the belt. 'Can I come through, please? That's my bag.'

'Which one, sweetheart?' a bulky, tattooed man asked. 'I'll get it for you.'

'No, thank you,' she snapped, 'I can do it myself. I just need you to *move*.'

Olivia launched forwards, almost toppling over and on to the belt herself. She grabbed the straps of her bag and hauled it off, struggling to maintain both her balance and her cool whilst doing so.

'These young people,' the man commented to his wife. 'Think they can do it all.'

Fury erupted inside her.

'These old people, always thinking they know best.' She tutted, swinging her bag on to her back and marching off towards the exit.

Her heart was pumping ferociously in her chest, the sour taste of her outbursts coating the inside of her mouth. She needed to get out of this airport and straight back to her flat, dump her godforsaken rucksack, and have a long, hot, relaxing bath—

'WELCOME HOME!'

Something had been unceremoniously shoved in Olivia's face, forcing her to stop dead in her tracks. A young family almost crashed into the back of her, narrowly avoiding the collision by millimetres.

'What the *hell*?' She felt the explosion building, the incandescent rage about to erupt from within her, when she noticed just who and what was standing in front of her.

There was Kyle, grinning from ear to ear, holding one end of a large, hand-drawn sign. The other, of course, was held by Kate, who was open-mouthed and shouting in celebration at her arrival.

'SURPRISE!' Kate squealed, letting go of the sign and rushing to greet her.

'I don't . . .' Olivia faltered, still standing frozen in place. 'I don't understand.'

Kate wrapped her arms around her. 'We're your welcome home party, silly.'

'But . . .'

Olivia felt the emotion begin to overwhelm her, the fire inside alchemizing into an ocean of tears.

'Olivia?' Kate looked at her. 'What's wrong?'

'I . . . it's all just . . . I don't . . .' Olivia's bottom lip began to tremble.

'Hey.' Her friend pulled her into a hug and steered her away from the crowd. 'It's OK.'

'It's not though.' Olivia's defences finally broke, the

pressure too much, the exhaustion too draining, the pain in her heart too crippling. 'It's not OK,' she sobbed into Kate's shoulder.

'Oh, my love, let's get you home. You're probably exhausted.'

Olivia nodded feebly, gingerly wiping her face with the sleeve of her top. She *was* exhausted – on every possible level – but the feel of her friend was enough to calm her racing thoughts and settle the turbulence in her chest.

'OK.' Olivia took a long, deep inhale. 'I'm OK.'

'Good.' Kate held her out in front of her. 'And you may look totally wiped, but at least you're tanned!'

Olivia couldn't help but laugh, as Kate lifted her arm into the air for inspection.

'It's more freckles than tan, but I'll take it.'

'I would.' She took the rucksack from Olivia's hands and slung it over her own back. 'Now let's get you home, shall we?'

'Please.'

Kate and Olivia made their way back towards where Kyle was standing. 'Just to let you know, your brother has been banging on about getting a McDonald's for the past hour. Do you fancy one?'

'No.' Olivia's stomach writhed in protest. 'But he won't shut up unless we get him one, so we might as well go.'

'Yeah, tell me about it, he's totally obsessed with the stuff. I don't know where he puts it.'

Olivia hesitated – something about Kate's words sent alarm bells ringing in her brain – but she was too tired and far too full of her own turmoil to fully register the meaning.

'Little Sis!' Kyle held his arms out wide as they reached him. 'Welcome home.'

'Thanks.' She managed a watery smile.

'Everything all right? You look a little . . .'

'Tired. I'm just tired.'

'Well then, I tell you what you need. A good old Maccy D's! That will get you energized again. Here, let me take that.' He took the backpack from Kate, an indiscernible look passing between them. Why were they being so weird around each other? Before Olivia had a chance to question it, Kate pulled her close.

'It's good to have you back.' She slipped her hand into Olivia's. It was soft and warm and felt like home. 'I've missed you.'

'I've missed you too.' Olivia squeezed her friend gently and smiled. 'Now please, *please* can we get out of this place?'

'As you wish, my love.' The three of them began to walk towards the exit. 'As you wish.'

*

Three hours and an order of two Big Mac Meals later, Olivia was so far past tired she felt catatonic. She lay on the sofa as Kyle and Kate flapped around her, shooting each other knowing looks, and giving each other tender and not so subtle touches of reassurance. It had taken Olivia a while, but finally she'd worked it out. The alarm bells had been going off for a reason.

'Right, I'd better be heading home.' Kyle stood, dusting the burger bun crumbs from his jeans. 'I have work later.' A lingering look at Kate. 'Liv, are you sure you don't want the rest of these?' He held up a half-eaten, soggy packet of chips.

'No, I'm good. You take them.'

'Great. Well, I'll see you at Mum and Dad's next weekend, all right?'

'Sure.' She stood and gave her brother a hug. 'And thank you for coming to meet me at the airport. It was . . .'

'Unexpectedly nice from me?'

'Yeah, exactly.'

'What can I say? I've kind of missed you.' He planted a kiss on her cheek. 'Kate, I guess I'll see you . . . well . . .' He shifted awkwardly, eyes darting everywhere but at the two of them. 'Yeah . . . whenever.'

'Great!' Her friend visibly tensed, her smile false and overly bright. 'See you around.'

'See you.' Kyle shuffled out, slamming the door behind him, leaving Kate and Olivia in silence.

'So . . .' Her friend inched closer to her on the sofa. Olivia felt the pain that she had been holding back begin to seep through the cracks in her defences. 'You want to tell me what's going on?'

Olivia's mind felt as though it had been pumped full of smoke: cloudy, impenetrable and completely disorientating. Jetlag and heartbreak were a potent combination.

Where the hell did she begin?

'It's Jacob . . .'

'What's happened? Is he OK?' Kate placed a hand over hers. 'Did he do something to you? Did he hurt you?'

Yes. But I hurt him too . . .

'Come on, Olivia, you have to give me something here. You were a complete state when you came through at the airport. Talk to me . . . please.'

Whatever else she was feeling towards Kate and Kyle and their new romantic dynamic, the look on her friend's face and the touch of her hand finally broke Olivia.

'Oh God,' she cried, letting the tears free at last. 'It's so messed up.'

'Hey, I'm sure whatever happened can be fixed. Nothing is ever that bad. Now' – Kate wrapped Olivia up in her arms and held her closely – 'tell me everything. From the very beginning.'

Olivia peeped her head out from the safety of her friend's embrace and began to tell the whole story. The surprise trip to the beach; the night they'd spent together. The beautiful candlelit dinner, the champagne, the walk afterwards, and then the argument. The fighting. The cruel words shot back and forth, scarring one another, hitting their marks where it hurt the most. If Kate was mad that Olivia had kept all this from her, she never showed it. Instead, she sat, hand never leaving hers, listening in silence the entire time.

'And . . .' Olivia wiped her nose with the back of her other hand. 'That's how we left it. I haven't heard from him since. There's been nothing.'

'Gosh, that's a lot.'

'I told you. It's completely ruined.'

'I wouldn't say that.' Kate tucked a loose strand of hair behind Olivia's ear. 'I know this might sound crazy, but have you thought of being the one to message him?'

Olivia jerked her head back in horror. 'What?'

'Look, you'd both had a bit too much to drink and you *both* said hurtful things.'

'He said worse.'

'Maybe . . .' Kate was evidently trying to navigate Olivia's emotional landscape with caution. 'And maybe he's being a typical man and waiting for you to reach out to him.'

'Well, then he'll be waiting a long time.'

'Come *on*, Olivia, at least think about it.' Kate cradled her cheek with her hand. 'He clearly means a lot to you; do you want this to be how it ends?'

'I don't know.' She shrugged. 'Some of the things he said . . .'

'Were completely and totally out of order. But remember, it was in the heat of the moment, and we all say things we don't mean. Even you.'

The truth of her friend's words sat like a weight on Olivia's chest. She had said a whole host of terrible, unforgivable things. Yes, she was hurt, and yes, she was feeling rejected. Did that justify her saying whatever she liked? Was she any more innocent than him?

'I wouldn't know what to say.'

'How about you start with "Hello and I'm sorry"?'

Olivia reluctantly reached for her phone and opened her emails. The minuscule spark of hope that his message would be waiting for her was put out instantly.

You can do this. You know you want to do this . . .

'I can't do this,' she announced, her anxiety spiking so high she felt sick. 'Not now anyway. I think I need to go to bed and sleep before I try to write anything. Do you mind?'

'Of course I don't mind.' Kate stood and gathered her belongings. 'But let's talk tomorrow – there's a lot we need to catch up on.'

Olivia saw the angst on her friend's face. Punishing her and prolonging the awkward conversation was unfair. At the end of the day, Kate was the closest thing to a sister she had left.

'Are you happy?' she asked. 'With Kyle, I mean.'

Kate's face dropped, her expression horrified. 'Oh my god, was it that obvious?'

'I'm jetlagged, heartbroken and in a McDonald's coma, and I still noticed. So yeah, I'd say pretty obvious.'

'*Fuck.* I am so sorry. I wanted to tell you as soon as I saw you, but then you were upset, and we didn't know what to do.' She clawed at her mane of hair. 'I'm such a bad friend, aren't I?'

'No, you're not. In fact, you're the very best. And all I want is for you to be happy. Are you happy?'

A bashful smile crept up on her face, the same smile that Olivia had probably worn a hundred times when she was with Jacob.

'Yeah, in a weird and unexpected and totally out of the blue way, I am. And nothing has even happened yet – I mean, we've just been talking loads, that's all. I said I had to speak to you before we even went on a date. I promise.'

The fierce and undying loyalty of her friend mended a tiny piece of Olivia's broken heart instantly. 'Thank you, I appreciate that.'

'So you're not mad?'

'I'm not mad.'

'You're sure?'

'Yes, I'm sure.'

'Thank God.' Kate exhaled, as though at last she could finally breathe. 'Like I said, we can talk about it properly another time. For now, just focus on sleeping and feeling a bit more human.' She kissed the top of Olivia's head. 'I love you, and whatever happens, you will be OK.'

'I know, and I love you too.'

The moment the door closed and Olivia was alone, she shut her eyes and let the full force of her feelings hit her.

You will be OK. We're always OK.

She looked down at her phone once more, before shoving it under the cushion and heading straight to bed.

Jacob

From: Olivia_Jackson@gmail.com
Subject: Hi

I've written and rewritten this email so many times that I'm not even sure what makes sense any more. I just want to say that I'm sorry about the other night. I hate how we left things and that we never got to say goodbye properly. I hope you're OK.

   Yours, incredibly apologetically, Olivia x

He rolled the dice in his hands. How much heavier they felt now. How much weaker he had become.

To reply to her.

Or not to reply to her.

He had been asking himself the same question continuously for weeks now. It had become second nature to him. More so than breathing. More so than eating. But every time he went to give an answer, he stopped himself.

It had been a mistake to open her email. He'd told himself

a thousand times not to do it. Wasn't thinking about her painful enough?

Pain.

How naive he'd been to think he'd known it before.

'Jacob! Is everything OK up there?'

The voice startled him, even though every fifteen minutes on the dot, the same call would echo up the stairs.

'Fine,' he replied, pushing himself out of his chair and making his way back to bed.

Another day, and the ache in his chest and the clouds in his head were growing stronger with every passing minute. What he would give to be back on that beach in Goa. What he would give to be anywhere but here right now.

'Jacob?' His mum was louder now, more urgent. 'Are you all right?'

'I'm fine!' he called back, as loudly as his weary body would allow. Then he whispered to himself, 'Everything is just fucking fine.'

Olivia

Olivia checked the time; she still had ten minutes before her next meeting. The board presentation was looming, and Phil was going into overdrive. Not only did he need to make sure the slides were OK, but also that Olivia wasn't going to have another one of her 'episodes', as he so kindly put it.

'Olivia, you good to go in a few?' he bellowed from his office.

'Yeah, give me five.'

She reached for her phone and clicked open her emails.

Nothing.

It had been a month since her email to Jacob, and she'd still heard nothing back. It had taken every bit of strength not to message again; what had Cece told her? Life was too short for playing games. And if he wanted to play silent, then he could do that on his own time.

Cece . . . Goa . . . Her entire time away now felt like a very distant and surreal dream. It hadn't taken long for her to settle into the swing of things back home. The grey skies and even greyer landscape seemed to suck every drop of Indian sunshine from her memory. Work had thrown her straight back into the thick of it once she'd returned from leave, Phil wasting no time in getting her back to busy again. In one way it was a blessing – there was less time to dwell when you had no time to eat, let alone think – but in another way, it was a cruel reminder of Jacob's words during their argument. Was this what she wanted for her life?

She clicked on her sent items and reread her message to him. Even if he replied telling her never to contact him again, at least she'd know he was alive.

Nerves ran their ice-cold fingers down her throat and began to tighten their grip around her ribcage. The unspoken fear that she had been carrying around with her for the last couple of weeks had reared its head once again. What if he was hurt? What if he needed help? Olivia closed her eyes and felt the frustration surge through her.

He's an adult and not your responsibility.

She clicked out of her inbox and straight into her junk mail. It was a ritual she'd adopted every time she searched for his reply, and there was no point in breaking the routine now.

She flicked her eyes back up to the time; three minutes to go.

Plenty of time.

'No, I don't want to get filler in my face, thank you . . .' She scrolled down the long list of trash messages. 'And yes, I would like to be a crypto billionaire, but I doubt you will help me get there, DreamMoneyMaker.com . . .'

Suddenly Olivia stopped.

Surely it couldn't be?

She'd never asked for his mum's name and even if she had, he probably wouldn't have told her. What were the chances of someone having the same surname as Jacob?

With a name like Green, extremely high!

She stared back at the unopened email.

Two minutes before she had to be up on the executive floor with Phil . . .

Against her better judgement, she clicked on the email.

One minute to go.

No.

Her entire body froze, the words on the screen blurring into one squiggled mess.

'No!' she cried out. 'No. *No.*'

'Olivia, let's go,' Phil barked, storming towards her like a balding pitbull.

'I . . . I'm sorry.' She looked up. 'I can't.'

Her hands were gripping her phone so tightly that all the blood had drained from her fingers.

'What do you mean, you can't?' Her boss's eyes ran up and down the length of her, searching for any obvious issues. 'What's wrong?'

'I need to leave.' Thoughts crunched around in her head like a thousand tiny shards of glass. 'I'm sorry, Phil.' She straightened up and switched her computer off. 'But I need to go. There's been an emergency.'

'Excuse me?' His piggy eyes were wide with confusion. 'You can't! You can't do this again.'

'Rob can cover – he probably knows it better than me

anyway.' She grabbed her bag and flung it over her shoulder, nodding to Rob, who looked equal parts shocked and grateful.

'You can't go!' her boss bellowed. 'We need you, Olivia.'

'I'm sorry, Phil.' She raced towards the door. 'But someone else needs me more.'

Olivia

'Where are you?' Kate asked. 'Are you nearly there?'

The second she was out of the office doors, she'd called her friend. Not only to panic about the fact she'd left work during the middle of the day with no warning, but also to fill her in on what was happening and to ask very kindly if she could borrow her car to drive all the way to Surrey.

Olivia peered out of the window and up at the iron gates she was parked in front of.

'I'm here, but . . .'

'What?'

Olivia took a deep breath. 'I don't know if I can go inside.'

'Are you *serious*?'

'What if it's weird between us?' Olivia leant back in her seat. 'What if he doesn't want me there? I don't think he even knows I'm coming.'

'Does it matter? His mum asked you to come. You've driven two hours to be there. You walked out of *work*, Olivia! Can I remind you how much of a big deal that is?'

Her voice quietened. 'And besides, you know more than anyone what it's like to be in this situation.'

Leah's tiny face appeared before her eyes. Olivia felt her insides knot.

'I know.' She exhaled, gathering up her courage from the corners it had hidden in. 'You're totally right.'

'What's the house like, by the way?'

'Kate!' Olivia remarked. 'What kind of a question is that?'

'I'm curious, that's all. From what you've told me about him, I can't picture it.'

'It's . . .' She looked out of the window at the towering mansion in front of her. No wonder he could afford to spend his days travelling the world, with a house like that. '*Huge*. Like, really huge. Super posh.'

'It's always the ones you least suspect, hey?' Kate sighed. 'Anyway, enough of me distracting you: get your arse in there.'

Olivia sat a little taller and took a short, sharp inhale. 'OK. I'll call you later?'

'You'd better. Now go!'

Kate hung up the phone before Olivia could even say goodbye.

You can do this. You can do this. You can absolutely do this.

She wound down the window and reached over to the intercom buzzer.

'Hello?' a lady's voice crackled.

'Erm . . . hi,' Olivia replied shyly. 'It's Olivia. Olivia Jackson. We spoke on the phone . . .'

'Olivia! Oh my goodness, hello. Come in, come in. Park anywhere,' she replied, buzzing open the gates.

Olivia pulled forwards slowly, trying not to gasp out loud

as the true grandeur of the house came into view. She pulled up next to a gleaming 4X4 in Kate's little Fiat.

Her stomach now felt so twisted she wanted to double over and weep. But there was no turning back now; Jacob's mum was already at the front door waiting for her. She looked older than she imagined, her blonde hair almost completely grey at the roots, her eyes marked with the tell-tale black circles of a mother who hasn't slept in weeks.

'Hi, Mrs Green.'

'Please, as I said on the phone, call me Helen.' She pulled Olivia in for a tight embrace. 'Thank you so much for coming.'

'That's all right. How is he?'

'So-so.'

Olivia knew that was the parent code for 'terrible'. She offered a consoling smile.

'And does he . . .' The question that had been plaguing her ever since she'd left London. 'Does he know that I'm here?'

'No.' Helen loosened her hold. 'But I know he'll be so glad you are. Come, he's upstairs . . .'

Olivia silently followed Helen through an enormous hall-way and up a sweeping staircase.

'Don't be alarmed at his appearance; he probably looks very different compared to when you last saw him.' She added sadly, 'He's still handsome to me though.'

'My sister was very sick not long ago, so I'm used to how quickly the body can change.' Olivia gave a small smile. 'And don't worry, he'll always be handsome to me too.'

Helen placed a hand on Olivia's shoulder. 'Oh my, I'd better not cry in front of him. He hates that.' She wiped her eyes and steadied herself. 'Here we are.'

They were standing outside a dark wooden door, one of

many down a long, narrow corridor. Helen knocked loudly, and Olivia felt her heart shoot up into her throat.

'Jacob, darling?' she called. 'I have a surprise for you.'

'Is it that life-sized chocolate sculpture I asked you for the other day?' a familiar voice croaked back.

'No. It's something much better.' Slowly, she opened the door and beckoned Olivia to follow her through.

'What on earth could be better than a giant chocolate statue of me?' Jacob laughed wearily.

'This!' Helen announced, stepping aside to reveal Olivia.

It was as though someone had flicked a switch and sent them all into slow motion. Jacob's face was mutinous, his charcoal eyes wide in his gaunt face. Olivia noticed his bony hands grip the edge of the duvet cover so tightly that his already ghostly white knuckles became luminous.

'Hi,' Olivia murmured, the tension of the moment making her voice audibly shrink.

'What the hell are you doing here?' He recoiled, turning to his mum. 'What the *hell* is she *doing* here?'

'Don't be like that, darling,' his mum purred sweetly, her hold on Olivia so firm it hurt a little. 'She's here to cheer you up!'

'Why?' he spat. '*How?*'

Olivia wanted the ground to swallow her whole. To chew her up and spit her back out somewhere far away from this awful situation. She was a fool for coming. What had she been thinking?

'I saw you looking at her email every day and how desperately sad you were becoming, so I messaged Olivia here and asked her to visit you.'

'No,' he hissed.

'Come on, sweetie,' Helen pleaded.

'I said *no*.'

Olivia felt her cheeks start to burn.

'But she's come all this way.'

'I don't *care*. I don't want her here. I don't want *anyone* here.' His skeletal chest was rising and falling rapidly, his fingers still clutching on to the covers as though his life depended on it. 'I don't need some pity party. I don't *want* anyone to see me. What part of that don't you understand?' He turned his hollow eyes to Olivia. 'Get out.'

'Jacob darl—'

'I said, *GET OUT*,' he screamed at the pair of them.

Helen began to sob, and Olivia felt the urge to join her. Instead, she swallowed hard and turned to leave.

'I'm sorry, Jacob. I didn't mean to upset you.' She stole one last look at him before walking as fast as she could from the bedroom.

'How dare you be like that, Jacob? How could you be so cruel?' Helen's cries could be heard all the way down the stairs, but within seconds Olivia was outside and sitting in the car.

'Why!' she shouted, slamming her hands on the steering wheel. 'Why, why, *why* did you think this was a good idea?' Tears were running thick and fast down her cheeks, her chest heaving for breath. His hollowed face haunted her thoughts.

You can't save everyone.

You can't fix everything.

A tentative knock on the window jolted her.

'Olivia?' Helen called.

'I shouldn't have come, I'm sorry.'

'Olivia, please.' She tapped again on the window. 'I'm the one that should be sorry. Can we at least talk for a second?'

Olivia wound down the window and sat back in her seat.

'I'm so sorry about that. He's just upset, he doesn't know what he's saying. I thought a surprise was a good idea, but clearly . . .' She sighed deeply. 'Anyway, at least come and have a cup of tea with me. You can't drive home when you're upset like this. It isn't safe.'

Through the streams of Olivia's tears, Helen's face began to blur into that of her mother. Lonely, tired and weighed down with grief.

'I have biscuits.' She smiled hopefully. 'And some cake.'

In that moment, it dawned on Olivia that maybe it wasn't Jacob who needed her today.

'Well, who can say no to cake?'

*

Olivia took the steaming cup of tea from Helen and let its warmth begin to soothe her.

'When my sister was really bad, I think we must have consumed about a litre of tea every day.'

Helen came to sit opposite her and placed a glistening Victoria sponge on the table between them.

'I'm not surprised. It makes you feel so much better about life, doesn't it?' She nodded to the cake. 'Can I cut you a slice?'

'Yes, please.'

Olivia took a sip and felt the emotional whirlwind inside her settle.

'How is your sister doing now?'

Olivia closed her eyes and took another sip of tea.

'Oh.' Jacob's mum nodded, her grip on the knife tightening a little more. 'I see.'

'She passed away a few months ago, actually.'

'I'm so sorry.'

'Thank you. She was sick for a very long time, so it wasn't unexpected.'

'But that doesn't make it any easier, I suppose.'

Helen placed the crumbling cake on to her plate.

'No, it doesn't.' The sweet smell of vanilla reminded Olivia of the softness of her sister's skin. 'How long has Jacob been sick for?'

The words still felt strange to say out loud.

'A long time too. He was first diagnosed when he was fifteen years old.'

'Wow.'

'Yes, I know. Gosh, it seems like a lifetime ago when I think back to it now.'

'Was it always . . .'

'In the brain?' Helen finished, squashing pieces of cake crumbs together with her finger. 'Yes. The first time he beat it quite quickly, but it came back. He beat it again, then it came back again. It was a constant war that he never seemed to win. Eventually, he decided to take himself out of the ring.'

'What do you mean?'

'He stopped treatment. On his twenty-fifth birthday, he decided enough was enough. He didn't want to do it any more; he was tired of fighting a losing battle for his life. Instead, he wanted to live whatever life he had left to the full. That's when he took off travelling.'

Olivia felt the pieces of the puzzle slowly slot into place.

'That must have been hard for you.'

'It was heartbreaking, but what could I do? He wasn't a child any more. He was a man, and a very stubborn one at that.'

Olivia tried to swallow down the lump in her throat. 'If it

352

helps, I can assure you that Jacob has certainly been living his life to the fullest.'

'It does.' Helen reached across and placed her hand over Olivia's. 'More than you know.'

'Do you mind me asking what brought him back to England?'

This question had been front of mind ever since she'd received Helen's email. What had been the turning point? What had happened for him to admit defeat and come home?

'From what he's told me' – Helen took a slow inhale – 'he started feeling unwell; headaches and clumsiness to start with, but it soon progressed into dizzy spells and severe migraines.'

The night on the moped.

'He ended up crashing his bike quite badly and was taken to hospital. They did a scan to check for concussion and found another tumour. He refused the operation but decided to come home.' She hesitated to gain some composure. 'He's been here ever since.'

The pair sat quietly for a moment, Olivia letting the information sink in, a niggling feeling of guilt gnawing at her conscience.

'We crashed,' she admitted, 'when we were coming back from the beach one day. Jacob was driving, and he went all quiet and lost control of the bike. I tried to make him go to the doctor's afterwards. I *knew* something wasn't right, but ... but ...' She shook her head, disappointment and shame clamping down on her chest.

'He refused to go? He laughed it off and pretended it was all fine?' Helen lifted Olivia's chin with her finger. 'Of course he did.'

'But maybe I could have done more? Maybe it could have been caught sooner.'

I could have saved him.

At least I could have tried to save him.

'My dear, please don't beat yourself up about this. Even if you had forced him and they had caught it sooner, who's to say he would have done anything about it except carry on as he was before? This is not your fault. My son is a master at playing pretend, and he's stubborn as anything.'

'I know that, but can't he see how serious it is?' The anguish in Olivia's voice was undeniable, and so too was the anger. 'Why won't he have the operation?'

How could he willingly give up his life? How dare he throw any extra day he had given to him away? Especially when other people didn't get that chance.

'I don't know. I've asked and pleaded and shouted and cried, but his answer remains the same.'

There was a brief silence, punctuated by Helen's unexpected laugh.

'I have to be honest with you, Olivia.' She ran her finger distractedly around the rim of her cup. 'Part of the reason I invited you here was to try and convince him to take the help. I thought, maybe if he saw you, realized how much he was about to lose, he would change his mind.'

'I could have told you that wouldn't have worked. He's already said he won't change for anyone. I'm not enough. Nobody is.'

The thought cracked the last remaining fragments of Olivia's heart that had been clinging together.

'But he loves you,' Helen implored. 'I know he does. That's why he won't let you see him. He's stubborn and afraid and doesn't want to upset you, but I hear the way he talks about you, and I see the look in his eye when he says your name.'

Olivia's heart tripped over itself. 'It's probably just the medication talking.'

'Now you're the one playing pretend.' She reached for her hand and grabbed it firmly. 'He loves you. And if one tiny part of you thinks you feel the same way, then please, before you go, at least say goodbye. Don't leave things like this. At the very least, for your sake.'

Olivia let the tears fall, each one dropping salty pearls into her tea.

'I wish it was just one tiny part of me that felt the same,' she cried. 'It would make this hurt a lot less.'

Helen squeezed her hand. 'Well, my darling, what are you waiting for?'

Jacob

He knew the knock would come. It took longer than he thought, but that was probably thanks to his mother plying the poor girl with tea and cake.

'Jacob, it's me.'

The sound of her voice made his already broken body hurt a little more.

'Can I come in?'

He tried to shift further up the bed, running his hands through his matted and dirty hair. He didn't need a mirror to know how terrible he looked. How the man Olivia once knew had disintegrated to leave a withered, gnarled and bitter version in its place.

'Fine.'

'I won't stay long.' The door creaked open and in she stepped, tentative, almost fearful.

And you wonder why, after you shouted at her like that?

'I just wanted to say goodbye.'

Her voice cracked on the final word, sending guilt tearing

through him. He watched as she finally allowed her eyes to lift, fully taking in the surroundings of his bedroom.

'Don't judge.' He nodded at the cartoon posters tacked to every available piece of wall. 'I was a big Spider-Man fan.'

Olivia hovered awkwardly, shuffling from one foot to the other, while Jacob stared down at his frail hands, shrivelled and shrunken like an old man's. He tucked them neatly under the covers and out of sight.

'You can sit if you want.' He gestured to the end of the bed, still unable to meet her gaze.

'Thank you.'

He felt Olivia perch, very tentatively, on the edge. She was like a frightened animal waiting to run at any given moment. Away from him. *Because* of him.

'How . . . how are you feeling?' she whispered.

'Really?' Jacob finally met her eyes, his glare incredulous.

'Yes.'

'Look at me, Olivia.' He ran his hands up and down the length of his body. 'I'm like a walking corpse that hasn't showered in days. How do you think I'm feeling?'

'I get it.'

'Do you?' he snarled.

He knew he was being difficult, snapping and fighting her kindness as violently as he could, but how could he not? How could he sit there and look at her face without feeling some kind of resentment? Some type of anger at the unfairness of it all.

'In a way, yes.' A single tear fell from her eye.

He took a deep breath in, remembering all too well how much she'd seen of this herself. This wasn't her fault; none of it was her fault. It just hurt so much to see her.

'How am I feeling?' He let down his defences momentarily. 'I feel tired. To the core of my bones. I feel depressed. I feel angry. I feel embarrassed that I shouted at you. I feel guilty that I didn't reply to your email. I feel . . .'

Say it. Say it now, while you can.

'I feel happy to see you.'

He saw Olivia visibly relax at his words, sinking more fully into the mattress.

'How about you?' he asked.

'Well, I also feel embarrassed because I turned up without you knowing. I feel guilty I didn't know you were sick, and . . .' she added shyly, 'I feel happy to see you too.'

'Even after my wonderfully welcoming hello?'

'Yeah, even after that.'

The sound of her laugh lifted his weakened heart.

'I think I was in shock – mainly at the fact my mum knew how to send an email, let alone organize a secret rendezvous behind my back. But also' – the truth dawned on him – 'seeing you meant I had to face up to the reality of my situation. And you know me: never one for real life.'

The echoes of their argument hung heavy between them.

'But I'm sorry I didn't reply to your email, and I'm sorry I didn't tell you what was going on. I guess I didn't know how. Every time I tried it sounded weird and wrong, and then it got really bad, and I didn't want you to see me like this. Plus, knowing what you'd told me about Leah, I just . . . I couldn't put you through that again.'

'I understand.'

'Really?'

'I understand why you didn't tell me, but I don't understand why you aren't accepting help.'

It seemed his mother had got her up to speed quickly.

'Is that the reason why my mum brought you here? As another persuasion technique? Bravo, Helen. I bet she's been filling you in on all the details.'

He turned his face away from her. He knew it wasn't fair, but a part of him felt betrayed.

'She only told me a bit.'

A small relief, but not enough for him to return her gaze.

'And look,' she continued, her voice more insistent now, 'I know it's scary, and I know everything feels unbearably hard right now, but don't you deserve to give yourself a *chance* to live?'

Jacob knew what was coming. He'd heard it a thousand times from his mother, and his doctors and the random family members that seemed to descend on the house in a constant stream. It was the same every time, and quite frankly he was fed up with it.

'You know what it feels like, do you?' Rage, fiercer than he'd ever experienced, raised its head from the depths of him. 'You know how scary it feels to be walking around with a death sentence hanging over you? A ticking time bomb lodged in your own damn head?'

He was close to shouting now, but he didn't care.

'I made a promise to myself to stop fighting. To stop putting myself through the operations and the chemo and the recovery. To stop beating up my body for – what? Maybe a couple of years more, at best? And what will my life be like after the operation, hey? More hospitals, more medication, more fucking *pain* for me and everyone around me.'

Hot, salty tears were burning his eyes, his brittle hands clutching each other as tightly as they could.

'I don't need another lecture. And I don't need another

person who doesn't understand what this is like telling me how to live my life.'

Abruptly, Olivia shot up to standing. Her eyes were wild with fury, and he could see the tension gripping her body.

'I understand more than you give me credit for. And I know that my little sister would have given *anything* for another minute on this earth. Another second with the people she loved.'

She let out a snort of derision, the resentment pouring out of her so freely that all he could do was watch in awe.

'You preached to me for so long about making the most of life. Throwing caution to the wind. And yet you're just going to give up? Put up your hands and surrender when you don't have to? When there's a chance that you can live? You took a chance on so much. Why won't you take a chance on yourself?'

'Because I'm fucking *terrified*,' he cried, the truth surfacing at last. 'I'm so scared of trying and dying anyway. Putting myself through *all* of it again for nothing. I'd rather die on my own terms. As my own man. Not cut up and pulled apart on an operating table, or attached to machines in a hospital ward.'

He didn't know when the venom turned to grief, but before he knew it, his whole body was racked with sobs, and Olivia was there. Holding him. Pulling him closer to her.

'But what if you got more time? What if . . .' She whispered now, her mouth so close to his ear. 'What if *we* got more time?'

Carefully, he pulled away, lifting his face to meet hers. Her blue eyes were ringed with sadness, but just as dazzling as he remembered.

'Olivia, how can there be a *we* with me like this?'

Her grip slackened a little and he felt her start to move away.

'Not because I don't want there to be.' He held on tightly, forcing her to stay with him. 'But because you deserve more than this. So much more. You've already watched one person you love go through this; you don't need to subject yourself to another.'

'That's not your decision to make. What about what *I* want?'

'Olivia, there wasn't a sick boyfriend in the plan you recited to me back in Goa. All those things you wanted to do, that you are *going* to do – you don't need anything holding you back. And that's what I will do. I will hold you back and I will become a burden. Maybe not straight away, but eventually I will.'

She tried to argue, but he cut her short.

'Don't you see? You can't *plan* a life with me, Olivia. Nothing is guaranteed. Nothing at all.'

'No,' she replied firmly, decisively. 'That's not true.'

'Yes, it is.'

'No, it's not.' She placed a soft hand on his cheek. 'Because what if I *plan* on being by your side for as long as we're both here? And what if I can *guarantee* that I will love you every single second we're together, and for a long time after that?'

At her words, the world around him dissolved. All he could see were a thousand shades of blue in her eyes, and all he could feel was the touch of her skin against his. She leant in, so close that he could taste the sweetness of his mother's baking on her lips. His body, which had become a barren wasteland devoid of anything but suffering, suddenly came alive, sparkling with a delicious and intoxicating feeling of hope.

'You love me?'

Her cheeks blushed in that beautiful, coy way they always did.

'I thought that was obvious.'

Jacob looked at her, a reel of images flashing before his eyes.

Him rolling Delhi for the third time, wondering why he was being brought back there again. Him literally crashing into Olivia on the street. Seeing her again at the market. Their dinner together. The emails. Him rolling Udaipur. Their snippet of time together. Snatched moments, leading to something more. Building to something bigger. And then the final throw. The die that lay undecided. A fork in the road.

And what did he choose?

Who did he choose?

'That's good to know.' He nodded solemnly, feeling the final, stubborn, ingrained piece of resistance melt away. 'Because if I'm even going to *consider* going through with this operation . . .'

Olivia's entire body froze in his arms.

'I'm not doing it for anything less than love.'

He pulled her face the final few millimetres towards his and kissed her.

It was a kiss that he hoped conveyed everything he felt in that moment. Everything he hoped they would feel for as long as they possibly could. A kiss that took his breath away. A kiss that meant if he were to die right there in that moment, it would have all been worth it.

For her.

Every hard, scary, terrifying thing that might come his way would be worth it – for her.

One year later

Olivia

As she stood on the beach and looked out to the ocean, time seemed to dissolve around her.

Had it really been a whole year?

So much had changed – in fact, almost everything had changed – but this place remained untouched, with its acres of sand and deep blue waters. The smell of smoky spices and metallic petrol still infused the dense, hot air, and the sounds of oncoming traffic still blasted over the slapping beat of the waves.

'Is it how you remembered it?' Cece came to stand next to her, the tinkling of her beaded hair signalling her arrival.

'No.' Olivia looked at her friend. 'It's better.'

'The company probably helps, right?'

The pair turned to look over to the group of bodies making their way towards them down the beach: a collection of people Olivia had never anticipated seeing all together, let alone halfway across the world in India. The trip had taken so much planning and countless hours of organization that at times Olivia was tempted to pack it all in and ship everyone off to Scarborough for the week. The logistics alone were a nightmare, and on top of that, trying to take time off work when she'd just started her own business was insane. But standing here, she knew it was worth every second.

'Yeah, it's been good for us to get away. I mean, don't get me wrong' – she dropped her voice – 'there have been some challenges.'

'Going on holiday with family is never easy.'

'No, and I'm not sure my mum knows what to make of Tracey and her parenting style.'

'Going out with your daughters until 4 a.m. drinking fish-bowls isn't what you and your mum like to do together?'

Olivia burst out laughing; the memory of seeing Tracey and her girls at breakfast that morning, heads hung low, eyes red-raw from lack of sleep, was something she wouldn't forget in a while.

'No, strangely not.'

'And how are you doing?' Cece nudged her gently, her tanned, inked skin so soft to the touch.

'I'm OK.' Olivia watched as the motley crew drew closer. Her mum and dad arm in arm, glimmers of happiness finally breaking through their walls of grief. Kate chatting animatedly to Tracey and her daughters, who appeared to have made a miraculous recovery from their earlier hang-overs. And then there was Kyle and Helen, one either side, supporting Jacob as he limped gingerly towards them.

Unfortunately, it hadn't just been one operation that Jacob had had to endure. They were now on number four, each one taking a little more out of him and making the recovery that much more challenging. Yet after months of pains-taking rehab and physical therapy, there was one thing they hadn't managed to take from him. One thing that Olivia knew they never would. And that was hope.

'It's obviously been tough, but we're getting there. Day by day, living in the here and now, and all that crap.'

'Ha!' Cece threw her head back. 'Still not a believer in the universe then, I take it?'

'I don't know.' She looked at Jacob, his jet-black eyes narrowed in determination. 'It did give me one good thing, I suppose.'

'Yeah.' Cece squeezed her hand. 'It looks that way to me.'

'Right, ladies!' Tracey bellowed, causing the other holidaymakers to practically jump out of their crispy red skins. 'Enough chatting – are we going in that ocean or what?'

'Yes!' Jacob cried. 'A woman who *finally* speaks my language.'

'No!' Olivia and Helen replied in unison, as the group finally came together. 'There is no way you're going in there, Jacob,' Olivia stated firmly.

'Come *on*. It's either that or the motorbike: you choose.'

'Motorbike?' Kyle's face lit up.

'Don't you *dare*,' Kate hissed, glowering at him with a look worse than death.

'Well, I don't know about you kids, but I reckon saltwater is the perfect thing to blow my cobwebs away.' Tracey ripped off her T-shirt and threw it over her head. 'Suze, Dave?' She draped her arms across Olivia's parents' shoulders. 'What do you say?'

'I'm not sure . . .' Olivia's mum faltered. 'Someone will need to stay here with the stuff.'

'Mum, I'll do that. You go.' Olivia took the beach bag from her mother's shoulders and shooed her parents away. 'Go! Have fun!'

'You don't need to tell me twice.' Kyle swept Kate up into his arms and charged towards the water, her legs kicking wildly and mouth screaming every step of the way.

'Helen, you fancy a dip?' Cece held out her arm for Jacob's mum to take.

'Why not? These legs haven't seen daylight in about thirty years – I might as well make the most of it.'

The pair walked off to join the others at the water's edge, leaving Olivia and Jacob to watch on from the shore.

'Well, it looks like you're stuck on dry land with me.' Jacob sighed, allowing Olivia to take the weight of him.

'I think I can manage that.' She planted a tender kiss on his cheek.

'Good, because I was wondering' – he reached into his pocket – 'if you fancied playing a little game with me?'

He held out a very worn and weathered-looking pair of dice.

'Jacob, you didn't!'

'Of course I did! It wouldn't have been right not to bring them along for the ride.' He waggled them in front of her face. 'Shall we?'

'Fine.' She helped lower him to the ground, shocked that even after a year he could still find ways to surprise her. 'How do you want to play it?'

'Let's keep it simple: we each get to ask the universe a question. Evens is yes and odds is no.'

'Simple yet totally ridiculous.' She sighed, grabbing the dice and shaking them. 'Will Jacob ever grow up?'

She let them fall across the sand.

A five.

'Aha' – he smirked – 'I could have told you that one for free.'

'One can always hope.'

'Now, my turn.' He scooped up the dice and held them close to his chest. 'What to ask . . . what to ask . . .'

After thirty seconds of him deliberating, Olivia became too exasperated to care. She lay back on the sand and stared out to the ocean. It was always best to leave him to it when he was in one of his particularly annoying moods.

'All right, I've got it!'

'At last . . .'

He gave his hand one last shake, before opening his palm to reveal something very different from the beaten-up pair of dice.

Olivia sat bolt upright.

'What's that?'

'Excuse me.' He smiled slyly. 'I thought it was my turn to ask the questions.'

'Jacob, I'm serious – what is that?'

'What does it look like?'

Olivia's mouth went dry.

It was a ring.

A dazzling, square-cut diamond ring.

'I don't understand.'

Olivia's palms were sweating. Her entire body was on fire, and her heart felt far too big for her chest.

'Well, let me make it a little clearer.' He awkwardly hiked himself up on to one knee. 'Olivia Jackson, will you do me the honour of becoming my wife?'

'Are you serious?'

'More than I've ever been in my whole, entire life.'

And in that moment – as she wrapped her arms around him, screaming her answer to the sky; as she agreed to marry the man who had become her best friend, the man that was fighting every single day to be here with her, who had shown her in so many ways what it meant to live, and above all else, what it meant to love – in that precious, magical moment, a tiny part of Olivia Jackson couldn't help but believe in fate.

ACKNOWLEDGEMENTS

I find that every book I write always contains pieces of me, but none more so than this one. Every time I read it back, I can't help but feel so connected to the stories and places on the page. It was during a solo trip to India in 2019 that my life changed completely. I was in Goa when I wrote my first book, *Before I Saw You*, and the people I met and experiences I had, have truly shaped the person I am today. When the idea for Jacob and Olivia's story came to me, there was only one place that felt powerful and magical enough for it to be set in – and it was through their love story that I got the chance to reflect on the one I had with such a generous, colourful and vibrant country. As ever, this book would never have become what it is today without the support and input from the people I am lucky enough to surround myself with.

Firstly, as always, to my friends and family who have been with me more than ever during the past couple of years. Riding the highs and the lows and being kinder to me than I ever am to myself. Thank you for believing, especially when

I find it hard to. How lucky am I to be in love with so many beautiful, caring and phenomenal people.

Secondly, to the incredible team of people I get to work with. Sarah – thank you for reading the ridiculous number of drafts this book went through! I think I wrote four different beginnings, and three separate endings? You are more talented, caring and supportive than I can ever hope to express. To Sally and Lara – a dream editorial duo! Thank you for everything you have given to Jacob and Olivia's story. To work with you both is an honour, you elevate everything to such a high standard and make me a better writer and storyteller with every book I create. Being part of the Transworld family is such a privilege and working with Rosie, Viv, Holly, Hana and Claire has been a dream. Thank you for all that you do – *Take A Chance On Me* wouldn't be what it is without you.

Finally, I would like to thank every reader who has been on this journey with me. Whether this is the first book of mine you are reading or the third, being able to share these characters and these worlds with you is one of the greatest privileges of my life. I am grateful and still pinching myself that I get to do this, so thank you.

And to anyone still searching for that great love – I see you; I feel you; I hear you – let's keep being hopelessly in love with ourselves until we find it.

TEXT ACKNOWLEDGEMENTS

p. 1: extract from *Lonely on the Mountain* by Louis L'Amour (Random House, 1999)

p. 105: extract from *Your Light is the Key* by Mimi Novic (Aspiring Hope Publishing, 2018)

p. 215: extract from *The Story of My Life* by Helen Keller (Simon & Schuster, 2005)

p. 327: extract from *An Intimate Collision* by Craig D. Lounsbrough (Ambassador-Emerald, 2013)

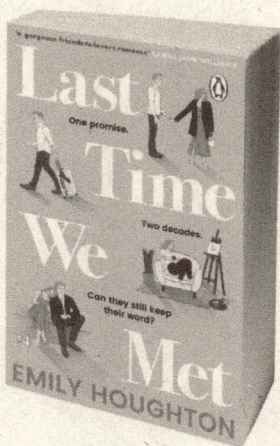

One Promise

Aged thirteen, best friends Eleanor and Fin are inseparable.
Convinced it will always be this way they make a pact to
go to university together, always live near each other, and if
they're both single at thirty-five they'll get married.

Two Decades

Eleanor and Fin haven't spoken in fifteen years. Life has
run away from them and they're both far from where
they'd dreamt of being all those years ago.

Can they still keep their word?

It takes tragic circumstances for Fin to come back
into Eleanor's life, but everything has changed since the
last time they met. Is it too late to mend their friendship?
Or is there a chance they can keep some of the promises
they made?

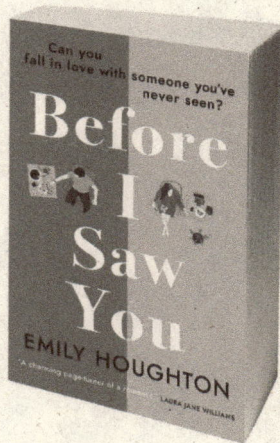

Alice and Alfie are strangers. But they sleep next to each other every night.

Alfie Mack has been in hospital for months recovering from an accident. A new face on the ward is about as exciting as life gets for him right now, so when someone moves into the bed next to him he's eager to make friends. But it quickly becomes clear that seeing his neighbour's face won't happen any time soon.

Alice Gunnersley has been badly burned and can't even look at herself yet, let alone allow anyone else to see her. She keeps the curtain around her bed firmly closed, but it doesn't stop Alfie trying to get to know her. And gradually, as he slowly brings Alice out of her shell, might there even be potential for more?

Great stories.
Vivid characters.
Unbeatable deals.

Page
TURNERS

**WELCOME TO PAGE TURNERS,
A PLACE FOR PEOPLE WHO JUST LOVE TO READ.**

In bed, in the bath, at the dinner table.
On your lunch break, at the gym, or while you wait for
your kids at the school gates. Wherever you are, you love nothing
more than losing yourself in a really great story.

And because we know exactly how that feels, every month we'll choose
a book we love, and offer you the ebook at an amazingly low price.

From emotional tear-jerkers to unforgettable love stories,
to family dramas and gripping crime,
we're here to help you find your next favourite read.

Join us on Facebook at
facebook.com/ThePageTurners

And sign up to our FREE newsletter for amazing monthly ebook deals at
penguin.co.uk/newsletters/pageturners

DON'T MISS OUT. JOIN PAGE TURNERS TODAY.